To
Andrea,

THE

DESCENDING

DARKNESS

MICHAEL CHULSKY

It was so
wonderful meeting you!
You have an excellent
sense of humor.
Have a safe trip,
God bless!
Michael
Chulsky

Rocking Horse Publishing
All on the Same Page Bookstore
11052 Olive Blvd.
Creve Coeur, MO 63141

Visit our website at www.RockingHorsePublishing.com

ISBN 10: 0989568563
ISBN 13: 978-0-9895685-6-2

DEDICATION

Nicholas Apicelli
Marjorie Chulsky
Veronica Frampton
Najah Wright
Dominique Apicelli
Vincent Dicristo
Niki Soto
Janette Hussey
Daniella Castro
Marlena Trento
Alex Martinez-Redondo
Amy Rice
Katelyn O'Callaghan
Daniel Yukob
Jessica Lentz
Teresa McNicholas
Paige Ferguson.

There aren't enough words in the world to properly express how happy I am to know each and every one of you. Each of you adds a dash of spice to the crazy soup I call my life. <3

ACKNOWLEDGMENTS

Nicholas:
The deepest, darkest parts of my soul that nobody knows or could ever understand, you love and embrace. You remain closer to me than anybody. Thank you for always being there.

Haidyn Hocklander:
An amazing beta reader/proof-reader. And an even better friend.

Kelsey Merritt:
For allowing me to use her song for the trailer and making really awesome music that I listened to thousands of times when writing.

Caleb Denecour, Andrew Pritchard, Toby Turner:
Three guys who through their inner light, always seem to cheer me up whenever I'm down. Thank you guys for putting yourselves out there.

Robin Tidwell/the authors of Rocking Horse Publishing:
You guys are amazing! I'm so happy to be a part of the family.

Cody Kennedy:
The kind-hearted and supportive. Thank you for your constant encouragement.

Jullian Roundtree, Henrique Lima, and Samantha S.:
I didn't have many friends growing up. I was always the weird kid that everyone avoided. You three made me feel welcome. At a dark time in my life, you guys helped me to laugh. It means more to me than any of you will ever know.

Gail Becker, Dan Alston, Kathleen Conley, Sandra Williams, Lisa Cybulski, Jennifer Elgrim, Candice Bidner, Joe Simon, and Joseph Ferraina. Lore MacDonald, Lynn Newbury, Suzanne Lomas, Ms. Baker:
My wonderful teachers. I have such fond memories of time spent with you all. Not everyone has the Opportunity to be taught by a good teacher who is passionate about their craft. I'm thankful for each and every one of you.

CHAPTER 1: THE CALLING

A figure draped in a flowing black cloak moved through the bustling city with great stealth, giving him the appearance of a fleeting shadow. The figure leapt skyward and landed on top of a small building. The wind created by his movement shifted the cloak partially off his face, revealing him to be a young man. He surveyed the crowd, searching for his target. After a few long minutes, his eyes locked onto the target at last.

He watched as the young girl walked into an alley. Her eyes seemed to pulsate with energy, beckoning him. He sniffed the air and breathed in the scent of her power. It was incredible. She had to be the girl he was looking for. He knew there wasn't much time left to waste.

He leapt off the building. His movement while falling was graceful; it was as if gravity simply did not exist. In mid-descent, he headed right towards her. He had expected the encounter to go as every other one had before it, but he was wrong, and it surprised him greatly just how wrong he was.

The girl whipped around in a blur of speed. She waved her hand in a circular motion, and cerulean specks of energy gathered towards her open palm. A shield of thick ice formed around her.

Before he could make contact with the ice, the young man put his hands out, and a black glow surrounded them. Thick tendrils of dark energy sprouted, the shadows themselves extending from his hands. The tendrils connected with the ice and launched him in the opposite direction.

The girl smiled condescendingly, almost sneering. She looked up at the young man who she had thought was attacking her. It sort of bummed her out to watch him just slowly land on the ground a few feet away; she had expected more of a fight.

"Hey, what's the matter?" she asked. "Scared you'll get beaten up by a girl?" She was trying to bait him; after all, life was much more interesting with the occasional fight.

He didn't say anything. His face was blank, he simply stared at her in mild amusement.

"Well?" she demanded, "aren't you going to say anything?"

"If I wanted to hurt you, you would be hurt," he replied, softly. "I can assure you, that wasn't my intention. I only want to talk."

"Whatever," she said, rolling her eyes. "I'm not going to listen to some weirdo in a cloak. I'm out."

He pulled off his cloak, and the moonlight illuminated him. He appeared to be no more than seventeen, with brown hair the color of melted chocolate, ruffled as if somebody had run their hand through it, and brown eyes so dark that they might be mistaken for black. "Wait, cloak's gone," he said, waving his hand in a voilà gesture. "See? Don't leave…I need only a few moments of your time."

The girl turned back around and looked him over before giving him the full weight of her gaze. "So it is. Tell me, do you greet everyone by jumping at them? It's original, I'll give you that."

He watched her with an almost curious look on his face. Admittedly, if he were a normal, average teenage boy, the type who only cared about looks, they probably would have dated, or he would have tried for it, because of her sheer and unedited natural beauty. Not even wearing an ounce of makeup, her face was pure and light, the color of milk, untarnished, like a porcelain doll. Her hair was bright turquoise, to her shoulders, but it was her blue eyes that made him realize he'd found the right girl, the one he was looking for. She was the infamous Ice Princess.

"Clearly, somebody likes the color black," she said, looking him up and down. "Black cloak, black shirt, black pants, and black shoes. Are you going to a funeral?"

Looking down, he almost blushed. "Perhaps you're right that my wardrobe could use a little color, but I'm not here for fashion tips."

2

"Then why ARE you here?" she asked. "Don't forget, I was just minding my business until you practically attacked me."

"I wasn't. . .I mean, I didn't intend for it to come off as an attack," he muttered. "It's just that I've been looking for you and wanted to make sure that you're you. . .or that you're the you that I thought you were. And I couldn't be sure that the you that you were was the you that I thought you were unless I made you think I was attacking you. If that makes any sense."

She blinked slowly. "Sorry, chief, you lost me."

He sighed. "What's your name?" he asked. "Tell me, and I'll be absolutely sure that you're the right person."

The girl glared and then turned her back to him. "Listen, whoever you are, I really do not feel like dealing with you tonight. It's way too late and I'm much too tired to play guess who."

"What did I do?!" he asked, confused. "I just asked for your name."

"First of all, you made me think that you were trying to attack me, which got me all excited for a fight," she replied, frowning slightly. "Secondly, I'm a girl, jerk. You're supposed to give me your name first. What, were you raised by wild animals or something?"

"Well, actually, no," he replied, trying to keep his temper down. "I was raised by humans."

She raised an eyebrow. "So what's your name?"

He paused, staring at her for a few awkward moments. "It's Shadow, okay?"

She smirked for a second, trying to gauge whether he was serious or not. After a few seconds, she turned back to face him. "Wow, you're not even kidding… My name's Ellie."

"Ellie," Shadow repeated. "Nice to meet you."

"I am known as the Ice Princess around here. But judging by your reaction, you knew that already, didn't you?"

Shadow nodded.

"I've heard some talk. A vigilante crime fighter, tough and powerful, yet only a teenage girl. Rumor has it you're pretty strong."

"So why did you try for me then?" Ellie asked, a sudden coldness surfacing. "Think I'd have an off day or something?"

"What do you mean?" Shadow asked. "I wasn't trying for anything."

Ellie frowned. "You said you were acting like you were trying to pick a fight," she said, then snapped her fingers, causing the ice to fade away. "If you weren't trying to fight, then what were you doing?"

"The thing is —"

A loud explosion from above interrupted him. Dark red and orange circles could be seen overhead, as if rockets were bursting in the sky.

Ellie glanced up. "Since when do they let off fireworks in the middle of January?"

"No, this can't be happening. I thought I had more time!" Shadow exclaimed, fear forming in his eyes.

"What's wrong?" Ellie asked.

Shadow sighed. "This was a mistake. I was a fool to think that you would understand everything, that I could explain it all before it was too late."

"Wait, what are you talking about, dude? You've explained nothing. And what do you have to do with the sky going all Fourth of July on us?"

"I don't have time for this!" Shadow exclaimed, shaking his head. "There's too much to explain and not enough time. I gotta hurry and warn the others." He turned and started to walk away.

"Oh, hell no," Ellie replied angrily, throwing her hands up. Light blue energy flowed from them, forming sharp icicles in the air. "I told you before, I am not in the mood for this cryptic mind game. Explain or be impaled."

Shadow smiled in spite of himself. "All right. I'll tell you everything. Just listen carefully because I don't have time to explain it twice. It's. . .kind of a long story."

"You've got my full attention," Ellie said, rolling her eyes. "Thrill me."

"All right. I'm assuming that you also know about all things preternatural, the creatures and demons that exist in our world. Correct?"

Ellie nodded, not breaking eye contact with him. "I'm guessing this has a point? Let me simplify it. Who, or actually, what are you, anyway?"

Shadow blinked at her coolly. "What do you mean?"

"Please, I'm not an idiot. You're definitely not human; humans don't just…fall like that. You know, when you were coming at me, you did everything but float down. I wasn't born yesterday. So what are you?"

Shadow frowned. "Well, for starters, I'm a vampire, although, not completely. I'm a Dhampir."

"You mean. . .like half-human, half-vampire?" she asked. "I thought that was a story, just a legend. You know, make-believe, imaginary?"

"I'm sure my real parents were equally as skeptical as you, but here I am. I don't have time to explain the logistics of it, but there it is. Anyway, haven't you ever wondered how you got your abilities, those powers you possess?"

Ellie shook her head. "No. I always thought they were a natural trait, like your brown hair or my blue eyes."

Shadow laughed. "Hardly, but I'll explain. The Bible talks about how God said, 'Let there be light,' but it doesn't talk about what existed before that.

"You see, thousands of years ago, before life as our ancestors knew it began, before God decided to create mankind, there was darkness. Stirring in the darkness were evil creatures. Some call them gods, others call them demons, but both names are wrong. Those evil creatures were the Valdemalum, or great evil. The Valdemalum existed then, and they exist now, but in lesser form.

"When our planet was created, those evil creatures, so powerful, which thrived in darkness, were bathed in light. They broke and shattered into pieces, no longer whole entities but separate lesser ones. Eventually, they found their way into our world, and they would attempt to bring back the eternal darkness that they once knew and loved.

"Angels themselves descended from the heavens to protect the humans, but even they could not fully withstand the evil and hate from the Valdemalum and humans. Eventually, some of the angels were corrupted. In fact, I believe one of them, who wasn't able to be saved from the corruption, became what is known by people today as Satan.

"But more on topic, our ancestors, after hundreds of years of being tormented and murdered by these Valdemalum, or demons, slowly began to adapt over time. They speak of evolution, but that doesn't even begin to cover it. After being exposed to the demonic and angelic energies over time, certain humans adapted and were naturally selected, given the ability to fight back, to save our world. You, Ellie, are one of those special few."

"What do you mean?" Ellie asked, her voice almost a whisper. "I'm one of what?"

"I thought you would be smarter than this," Shadow said, shaking his head. "I mean that you're one of the humans who lucked out. You were chosen by luck of the draw to be a protector, a guardian for your race. You, and less than two percent of the world, were given abilities to defend against the demons and other creatures. Look at it as nature evening the playing field."

"I see," Ellie muttered, attempting to process it all. "What about you?"

"Me?" Shadow asked. "What do you mean?"

"You say 'our ancestors,' but you're not fully human. I mean, unless you're suggesting that vampirism is a gift passed down?"

"No, that's not what I'm saying," Shadow replied, crossly. "Vampirism is both a disease and a curse. Don't ever think of it as a gift, but a contagion."

"Then how does vampirism fit in your theory of abilities being a gift?"

Shadow smiled darkly. "People in ancient tribes thought that if they consumed the blood and flesh of fallen demons, they could capture their power. Idiots, that's what they were. All that they gained by consuming the demons was corruption. The moment that the demonic essence entered their bodies, they lost their souls and became the first human-demon hybrids, the first vampires."

"Well, this was a nice history lesson and all, but why does any of this concern me?" Ellie asked, glaring. "All you've done is explain things that are interesting, but hardly relevant, and made bright lights go off in the sky. Which is a neat trick, I'll grant you, but hardly end-of-the-world-worthy."

"Funny you should pick that choice of words. Those fireworks, as you so aptly call them, are a major omen. They are an omen signaling that all hell is going to break loose soon. I can't be sure of the exact time, but rumor has it that it won't be until the end of spring. That gives us all about three months, maybe less, to prepare for it."

"There you go again, talking in plural pronouns again. Who's 'we'?"

"You, myself, and the rest of the teenagers with special abilities that I've already recruited. You were one of the last that I had to find on my list, which I'm glad I did. . .find you, that is, because time's running out."

Ellie frowned. "So you've been, what, adopting us like puppies?"

Shadow smirked. "I wish it was that easy. I got attacked by demons and other beings a few times along the way, not to mention you trying to fight me, so hardly as simple as that."

"So where are the others?"

"They're waiting for me to come back after I recruit the last few on my list, at my. . .home."

Ellie nodded. "Well, you seem like you have everything figured out. I'll give you that, at least. This all just seems like it's happening so fast."

Shadow nodded, then pulled a small device out of his pocket. He threw it to her, and she caught it instantly, without hesitation. The object slightly resembled a cell phone. It was black with blue streaks around the sides, strange buttons on the bottom, and a large screen in the center. "Take that. It will come in handy later," he said. "It will allow you to communicate with the others, and with me."

He opened his mouth to speak again, pausing as he saw the confusion in her eyes. "I understand that you're confused and that my explanation has probably left you with a lot more questions than answers resolved. But for now, you'll just have to trust me." He waved a hand over the ground and a large, glowing, black hole appeared.

"What is it?"

"It will take you to where I live. Please wait there. You'll find people like us, people with special abilities to fight the evil that's coming. I have to go find the last two before someone or something else does first."

Ellie frowned, throwing him a dirty look. "What makes you think I'm that naïve? This is like a whole new level of taking candy from a stranger."

Shadow shook his head. "I wasn't aware that I was offering you candy. But humor me by doing a small favor?"

"What is it?"

"Look into my eyes and tell me if you think I could or would hurt you. People say that eyes are the gateway into the soul. If I have bad intentions, you should be able to see, just by looking into my eyes."

Ellie shook her head and sighed. It was a small request - trivial, even. She gazed into the eyes of the young man. She wanted to fight it, but couldn't ignore the feeling that was flourishing deep down inside of her. She just knew he meant her no harm and decided, against her better judgment, that it was okay to trust him.

"Fine." she said. "I'll go to your. . .house, base, or whatever."

"All right." Shadow gave her a small nod. "Go ahead, jump in."

Ellie let out a huge breath. "I must either be very trusting or very stupid to believe you, but I do. I know that you're sure as hell going to give me a better explanation later," she said, then jumped into the black hole. She sank into the shadows and disappeared.

"Tonight really is the night," Shadow thought. *"The night that I was warned about by that shaman. This is the beginning; what must be done to protect the world. I will do what I can to make you proud of me, Mother."*

He closed his eyes and bowed his head in remembrance. Suddenly, a jolt ran down his spine; he sensed something calling to him from a short distance away. "One of the kids on my list is in trouble. I'd better hurry." Slowly, the wind began to pick up around him and twisted. In less than an instant, he was gone.

CB EO CB EO CB EO CB EO

A few miles away from where Shadow and Ellie met, a small boy was running from someone in pursuit.

"Leave me alone!" he yelled. He threw his hand behind him, and gigantic rocks broke away from the ground and rushed towards his attacker.

The person chasing him, a woman, dodged the rocks and laughed mockingly. Tired of the chase, she fired a bolt of energy at him. It slammed into his back, propelling him forward, knocking him onto the ground. "Bull's-eye," she announced, throwing her head back and laughing. "It's always more fun when you have a moving target."

"No. . . please," he whimpered. He pulled himself off the ground and edged backwards away from her.

"Tereya, you stupid child," the woman said scathingly, licking her lips. "You should know better by now than to cross me. You know that I always get my mark."

"Please, stop! I didn't do anything wrong! Somebody help me!"

The woman laughed again. She pointed a finger at him, and a bolt of lightning shot out of it, striking him in the shoulder, sending him spiraling onto the ground. "You know, you're proving to be much more difficult than you're worth."

"No. . . please!"

The woman flexed her outstretched hand, and electricity gathered, forming a whip within it. The woman raised her hand and thrust the whip down, but as Tereya prepared for the final blow, a hand caught it.

"Didn't your mother ever tell you not to play with electricity?" Shadow asked. "You might get shocked."

The woman's eyes widened. "How in the world did you do that? You shouldn't have been able to touch that whip. Nobody could have survived that. It's impossible."

Shadow jerked the whip out of the woman's hand and tossed it to the side. It landed on the ground and disappeared. "Apparently, I just did, so it's not," he replied curtly. He threw her a scornful look and then walked over to the child. "Hey. . .are you all right?"

"Y-yes, I'm f-fine. W-who are y-you?"

Shadow smiled and kneeled down. Before he could respond, he moved to the left and caught a knife by its hilt that would have pierced his back. "And now you're throwing knives at me," he said. "You know, lady, you're not making a very good first impression. If I didn't know better, I'd say your hostility means you don't want to be friends."

"You shouldn't turn your back on people," she said. "You might get stabbed in it someday." She laughed at her own joke.

Shadow stood up. He walked over and threw the knife down at her feet. "I'd leave, if I were you."

"You don't intimidate me, you uppity punk."

"I'm not trying to scare you; simply forewarn you. So why don't you do the smart thing and walk away. . .before I feel the need to prove my point."

She studied him and then growled. "Fine, I'm leaving. And don't worry, Tereya, I'll be back for you soon, and this little vampire won't always be there to protect you. And then, when you least expect it, I'll strike!" With a wild laugh, she disappeared.

Tereya grunted as he sat upright and stared at the man in front of him. "Y-y-y-you're a vampire?"

Shadow frowned. He looked down at the kid and gave what was a strong attempt at a reassuring smile. "Yes, they call me that, but you'll find that there are certain things that differ between a normal vampire and me," he said calmly. "Here, let me help you up." He extended a hand and pulled the kid off the ground. "Don't be scared. I won't bite."

"Thanks. And hey, I never got your name. Mine is Tereya."

"I know your name," Shadow replied. "That woman used it very freely. My name is Shadow."

"Well, nice to meet you, Shadow!" Tereya exclaimed.

Shadow nodded. He reached into his pocket and pulled out a device similar to the one he had given to Ellie. Instead of it being blue and black, it was brown and black. "Here, take this, kid. You can't be left here alone," he said, handing the device to Tereya. "It's a way of keeping contact. You'll need it."

"Th-thanks," Tereya muttered. He grabbed the device and pocketed it. "I don't want to be by myself. She'll come back and attack me again. . . I know it." he said, grabbing Shadow's arm.

"You're right," Shadow said, waving his hand, and the glowing black hole appeared again. "It's why I'm taking you where there are others like you. You'll be safe now."

"Thanks. Thank you so much," Tereya said. He hugged Shadow.

Shadow tensed and smiled awkwardly, pulling away a second later. Although a normal thing to do, hugging wasn't on the list of things that he was comfortable doing.

He looked Tereya over properly for the first time. The boy had brown hair, much like his own; however, it was much longer, and it fell down around his face. His eyes were hazel, green with specks of grey floating in them like storm clouds.

Shadow waited and watched as the young boy jumped into the black hole and was transferred to the base. "Thank God," he said, then pulled the list out of his pocket and looked it over. "Two down, one more to go." Within seconds, he faded away.

ଓଞ୍ଚଓଞ୍ଚଓଞ୍ଚଓଞ୍ଚ

Shadow appeared in a ruined city. The shaman who had warned him of what was to come had also given him the ability to sense where the special children were located. It had worked thus far, but the town he was drawn to seemed deserted. "It's just a ghost town," he said, thinking aloud. "I don't see anybody here; in fact, I don't see anything strange here."

A loud blast rang out, followed by screeching and a girl yelling. *"I guess I spoke too soon,"* he thought, running towards the commotion. He came to a clearing and saw a young woman.

She had jet-black hair with vibrant blonde bangs. She was wearing a long-sleeved shirt and jeans with slits up the sides. As he continued forward, Shadow watched as her eyes flashed blue and bolts of electricity fired out of them, engulfing a skeletal figure, reducing it to a pile of yellow goo. "Let me guess. You're Kay, right?"

Kay paused, taking a few steps back. "How do you know who I am?"

"My name is Shadow. I am searching for teens like you, with special powers." He watched her carefully, trying to gauge her reaction. "Something is happening soon, something big. I don't know all the details yet, but from what I have heard, I'm going to need all the help I can get."

"So why are you gathering people with special powers?"

"I am gathering those who will one day be known as the greatest heroes of our time so that we may fight together as a group and overcome the evil. It's definitely not a one-person kind of job."

"Okay. Well, you seem pretty cool," Kay replied, shrugging. "I think me and Isaac can trust you."

"Who's Isaac?"

"Isaac is a kid that I'm close to. I've been taking care of him ever since I saved him from a demon two years ago," Kay replied. "If you do anything to hurt him, I'll destroy you."

"And I thought that that Nicki Minaj lady was crazy," Shadow thought. But he said aloud, "Calm down. I don't wish to hurt him at all. All I want to know is who he is and why I can't sense him. He is one of the special kids I was talking about, right?"

Kay nodded. "Yeah, sorry. I get worried about him; he's really young and practically helpless without me. Isaac can manipulate different types of energy, while I can only do electricity. As for why you can't sense him, it's because his powers shield him from stuff like that. Unless he wants to be found, he can't."

Shadow nodded. It made sense after all. "Let's go. I can't wait to meet him."

"No worries. I can give him the signal and he'll come to us," Kay said. She then put her hand up, pointing at the sky, and a bolt of lightning struck the ground a few feet away from them.

After a few minutes, a boy could be seen in the distance, sprinting up the road towards them.

"Isaac!" Kay called as the boy got closer.

Isaac caught up to them at last, smirking halfheartedly. He was short for his age, being thirteen and barely over five feet tall. He had jet-black hair; his eyes hazel, with gold framing them. "Kay, you won't believe—" he began, but paused, catching sight of Shadow for the first time. "Wait. Hold up. Who's he?"

"Don't worry. He's all right," Kay said, leaning against a wall. "Now, cut to the chase and tell us what took you so long."

12

"Let me take a wild guess. You were attacked by creatures?" Shadow asked. "Big ones, all bones and little skin?"

"Yeah. How did you know that?" Isaac asked. "How did he know that, Kay?"

Shadow shrugged and pointed at Kay. "Well, she was attacked too. I assumed the same people who attacked her would attack you," he said. "Besides, anyone who has even the slightest touch of power in our world is in trouble. The forces of darkness are trying to prevent me from succeeding."

"What do you mean?" Isaac asked.

"Well, you see, as I already told Kay, something bad is going to happen, and the evil that will cause it will reveal itself soon. I intend to stop it, but I need help. I can't fight it alone. I have tracked down others, like you two, in order to fight. If we all work together, we can—"

"Hold on a second. What makes you think we want to help you?" Kay asked. "I mean, getting attacked by creatures is fun once in a while, but today has been the most attacks ever, like four in a row. You and your evil must be causing it."

Shadow frowned. "You can blame it all on me, if you want. I don't care. But know one thing: If you guys choose to stay here, yes, you can choose to stay here, but it isn't in your best interest. "So it's up to you. If you want to keep fighting off hordes of creatures and demons by yourself, be my guest."

"Kay, I don't know about you, but I want to go with this guy," Isaac said. "Please. I don't want us to fight all these creatures by ourselves."

Kay scowled. She opened her mouth and then immediately closed it, seeing the look on Isaac's face. "Seeing as how you won Isaac over, my hands are tied. So count us in."

"Thank you, Kay," Isaac replied, sighing in relief.

"Well, it's for the good of the world, right?" Kay replied, shrugging.

Shadow pulled a device out of his pocket similar to the ones that he had given to Ellie and Tereya before, except this one was black and yellow. He handed it to Kay. "It's a special cell phone. It's how I stay in touch with people on the team."

Kay stared at Shadow expectantly. "What about Isaac?" she asked. "Doesn't he get one of your magical cell phones or whatever?"

Shadow blinked. *"I didn't know he even existed, so of course I wouldn't have one for him. I only had enough for the kids on my list,"* he thought, frowning. That wasn't entirely true. He did have an extra one. How could he have forgotten?

"Actually, I do happen to have a spare one. It was... meant for another kid."

Kay raised an eyebrow. "What happened to him?"

"It doesn't matter," Shadow said blankly, pulling out a gold-and-black cell. "It's Isaac's now."

"Thank you," Isaac replied, taking the phone.

"Lastly. . ." Shadow said, waving his hand, and a hole like the ones before, with Ellie and Tereya, appeared on the ground.

"What's it do?" Isaac asked, looking in awe.

"It will take you to my home," Shadow replied. "I'll be there soon."

Kay shrugged. "So. . .we just jump in?"

"Yeah," Shadow urged, waving his hands at them. "There will be others waiting for you. Don't worry, they're friends."

Kay gave Shadow a mock-salute and then jumped into the hole, Isaac following her.

Shadow closed his eyes, focusing one last time, trying to sense if he had missed any, but he came up dry. "Now I can finally get some rest and relaxation."

CR&OCR&OR&OCR&O

A short while later, Shadow appeared at the front gate of his castle and walked up the steps leading to the front door. He had begun his conquest at sunset, only to come home around two in the morning.

"Home, sweet home," he said out loud, glad to finally be home and done with the tedious process. He pushed open the door. He was looking forward to some well-deserved peace and quiet.

"No, I want this room!" Kay screamed from the hallway and a large bolt of lightning shot out of her hand, narrowly missing Ellie.

14

"Touch my stuff and I'll kill you!" Ellie screamed, sending orbs of ice flying in response.

Shadow sighed as he went to break up the fight. On his way over, he saw Ryan and Tristan, two other kids he had recruited, fighting over the TV, and he frowned as a pillar of flames engulfed his favorite statue. Meanwhile, Faith, Tristan's twin sister, was blasting her radio, sprawled out on the couch. In the kitchen, Isaac was rummaging through a cupboard as Crystal and Ethan, two other recruits, were making a mess of the refrigerator, looking for something to eat.

"What did I get myself into?" Shadow wondered, shaking his head as he watched the scene. He waved his hands, and the castle doors were surrounded with a glow of black energy, then closed.

CHAPTER 2: THE DARK CASTLE

Shadow awoke early in the morning. It had been only three weeks since he had recruited the last few teens, and he still hadn't quite adjusted to the new sleep schedule. He couldn't believe he actually thought it was a good idea to be awake when the rest of them were. Rubbing his eyes, he yawned and, with reluctance, got up. He changed into his spare clothes and then left his room, stepping out into the hallway.

Shadow heard noises coming from the recreation room and decided to indulge himself in some television. Entering the rec room, he saw Ellie and Crystal listening to music in a corner together. Ellie had one earphone in, and Crystal had the other. Crystal, whom he had found a few weeks ago, was a very unique person, to say the least. She was incredibly spoiled and finicky, but, being the daughter of a millionaire, this was typical and expected behavior. Her blonde hair was twisted back into a ponytail, French-braided.

Crystal turned her head and noticed Shadow's presence. Her grey eyes filled with warmth, and she waved to him. Shadow waved back as he passed, slightly hoping deep down that Ellie would notice him too, and wave, but it was in vain. She was apparently too wrapped up in the song to notice.

On the other side of the room, Tereya was playing chess with Ryan. "Hey, guys, how's the game going?" Shadow asked as he walked over. He felt slightly awkward, not being one to socialize. He looked at Ryan, whose adolescent face was screwed up in concentration. Aside from the slightly abrasive personality, Ryan was actually a decent-looking guy. He had slightly

16

long, messy, brown hair and blue-green eyes that were always shining mischievously.

"Just fine. About to kick Reya's butt," Ryan said finally, smiling. "He's terrible at this game."

"Am not!" Tereya exclaimed. "Ryan's just really, really good at this game, and I'm just learning."

Shadow held back a laugh and shook his head. "Don't worry, Reya. Chess is a very strategic and challenging game. It takes time to learn properly. You'll get it eventually."

"T-thank you," Tereya muttered.

"Don't mention it," Shadow replied. He looked from Tereya to Ryan and then leaned over and whispered something into the younger boy's ear.

"Cheater!" Ryan bellowed, pointing his finger at Shadow.

Shadow made a reprehensive sound. "He's much younger than you. Don't be a baby."

Ryan scowled. "Whatever. It won't make a difference. I'm still going to win."

"I'll be sure to have a trophy made and an award ceremony prepared for your momentous win," Shadow replied, rolling his eyes and walking away. He walked over to the girls and saw that Ellie had removed her earphone and was watching him.

"Hey, you two, what's up?"

"Nothing much," Ellie replied. "We were just talking about music and then thought of going to spar, you know, practice our skills and whatnot. More training never hurt anybody."

Crystal turned the iPod off and gave Shadow a nasty look. "You did say that with all of us fighting together, this evil that we're supposed to fight would be easy, right?"

"Well. . ." Shadow muttered, at a loss for words. This hostile manner was an extreme difference from the warm and happy greeting she gave him earlier, which was standard Crystal behavior. Happy one moment, ready to declare nuclear war the next.

Crystal exhaled loudly. "Fine, don't answer. It's quite obvious you don't know how to be a leader. That, I can handle. But at least have the common courtesy to answer me when I am speaking to you!" she yelled, then huffed out of the room.

"Whoa," Shadow said, confused. "Somebody please explain to me what happened there, 'cause I'm lost."

"It's quite obvious, Shadow," Ryan said, looking up from his game. "That girl is loonier than the cartoons of the same name."

Ellie frowned. "Shut up, Ryan," she said, patting Shadow's shoulder. "It's not your fault, dude. She's just scared. In fact, we all are. But if I know anything, it's that fighting for what's right is well worth any sacrifice. I'm sure she'll come around eventually."

"Thanks," Shadow said. "It... means a lot that I can count on you."

"Don't mention it," Ellie replied, smiling. "Now, if you'll excuse me, I have to go make sure Crystal isn't taking out her frustrations on poor Ethan again."

Shadow watched as she left the room. He definitely didn't envy Ethan, especially considering the job he was tasked with. Ethan was sent by the forces of light to be a guide for Crystal and protect her from evil. He was, ironically, her guardian angel. So, no, he didn't envy the bond shared between Ethan and Crystal, because she was much too complicated and confusing. *"I guess I'll never understand girls,"* he thought, *"especially ones like Crystal with mood swings."*

Shrugging, he decided to rally everyone together for their first meeting. He wanted them all to know exactly what danger lay ahead for them and wanted them all to properly prepare for it. He pulled out the small cell phone, not unlike the ones that he handed out to the others when he recruited them, and hit a button.

"Everyone to the Rec Room, now!"

"But I'm already here," Ryan said.

"Shut up, Ryan," Shadow replied, shaking his head. "You and Tereya just continue your game and wait for everyone else to arrive."

After several minutes, everyone began filing into the Rec Room from various directions. Some of them looked worried, while others simply looked annoyed.

"What's wrong, Shadow?" Ethan asked, his brow furrowed. "Has anything happened?"

"Don't worry, Ethan," Shadow said reassuringly. "Nothing bad has happened. I just need to talk to everyone."

"You do realize that me and Ellie were just in the room, right?" Crystal asked, frowning. "I don't see what the point was in letting us leave if you had to speak to all of us."

Shadow's mouth opened wide. "Let you leave?" he replied, awestruck. "I didn't let you leave. You walked out!"

"Crystal, dear," Ethan interjected, "perhaps it's best for you to not interrupt Shadow and let him say what he has to say. I'm sure it's very important."

Crystal paused and took a second to think it over. "You're probably right, Ethan." She turned to Shadow. "But make it quick. I have online shopping to do."

Rolling his eyes, Shadow turned so that he faced everyone in the room. "Listen, guys, I'm going to need you all to learn how to work together as a team. If you don't, then we lost the battle before it has even begun. We have a lot of work to do and far too little time. It's prudent that we get our acts together before things get rough. Okay?"

"Sure. It's cool," Ryan replied.

Shadow looked around. He was glad to see that everyone was nodding in unison. Another plus was that Tristan hadn't said anything, which was one step towards a headache-free day. It wasn't that Tristan was stupid, per se. It was just that the kid had a tendency to say really, really, incredibly stupid things.

"Uh, Shadow," Tristan said, "I have a question."

Damn it, Shadow thought angrily. He expected Tristan to say something annoying, but since he hadn't spoken up earlier, he thought he was in the clear. Looking over the kid, he knew that there was nothing about Tristan's appearance that would make anybody immediately dislike him. He had hair the color of flames, almost too red to be natural, but oddly enough, it was. He had bright blue eyes that reminded Shadow of a Siberian Husky's.

No, it was definitely not Tristan's appearance that made him annoying; it was his mouth and extreme lack of common sense.

"You awake in there?" Tristan asked, poking Shadow's arm.

"Tristan, how can I help you?" Shadow replied, struggling to maintain a calm and collected tone.

"Well. . .why should we train for this 'great evil' or whatever, if we don't even know who or what it is?" Tristan asked. "I mean, it could be a weakling or whatever, like an evil rabbit or something. We're all tougher than average kids our age; we can handle anything. So why should we struggle to prepare?"

Shadow sighed. He had expected this question from most of them, it being an intelligent one. Though, out of all of them, Tristan, he thought, was the least likely to ask. He thought, however, it would be best to reply to it with all of them there.

"I know what's coming because a powerful shaman had a vision of everything. It was that shaman who told me to gather all of you and gave me the ability to sense your locations. It was also she who helped me make these communicators that we all have. I know that what she said was true because of my own experience with her and also because she accurately led me to all of you," he said.

"The prospect of a powerful and evil being after us might scare some of you, but that's what the training is for. That's what we're all here for. I promise that, as long as I'm here, I'll try my best to see that none of you will get hurt."

"You can't promise that," Crystal said. "You have no way of making sure that we're all okay. You're just one person."

"Crystal," Ethan began.

"No, Ethan, she's right," Shadow interrupted. "I can't make that promise, so I shouldn't, but I am. I promise that I will try my absolute best to make sure that nothing harms any of you. If I have to give my life to ensure that you're all safe, then so be it."

"I trust you, Shadow," Tereya declared. "You've already saved my life once. If you hadn't stopped that lady, I wouldn't be here now. I know you'll try your best, and that's all that really matters to me."

"Yeah, you don't need to do any convincing here either," Ryan chimed in. "You've saved my vivacious butt many times, even before you 'gathered' me for this mission, so I know that I can count on you."

"Ryan's vivacious butt aside, I know that you won't intentionally let us any of us down, Shadow," Ethan said. "You're a good person. It's simply not in your nature."

"Thanks, Reya," Shadow said. "You too, Ryan and Ethan."

"If Ethan trusts you, I guess I do too," Crystal said, with a shrug. "But just so you know, if I die, I'll kill you."

"But won't you be dead?" Tristan pointed out.

"Nobody asked you!" Crystal yelled, turning on the spot and rushing out of the room. Ethan, bemused, frowned apologetically to Shadow and followed her.

That girl will be the death of me yet," Shadow thought, shaking his head.

"Checkmate!" Tereya exclaimed, moving his piece to take Ryan's king.

"Congratulations, Reya," Shadow said. "For your first game, you did really well."

"He only won because you helped him," Ryan rumbled through clenched teeth.

Shadow rolled his eyes. "I don't know what you're talking about. Anyway, I'm going to my room to do some personal training," he said. "I hope all of you do the same, because trust me, we'll need it. I don't know how soon it will be until our first mission, but I sense it's soon. Get in as much training as you can." With that, he faded into the darkness, teleporting away.

Shadow appeared in his room and opened the door. He looked out of it to see if anybody was around. Seeing that the coast was clear, he gently pushed the door closed again. He walked over to the closet and opened it, examining a dusty bookcase. He picked up a book from the shelf and put it back in a different place on another shelf. No sooner had he done that than the entire bookcase flipped forward, revealing a hidden hallway. He hurried down the secret passage and arrived in a room, his private meditation chamber.

Suddenly, he stopped moving and froze, sensing that someone was following him. *"How did they find me?"* he wondered. *"I teleported, and then I closed the door behind me. There's no way that anybody but me could know where this room is hidden."*

In mid-thought, it hit him. In his haste, he hadn't shut the door behind him. Sure, he had pushed it shut, but the door to his bedroom had been left slightly ajar. Somebody could have very well seen him enter the passageway.

He decided to act like nothing was wrong and wait for the person to show themselves. It didn't worry him so much as it made him cautious, wondering why somebody would follow him. At the very least, they were curious. Admittedly, a secret passageway would be cool to any teenager, perfectly understandable. If it was anything but mild curiosity, it had to be mistrust. It was now important to discover which one of them didn't trust him. He decided it was best to just continue on.

He walked inside a deserted room that had two chairs and a fancy-looking machine. *"Once I activate the training machine, my hidden 'stalker' will be revealed,"* he thought. He walked forward to one of the machines and inputted some codes. He prepared himself as he waited for the machines to take effect.

A few moments later, Shadow felt the machine activate. The air in the room became heavy as the temperature in the room rose higher and higher. He used this room to get his body used to varying temperatures and also modified it so that he could train against the powers of his teammates.

Looking around the room for signs of the hidden person, he heard a girl cry out and saw Kay by the door, leaning against the wall for support. As he approached her, he saw that she was out of breath and gasping for air. "Kay…" he said blankly. He raised his hand, and a black, transparent bubble formed itself around her, shielding her from the room's effect.

As Kay was recovering, she glared at him. "What are you trying to do, kill me or something?"

Shadow laughed in a mocking sort of way and then sat down by the bubble, amused. "You do realize that you were stalking me in my own home, right?" he asked. "So don't get all high and mighty."

Kay rolled her eyes at the question and then sighed. "I was just curious and wanted to explore, is all. And it's not like you said that we couldn't follow you."

Shadow smiled in spite of himself. Her brash personality was amusing him. "Yes, I suppose that I didn't directly say that you couldn't stalk me in my own castle. Please excuse me for my extreme lack of perception."

Kay glared harder. "Fine. I guess I'm sorry for invading your privacy. But look at it from my point of view. You have a secret room. That's like five kinds of cool."

Shadow nodded. "Five kinds, really?" he remarked. Shaking his head, he pointed his hand towards the machines. Darkness wrapped around them, and they beeped, switching off. "There. You're free."

Kay rose to her feet. "Thanks," she said. "That was intense. So this is where you go to train, huh?"

"Don't mention it," Shadow replied. "And yes, this is my private training room. I have to warn you... Since you've seen my secret training area, I'm going to have to kill you."

"Really?" Kay asked, eyes wide.

"Kidding... I was just kidding. Like in the not-serious and facetious sense."

Kay smiled. "Oh, right. Duh. Sorry about that. Usually when a vampire says that they're going to kill you, they mean it. Not to be all discriminating or anything."

"I'm half-vampire. Half. People always seem to forget that part."

"Well, I'd better be going. I have my own training and whatnot to do," Kay said.

Shadow nodded. "All right. I hope your training goes well."

Kay waved goodbye and left.

Shadow smiled in relief as she left, glad to finally have some time to himself. He sat down on the floor of the room and closed his eyes; he began concentrating, channeling the focus of his mind. Suddenly, the very shadows in the room seemed to whisper to him. He lifted both of his hands and held them out to his sides. The dust that had gathered on the floor of the room began to swirl around him.

His eyes opened and were filled with darkness. He was in a trance. Different visions flashed around him, inside of his mind like scenes from a movie. He saw a tall demonic figure walking towards a portal, then thrusting his hands up into the air. The figure's hands began to glow bright green. Hordes of demons and creatures began walking through the portal. The figure gave a dark laugh, fire raining from the sky in the background.

The vision faded, and a familiar voice echoed in his head. *"It's time, Shadow. It's time. Go to the dragons' rest."*

Shadow awoke in a sweat on the floor, the visions fading from his eyes. *"Was that my. . .our... future?"* he wondered. *"But I can't see the future. I don't have that ability. . .unless she wanted me to see this."*

He got up. *"That voice. . .It must have belonged to her, to that shaman. She could never stay out of my head. She told me to go to the place where the dragons rest. She's mentioned it to me before. Draconia?"*

He rushed to the exit and came out from the hidden bookshelf, finding himself back in his room. He then walked over to his bed, picked up his own communicator, and looked at it. No messages, none at all. *"It's been too quiet around here for a good hour. . . Something must be up,"* he thought. He left his room.

As he went into the dark and empty hallway, he couldn't help but admire the silence, but it was making him increasingly nervous. He didn't see signs of his teammates anywhere.

Shadow entered the living room and saw the TV on. But, strangely, it was muted. Not shut off. The room was deserted. After searching all of the main areas of the castle, he couldn't help but feel uneasy. He stood perfectly still, and then his body began to emit light grey energy rays, which flew around him in ripples. This technique, although physically draining, allowed him to sense any life forms in the area. It would tell him exactly where his teammates were.

After many long seconds, the ripples came back through the floor and ceiling and retracted back into his body. A smile spread across his face as the knowledge of where his teammates were imprinted in his mind. *"No. . . It couldn't be,"* he thought. *"They actually followed my orders. That's almost too good to be true."*

He walked along the corridor leading to the east wing and came to a door, which was adorned with sapphires and emeralds. He turned the knob and entered the room. It led to a long hallway, which spiraled upwards and turned into stairs that led to another door. This one was ancient and less ornate than the previous. He pulled on the handle, and with a loud creaking sound, the door wrenched open and he was on the roof.

Loud noises told him he was getting closer. Since the roof of the castle was so large, he had made a training facility there, a place to improve skills and powers. The training area was covered with a thick layer of special glass to block out UV rays. It spanned out almost a mile in radius and was big enough for many people to train in at once. He looked through a window.

Ellie and Tristan were training together. She was throwing up thick ice shields as he threw large fireballs to melt them. Shadow looked to the left and saw Tereya and Faith training together in the earthen area. As Tereya would use his geokinesis to throw rocks at Faith, she would use her senses to avoid them. Otherwise, he saw the usual people pairing up with each other: Isaac with Kay and Crystal with Ethan.

He walked over to the training room door. As he pulled it open, everyone immediately stopped what they were doing, and all eyes fell on him.

"Well, this isn't awkward or anything."

"Shadow!" Ellie called, causing the looks to shift from him to her. She blushed slightly and smiled. "What's up?"

"A robbery, one that we're going to stop," Shadow replied.

"You have to give us more to go on than just a robbery," Tristan said. "I mean, is somebody shoplifting from the local donut hut or. . .is there an actual crime in progress?"

"Tris, you're being stupid again," Faith began, shaking her head. "I highly doubt that Shadow would want us all to train to stop a bakery from being robbed. While stealing is bad, somebody stealing donuts hardly counts as end-of-the-world-worthy."

"Faith, I'm appalled by your gross oversimplification of donut-related delinquency in the world. Don't you know that donut theft is a gateway crime?" Ryan replied, waving his finger. "First, it's simple. You steal a donut.

Then, you move on to stealing a car, then arson, and then murder! It's a vicious cycle."

"Ryan, shut up," Ellie said, sighing. "Shadow, please clarify what you're talking about before I backhand Ryan and Tristan into the next century."

Shadow looked up at the clock on the wall, which read 7:37. Shocked, he looked back down at them. "There's no time to explain, because it's time. I know it's sudden, but I trust that you all are prepared. Tonight wasn't the first training session, nor will it be the last, I'm sure."

"Where is this whole thing going down?" Isaac asked.

"I don't know the exact location, but it will be taking place somewhere on the island of Draconia," Shadow replied.

"Draconia?!" Ryan exclaimed.

"Yes, Ryan, I believe he said Draconia," Faith replied curtly. "What's so shocking about that?"

Glaring at Faith, Ryan continued. "Isn't that the island of legends? I thought it didn't exist, just a myth."

"Yes, the legends all speak of a powerful artifact being held there and guarded by a powerful dragon. It just so happens that we are going there to intercept someone from stealing it, since the guardian dragon is sleeping. It sleeps once every thousand years, so now something or someone is going to try to steal the artifact," Shadow said.

"What is the artifact? And what does it do?" Kay asked.

"Is it the Dragon's Eye?" Ethan asked, in a voice that said he hoped he was wrong.

"Yes," Shadow replied blankly, looking curiously at Ethan. "How do you know about the Dragon's Eye?"

"I'm familiar with most legends. Let's just leave it at that," Ethan said briskly. "All that matters is that we need to prevent the forces of darkness from grabbing hold of it. The last time a mortal got his hands on it, the results were disastrous."

"Let's go. We haven't time to lose," Shadow said.

"How are we getting to this island?" Tristan asked. "Islands are typically surrounded by miles of water on each side. So it's not like we can just walk to it."

"Typically?" Ryan replied. "Try always. Islands are always surrounded by water."

"We will be taking my jet," Shadow said. "Let's head to the flight bay." He motioned the others to follow him down the long stairwell which led to the ground floor.

Faith cleared her throat, causing everyone to stop. "I don't mean to question your methods, but. . ."

"Yes?" Shadow asked. "Go on."

"You do realize that we could cut about twenty minutes of travel time if we just take the elevator that's just over there, right?"

"Faith. This is my castle, I've lived here for quite some time, and I think I would know if there was an elevator."

Faith pointed out a small door over to the side that was clearly labeled "elevator," then made a voilà gesture.

Shadow frowned. "Okay. Well, that's new," he replied, frowning, as Tristan, Ryan, and Isaac laughed in the background.

"No, it isn't. You just didn't notice it, oh, unperceptive one," Ryan said, shaking his head.

"Whatever, I guess we're using it," Shadow said, then led the way to the elevator. He pressed the button, and the doors opened. It was clear to him that the elevator was big enough for them all; it was five times the size of a standard one. After they got in, he pressed a button to close the door and then pressed another button labeled 'Flight Bay' and waited for it to start moving.

CBEOCBEOCBEOCBEO

The elevator came to an abrupt halt and Shadow exited, with the others following closely behind. "So where is our ride?" Crystal asked.

"That one over there," Shadow replied, pointing to the jet. No secret, it was his pride and joy.

"Eww, come on. Why do we have to take that piece of junk?" Crystal asked in disgust. "It's so small, like traveling in coach. I only travel first class."

"You'll fly in whatever we have and like it. I'm not going to put out a red carpet and have a friggin' parade just to get you on this jet."

"Looks like you'll just have to shut up and deal, Princess," Ryan said.

"Whatever," Crystal huffed. She threw Shadow a final scathing look before boarding with the others, leaving Ethan and him outside.

"Sorry about that. You must forgive her. She's still not quite used to living here and dealing with everything yet," Ethan said.

"Well, she'll have to get over that now, won't she?" Shadow replied, with a hint of anger in his voice.

"Yes. . .I'm aware," Ethan replied, "though you must also try to work on your own temper. Do not be so quick to let your anger rise. Dealing with teenagers is like most things; it requires patience."

Shadow nodded. He and Ethan walked inside, parting ways at the entrance. He walked into the cockpit and sat in the pilot's seat. He punched the coordinates for their destination and prayed that they would have enough power and luck to fight back the evil force that they would be confronting that night.

Cৠৎৠৎৠৎৠৎ

During the flight, Shadow tried to think of ways to boost morale. After a few moments of thinking, he decided that the best course of action would be to talk to his teammates and see how they were holding up. Putting the jet on autopilot, he went through the door and into the seating area. Walking into the aisle, he saw everyone except Tereya and Ellie fast asleep.

"Hey, Shadow," Ellie said, "have you looked outside lately?"

Shadow rushed over to her. "What do you mean?"

"Look at the sky. It's acting all weird. It's like what happened that night when we first met. Remember?"

Shadow moved over to the next window, leaning over a now-awake and very annoyed Crystal. He gazed out and saw the sky flash red as it turned dark.

"The second sign," he whispered, his voice flat. He didn't want to worry them by acting scared, but this was definitely something to be feared. He was told to watch out for three signs, and this was the second.

"Okay?" Crystal asked. "So what does that mean? And it had better be something dire 'cause you just wrecked my beauty sleep and messed up my makeup when you leaned over me."

Shadow sighed and then turned to the rest of the group.

"Once again, pardon her," Ethan said, noticing how tense Shadow was getting.

"It's all right. It's my fault for not explaining things better than I have. It's a bad habit that I need to break," Shadow replied. "I was warned that there would be three signs to watch out for, and the real test will commence following the second sign."

"Well, duh," Ryan said, yawning and rubbing his eyes. "I'm sure we've gathered that this had to do with this 'great evil' that we are supposed to fight. We're not stupid. I don't think any of us, aside from Tristan, are thinking, Oh, no, it can't be the great evil that's making the sky go all crazy; it's probably just global warming."

Shadow scowled. "Look, now isn't the time for jokes or–"

"But what if I break a nail?!" Crystal interrupted angrily.

"–or interruptions!" Shadow added, glaring at her.

Ethan stood up at Shadow's side. "Listen, everyone, we must all work together or we're going to be finished before we've even started," he said in a calm and soothing voice. His words seemed to have a positive effect on everyone in front of him. Crystal's anger seemed to ebb away like the ocean's tide.

Shadow grew tense, seeing the power that Ethan had over everyone just using his voice. "What did you do to them?"

"Oh, nothing much," Ethan replied. "It's just an ability of mine. I can spread an aura of tranquility around me, which can calm down almost anyone."

"Then why didn't it work on me?"

"It's probably because of your vampire side. I'm guessing it makes you immune to some, if not most, forms of mental alteration," Ethan said. "That's pretty handy, mental immunity."

"Well, I guess there is a bright side to being cursed then," Shadow replied darkly.

"I didn't mean anything by it," Ethan said. "My sincerest apologies."

Shadow shook his head. "No, it's fine. I know you didn't. It just doesn't ease the bitterness up any. I hate being half-vampire; not really the life I would have chosen for myself, you know?"

"What's wrong with being practically immortal, and having enhanced senses, in addition to super speed and strength?" Ethan asked. "Most would sell their soul for a fraction of the power you have."

"Well, besides being deathly allergic to sunlight, it sucks that I'll never be able to get into a real relationship. Say I find somebody special. I can't date them. They'll age and eventually die, and I'll be this young forever," Shadow replied, closing his eyes. "I wouldn't ever ask anybody to condemn themselves to a life with me anyway. I'd only bring them pain and heartache."

Ellie went very still, as she listened to Shadow's words. It had occurred to her before, what his being half-vampire meant, but the pain of hearing him say it aloud was almost like being stabbed. And she wasn't sure why.

"You are truly a romantic," Ethan said.

Shadow nodded, staring blankly outside into the dark sky. "You say that like it's a good thing. It's not. It just makes me weak."

Ethan sighed. "'Love never fails. But where there are prophecies, they will cease; where there are tongues, they will be stilled; where there is knowledge, it will pass away. For we know in part, and we prophesy in part, but when completeness comes, what is in part disappears. Now I know in part; then I shall know fully, even as I am fully known,'" he said. "'And now these three remain: faith, hope, and love. But the greatest of these is love.'"

"Are you quoting something?" Shadow asked, raising an eyebrow. "It sounds familiar, but I don't know where it's from."

"It's from a book, one of the best I know," Ethan replied. "The Bible."

Shadow smiled. "With you, I should have figured. Well, regardless, nobody will ever love me," he said, waving his hand. "So love doesn't matter to me."

"Don't be so quick to throw out the plan that fate has for you," Ethan said. "You never know what is in the grand scheme of things…."

"Not to throw out your whole grand-scheme theory, but I've never been one to think of my future. I just take each day as it comes, living to the best of my ability. Life is wasted on me and the rest of my brethren who have been subjected to this… life."

"Don't let yourself become so cynical. You're doing great good here, whether you believe it or not. Fate has been dealing more cards into your hand. Are you truly ignoring them? Or pretending they don't even exist?"

"I'm ignoring nothing. I'm just saying that fate has never been on my side, so I don't believe in fate. I know that there is a higher power, yes, but I don't think He's my biggest fan, not by a long shot. He's shafted me at every turn."

"I'm sorry that you feel that way. Just know that something doesn't happen for nothing. There's a reason behind every single event that occurs in this world, from the fruit growing on a tree or the rain falling from the sky. Small occurrences happen to contribute to the bigger picture."

"Oh? And what's in my bigger picture? Can you, with your connections, tell me? Because so far, it looks like it's one big nothing."

Ethan shook his head. "I'm afraid it doesn't work like that. I can't tell you what will happen because it's not in my power to decide that. Fate and future are two different things. The future isn't set in stone. Fate is. One day you'll understand your place in the world, and you'll find the happiness which has eluded you for so long."

"It doesn't even matter. Nothing is more important than right now. We've got to kill this evil, or Earth, as we know it, is done for," Shadow said, in a tone that clearly said he wanted Ethan to drop the conversation.

Ethan nodded. "I can sense that you wish to be left alone. I will comply with your wishes," he said. "Just try not to worry too much. You're a good person and things will work out in the end. They always do." He left Shadow's side and sat down in the seat by Crystal.

Shadow, still slightly wound up by the conversation with Ethan, walked over to an empty row and sat in the second seat in. He rested his head on the window and gazed out solemnly. He ignored the conversations held by the other members in the background, and tried desperately to drown out the noise.

"Hey. . .Shadow, uh, like, can I talk to you for a second?" Crystal asked, moving to stand next to him.

Shadow raised an eyebrow. For the first time since he had met her, Crystal had an apologetic look on her face, as if she knew that she had done something wrong. Intrigued, he blankly nodded and motioned towards the free seat by him. "What's wrong?"

Crystal sat down. "Listen, I…uh…spoke with Ethan, and I just wanted to say that I'm sorry for causing problems before. I was being a brat, and you didn't need to deal with that."

"It's fine, Crystal. I'm not mad. Just being where we are now and having everything on my shoulders is very intense, you know?"

Crystal nodded and smiled. "I know. But I'm still sorry for putting extra stress on top of you." She leaned over and gave him a quick hug. "Thank you for doing everything that you have been doing just to protect all of us."

"Er. . .thanks, Crystal," Shadow said, eyes widening in surprise, mouth gaped in disbelief that she was hugging him instead of biting his head off. "This is definitely a nice change from how you usually act."

Almost immediately, Crystal regained her usual composure and flicked her hair. "It was nothing, and don't make it out to be more than it was," she replied in her usual tone. "And what do you mean, a nice change from how I usually act? Are you saying I don't act nice all the time?"

"Are you sure that you're feeling okay?" Shadow asked wearily. Her mood swings were beyond tiresome.

"Shut up!" Crystal huffed, rushing back to her seat.

"Crystal?" Shadow called once more, but she threw him a nasty look and turned her head in the other direction, avoiding him.

"Ethan," he said, struggling not to get angry; after all, dealing with Crystal was sometimes like nails on a chalkboard. "Do something?"

"I can try, but I can't make any promises," Ethan said.

Shadow sighed. Since Ethan was Crystal's guardian angel , he had wrongfully assumed that if anybody could control the bipolar-acting girl, it would have been him.

Ellie let out a soft laugh. She got up and sat in the empty seat next to Shadow, who was glaring at her. "May I help you?" she asked coolly, privately enjoying his temper, which he wasn't able to hide.

"You're laughing at me. Why?"

"No, no. It's just kind of cute how worked up you get when you deal with Crystal," Ellie said. "It's not your fault. It's just who she is."

Shadow sighed and dismissed her attempt at justifying Crystal's behavior. "I don't need you to provide excuses for her. It's obvious that she's losing what's left of her mind, and trust me, it didn't seem like she had enough to spare."

Ryan, who had overheard the comment, laughed. "If that isn't the understatement of the century, I don't know what is."

"If you don't shut up right now, Ryan, you'll find out exactly why I'm called the Ice Princess," Ellie said darkly, her eyes narrowed threateningly.

"Whatever is wrong with Crystal, I'm done caring," Shadow said, interrupting their showdown. "It's the mission that matters; the mission is what counts. Unless I'm focused, we don't stand a chance."

Ellie nodded. "You're right, but don't worry too much about it. She'll come around on her own time. Until then, leave it alone and get some rest. We have a big night ahead of us." She rested her head on his shoulder and closed her eyes.

Shadow's eyes widened. He didn't expect her to fall asleep on him, not then, not in a million years. Yet it was happening, and he couldn't help but think how soft her skin felt against his arm or how light she was, not to mention how good her hair smelled. It smelled floral and reminded him of freshly-picked oranges. He sighed, but muffled it so it wouldn't wake her up. After a while, his anger with Crystal faded, and he fell asleep.

ଓ*ୈଓ*ୈଓ*ୈଓ*ୈ

"Ahoy, Captain, I think we're here," Ryan declared about twenty minutes later. He nudged Shadow.

Shadow's eyes jolted open. "Sorry, I must have fallen asleep." He yawned, turning to Ellie and giving her a gentle nudge.

"What is it?" Ellie asked, slowly opening her eyes and yawning.

"It's time, Ellie. Wake up. We're here. . .Draconia Isle."

Ellie sobered up instantly and nodded. Her determination filled her with newfound energy. She turned back to him and smiled confidently. "You ready to do this?"

Shadow nodded and returned her smile. He couldn't ignore the feeling that this could all end very badly. He moved past Ellie, and he saw that the rest of his team was getting up. Some of them were stretching, others yawning, and others looking alert and ready.

"I'm glad to see you are all up," he announced, moving to stand by the door. "Whatever stands ahead in our way, just know that you all will conquer it as long as you become one. Fight together and stand together. It's the only way we stand a chance."

"Quick question, Captain," Ryan said. "If you were sleeping, who landed the jet?"

Ethan raised his hand and moved forward. "Guilty, I'm afraid," he said. "While you were all sleeping, the jet's GPS gave a notification that we were near our destination. So, rather than wake you, I decided to land it."

Shadow smiled. "Thanks. I appreciate it."

"Don't mention it," Ethan replied.

"So this is it?" Tereya asked. "We're here… and we're about to fight the evil that was so powerful that you needed to recruit us all?"

"Yeah, this is it," Shadow replied. "But don't worry, we'll stop the evil and—"

"Then get some food?" Ryan asked hopefully.

Shadow sighed. "We'll see, okay?" He took a deep breath, motioned for them to follow him, and they set foot out onto Draconia Isle.

CHAPTER 3: THE WARNING

"It's so freaking hot here!" Crystal whined, her face screwing into a pout. "I can hardly breathe!"

"Then why are you talking?" Ryan asked, sticking his tongue out at her. "We wouldn't want you wasting your ever-so-precious air."

"Ryan, don't instigate," Shadow said shortly. "Now is not the time. And Crystal, you'll just have to deal. The temperature won't change just because you whine at it."

Tristan laughed. "You guys are stupid. It's not hot here at all."

"I didn't think it was possible to be too dumb to feel things," Ryan remarked, throwing a sideways glance at Tristan. "Apparently, I was mistaken."

"Ryan, shut up! Stop picking on my brother. And Tristan, stop giving Ryan an excuse to pick on you," Faith said, shaking her head.

Ellie wiped the sweat off of her forehead. "She's right. This heat is crazy," she said, waving her hand like a fan.

"Well, it's not too bad out here for me," Tristan replied, arrogance filling his voice.

"You do realize, of course, that a hot environment wouldn't bother you because your powers are fire-based?" Shadow asked.

Tristan blushed and then turned to face Shadow. "No, I guess that thought hadn't crossed my mind."

Shadow opened his mouth to make a remark, but Faith beat him to the punch. "Maybe you should allow a thought to cross your mind now and then; might be a good change for once."

Ryan laughed as Tristan's face flushed a deep red. "Nice one."

"Nobody said you could laugh," Faith snapped. "So why don't you just do us all a favor and shut your mouth."

"So, apparently, I need your permission now?" Ryan replied, holding his hands up. "Somebody call the laugh police. I've broken a law!"

"Okay, stay focused, guys," Shadow said before Faith could reply. "You don't know what could happen. At any moment, something could jump out at us."

"Maybe we should begin searching?" Isaac suggested. "I mean, the object we're supposed to guard could be anywhere, right?"

"Isaac's right," Kay said. "We have no idea where the darn thing is. How can we protect what we can't see?"

"Take it easy, Kay," Shadow said. "I believe the Dragon's Eye resides somewhere in the middle of the island. . .perhaps underground, probably in a sacred shrine or something."

Faith nodded. "Didn't you say that there's a dragon guarding the Dragon's Eye?"

"Yes, I did," Shadow replied. "As I've said, the dragon sleeps only a day out of every thousand years. And I highly doubt that it's a huge coincidence that some evil being is coming here tonight."

"Tonight just so happening to be the night that the dragon is sleeping," Ellie stated, and Shadow nodded in confirmation.

"What if we're fighting this person or thing and the dragon wakes up?" Isaac asked, almost shaking in fear.

"Yes, that was a fear of mine for some time," Shadow admitted. "But not to worry, Isaac. I'm sure that the guardian dragon will not attack us. All dragons are supposed to have high intelligence, so it should know we're trying to protect the artifact. We just need to find the shrine."

"I'm afraid that you guys are never going to find what you're looking for," a voice called.

Shadow paused and looked around as he tried to make out which direction the voice had come from. "Hold on, guys. I don't like this," he said. He continued to survey the area. "Come out now!"

Laughter rang out all around them as the unknown party came closer. He was an older man who appeared to be in his mid-thirties or early forties. He had blonde hair and bright blue eyes. Dressed as though he was going to a fancy party, he moved slowly and confidently as he walked up to Shadow. "Hello," the man said, with a condescending smile.

Shadow looked the man up and down; a slow, calculating look. *Where did he come from?"* he wondered as the man eyed him back.

"So who are you, and what do you want?"

The man shook his head, and his smile broadened. "Temper, temper. Anger only clouds the mind. You can't allow your mind to be clouded, especially not if you wish to succeed."

This time it was Shadow's turn to smile and it wasn't pleasant. "Excuse my hostile disposition, but I don't like surprises."

"Very good, very good!" the man laughed. "You're playing the game. You've drawn your hand. . .Was it a good one? Can you win?"

"I live life; I don't play it. I don't play games, period. They're for fools, which I am definitely not." Shadow replied. He watched, slightly satisfied, as the laughter faded from the man's face.

"So you think you can handle what's to come?" the man asked.

Shadow shrugged. "I'm always looking for a challenge."

The man's smile returned. "To answer your question," he began, "my true name is not your concern. You, however, may call me Zach."

Shadow rolled his eyes, but his irritation didn't match his rising curiosity. "Okay, what message do you have to deliver?"

Zach gave Shadow a look as if he were an annoying insect. "My, you certainly aren't one for pleasantries, are you? I'll bet you always do that, just cut right to the point. Don't you? Recklessness is not an endearing quality."

"We're on a mission, and we don't have time for your childish games!" Shadow growled. "Don't you understand that there are lives at risk?"

"You're lucky I'm such a nice guy, or I would just leave you hanging and not deliver my message," Zach said, taking obvious delight in Shadow's rising anger. "So, anyway, I was sent by a higher power that wants you guys to succeed."

"Wait a moment, a higher power? You seem vaguely familiar," Ethan said. "Do I know you from somewhere?"

"Please don't interrupt me." Zach replied, brushing Ethan off. He then pointed at Shadow. "One amongst your number will betray you."

Shadow turned and looked at his teammates, and shook his head. "I trust all of them. They wouldn't betray me."

"Trust is a fine virtue, as long as it's not misplaced," Zach said. "And you, my friend, had better hope yours isn't. But, for now, just remember one thing: The person that's after the Dragon's Eye, she's nothing. Nothing at all compared to what's to come." He turned and walked away.

"Wait a second," Shadow called.

Zach turned back to face him. "What?" he asked curtly. "Wasn't I clear enough?"

"No, you weren't!" Shadow growled, his temper rising once again. "You've explained nothing."

"Be more specific," Zach said. "What is it that you don't understand?"

"The person we have to watch out for, who is it?"

"Oh," Zach replied thoughtfully, scratching his head. "Well, I'm not able to tell you that. It's not my place. Just know that the thing you'll fight here today is just a minion, or lesser being, if you will, compared to a more devastating evil that you guys will soon face," he said, turning to leave once more.

"Wait," Tereya said.

Zach stopped once again, though he didn't turn back around. "Yes, Tereya?"

"If you're so powerful, why aren't you helping us fight?"

"I'm afraid that's not my job. And…."

"And…?" Ryan asked, eyebrow raised.

"I just don't have the time. Good luck, though," Zach said, and he faded more and more with each step he took until he was gone.

"Wow, that was different," Faith said quietly. She turned to Shadow. "What's your take on him?"

"I don't know. He was definitely unique, to say the least."

"So, basically, once again, you're clueless?" Tristan asked.

Faith sighed. "Brother, please. Be respectful. You're not helping anyone or anything by acting like a jerk."

Shadow waved his hand at her, as if telling her to be quiet. "No, he's saying what a lot of you are probably thinking by now. Right?"

Tereya shook his head. "Not me!"

"Don't lie!" Shadow snapped, his anger causing the younger boy to burst into tears.

Before a tear could even hit the ground, a beam of sparkling blue energy smacked into Shadow, lifting him off his feet and throwing him backwards onto the ground.

Ellie walked towards him. Her hand was still glowing with energy as she lowered it to her side. "Don't you dare yell at Tereya," she said coldly, and, for the first time, anger appeared in her eyes as she looked at him.

Tereya sniffled a bit, wiping his eyes gingerly on his sleeve. "I-I'm fine. I just want us to stop fighting. We're friends. Friends shouldn't fight."

Ellie nodded, and turned to Shadow. "Here," she said softly, holding out a hand.

Shadow took her hand and was pulled back onto his feet. His eyes met hers, and their gaze lingered.

Ryan whistled. "Hey, you two, Tereya's too young for this. Let's keep it PG."

Shadow's lips tightened. He rubbed his arm nervously. "If we're done playing around, we can actually be saving the world right about now."

"Well, lead the way, oh, leader of ours!" Ryan exclaimed in a mocking tone.

"Can you pick up something, like a psychic vision or something?" Shadow asked Faith, hope filling his voice.

"I'll try my best." She stared off into the distance, her dark purple eyes instantly flashing the darkest shade of gold. The world began to spin from beneath her; she felt an intense shock surge through her. She felt like she was being ripped from her own body. Everyone disappeared. Everything went black.

CB&CB&CB&CB&

Faith stirred. She opened her eyes slowly, and she struggled to get onto her feet. "What happened?" she asked, hoping someone would answer her. She looked around and saw that her teammates and Draconia Isle were both gone.

She was in a temple, or what was left of a temple. The walls were covered with a thick kind of plant, which she took to be moss. The ground was cracked in places, and bones were scattered around the ground, making her think a battle must have been fought there. *What is this place for?* she wondered.

At once, as if a mysterious force was sending the information into her mind, she knew the purpose of the place. She continued thinking for a few moments, and then she finally knew the answer.

"Show me what's going to happen to me and my friends!" she called out desperately. As she spoke, waves of bright-colored beams danced around her like a strobe light. The falling pieces of color began joining together, fitting in place like puzzle pieces, forming into individual distorted images.

She willed them to take a clearer form. As the pictures slowly became pure, she knew what they were. They were pictures of future events. They circled around her and then rushed through her body, echoing in her mind like flashes of light.

Flash! A bunch of old objects sitting on an altar, sparking in the light.

Flash! Kay laughing and looking down at a ring on her finger.

Flash! A group of women sitting at a table.

Flash! A dark figure crying over a girl's body.

Flash! The sky black and raining fire.

Flash! The team walking across a bridge, lava beneath them.

Flash! A woman with long, wild, red hair, walking towards Shadow.

Flash! A dragon sending a blast of flames at a demon.

Flash! Herself pointing out a path leading to the temple, turning and winking.

CʒʔʘCʒʔʘCʒʔʘCʒʔʘ

Faith's body jerked. Her eyes fluttered open as Tristan kneeled down next to her. "What happened?"

"Are you all right?" Tristan asked.

"Yeah, just peachy, Bro," Faith replied weakly as she rose from the ground and back onto her feet. "I mean, I feel like I got hit by a truck, but aside from that… I'm just chipper."

Tristan hugged her. "I was worried; you have no idea. All I could think of is how much I would miss you if anything happened."

"Oh, Trist," Faith exhaled softly. "If I knew that me being in dangerous situations would bring out the nice guy in you, I'd do it more often."

"What did you see?" Shadow asked suddenly. "Anything that could help us?"

Ellie scowled. "Shadow, please at least try to hold back your excitement until we find out if Faith is okay or not."

Shadow blushed slightly. "You're right. I'm sorry."

"It's okay, guys. I'm fine, really," Faith said hurriedly, looking from Ellie to Shadow. "Don't go fighting on my account."

"You sure, Sis?" Tristan piped up, concern still filling his voice.

"I said I'm fine," Faith said. "Now, please. . .can we just go find this place?"

"Hold on. First, tell us exactly what you saw," Shadow said. "Leave out no detail. Anything could be important, even if it doesn't seem like it."

"Well, I saw a couple of things. They were like pictures flashing in front of me," Faith said. "I saw… somebody crying over a dead body. Then I saw. . .lava and fire. I saw a dragon, and then I saw a dark figure approaching you, Shadow."

"Is that all?" Shadow asked.

"No. I saw myself. I was pointing out the way to the temple."

"Well, as long as you saw where this temple is, we can go to it," Ethan said.

"What about the rest of the things that she saw in her vision?" Isaac asked.

"As troubling as those things are, we cannot worry about them right now," Shadow said. "You can't prevent the future from happening just by worrying about it. You'll only drive yourself crazy."

"Shadow's right," Ethan said. "If you allow yourself to fret about things that haven't happened yet, then you'll waste the time you have right now in the present."

"I knew you would agree," Shadow said. He was glad to have someone like Ethan around, someone who would never be the difficult one or the one who disagreed at every turn.

"We need to go to the temple and protect the Dragon's Eye. Time is running out."

"Why should we risk our lives for some stupid jewel?" Kay asked, and her tone strongly suggested that it had been on her mind for some time. "I mean, this all just seems so pointless."

"I would never ask you to risk your life," Shadow began, and turned to face them all. He saw, reflected in their eyes, exactly how young they were; innocent and whole. He knew exactly how much they stood to lose if any of them perished in the upcoming battles.

"If there's anything I know, it's that the greater good is the most important thing, what's always worth fighting for in the end. By us fighting to defend the Dragon's Eye, we can save lives. Innocent lives."

Ellie nodded and smiled. "And I don't know about you guys, but I'd gladly risk my life to save millions, if not billions, of people," she said. Ethan, Faith, and Tereya nodded in agreement.

Shadow took the following silence as an opportunity to continue. "Once again, you guys can leave, if you want. But know that fighting the good fight and losing is better than not fighting at all. We were all blessed with these abilities, and that's what separates us from the bound."

"What are the bound, anyway?" Kay asked.

"Not what, but whom, Kay. They're everyday people, the ones who are average and normal," Shadow replied. "They are the people we protect and fight for. We fight the great battle, not because we want to, but because we have to, and because it's the right thing to do. They can't protect themselves."

"I've never heard them called that before," Faith said. "I mean, they're people like us. Why call them anything but?"

Shadow paused and then smiled. "It's the name given to them by the gifted people of the past. Yes, they are people, as are we. However, we're gifted with abilities. What better to do with our abilities than to protect the less fortunate?"

"But what makes them so important?" Kay asked, rolling her eyes. "I mean, it's survival of the fittest. If they can't survive by themselves, maybe they're not worth keeping alive."

Shadow blinked in disbelief at her cruelty. "They are important because they are people just like us. They feel pain, love, and fear, and they need us, and we need to protect them," he replied, with a note of finality.

"But wait. . .don't you feed off of them?" Ellie asked, playfully.

Shadow's face flushed scarlet, but he shook it away as he turned to face Ellie. "Yes, I require them for sustenance, which makes them even more important. . .to me, at least."

Kay frowned, but then nodded. "Fine."

Shadow smiled, satisfied. "So," he began, turning to Faith, "to the temple of the dragon god. Lead the way!"

Faith nodded. "Aye, aye, Captain!" she replied, then began walking. The others followed directly behind her.

CB&OCB&OCB&OCB&O

They walked on past overgrowth and thorny brambles to the foot of an ancient set of stairs. These stairs were crafted from what seemed to be diamond, carved and cut in different patterns that changed as one walked up them. If someone looked up the stairs, they could see a solid gold door with strange patterns carved into it.

They walked up the stairs quickly, but carefully. Shadow walked ahead by a few feet in case anything dangerous was ahead. The others followed closely behind until they reached the top. He held out his hand to stop them.

"What's wrong? Why are we stopping?" Tristan asked. "It's only a stupid door, not rocket science."

"As if you could recognize rocket science," Ryan remarked. "I bet you couldn't even recognize elementary science."

Faith's eyes narrowed. "Ryan, I'm not going to warn you again. Leave my brother alone, or else."

"Or else what?" Ryan scoffed. "You gonna psychic me to death?"

"No, but my fist will make best friends with your face."

"Guys, chill. There's no reason to fight," Tristan said. "I'm going to demonstrate exactly how paranoid Shadow is by opening the door and proving that there isn't anything dangerous about it."

"Tristan, I really wouldn't do that if I were you," Shadow said. "It could be a trap of some kind."

"Whatever," Tristan replied. "You think you know everything, but you're bound to be wrong one time."

He placed his hands on the door and pushed with all of his strength. When the door didn't budge, he simply stared at it and then sighed.

Faith shook her head. "Trist, when will you learn?"

"Well, how was I supposed to know the door wouldn't open?" Tristan replied, kicking aimlessly.

"Tristan, your brain, use it," Shadow said, rolling his eyes. "Of course, it wouldn't be that easy. Nothing in life is easy."

'How come Shadow can make fun of your brother and I can't?" Ryan asked, frowning.

"Shadow's the leader. It's his privilege," Faith replied, with a small smile.

"Shh, guys," Shadow said, frowning. "Let me figure this out."

"What do you mean?" Crystal asked. "You said you would need our help, but now you're trying to do everything by yourself!"

Ethan threw her a "be quiet" look, and she immediately hushed up. He tapped her shoulder and then pointed at the door.

Shadow stared blankly at it. Strange writing covered the surface.

"Salenrz ezril peouna, salenrz rfalelhnz dsoekwpa. Salenrz aprjosa rweka-zzar, salenrz aorezlza oezha?"

44

Above the strange writing there was a socket filled with a lifelike diamond eye. The eye rotated ominously.

"I see the problem," Ethan said. "It's a riddle. We must solve the riddle to enter the temple."

Shadow sighed. "I don't know what language that riddle is in. Does anyone know what language it is?" he asked. When no one spoke up, he cursed under his breath. He refused to be stopped by a door, of all things.

"It's Demonic," Faith said quietly. "I think. . .I can read it. It will be somewhat of a challenge, though. Demonic isn't very straightforward."

Shadow looked confused and slightly worried. "Faith, how do you know how to read Demonic?"

Faith bowed her head. "Does it really matter?"

"Yes, it actually does," Shadow replied. "What aren't you telling us?"

Tristan growled. "Don't worry about it!" he said, glaring. "All that matters is that she can read it and get us inside there."

"Shadow," Ethan said, gesturing to Faith, "don't push this."

Shadow was going to press the issue, but seeing how distraught Faith was getting, he decided to drop it. "Faith, I'm sorry. Tristan and Ethan are right."

Faith smiled. "Don't worry about it. Tristan is bound to be right sometimes," she joked.

"Hey!" Tristan exclaimed. "Are you going to read that or insult me?"

"Why do the two have to be mutually exclusive?" Ryan asked. "Both are equally helpful."

Faith, using a great amount of self-restraint, ignored Ryan and studied the ancient writing on the door for several moments. After several minutes, she finally recited the riddle:

"The clouds are my castle; the wind is my guide.
"The colored bow is my bed; the Earth where I fall to hide."

"Interesting," Shadow said, his face screwing up in thought. He wasn't much for riddles, or any kind of puzzle, for that matter. "Does anyone have any ideas?"

Crystal stared off into space for a moment and then smiled. "I know what it is!"

"Well?" Shadow asked.

Crystal raised an eyebrow. "Well, what?"

Shadow blinked. "What is it?"

"What is what?"

"The answer to the riddle!"

"Oh," Crystal replied, "it's me. I'm the answer to the riddle."

Shadow's eyes bulged slightly. Now he was getting annoyed. "Does anybody else have an answer for the riddle, a real answer?"

"No, really, it is me," Crystal said adamantly. "I'm heavenly, which means the clouds are my castle. The wind in my hair makes me look absolutely radiant. I love wearing colored bows, and I live on the Earth!"

Before Shadow could tell her off, Ethan spoke. "Crystal, dear, while you are special in your own way and very well-received, I don't think that the ancient people who wrote this riddle were thinking about you at the time. . .or even knew who you are," he said, patting her on the shoulder. "So the likelihood that you're the answer to the riddle, I'm afraid, is slim to none."

Crystal flushed bright red. "Right." She sat down at the top of the stairs, placing her face in her hands. "Well, then I'm out of ideas."

"Does anyone have an intelligent answer?" Shadow asked, rolling his eyes.

"Hmm," Ethan said, looking at the riddle over and over again. "One might assume that it would be something that was around back then and would still be around today. I doubt the riddle would be about something that isn't eternal. They wouldn't want people to never be able to enter - just to make entry difficult."

"Well, what about something like the seasons or whatever?" Tristan asked.

Faith smiled. "You may be onto something, Brother," she replied. "Perhaps something that happens at a specific time?"

"Maybe we should just go to the mall instead." Crystal said.

Kay roared in frustration. "Can you ever add something to the dialogue besides mindless nonsense?" she asked, whipping around to face Crystal.

"Kay, don't…" Isaac said, tugging on her shirt.

Crystal stood up and got within inches of Kay and stared her right in the face. "Excuse me, but I don't think I asked for your opinion."

Kay smiled. "I don't need to be asked for my opinion, 'cause at least I have one that's worth giving," she replied, moving closer.

Crystal gave Kay a look which clearly said, 'Oh, no, you didn't,' and the other girl backed up slightly.

Shadow whistled loudly. "Girls, calm yourselves!"

"Rain. . ." Tereya mumbled.

"What did you say?" Ellie asked.

"I asked them to calm themselves. They're acting ridiculous," Shadow replied, shaking his head.

"No, not you, Shadow," Ellie said, rolling her eyes. "Reya said something."

"Oh. Well, what did you say, Tereya?" Shadow asked, turning to face him.

"Maybe we would have heard him if Crystal kept her fat mouth shut," Kay said.

"Oh, no, she didn't!" Ryan exclaimed, snapping his fingers in a "z" formation.

"Did you just call me fat?" Crystal asked, narrowing her eyes. "Because, I swear, you won't have to worry about being killed by evil because I will—"

"Rain!" Tereya yelled loudly, interrupting Crystal. Everyone's eyes fell on him.

Suddenly, the eye that was embedded in the door shone bright red and began spinning around in the stone socket. After a few seconds, the entire floor started rumbling, and deep cracks appeared in the door.

Shadow watched as the door slowly disintegrated away, revealing a long, dark hallway. "I guess the answer was 'rain'."

"Well, that was anticlimactic," Ryan said, feeling the empty space where the door once was, checking to see that it was really gone. "Good work, Reya."

Tereya blushed. "Don't mention it. I just got lucky or something."

"Nonsense. You were brilliant," Isaac said, patting him on the back.

"Yeah, you were great, Reya," Shadow said. "Let's go, guys. I hope we're not too late."

A loud grumbling rang out under their feet from deep inside the temple. Then came the sound of something heavy hitting the ground, followed by a tremor.

"I'm guessing that the event is starting without us, eh, Captain?" Ryan said. "Does this mean we can skip the pleasantries and just go out for food? Because I could really go for –"

Shadow slapped Ryan on the back of his head. "Ryan, please."

"Ouch!" Ryan said, gingerly feeling the back of his head. "What was that for?!"

"I don't need you making sarcastic remarks," Shadow replied. "Just hush."

"Enough," Faith said. "We have a deadline, remember?"

"You're right," Shadow replied. "Tristan, lead the way."

"Why me?" Tristan asked, frowning.

"Because it's very dark ahead and you can brighten the way. Or because if you don't, I'll slap you harder than I hit Ryan. Take your pick."

Tristan led the way. A bright red aura of heat surrounded him, lighting the path. Everyone followed him along the route, down some stairs, and through sloping hallways.

"Faith, how close do you think we are to the inner chamber?" Kay asked.

Faith closed her eyes for a second. Then, as if she'd been doused with cold water, her eyes jolted open. "Not much further."

"It will be nice when we get done," Ryan said. "I'm thinking we should seriously consider stopping for cheeseburgers after this."

"Cheeseburgers? Ryan, you've got to be kidding," Crystal said, disgusted.

"What's wrong with cheeseburgers?" Ryan asked. "I like them."

"That does sound nice," Ellie admitted. "I didn't get a chance to eat before we left, it being so abrupt and all."

"Me either!" Tristan added.

"They're so nasty and fattening. All meat is," Crystal replied.

"Whatever," Ryan said. "All I know is, I want a cheeseburger, and I'm getting one."

CRORCRORCRORCRO

At last they came to a blackened chamber which appeared to be made out of a glass-like substance.

"Shadow," Ryan said quietly, "I think we found that dragon you were looking for."

"Mortals in my temple," the great beast rumbled in a deep, thundering voice. "Approach me, or perish."

Shadow knew a bit about dragons. He knew that they did not tolerate secrecy and preferred direct approaches. He motioned his team to follow his lead and slowly walked into the great chamber.

"You must be the great guardian," he said. Everyone was at his back, waiting for a command.

"Yes, mortal. I am Xalchraios, the Neo-Guardian," the dragon replied, smoke jutting from his snout. The dragon was as tall as the temple room, which itself was over one hundred feet high. He had pale purple skin. The bony parts of his wings were purple, while the fleshy parts were of the deepest cerulean blue. His teeth were long and sharp. His horns pointed straight in front of him like a bull. His tail flicked back and forth, the tip littered with long spikes.

Shadow smiled. He loved dragons. They were noble and powerful beasts. He could appreciate them. "Nice to make your acquaintance, Xalchraios," he replied, bowing. As he spoke to Xalchraios, he couldn't help but notice that a large gemstone, which was obviously the Dragon's Eye, sat behind him on a pedestal. It gleamed in the light that was cast by the torches.

"Why have you come here?" Xalchraios asked. "The only ones who dare enter sacred shrines are thieves. Are you thieves?"

Shadow shook his head. "No, we aren't. We're friends. . .allies, if you will. We mean you no harm. We know how powerful you are. We don't want a fight."

"You're correct, mortal," Xalchraios responded. "You all are insignificant to me. . .like insects. With one flap of my wings, I could destroy you."

"Its wings are smaller than its body," Tristan said. "How does it fly if it has such tiny wings?"

"Brother, hush," Faith whispered. "Do not draw attention to yourself."

"If you are not thieves, then why do you trespass in my midst?" Xalchraios grumbled, flicking his tail. "Usually prey doesn't come to me. I have to go searching for it."

"We're not food!" Tristan cried.

"Will you shut up?!" Crystal exclaimed, punching him in the ribs.

Shadow laughed nervously. "Great dragon, we don't want any trouble. We came to warn you about danger. There's great danger after you."

"You dare disturb my sleep over this?" Xalchraios roared.

"But you weren't even sleeping!" Ryan said pointedly. "In fact, you practically invited us into this chamber."

Xalchraios growled. "It is not for you, mortal, to decide what I was or wasn't doing. Did you ever consider that I wasn't sleeping because of the noises you've all been making throughout my temple?" he said, gazing down at all of them.

"It is true, I usually sleep on this day, but I've sensed a great evil coming this way. Your assistance wasn't wanted nor needed. To think that you all have the audacity to think that I would need the help of mortals is laughable."

"Well, obviously, Xalchraios has things under control. Can't we leave?" Isaac asked hopefully, eyeing the gigantic dragon.

"No," Ellie replied, before Shadow could respond. "We must protect him and the Dragon's Eye," she said. Ethan and Shadow nodded in agreement.

Kay blinked and clenched her fists. "But there's no point in us being here. The Dragon obviously doesn't want our help, so why should we stay?"

"If he wants our help or not, we still can't leave," Ethan said. "We can't take the risk that the forces of evil will get their hands on the Dragon's Eye. It's a powerful artifact."

"But wait," Tristan said, making sure that Crystal wasn't in touching distance before continuing. "Isn't he a dragon? Aren't they immortal? So why would he need our help?"

"Yes, dragons are immortal. But as a general rule, all dragons share the same weakness," Shadow replied matter-of-factly.

"Ixnay on the eaknessway," Ryan whispered, eyeing the dragon. "I'm sure he's a bit self-conscious about that."

Suddenly, Xalchraios snorted out a large puff of air, sending Ryan flying backwards onto the ground. "Do not test my patience, mortal."

Ryan growled, "I didn't even do anything, you big bullying lizard."

"Great Xalchraios, he didn't mean to offend," Shadow said as the great dragon glared at Ryan hungrily.

"The damage was done," Xalchraios said, stomping his foot on the ground, causing the whole room to shake. "I didn't intend to have an early meal, but he seems like he would be a delicious choice."

As Shadow opened his mouth to speak in Ryan's defense, a loud explosion rang out. The temple shook, and specks of dust rained from the ceiling.

"What was that?" Tereya asked, frightened. "It sounded like somebody was crashing through the walls."

Shadow motioned them all to move away from the door. "I think it's showtime," he said, pulling out a small sword from a sheath on his waist.

Xalchraios growled and looked down at Shadow. "Somebody comes to steal the Dragon's Eye," he said. "You aren't as dishonest as the rest of your kind."

Shadow nodded. "Yes, something is coming this way. It's why we came here to protect it."

"But why, mortal, do you try to protect an artifact that you have nothing to do with, and how did you know something would be coming for it?" Xalchraios asked, staring at him curiously.

Although Shadow heard the question, he ignored it. "Just know we're here to help. I just don't know what we're up against," he replied, as more explosions were heard, considerably closer than the last ones. "Plus, it's the right thing to do."

"Clearly, you are different from most humans," Xalchraios said, giving Shadow a long and calculating look.

"Thanks," Shadow replied, watching the door. A figure appeared and was forcing itself through it. Although the door was quite high, the figure had to duck to avoid hitting it. "A Neseptra demon!" he exclaimed. And, for the first time, fear spread across his face.

The creature was made like a bodybuilder. Its skin was a sick, pale green, with red markings across its body. Its head resembled a snake; red eyes and thick fangs could be seen in its open mouth. A large black tongue flicked around inside. It had two arms, each of which was equipped with a sharp spike protruding out from where its elbow would have been, and razor-sharp claws on its hands.

"I'm guessing Neseptra is a code word for ugly snake creature, right?" Ryan asked, although he didn't smile as usual.

"Yeah," Shadow said. "You could say that."

"I come for the artifact," the demon hissed, baring its teeth. "Give me the Dragon'ssss Eye or I'll resort to violensssse." Its attention was all on Xalchraios, as if the rest of the people in the room were insignificant.

"You were a fool to come here, demon. I am one of the five Neo-Guardians. You are no match for me!" Xalchraios boomed. He thrust his tail towards the demon as Ryan, Shadow, and Tristan jumped backwards to avoid being hit.

"Foolissssh dragon," the demon said, jumping to avoid Xalchraios' tail. It swiped at the tail with its claws and left two deep gashes. The cuts instantly bled, heavily; thick drops of yellow blood fell onto the stony floor. Ellie gasped, and Crystal put her hands over her mouth as the dragon screamed in agony.

The Neseptra demon licked the blood off of its claws. "Foolisssssh dragon god, you are no match for me. I get my powersssss from an even greater entity than yourssssself!"

Shadow stared at the scene before him, puzzled. *From what I heard, Neseptra demons are supposed to be strong, but nowhere near this strong. Xalchraios should be able to take this demon down with no problem,"* he thought. *"Who or what could this entity be that is giving this demon so much power? It's unbelievable."*

"You will pay!" Xalchraios roared, blood still flowing from the deep cuts on his tail. He opened his mouth wide and sent a pillar of flames straight at the demon. The demon opened its mouth and stood directly in the path of the oncoming flames, which it then consumed. It licked its lips greedily.

"Tasssty," the Neseptra replied. "I love a good ssssnack."

Shadow frowned. He knew full well that if he didn't step in now, Xalchraios was going to die. He couldn't let the dragon die. He had to do something.

The Neseptra demon walked forward, holding its claws outward in a threatening manner, preparing to slice open the dragon's chest. As it came within a few feet of Xalchraios, it was hit by a ball of shadow energy and thrown backwards, slamming into the wall. "Who daresss to hit me?"

"Oh, I dare," Shadow replied. "Did that hurt? If so, I'm sorry."

"You fool! I ssssshall inflict pain on you ten timessss worsssse than what you have causssssed me!"

Shadow smiled. "Sorry. I'm honestly not in the mood to feel pain. But causing it? Always fun." His glance flickered to his team. He knew that this demon was tough and that he would probably need help, but he didn't want them to get caught in the crossfire. He just didn't think they were ready yet. "Guys, let me handle this one alone."

Ellie laughed incredulously. "Sorry, Shadow, but not going to happen." She cupped her hands and air swirled into them like a vacuum. She willed the moisture in the air to take form, and a ball of a snow-like substance appeared inside her hands, ice forming around it. She threw the ball at the demon, and it smacked into its chest, causing the demon to double over in pain. The area where the ice hit was bright red.

"Guys, I said to stay out of it!" Shadow yelled, and was caught off guard. The demon swiped at Shadow with its claws, slicing his arm open. It then grabbed Shadow with its other hand and threw him across the room, where he rolled and then lay still, not moving.

"Hey!" Tristan cried angrily, getting off the floor. He flicked his hand forward and sent a ball of flames soaring at the demon.

Yet again, the demon opened its mouth and devoured the fireball. As the demon finished consuming the fireball, the frostbite on its chest vanished.

"Tristan, you idiot!" Faith yelled. "Of all the stupid things you've ever done in your life, this really takes the friggin' cake."

"What, Sis?" Tristan replied, confused and a bit shocked that his sister would take such a tone with him.

"Neseptra demons are obviously impervious to fire! Didn't you happen to notice that when Xalchraios' flames did absolutely nothing to it?"

"Crap. You're right," Tristan said. His face reddened in embarrassment. "I'm sorry!"

The demon smiled. "Don't be upsssset, boy. You helped me. Let me return the favor!" It spit up a ball of fire, which headed straight for Tristan. Before he could respond, a silver shield appeared around him out of nowhere, and the fireball smacked against it and evaporated.

"How?" Tristan asked, looking around.

Crystal, who had created the shield, stepped forward and faced the Neseptra demon. "You don't get to attack my friends!"

The demon growled. It regurgitated a larger ball of fire, which sped much quicker towards Crystal than the one that was launched at Tristan.

Crystal waved her hand, and another shield appeared. But when the fireball hit the shield, it broke under the impact and she was knocked backwards. She smashed into a wall and lay unmoving on the ground, bleeding out of a fresh cut on her head.

"Crystal!" Ethan yelled, rushing over to her.

Isaac stepped forward, but Kay put her hand on his shoulder. "Stay out of it," she muttered. "I won't let anything happen to you."

"But they're in trouble," Isaac replied. "If we don't do something now, they could get killed!"

"You can't do anything for them but get hurt. Just stay out of this one, Isaac."

"Kay –"

"This isn't up for discussion. I'm telling you, do not get involved." Kay said adamantly, and Isaac nodded.

Ethan kneeled down by Crystal's side and pulled her into his lap, checking her pulse. "She's still alive, but the bleeding must stop," he said. "Faith, please... heal her."

Faith nodded and started towards them, but the demon got in her way. "Move, or be moved!" she yelled, raising her fists.

"I don't think sssso. You sssshall not be healing anyone elssse today!"

"How does this demon know so much about us. . .about our powers and abilities? This doesn't add up," Shadow wondered, moving between Faith and the demon. He had recovered from the earlier attack. The wound on his arm was no longer bleeding.

"Sssso…you're back, I ssssee," the demon said. "You're not even hurt. How issss that?"

"What can I say? I eat my Wheaties," Shadow replied. "Now, you tell me something. How do you know so much about us?"

"My massssster keepssss me well-informed!" the demon said. It took a few steps towards him. "You are no match for me. You're just a weak, pathetic human."

Shadow smirked. "I guess you and your master don't have your facts right, because I'm not human. I'm a tiny bit beyond the limitations of standard mortality."

"You're sssso ssssure of yourssself, aren't you?"

Shadow didn't reply. He shifted his gaze to Xalchraios. The dragon was now lying down, severely weakened, breathing slowly. "Faith, I need you to heal Xalchraios."

"I'll kill her before sssshe doesss anything," the demon said, motioning towards Faith.

"You won't do anything," Shadow said, the torchlight of the room flickering with his voice. "Faith, ignore him. Just go heal Xalchraios."

Faith glanced at the demon, then back at Shadow, and nodded. She walked over to the wounded dragon, placed her hands on his tail, and began to channel her energy into him.

"I did the best I can do, Shadow," Faith said, after a few seconds. "I closed the wound, but my powers aren't great enough to heal him fully. He's still severely low on energy."

"It's fine," Shadow replied, turning towards Ethan. "How's Crystal doing?"

"I've stopped the bleeding," Ethan said, Crystal still on his lap. He paused, checking her pulse again. "She'll be all right."

"Good. Now, as for you," Shadow said, pointing at the demon, "your time in this realm is over. I'm going to send you back to hell where you belong."

"Liar! You have no power," the demon said. "You're nothing compared to my massssster. Nothing at all."

Shadow's eyes turned black, and he slowly walked towards the demon. The light in the room dimmed with each step he took, and the shadows seemed to whisper promises of pain and misery.

The demon backed up slightly, fear filling its eyes. "You can't do anything to me. Massssster promisssssed me power. I'm indesssstructable!"

Shadow laughed coldly and continued to walk forward. The demon took a step backwards for every step forward that Shadow took. "Why are you backing up, demon?" he asked, "unless you know that your master was lying, that you have no power?"

Shadow took one final step forward. He watched with a smile as the demon tried to step backwards again, only to realize that it was against a wall. "Looks like you have no more room. What are you going to do now?"

"You won't kill me, Dhampir!" the demon hissed, throwing a punch.

Shadow stepped to the right, catching the fist, and paused. He then jerked his hand backwards, ripping the demon's arm off. Green blood exploded out of the hole where the arm used to be.

The demon screamed in agony.

"Now. . .tell me, who is this master of yours?" Shadow asked, throwing the demon's severed arm onto the floor. "And don't make me ask again, for your own good."

"I'll never tell you!" the demon spat as it coughed up blood. "What you can do to me is nothing compared to what sssshe'll do if I fail her!"

"Hmm. Maybe I should take another limb?" Shadow asked, shrugging. "After all, you don't seem to mind very much."

"You wouldn't dare!" the demon roared.

"Ooh, are you taking requests?" Ryan asked. "Can it be a leg this time?"

"Ryan, shut up," Ellie said, turning away from the scene. It wasn't that she was squeamish. It was just that she wasn't used to how cruel Shadow was being. A fight, she could handle, but torture? Not so much.

Shadow sighed, ignoring Ryan. "Is that a dare or a double dare?" he asked, grabbing the demon's still attached arm. "Because if I have to, I'll keep taking pieces of you off until you start talking."

"No!" the demon shouted. "Sssstop it!"

"Then tell me who you work for, now. I want a name, damn it!"

"I work for. . .a woman. Ssshe ssssummoned me, gave me tremendoussss power," the demon whispered. "But I'm nothing compared to her. Her power is over ssssixty timessss that of mine."

Shadow lost his focus for a moment. "How can she be that much stronger than an upper-class-level demon?"

The demon took his chance while Shadow was deep in thought and made a quick swipe at him.

Shadow, however, was prepared for this. He dodged the blow quickly and, in a lightning-fast motion, unsheathed his dagger and plunged it into the demon's chest.

"T-t-thissss. . .cannot be. Massssster promissssed that I was invinssssible!" the demon spluttered as Shadow wrenched the dagger out of its chest.

Tereya closed his eyes at the sight of the bleeding demon, but Tristan and Isaac stared at the scene, transfixed. Faith took this as an opportunity. She ran over and put her hands on Crystal's face, healing her.

"Even if you kill me, my death accomplisssshessss nothing! You won't win. Ssshe will make ssssure of th-th-that!" the demon choked, drawing its last breaths. "Ssshe will tear you all apart with her bare handssss. . ."

"Who is 'she'?" Shadow asked. "I need a name."

The demon opened its mouth to answer. Then suddenly, its eyes widened in shock. Its whole body began to glow red. "Massssster, no. . .pleasssse don't hurt me! I wassssn't going to tell. I did nothing wrong!" the demon cried. Its cries seemed to fall on deaf ears. The red glow began to crackle around it, and the demon melted into a pool of green, acrid liquid.

"Whoa!" Tristan exclaimed. Faith removed her hands from Crystal, who was now stirring in Ethan 's lap.

"Whoever was the master of that demon has to be extremely powerful to destroy it from here," Ethan said.

"Yeah, but how powerful?" Shadow wondered. *"And why would she kill her own demon? Maybe she thought it was going to run its mouth."* He got off the ground and wiped the blood off of his dagger onto the ground.

"It wasn't just any demon, though," Faith said, "It was an upper- class demon. How can we possibly expect to survive against somebody who has that type of power at their disposal?"

"We'll need to get stronger. That's the only way," Shadow replied.

"Is the dragon okay?" Tereya asked.

"I almost forgot!" Shadow exclaimed. He turned and ran over. "Xalchraios!"

"Mortal," Xalchraios said, its powerful voice reduced to a whisper, "I am greatly weakened. I need rest. Whatever you require, make haste."

"I wanted to know if you're going to be okay. You took a lot of damage in that fight. The Dragon's Eye needs its protector. We can't leave you here to die."

The dragon made an attempt to get up but fell back onto its stomach. "I will be fine. Now that the Dragon's Eye is safe. I can rest to regain my strength. Thank you, heroes," Xalchraios said, breathing heavily.

"If I wasn't so damaged, I would grant you something… some kind of blessing or power. Unfortunately, that is not the case. However, I can offer you something small."

"What?" Shadow asked.

Xalchraios nodded towards several bright blue specks on the ground. "During the attack, the demon knocked some of my scales off. Take them. They're magical in essence, and you never know, they may come in handy."

Shadow blinked, but nodded. He walked over and picked up the seven scales, putting them into a pocket. "Is there anything else we can do for you before we leave?"

"Actually, I am incredibly hungry," Xalchraios replied, looking down at Ryan. "And that annoying one still looks tasty."

"Uh, gang, maybe we should be leaving," Ryan said quickly, making his way to the door.

Shadow smirked and then nodded. "Yeah, the danger is over here, so we can go home."

Ethan lifted Crystal into a standing position and allowed her to lean on him. "Are you all right, Crystal?"

Crystal nodded and smiled. "Yeah, thanks to you."

Ethan blushed slightly. "It's my job," he said, smiling. Crystal returned it.

Kay sighed. "Okay. Enough with the after-school special, people. Let's get a move on."

"Yeah, I could really go for that cheeseburger," Tristan moaned, his stomach rumbling.

Faith sighed. "Brother, can't you at least try to act like you have some class?" she asked, shaking her head.

"I'm sorry, Sis, but I haven't had dinner since, like, six hours ago. We've been on this stinking island since, like, ten o'clock, and it's now almost three in the morning!"

"Faith, he is right. I, too, am feeling a bit famished," Ethan admitted, which Crystal agreed with, so Faith just shrugged and looked at Shadow.

"Yeah, I guess you've all earned a dinner for such good teamwork," Shadow said, with a smirk. Ryan, Tristan, Isaac, and Tereya cheered.

Kay smiled. She placed her hands behind her back, and a tiny white ball of energy fell out of them. It stuck to the floor and vanished. "Yeah! I'm hungry too. So we're ready?"

"Well, what do you think, Ellie?" Shadow asked, yawning.

Ellie didn't answer right away, still a bit shocked at how cold he was during the fight with the demon. Part of her wanted to talk about it. The other part only wanted to forget that it ever happened. Deciding to keep quiet, she shrugged. "Dinner would be nice. . .especially a cheeseburger."

Tristan shouted in excitement. "Yes! I win!"

Ryan rolled his eyes. "The only thing you win is the idiot of the year award," he said, causing Tristan to blush and everyone else, except Faith, Shadow, and Kay, to laugh.

"Ryan, I swear," Faith said through clenched teeth, "you've got one more time...."

"Okay, that's enough. Let's go, gang," Shadow said. He gave a curt nod to Xalchraios, who returned it, and he led them out of the room. They began the long walk back to the surface. After a few minutes passed, a loud explosion erupted from behind them.

"What the hell was that?!" Ellie exclaimed, looking back down the stairwell that they just came up from. "It sounded like it came from Xalchraios' chamber!"

"I'll check it out," Kay said. "You guys go ahead. I'll meet you at the jet."

"But Kay, it could be dangerous!" Isaac said, looking worried.

Shadow nodded. "Isaac's right, Kay. I wouldn't be comfortable letting you go back there by yourself. Something could happen and you could get hurt."

Kay frowned. "Is it because you don't trust me or because I'm a girl? I'm just wondering which of the two is why you don't think I'm tough enough to handle it."

Shadow sighed and rubbed his forehead. "It's nothing to do with either of those things, and you know it."

"Then let me go and check it out," Kay said. "If you truly trust me and know that I can handle myself, you'll let me go."

"Fine, but if there's any trouble, any at all, use the communicator to contact us," he said, turning away from her. "Let's go, guys." And he continued to lead the others out of the temple.

☙❧☙❧☙❧☙❧

Twenty minutes later, when Kay exited the temple, she took a deep breath, taking in the dense air. She quickly descended the stairs. When she reached the bottom, the temple slowly faded away into nothing, as it if had never existed. *Maybe no one will notice it's gone,* she thought hopefully as she stared at the area where the temple once was. She began to run, pushing through vines, bushes, and branches, until she heard somebody shouting overhead.

"Kay?!" Isaac yelled, high up in the air, standing in the doorway of Shadow's jet.

"Isaac!" she called, hoping that he would hear her. "I'm down here!" she added as the jet descended a bit lower.

Isaac waved, indicating that he saw her. "Kay, Shadow's going to lower down a rope. Grab it!" he said, and she nodded. A rope ladder was thrown down to her. It was a tough reach, being almost three feet higher than her, but she jumped and grabbed on to it. Pulling herself up, she began to climb up the ladder slowly but steadily.

"Thanks," she muttered to Isaac, who breathed a sigh of relief that she was safe.

"What was that explosion in the temple all about?" Shadow asked as she walked into the aisle. Kay could feel his eyes searching, reading her.

"Well, you see, it was Xalchraios. He made a noise to get our attention. He forgot to tell us something."

"Which was?" Ellie asked.

Kay pointed down to the island. "Take a look for yourselves."

"What happened to the temple?!" Shadow asked.

"Xalchraios wanted to protect the Dragon's Eye and himself, since that last battle weakened him. He decided to seal away the temple deep underground," Kay replied. "That way, nobody can ever try to get the stone."

Shadow nodded. "Makes sense."

"Speaking of the temple, who is this master that the Neseptra demon spoke of?" Ethan asked.

"Yeah! He was able to break one of my strongest shields without breaking a sweat," Crystal noted, a hint of fear in her voice.

"If the master is as strong as the demon claimed, I wouldn't be surprised if she had thousands of demons, equally as powerful, at her disposal," Kay said. "Any idea how we're going to handle that, leader?"

"Thousands?!" Tereya exclaimed.

"It's nothing, guys. Don't sweat it," Shadow said, although his words were far from what he was actually feeling inside. While he didn't want them to freak out, he couldn't help but be afraid.

"Well, I, for one, am glad that we beat that demon silly," Ryan said, putting his feet up on the back of a chair in front of him.

"You mean Shadow beat the demon silly while you watched, right?" Ellie replied. "Because, unless I'm mistaken, you didn't throw a single punch."

"Hey, there's no 'I' in team," Ryan said, shrugging.

"If anything, this battle proved that we are strong, and we'll be able to overcome any obstacles if we work together." Shadow said.

"Yeah. One question, though," Ryan said, motioning towards Crystal. "How come you can create shields when there's no metal around?"

"What do you mean?" Crystal asked.

"When we were down in the temple with Puff the Magic Dragon and that snake demon, there was no metal around. You can manipulate metal, so where did you get the metal to make your shields?"

"Oh," Crystal replied. She tugged at a chain around her neck, and a grand silver locket popped out of her shirt. "This lets me do it."

Seeing the confused look on Ryan's face, Ethan spoke up. "That locket was given to Crystal by her mother when she was a little girl. The locket is made out of pure iron, so if there's no metal around, Crystal can use it to form shields to protect herself or others around her."

Shadow grew somber, listening to the explanation. *What I wouldn't give to have grown up with my mother,* he thought. *To have something of hers, anything, just to know that she loved me.*

"So this evil woman. . .or lady or girl or whatever," Tristan said suddenly, grabbing everybody's attention.

"Yeah?" Shadow asked, feeling himself slip back into the serious attitude that he knew so well. "What about her?"

"Well, I wonder what happened to her. I mean, like, why is she so evil?" Tristan asked.

"God, Tristan, you can't just ask people why they're evil," Crystal said.

"Did you just quote *Mean Girls*, Crystal?" Ellie asked, laughing. "Because if you did, that would be so fetch of you."

"Yeah, I did," Crystal replied, smiling. "And yeah, stop trying to make fetch happen, because it isn't going to."

"This idiotic behavior is going to get us all killed," Kay thought, digging her nails into the palm of her hand.

"Shadow, we've been flying for a few hours now. It's almost near sunrise! Are we almost there?" Tereya asked worriedly.

Shadow gasped as he was jolted back to reality from his thoughts. *"How could I be so careless? How could I forget that it's almost sunrise?! My curse. . .my death warrant,"* he thought. "It's getting close to sunrise. I can feel it. I hope we make it back in time."

"Don't worry. You'll be fine," Ellie said. "I checked the map. We'll be back at the castle in twenty-five minutes. That leaves you with an extra fifteen minutes to get inside the castle until sunrise."

"Thanks for looking out for me, Ellie," Shadow said, tossing smile in her direction.

Ellie almost blushed. "No problem," she said, leaning back in her chair and yawning.

"Uh…Shadow, do you pay overtime?" Crystal asked suddenly.

Shadow sighed. "You're serious, aren't you?"

"Crystal, are you really asking for monetary gains?" Ethan asked. "But why? Your parents are multimillionaires."

"That would be like Willy Wonka asking for chocolate," Ryan remarked.

Crystal pouted. "But you can never have enough money," she said. "There are so many nice things I need to buy!"

"No, Crystal, it just so happens that I don't pay overtime," Shadow said. "I'm not even paying you guys at all."

Crystal's mouth opened, her eyes widening. "B-b-but. . .we're risking our lives. The least you can do is throw us some money!"

"Um, you get free food and free housing, not to mention you get protection from demons who would hunt you down and kill you to take your powers," Shadow replied.

Crystal blinked. "Oh, right. Well, that's fair enough."

"I think so too," Shadow replied. Ellie, Tristan, and Ryan laughed.

CRBOCRBOCRBOCRBO

"Hey, Shadow," Tereya called.

"What is it, Tereya?" Shadow asked.

"Well. . .where do you think that this woman is?"

"Don't concern yourself with that, Reya. That's my job, and I promise I'll find out," Shadow said.

"The evil, mysterious woman," Ryan said as they all exited the jet. They entered the castle in the nick of time, the sun just barely starting to rise in the distance.

"What about her, Ryan?" Ethan asked, with a yawn.

Ryan shrugged. "I'm just betting that she's probably doing something evil."

"Well, isn't that the statement of the century," Shadow remarked. He smacked Ryan playfully on the back. "Everyone get a good night's sleep. You've all earned it."

The team all said their good nights and parted ways, heading to their respective rooms.

CRBOCRBOCRBOCRBO

Over a hundred miles away, in Kreashe La-Femme, a very expensive shoe store, a woman paced back and forth. She had slightly below waist-length, wild red hair. Her eyes were cold and empty, their color a mix between the sky and a sheet of ice. She pointed at a pair of red high-heeled shoes, her three-inch nails toxic green. "So I totally decided," she said, "and I'll take those!"

The salesman, who looked as though he didn't want to be working, it being six in the morning, walked over to her. He looked the woman up and down, taking in her appearance, and frowned.

"Um, excuse me," he said, trying not to be rude. "Those shoes are over $6,000. Are you sure you can afford them?"

The woman laughed. "Uh, duh," she replied, rolling her eyes. "I saw the tag; I know the price. I wouldn't have picked them out if they weren't that expensive. If it doesn't cost almost as much as a car, it doesn't go on my feet."

"I see," he replied. He retrieved a step stool and climbed up to get the shoes in question. "These?"

"Yes!" she exclaimed, almost giggling in glee. "Do you have them in my size? It's nine. I'm a small, delicate flower, you see."

The man raised an eyebrow. "Of course, you are. Wait one moment," he said. He left to check the storage room.

"Lady Maedara?" a small creature called, walking up to the woman's side. It was a demon that looked like some sort of spider. It had tiny red eyes and large fangs. It was also considerably short, barely as tall as a six-year-old child. It was covered in soft black fur.

"What do you want, you friggin' idiot?!" Maedara asked sharply, clenching her fists and sucking in her lip. "You know that I love my 'me' time, Mezmir. It's the only time I get to enjoy myself. And you know I don't get nearly as much of it as I'd like."

Mezmir recoiled in fear. "Master, my apologies!" he replied, taking a few steps back. "I only wish to tell you that the Neseptra demon failed to acquire the Dragon's Eye."

"What?!" Maedara cried. Her eyes tinted red, and the lights in the room began flickering. "I know you are not doing this to me. No, you're not, not right now. You are not interrupting my 'me' time and delivering upsetting news, both at the same time... not this particular moment. I can't even deal with you right now. Tell me, are you suicidal?"

"Please, Master!" Mezmir cried, bowing at her feet. "I didn't. . .I. . ."

"I despise your mother, Mezmir," she said coldly.

"M-my mother?"

"Yes, Mezmir, your mother. She gave birth to you; therefore, by extension, she is the cause of all my suffering. It's all her fault, and I just want her dead."

"Master, my mother is already dead. You killed her yourself, remember?"

Maedara frowned. "Oh, isn't that just great. You're motherless, and I'm unhappy. This world sucks."

"Master, don't upset yourself. I promise, this is only a minor setback. Your plans will not be halted!"

"You'd better be right, Mezmir. I'd hate to litter the sidewalk with your insides." She ran her hands down her long black dress. "Now, stop your blathering and tell me how pretty I am."

Mezmir blinked. "You're the most beautiful and gorgeous woman in all the land. The sun rises and sets just for you."

Maedara smiled. "Oh, Mezmir, you know how much I love your random compliments. They make me feel all tingly inside."

The salesman returned from the storage room, empty-handed. "Ma'am?"

"Did you find the shoes I wanted?" Maedara asked, any hint of her previous anger gone.

"What the hell is that?" the salesman cried, looking disgusted.

"What's what?" Maedara asked, confused. She followed his eyes to Mezmir and then nodded in understanding. "Oh, that. That's a Mezmir. Revolting, isn't it?"

"Indeed," the salesman replied, looking at the demon in disgust. "I'm sorry to say that we don't have your size in. It's completely sold out. If you wish, I can put you on the waiting list, and you can—"

"Well, thank you for ruining my day," Maedara growled. She kicked Mezmir and then turned to walk out the door.

"Have a nice day," the salesman muttered.

"Oh, but wait!" Maedara said suddenly, turning back to look at the man. "I must thank you for helping me!"

"Master," Mezmir began, knowing full well where this was going. "I'm not sure we have time for this."

"Mezmir, you're giving me worry lines," she snapped, throwing a threatening glance at him before looking back at the salesman. "You see, I repay those who do me favors. I do them favors in return." She smiled suggestively.

The salesman blushed. "So how, exactly, will you be repaying me then?" he asked, licking his lips nervously.

She winked. "I'll. . .release you, set you free."

Before the man could respond, she lifted her hand as if she were going to caress his face. Her fingers danced sensually down the side of his throat.

Suddenly, her nails extended six inches longer. They pierced his neck, and she dragged them across in one fluid motion. The man brought his hands to his throat as she retracted her nails out of it. He tried to speak; all that came out was blood. He fell to his knees, his mouth agape, his eyes wide open in shock. Emptiness filled them. He fell to the ground and moved no more.

"Pity," Maedara said, licking the blood off her nails. "I really wanted those shoes. They were such a pretty color and would have been lovely with this dress, which I now have to replace because of the blood."

"Master?" Mezmir questioned, getting off the ground.

"No, you fool, I won't kill you. But count your lucky stars that I took out all my rage on that innocent bystander."

Mezmir sighed in relief. "Thank you, Master."

"Don't thank me. We have planning to do, and I might need you in the future," she said. "Besides, I need somebody to accompany me to the next store. A lady simply does not carry her own packages."

Mezmir watched as Maedara happily skipped out of the shoe store. He walked over to the light switch, flicked it off, and strode out after her.

Michael Chulsky

CHAPTER 4: UNFORGIVING FLAMES

Shadow paced back and forth in his room. It had been about four weeks since his visit to Draconia Isle. He had barely gotten any sleep; his mind was much too busy for that. He feared how powerful the evil woman was and, for the first time, wondered if he and the others actually stood a chance.

Shadow?" Ellie's voice called. "Are you in there?"

"Yes," he answered hotly, opening the door.

"Sorry to bother you, but you haven't left your room much since we got back from Draconia Isle. It would be nice to know you're still alive." She paused for a second, as if thinking how to place into words exactly what she was feeling. "Your seclusion isn't helpful for morale. The others are worried about you, and I am too."

"I've just been busy... working on things. You know how it is."

Ellie shook her head. "Yeah, I know all right. You're being stupid again. You always do this, overwork yourself. It's not healthy, mentally or physically. You're going to drain yourself, and then what good are you?"

Shadow shrugged. "I promise, Ellie, I'm fine. You and the others have absolutely nothing to worry about. I'm not going to burn myself out just by getting a few sleepless nights."

"If you say so," she replied, rolling her eyes. "But try not to be so hostile towards the people who care about you, okay?"

Shadow blushed. This was new to him, someone actually giving a damn about him. It was refreshing and confusing. "You're right, and I'm sorry," he said. "Ellie, do you remember that strange guy that appeared to us a few weeks ago on Draconia?"

"Yeah. What about him?"

"He was in my room few minutes ago."

Ellie grew tense. "What happened?"

"He told me about a boy in trouble in a nearby village."

"What's so special about this kid?"

Shadow shrugged. "Apparently, he's a pyrokinetic."

"Like Tristan?" Ellie asked.

"Not exactly," Shadow said. "Tristan's power is creating fire from thin air. This kid can ignite and make them explode."

"How is this even possible? I thought you scanned the entire continent for kids with special abilities. Why didn't he come up?"

"His parents cloaked him," Shadow replied. "They're both powerful high priests, and they're putting spells around him. I'm guessing whatever magic they're using is strong enough to interfere with the energy of the sensing power I was given."

"Well, I think it's time for a rescue mission. Where is this town, anyway? We have to do something."

Shadow nodded and walked over to a map on his wall, pointing to a location. "The village is Derelyn, in the western providence of Arkovia."

Ellie blinked. "Dude, you serious?" she asked, raising an eyebrow. "That's only, like, what, a few miles away from this castle. He's been practically under our nose this entire time."

"I'm aware. What's more annoying is the fact that somebody is in trouble, somebody so close, and I haven't saved them yet. It's unforgivable." His body tensed up and then he punched the wall, his hand going through it with a loud crunch.

Ellie took in a deep breath and then let it out. She turned to him and placed her hand on his back. "I understand you're angry, but taking out your anger on the wall isn't going to help. The most important thing now is saving that kid."

"I know. I just hate it when kids are in trouble."

"Speaking of trouble," Ellie said suddenly, "did you hear about what happened the night we went to Draconia?"

"No. What happened?"

"Are you serious?" Ellie asked in disbelief. "I mean, it was in the paper and on the news, practically on every station."

"Yeah, because I totally read the newspaper or watch the news," Shadow said.

"Well, maybe you should start. Then you would know about this," she replied, pulling a folded newspaper article out of her back pocket and handing it to him. "You may want to take a look. It's an interesting read."

Shadow unfolded the newspaper article, and his eyes darted back and forth as he read it. "One month ago, a brutal murder occurred in Kreashe La-Femme?" he read aloud, confused. "What's that supposed to mean to me, besides the fact that people can't come up with normal names for stores?"

Ellie scowled and then turned the page, reading aloud. 'Store cameras saw a woman attack the man and kill him in what police are calling the strangest murder of the year. Her nails appeared to have magically extended and sliced his neck right open."

"So. . .This evil master lady is finally showing herself," he said slowly. "It has to be that, because the chances that this occurred the same night that we were on Draconia are slim to none."

Shadow growled. He crumpled the paper in his hand. It became surrounded with shadows and then disintegrated. "I will personally make sure that this monster doesn't harm another living being."

"Shadow, please!"

"Ellie, what's wrong?"

"I'm sorry. It's just. . .you're trying to save everyone. You're only human!"

Shadow raised an eyebrow. "Only human, really?"

"Oh, hush, you know what I mean," Ellie replied, rolling her eyes. "I know you're not technically human, but still. . .You're not a superhero or anything. God, sometimes you can be so dense!"

"So who's going with us to Derelyn to save this kid?"

"If that's your attempt at changing the subject, you're doing a poor job, because that's not changing the subject," Ellie said pointedly. "You're still talking about saving people. You're not listening to a word I've said, are you?"

"Ellie, drop it," Shadow said, any hint of humor or room for compromise absent. "I mean it."

Ellie scoffed. "Fine. Whatever. Who would you like to come with us on our rescue mission then?"

"I guess it would be just you and me. Oh, you think we should take either Tereya or Ryan, maybe? It never hurts to have backup."

"Ryan would probably get us all killed with his smart mouth," Ellie replied thoughtfully. "I'm thinking Reya. We could use his powers in case the village people decide to get violent."

Shadow almost smiled. "You read my mind." Taking great care to avoid the windows, he left his room and followed Ellie to Tereya's to ask him to come with them. "Do you think he's up?"

Ellie shrugged. "Maybe, but how should I know?" she asked. "I mean, do I look like his keeper?"

"Real funny," Shadow replied before knocking on the door.

"Come in," Tereya answered.

Shadow twisted the handle and pushed. Immediately, he was showered by rays of sunlight. He shrieked and covered his face with his hands.

Thinking quickly, Ellie threw herself in front of Shadow as Tereya pulled down the window blinds.

Thanks. That was close," Shadow said. "I was almost deep-fried."

"Sorry, Shadow. I didn't expect you, of all people, to visit me," Tereya said. "I'm glad you did, though."

Ellie turned to face Shadow. "Are you all right?"

"Yeah, I'm fine, just stupid," Shadow replied. "I keep forgetting that things are different now and I'm not alone anymore."

Ellie looked him over and gasped. All of the bare skin that was hit by the sunlight on his face and arms was now covered in red, blistering, peeling skin, much like a bad sunburn. "Are you absolutely sure that you're okay?"

Shadow smiled reassuringly. "Yeah, trust me. Just watch."

Ellie watched, and her mouth opened in awe as his increased regeneration kicked in. The skin that was damaged was now blister-free and no longer red. A few seconds more and the peeling skin hardened and then smoothed out like candle wax, leaving his arm unblemished.

"Whoa!" Ellie exclaimed, running her fingers across his arm, trying to feel if it was real or not. "This isn't an illusion, is it?"

Shadow moved his arm back, flexing it. "Nope, it's real, I promise. I'm good as new. There are some bonuses to being half-vampire, 'some' being the key word."

"So what's up?" Tereya asked. "Not that I'm not happy you're here. It's just that I doubt if you came just to visit me."

"Nonsense, Reya. You know you're fun to be around," Ellie replied. "But we're here because we need your help with something."

"You need my help?"

"We want you to come with us on a mission," Shadow said, gazing directly into the younger boy's eyes. "There's a boy around your age who is in trouble. His parents are torturing him. And if we don't rescue him, he'll die."

Tereya's eyes widened, and his bottom lip quivered. "We gotta help him," he said, the entire building shaking slightly, just by the power of his voice. "We can't just leave him there…"

"Glad you're on board, Reya," Ellie said, giving him a thumbs-up.

"Well, if there are no objections, let's go," Shadow said.

"How will we be getting there?" Tereya asked.

"Well, we could take the jet," Shadow said, a thoughtful look in his eye. "Or I have a better idea."

"What's that?" Ellie asked, but her question was answered. The area of ground that they were standing on flashed black and became hollow. She and Tereya both let out screams as the ground disappeared out from under them. They fell for what seemed like forever. However, less than a minute later, they appeared a couple inches off the ground, inside a strange building.

Shadow landed on his feet, while they hit the ground hard. "Yeah, the landing takes some getting used to."

Ellie growled. She lifted herself off of the ground and then helped Tereya up. "You could have warned us first, jerk."

"Yeah, I could have," Shadow said, "but where's the fun in that?"

"Where are we?" Tereya asked, looking around.

"We are in the purification house of Derelyn," Shadow said. "This was the only place I could teleport to because the entire town is ultra-consecrated ground, meaning that my powers are slightly reduced."

Ellie slapped him upside the head. "You idiot! If you could teleport us here that quickly, then why didn't you just teleport us all to Draconia Isle to save time?!"

"Teleporting takes energy, more with each person I teleport with. I couldn't risk depleting all of my energy and leaving me too weak to fight," Shadow said, rubbing the back of his head. "Even now, after teleporting and being in this town, I feel weakened."

"Um, Shadow, what do you mean by 'purification room'?" Tereya asked.

"Look at the ground and it should become obvious, Reya," Shadow said. Under their feet were hundreds of bones as well as piles upon piles of ashes. They littered the floor like dirt.

"Gross!" Tereya exclaimed, backing up until he hit the wall.

"Calm down," Shadow said, putting a hand on his shoulder. "Nothing in this room can hurt you. Besides, they weren't evil. They were innocent people who just weren't pure enough for the residents of this town. If anything, they should be pitied, not feared. Never feared."

"Shadow," Ellie said, rubbing her hands together nervously, "how do you know so much about the people in this town?"

"What are you implying?" Shadow asked, avoiding her eyes.

"It's just that you knew where the town was located, and you know a lot about their rituals and whatnot," Ellie said. "It's like you're really familiar with everything. You wouldn't be, unless you've been here before. So have you?"

Shadow sighed and shook his head. He didn't want to remember all of this. He wanted to forget, to place it deep in the dark crevices of his mind. Yet here fate was, bringing him back to the last place on Earth he wanted to be, forcing him to remember and relive the horror of it all. Yes, fate was cruel.

"Do we really have to go over this right now?"

"You have to learn to trust us, Shadow. Like it or not, we're your friends and we're here for you, no matter what," Ellie said. "So, yeah, if something is bugging you, I want to know about it. You can't just keep everything bottled inside of you."

"All right, let's play therapy," Shadow replied derisively. "About two or three months ago, when I first started tracking down all you guys, there was a kid just like you. His name was Josh. He was able to project his thoughts into reality. I had run into him a few times, and we got along great. He wanted to travel with me to do the recruiting. I should have said no, but I didn't. God, I was so stupid. . ."

"You don't have to continue!" Tereya exclaimed.

"Reya's right, Shadow," Ellie said, grabbing him by the arms. "You can stop. We get it."

Shadow shook his head and pulled away. "No. I need to," he said, taking a deep breath. "It was a few days before I found you two. Josh and I were tracking Faith and Tristan. Our search brought us near this village. Josh was hungry, so we decided to try to find a local place where we could rest for a few minutes and get him something to eat.

"We came during one of their prayer sessions. It was almost like they sensed what I was. They were coming after me. Josh could have gotten away. They caught me. I was tied down and about to be bathed in holy water. Josh used his powers, imagining me safe and out of there, and teleported me away from them. He was so busy focusing on my safety that he didn't see the person come behind him with a knife."

Shadow paused, balling his fists. "I made my way back to try to save him, but I was too late. I found his body nailed to a cross…"

"Shadow," Ellie breathed, tears in her eyes. "I had no idea. None of us did."

"Not true," Shadow replied. "Ryan, Ethan, and Crystal knew. They had all met Josh. He lived with us for a few days before it happened. I told them to never mention his name to me, ever again. Why? Because every time I hear it, I think about how I should have been the one who was crucified, not him. He did nothing wrong except care about me. And now he's gone. It's all my fault."

"I'm sorry," Ellie replied, brushing her tears away.

"Me too," Tereya said, his body shaking.

"Whatever. Let's just find this kid and save him," Shadow said. "We don't have the luxury of getting all emotional right now.

"Where do you think he is?" Ellie asked. Normally, she would have noted the abrupt change in subject, but this time she had to let it slide. She kicked a cracked skull on the ground. It flew from the force of her kick and shattered when it hit the edge of a coffin.

Shadow didn't reply. He closed his eyes and reduced his breathing to slow, deep breaths. He was using the ability to sense power sources with his mind. A few moments passed by, and then he smiled triumphantly. "I can feel his energy. It's getting weaker, fading by the moment, but it's there. It's coming from the north."

"Let's go," Tereya said. "There's not a second to waste."

Shadow nodded. He pulled open the door, taking a few glances to sweep the area. After seeing that the coast was clear, he motioned for them to follow him. He led them out of the purification room, pushing the stone door closed behind them, making a loud banging sound.

"Well, there goes the element of surprise," Ellie said.

"You know, if I wanted witty repartee, I would have brought Ryan," Shadow replied.

"So where exactly is this kid being held?" Ellie asked, ignoring him.

Shadow pointed straight ahead at the only well-lit building in the town. A crowd was gathered around, crying out a faint but steady chant. "I think we should get closer. Maybe we'll be able to overhear something useful. It's worth a shot."

The building was ancient in style, with the bricks a bright yellow. It was tall, putting a three-story house to shame. If the height itself wasn't impressive enough, it stretched out six to seven times wider than the average church.

"Listen," Shadow whispered, pointing to the cathedral steps. Two people stood behind a podium: a man and a woman. The man was wearing robes of dark green and holding a book in his hand, while the woman was wearing robes of purest white, with yellow lining.

"Citizens of Derelyn! We begin a glorious age today. Such a glorious age requires a sacrifice!" the man exclaimed, receiving loud applause in response.

"The hell-spawned child will finally be eradicated. We begin anew, and our town will finally achieve purification. We finally will gain redemption for our sins. Our goddess, Maedara, will finally smile upon us with the destruction of the unholy one. So it is written in the book of Azradeau, so shall it be!"

Loud roars were heard from the crowd: cheering, applause, and shouts of praise.

"What we need," Shadow said, "is a distraction or something, unless you two think we can take on the entire village and save him in time."

"Let me handle this," Tereya said. "I can make a good distraction. Trust me."

"No, Reya," Shadow replied. "I already lost Josh to these freaks. I won't lose you too. If anybody is going to be bait, it will be me."

"Shadow's right," Ellie added. "We can't let you go alone. It's too dangerous."

"Don't treat me like a baby," Tereya said, frowning. "I can do it; it's what I've been training for. We all can't go save the kid, because there are too many townspeople. And if they aren't distracted, then they'll swarm and corner us in. Only I can cause a distraction big enough to take their focus away from that building."

"But Tereya –" Shadow began.

"No," Tereya interrupted, and Ellie's and Shadow's eyes widened in surprise. "Don't try to talk me out of it, Shadow. You've told us that we have to train and we have to get stronger. How can we get stronger if you keep us out of harm's way and never let us get any experience? You kept most of us out of the fight on Draconia Isle out of fear of us getting hurt, and your fear of us getting hurt is going to cause the most problems in the long run. How can we grow if you keep holding us back?"

"Reya, this is crazy," Ellie said.

"No, Ellie, it isn't," Shadow declared, his lips pursed. "Tereya's right. I'm being stupid. I always say that I don't want you guys to get hurt. But if I don't let you get hurt every now and then, then when you guys do fight and I'm not there, something huge can go wrong. I can't let that happen."

"So what are you saying?" Ellie asked.

"I'm saying Tereya's our best shot, and I know he won't let us down."

"You're darn right, I won't," Tereya replied, smiling. "Now, let's make up our game plan."

CΒΏΔЄΏΔЄΏΔЄΏΔЄΏ

"So. . .we're all clear then?" Shadow asked a few minutes later.

"Yeah, I know what I'm supposed to do," Tereya said. "You two go and get the kid, and I'll do the heroic thing. . ."

Shadow nodded. "We'll wait for our opening, and then we'll go get him."

They fell silent for a few moments and watched as the speakers retreated back inside the cathedral and closed the big, iron doors with a loud shudder, which echoed all around them.

"Ready, Tereya?"

Tereya nodded. "I'm on it."

"Be careful, Reya, please," Ellie said, pulling the boy into a hug.

Tereya blushed slightly. "Don't worry. I'll be fine." He walked out into the open, Shadow and Ellie giving him nods of encouragement. He reached the center of the town, and a few stray villagers gave him odd looks. He was a stranger, and it had been a while since an outsider had visited the village.

"Hey, are you lost, little boy?" a villager asked, walking up.

"No, I know exactly where I am," Tereya said.

"You look like a stranger," the villager replied. He whistled, and guards started moving in.

"No. The whole plan will be ruined," Tereya thought frantically. He backed up as the guards advanced, their swords drawn. *"Shadow will be angry, Ellie will be disappointed, and the kid will die. I can't let this happen."*

"He's cornered," another guard said.

"You're right!"

"Let's get him!"

"You're dead, kid!"

When the first guard was within touching distance, the whites of Tereya's eyes disappeared as the brown spread out and filled the entire eye. He lifted his hands up, and the ground began to shake and crack. The ground below the guards broke free from the Earth and lifted them all up in the air.

He moved his hands once more, and the sledge of rock that held the guards crumbled and liquefied in midair, tossing and churning. The guards were thrown up into the sky, and the mud caught them before they fell, encasing them like a bubble. He moved the thick mass through the air, and the men could be heard screaming from inside.

"I'm guessing that's our cue," Ellie said.

Shadow nodded and motioned for her to follow him. They both sprinted past Tereya and headed for the great iron doors.

"Think it's open?"

Shadow shrugged and pulled. To no surprise, it was locked. "Should have seen that coming."

"Well, what are we going to do?" Ellie asked. "We came all this way, and I refuse to be stopped by a locked door."

"We could just use the key... or something."

Ellie gave him a puzzled look. "You have the key?!"

"Nope."

"Then how are we going to–" Ellie began, but paused, watching him move. Shadow thrust his fist into the door and made a large hole. Through that hole, he unlocked the door. "I said, 'or something'." They walked through the now-open door into a new room. It was a typical church-like cathedral, several rows of pews lined perfectly across the floor, and gigantic panes of stained glass hung from the walls and ceilings.

Ellie nudged him.

"What is it?"

"Never mind. It's stupid."

"Oh, come on, Ellie. You know you can ask me anything. I won't get angry or offended, no matter how stupid - unless you're Tristan."

Ellie sighed, but smiled. "Okay, fine," she said. "If you're part vampire, how can you be in a church without getting hurt?"

"That's actually a very good question. Due to my half-human blood, holy objects only hurt if they come in contact with my skin."

"Oh," Ellie replied, looking at the floor fixedly.

"Ellie, it's okay, really. Why are you acting so weird?"

"I don't know. I mean, I guess it's because you make it obvious that being part vampire isn't exactly something you're thrilled about."

"Yeah, and it's not something that I hate either. It has helped me more than you could possibly imagine. You wouldn't believe how most people don't even think to stick a wooden stake through someone's heart. They just shoot you with a gun or stab you and call it a day," he replied, smiling. "Anyway, let's go. The sooner we find this kid, the sooner we can go home."

"Well, don't just stand there," Ellie said, motioning to a new door they had come to. "Use your vampy door-smash thing."

Shadow chuckled. "Vampy door-smash thing. That's totally proper grammar." He punched a hole right through the solid wood door and felt around the back for the lock, which he turned, and it clicked. He pulled open the door, and they continued through it.

The door took them to a hallway. The floor was composed of many different colored tiles arranged in strange patterns.

"I don't like this," Shadow said, keeping himself and her in the doorway, not allowing either of them to touch the new room's floor.

"What's wrong?" Ellie asked. "Is the floor not safe or something?"

Shadow put a foot forward, stepping on a white tile in the new room. "It's solid, whatever it is," he said, motioning to the floor. "So let's continue to the next room. I can sense that the kid is close."

Ellie walked forward, stepping on a blue tile. The tile sunk into the floor, and a metal pole shot out of a crack in the wall, heading straight for her.

Shadow used his inhuman-like speed to pull her back, causing the pole to impale his left arm. "Agh," he gasped in pain, the brunt of the impact forcing him to take a step backwards. His foot landed on a red tile, and he had to jump backwards by the doorway to avoid a torrent of flames that shot down from the ceiling.

Ellie gasped. "You idiot!" she exclaimed. "If you hadn't pulled me out of the way, you wouldn't be hurt right now."

"And you would be dead. Are we really arguing about this?" he asked, shaking his head. "I could take the hit and it wouldn't damage me. You, on the other hand, it may have permanently damaged your arm or punctured an organ."

"But—"

"It's fine," Shadow said, holding up a hand and interrupting her. He closed his eyes tightly and ripped the pole out of his arm in one swift motion. Blood slowly trickled down his arm. "It's not a serious injury. It's already healing."

Ellie looked at him. "How can I ever thank you for saving me?"

"Don't worry about it. It's fine. I just really hope that there are no more traps like that. I don't want to be impaled again."

"What do you think caused it?"

Shadow looked at the floor for a couple of seconds, then pointed to a red tile. "The red tiles cause flames to shoot out." He then pointed to a blue tile. "The blue tiles cause projectiles to shoot out. And—"

"But what do the other colors do?" Ellie asked, interrupting him.

He shrugged. He looked at the other colored tiles: white, green, and black. "I don't know. I'm going to assume that the white tiles are safe, since I stepped on one when we first walked in and nothing tried to kill me."

"Let me go first this time. I don't want you to get hurt any more than you already are," Ellie said.

"No. I don't want you to get hurt. It's out of the question. I will go first," Shadow said, and he started forward before she could object. He gingerly pressed his foot on a white tile and looked around. "They're safe."

Ellie nodded and followed his path. She reached the door and went to push it open.

"Wait," Shadow said, grabbing her hand. "Okay, listen. I sense that the kid is beyond this door, as well as our two psycho friends. We must be careful - and quiet. We don't want them to know that we're here just yet. Okay?"

Nodding, Ellie pushed open the door.

They both slipped through and closed it behind them, careful not to make the slightest sound. The room they entered was like a Grecian temple. Large, white stone pillars held up the ceiling, and the pews were carved from solid marble. Hearing voices coming from a short distance ahead, they darted behind a pillar.

"Finally, today, the day of cleansing is upon us, Leon," a woman said. She was wearing bright white robes, and her hair was wrapped tightly in a bun. "The unholy child will be lifted into God's graces, and his foul stench of evil shall be eradicated!"

Leon, standing next to her, was wearing dark green robes the color of poison. He shifted some bottles around and looked down at a large surgical table they were both standing over.

Ellie peered from behind the pillar to take a look at what was on the table. When she saw what it was, she placed her hands over her mouth to mask a scream.

Shadow, having improved senses, heard her muffled cry and knew that something had upset her. He too looked out from behind the pillar, and despite seeing as much pain, death, and violence as he had in his life, what he saw caused his stomach to wrench.

Lying face up on the table, a young boy could be seen. His skin was light tan, like coffee with too much cream. He had light brown eyes, which seemed to shine like liquid amber. His hair was short and dark brown, just a shade lighter than jet-black, contrasting beautifully with his eyes. Dried tears could be seen on his cheeks, and new ones were quickly forming.

His shirt was ripped open down the middle. Holes could be seen in his pants and the areas of his shirt that weren't already torn. It was as if somebody had taken a lighter to his clothes and skin. Burn marks covered his chest and legs.

With Shadow's keen eyesight, he could see fresh scars on the boy and a cross-shaped burn on the area of skin right above his heart. "Oh, my God."

"This can't be real," Ellie whispered, on the verge of tears. "Nobody's this cruel. Nobody could ever be."

"Ellie, we'll do something about this, I promise." Shadow whispered. "We'll wait and then—"

Suddenly, a scream rang out, echoing all around the room. The scream had come from the young boy lying on the table. Smoke was rising from his chest.

The woman held a small bottle of liquid in her hand; she had been pouring something onto him. "Now, now, now, Cameryn, don't you scream. You know that you're evil, and you must be cleansed," she said, caressing the side of his face. "A person like you is against God, and you need to be punished in order to be saved. You must be cleansed."

"Get on with it, Mary," Leon said. "We don't have time. We need to finish this now. The day of cleansing is almost at an end."

Mary nodded. "Forgive me. I almost forgot myself. I don't know why I keep trying to talk to it like it will see reason.

"Cameryn, this is all your fault. I don't know why I let you get to me like this." She poured more of the strange liquid onto the boy's chest. His scream was powerful. The scabbed flesh on his chest was burned away by the liquid. It became raw and red and started to bleed again.

"Enough!" Shadow yelled, jumping out into the open.

"Who are you, and what are you doing here?" Mary exclaimed. "Nobody is permitted inside this building once the rites have begun."

Shadow laughed coldly. "I don't care. But if you touch that kid again, I promise, it will be the last thing either of you ever do."

Leon glared. "Don't threaten us, heathen. This is a holy sanctuary; certainly not a place for the likes of you. Filthy scum, I can smell the impurity within you."

"What do you mean, you can smell my impurity?" Shadow asked, raising an eyebrow.

"The goddess gives me grand insight. You're a vampire. What guts you must have to come in here. Your very presence defiles our sacred ground." Leon picked up an athame from the table. "Pray for forgiveness, and perhaps we'll have mercy on you both."

Ellie rolled her eyes and walked up onto the platform. "Hey, preacher, how about you pray that I won't kick your ass up and down this aisle? Who knows? It may not happen if you close your eyes and believe."

"You dare defile the goddess's house of worship with your foul tongue?!" Leon asked in disbelief. "Have you no respect, wench?"

Shadow shrugged. "Oh, we dare. Idiots like you need to remember that respect isn't given. It's earned."

"Really, now?" Leon replied thoughtfully, rubbing the dull side of the athame with his fingers. "Well, Mary, why don't you give them something they can... respect."

Mary look at him for a few moments, then nodded when comprehension dawned on her. "Perhaps you're right," she said, a smile curling on her lips. "I agree, these kids need to learn a lesson in obedience. Maybe a small demonstration is in order."

"What are you two wackos going on about?" Shadow asked. He felt, more than saw, the woman moving, and his eyes flickered over in time to see her pour some of the liquid onto Cameryn's legs. The places where the liquid hit melted away more of his flesh, and a loud scream escaped his lips.

Ellie let out a shriek of pure frustration. The air around her became thick and dense as her power flowed from her body and lashed out. The pillars in the room covered with frost. "Don't you dare touch him, ever again!"

Cameryn turned to face Ellie as he struggled to retain consciousness. "H-h-help. . .m-me. . .p-plea. . ." he stammered before his eyes closed and his body went limp.

"Is he...?" Ellie asked. She feared the worst, though silently she begged, hoped, and prayed that he wasn't dead. She'd have given up almost anything in that one moment for the boy to still be alive.

Mary lazily placed her hands on Cameryn's neck. Far from gentle, she moved it up and down, searching for a specific spot. Finding it at last, she placed two fingers there for a few seconds and then sighed, moving her hand away. "The child lives. We'll just have to try harder in the future."

"Let me tell you, you're making way too many assumptions," Shadow began. "You're assuming that he'll still be around for you to hurt. You're also assuming that you'll both still be alive after I get through with you. Seems to me like you two are putting a whole lot on chance."

"You smug little brat!" Mary shouted, her face flushed. "That boy is our son, shameful as it is to admit it, and we will raise him as we see fit."

Shadow's face hardened. "Is this what you call raising a child?" he asked as he took a few steps forward, unsheathing his sword. "Torture, food deprivation, and mental abuse? Feral animals would make better parents than you two."

Mary spat on the ground in Shadow's direction. "You disgusting creature, how dare you talk down to me?" she said, eyes wild. "You have no idea what I've done, the pain and suffering I have endured.

"Leon and I were the leaders of these people, the purest. Then suddenly, one day I was pregnant, and we were both overjoyed. We loved him and treated him with respect and care, as good as any parents out there. Then, when he became a teenager, his true disgusting nature came out. He started acting differently. He was reclusive. He wouldn't talk to us or his friends. He wasn't even interested in dating the local girls. Then we found out why our perfect son was acting so strangely. He was a freak."

Shadow frowned, but he didn't respond. He couldn't wrap his head around the fact that people like them actually existed, people who would hate their child just for being different.

Ellie was shaking. "Parents are supposed to love their kids no matter what…no matter what," she said, tears rolling down her face. "How can you two live with yourselves?"

"Are you a parent?" Mary asked.

"Well, no," Ellie admitted.

"Then don't you preach to me about what a parent should and shouldn't be. You have no idea what it's like trying to raise a child who refuses to change for the better. We told him countless times that if he would just try to make a change, perhaps we could love him again. We cannot and will not love him if he continues to live in this lifestyle."

Ellie shook her head. "You're wrong, wrong in so many ways. I may not be a parent, but I know that if you're a parent, you are supposed to love your kids, no matter what. Not only that, but you're supposed to support them and care about them, even if they make decisions that you personally disagree with.

"It's not about having the perfect child; it's about loving that child with all your heart. It doesn't matter if the child loves sports and you don't, or plays games and you don't, or if the child is gay, straight, lesbian, transgendered, has powers or doesn't, or is an alien from Mars. What matters is that you love them."

"It's pretty to think that way, little girl, but we cannot support somebody who chooses to be so disgusting," Mary said.

"It's not a choice. He can't control it!" Shadow retorted indignantly. "You can't choose to be what you are or who you are. You're born with it!"

Ellie asked, wiping her tears away. "Hating and being ignorant. You can choose to hate somebody for something they cannot control. You can also choose to be ignorant."

"Enough!" Leon shouted, slamming his free hand down on the table. "We've heard enough from the both of you. Leave now, or we'll have to make another sacrifice."

"I guess we'll have to see if your 'god' can protect you from being stabbed," Shadow said, raising his sword. "Don't worry. I'll make sure it won't hurt… too much."

"You shall not take my life easily, vampire. The goddess has given me her blessing," Leon said, pulling a glass vial filled with a dark green liquid out of his pocket. "All I need to do is drink this potion, and I will be imbued with great power."

Shadow shrugged. "Drink your silly potion. It won't make a difference."

Leon laughed. "You fool. This will give me a portion of her power," he said, flicking the top off of the vial and bringing it to his lips, "giving me more than enough strength to kill a weakling like you." He poured the contents into his mouth.

"You're going to get it now," Mary said.

86

"No, I actually don't think we are," Ellie said, moving forward. She rolled up her sleeves. "But I'm happy. This is the part I've been waiting for."

Mary raised an eyebrow. "You want to say something, little girl?"

Ellie smiled, unpleasantly sweet. "Yes, I do," she said. "First off, don't call me little girl. Secondly, we're taking Cameryn, and you will never harm or see him ever again. Thirdly, I'm going to beat you so hard that your face will rival a Picasso painting."

"Big words, for such a little girl. Besides, once the potion takes effect, Leon will destroy you both single-handedly."

"It's done," Leon announced. His eyes were deep red. His skin was tinted a yellow color; strange runic symbols littered his body. "The goddess has granted me her blessing and infused me with her strength."

Mary smiled triumphantly. "You two are finished," she said. Her breath quickened. "The goddess smiles upon her truest followers. Unfortunately for you two, there are none truer than us."

"Couldn't they just... drop dead or something?" Ellie asked.

"No, because that would be easy," Shadow replied, "and my life is not easy."

"You two are in no position to be joking," Leon said. "I still cannot fathom why anyone would risk anything for the likes of him. He's hardly worth the time it takes to torture him."

"You're wrong," Shadow replied.

"Oh, so you disagree?" Leon asked. "Fine. Then tell me one thing: Why risk your life for someone you don't even know? Why risk anything for him at all? You don't know him. You don't owe him anything."

"Sometimes there are things worth fighting for, people worth fighting for, things worth dying for," Shadow said, pointing his sword towards Leon. He moved his left foot to the side, preparing for battle.

"Oh, that's real sweet. But when you die, who will take care of your lady friend?" Mary asked. "Soon you will be dead and she will be all alone... with no one to protect her."

Ellie laughed. "Lady, I hate to break it to you, but this isn't some fairy tale and I am not a damsel in distress. This ain't the 1950s. I don't need anybody to save me. I can handle myself."

"That's my girl," Shadow thought. *"She'll never need me to come to her rescue. She'll never die waiting for me."*

"Shadow, you take him," Ellie said. "I'll handle her." Shadow nodded in agreement. They both charged at their respective targets.

Mary grabbed another athame from a table and threw it at Ellie.

Ellie took a deep breath and then blew it out. The moment her breath left her mouth, it chilled the area in front of her, and the dagger froze in midair and fell to the ground. She flicked her hand forward, sending hundreds of tiny icicles shooting towards Mary. Mary just barely jumped out of the way in time as the barrage of sharp ice grazed her arm. Blood started soaking through the soft, thin material.

Mary placed her hand over her wound, brushing it softly, and then frowned when she brought her hand up and saw blood on it. "You brat. You made me bleed."

"I guess you're a Bloody Mary now. Get it?" Ellie replied, snickering.

"You'll pay for this, I promise you," Mary said, rushing at her. She pulled another dagger out of her waistband and thrust the blade forward, aiming for Ellie's stomach.

Ellie grabbed the woman's wrist as it came down and twisted it until she dropped the knife.

"You're good, little girl, but not good enough," Mary snarled through clenched teeth. She threw a punch at Ellie's stomach. It connected. Ellie buckled forward. She thrust her leg across Ellie's face, which knocked her backwards onto the floor.

"Not bad," Ellie said, lifting herself off the ground and wiping away a thin line of blood from her nose. "But I'm still going to kick your ass."

Shadow was locked in combat with Leon. Leon was slashing at him with an athame, Shadow dodging every blow. Shadow slashed his sword forward, and it cut deeply into Leon's chest. With the first strike landing, he used the opening to his advantage. He made two more quick slices, leaving deep gashes in Leon's chest, and then jumped in the air, sending his leg soaring towards the man's head.

Leon backed up with each hit. As Shadow's leg came at his face, he caught it with both hands and flipped him backwards. Shadow landed on the ground a few feet away. He threw his hands forward and sent a blast of energy, which hit Leon's arm. The shadows ate right through the limb, and the arm fell to the floor.

"Impressive," Leon said, holding a hand to the bloody stump.

"Thanks," Shadow replied. "Good to know that years of tedious training haven't been wasted."

Leon closed his eyes, and the deep gashes in his chest knit themselves closed and healed. His severed arm twitched on the ground for a second, then flew back to the stump, reconnecting itself. The skin smoothed out like clay. "Oh yes, you're impressive… but not impressive enough."

Shadow looked scared for the first time since entering the cathedral. He cursed under his breath. "Well, I guess, if at first you don't succeed, try, try again." He started to move forward, but he was forced into defense as Leon began a relentless assault. He was dodging punches left and right. Each punch seemed to be faster than the one before it.

Getting tired, Shadow suddenly ducked, a fist whizzing past his head. He took this opportunity to smash his elbow into Leon's chest, winding him. Finally, he put all of his preternatural strength into one final uppercut, hitting Leon under the chin. The force of the hit was so powerful that Leon's body left the ground for a few seconds before smashing to the ground.

Ellie whistled in appreciation. "Nice one!"

Mary growled. "Don't be so quick to cheer, little girl. You'll be burning in hell soon enough, and your boyfriend will join you."

"I think hell is reserved for monsters like you."

Mary screamed in frustration. "I've had enough of your mouth, brat!" she bellowed, slapping Ellie hard across the face.

Ellie's head moved slightly to the side due to the force of impact. A red handprint slowly appeared on her face. "Game over," she growled. She walked up to Mary and punched her squarely in the face. While she was recovering, Ellie spun around and smashed her leg across Mary's chest, sending the woman flying. Mary flew over the table on which Cameryn still lie unconscious, and she was impaled onto a candle bracket.

"Mary!" Leon screamed. He ran to her and grabbed her hand. "What did these heathens do to you? Speak to me!"

89

"L-Leon…" Mary said weakly, spitting up a thick glob of blood. It trailed down her chin and splattered her robes.

Leon, trembling with fury, turned back to face Shadow and Ellie. "You brats killed her. I'm going to kill you!"

"Not to be childish and whatnot, but that psycho tried to kill me first," Ellie said. "And besides, you were going to kill us anyway. Remember? You can't double-kill somebody. It's not like they will be any more dead."

Shadow tried to mask his smile by pretending to yawn and putting his hand over his mouth. The gesture was entirely noticed by Leon, who growled. "Sorry?"

"You brats are dead. I'm through playing games," Leon said, rushing at Shadow, catching him off guard. Leon plunged his fist into Shadow's shoulder, knocking him off balance, and then backhanded him, knocking him to the ground.

Before Ellie could react, Leon was suddenly charging at her. He was like a blur. He threw a roundhouse kick, catching her in the thigh, and she huddled forward in pain.

"I told you," Leon said, grabbing Ellie by the throat, a triumphant smirk forming upon his face. "You two are no match for me now. The goddess has been good to me!"

"You know what hurts more than getting punched in the chest?" Shadow asked, lifting himself off the ground. "Having to constantly hear your annoying voice." His eyes shined black, and a wave of power radiated off of him, all directed at Leon. The force of power was so strong that Leon's hand was forced off of Ellie's throat and he was thrown backwards away from her.

"How did you…" Leon stammered. "Where did you get that power from?"

Shadow didn't respond. He walked over to Ellie and helped her off the ground. "You all right?"

"Yes," Ellie said, "I'm fine."

As Shadow moved forward, the shadows in the room seemed to come alive and hiss. "I have a trick for you," he said, placing his hands in front of him. The shadows in the room flooded up to his hands and formed into a sword. "My trick is to make you disappear."

"Fine, then, vampire," Leon said, picking his knife off the ground. "Time to see how your darkness can stand up to the light."

Shadow rushed Leon, who tried to thrust the dagger into Shadow's chest, but Shadow blocked it with his own blade. Leon took his chance and made another slashing motion with the dagger, but Shadow parried the slash and aimed a strike at Leon's legs. Leon jumped up into the air and did a back flip, landing a few feet away from Shadow.

Leon rushed at Shadow this time, throwing the dagger as he was charging. Shadow caught the dagger mid-flight and threw it back at him. Leon attempted to move out of the way to dodge the dagger and almost did so, but his shadow seemed to "trip" him, causing the dagger to graze his arm. A long cut opened across his arm, this one not healing instantly.

"How is this possible?!" Leon asked, surprised. "This is impossible. I am immortal. You aren't supposed to be able to hurt me!"

"How did I just hurt him?" Shadow wondered.

Ellie looked from Shadow to Leon, and then realization dawned upon her. "Shadow, he can only be hurt by his own weapons - weapons blessed by him or that woman!" she yelled. She picked up the dagger that Mary had dropped earlier and threw it to him.

Shadow caught the dagger by the hilt and waved it at Leon. "Hey, Superman, guess who found your kryptonite?"

Leon growled angrily. "You won't make a fool of me!" he said, and then he blindly charged at Shadow.

Shadow stepped gracefully out of the way and, without hesitation, sank the dagger into Leon's chest, the blade going in hilt deep, grazing the man's heart. In that split-second, life flooded away from Leon. His body fell to the floor, nothing more than an empty shell.

"Is he dead?" Ellie asked.

Shadow bent over and ripped the dagger out of Leon's chest, then checked him for a pulse. "It's over. I can only hope he suffered half as much in death as he made Cameryn suffer in life."

"What's going on?" a voice called. It was Cameryn, who had just regained consciousness.

Ellie rushed over to the boy, Shadow following closely behind. "Are you all right?"

Cameryn blinked a few times, absentmindedly brushing his chest with his hand. He flinched in silent agony and moved it away. Areas where the liquid hit resembled burns. Fresh blood dripped out of the wounds, rolling in little droplets down his sides.

"Damn it," Shadow muttered, checking out the wounds. "They're pretty bad. I've never seen anything like this before."

He glanced at the half-empty bottle sitting on the table, the same bottle of liquid that Mary had been pouring onto Cameryn. "This stuff, I'm not sure what it is, but it apparently has corrosive properties. Maybe hydrochloric acid?"

"It. . . it hurts," Cameryn whimpered, struggling to a sitting position.

Ellie shook her head and placed her hand on his shoulder. "Try not to move too much. You're too weak. We'll get someone to fix you."

Cameryn frowned and pushed her hand away. "Don't touch me! You're just trying to set me up so you can hurt me like they did!" he yelled.

"That is just nonsense," Shadow said. "Listen, I personally have no reason to hurt you. I've seen that you've been hurt before, and I wouldn't want to add to that. Besides, why would I risk my life to save you, just to kill you? I promise, I'm not that clever."

Ellie nodded. "He's right. He really isn't."

"Everyone in my life, since I can remember, has only wanted to hurt me. Why should you guys be any different? Why should I trust you?"

"Well, for one, we rescued you," Ellie replied. "And for two, sometimes you just need to trust people. If you never let anybody in, you can't expect them to let you in."

"She's right," Shadow said. "You have to trust us. I promise that we have no intention of hurting you, at all. Once again, I'm not that clever."

Cameryn smiled. "Thanks for the honesty. Finally, someone being honest with me... It's a nice change."

Ellie returned his smile with one of her own. "So why did they want to harm you, anyway? The whole town seemed to be helping them. Why?"

Cameryn shook his head. "You'll just think I'm a freak. Not everyone is like I am. Most people would hate me for it, especially my parents. They always hated me for it. It prevented me from being the perfect son they wanted."

Shadow gave him a puzzled look. "What do you mean?"

"They always wanted a normal son. They couldn't handle what I am. They regarded it as a sin; that I was evil," Cameryn said, checking Shadow and Ellie's faces for hints that they, too, would reject him, like everyone else in his life had.

Ellie frowned. "You're going to have to give us more than just that to go on. Show us what you mean."

Cameryn hesitated for a moment before lifting his hand up. He pointed at a candle hanging on the wall, and it exploded in a burst of flames.

"So. . .the rumors are true," Shadow muttered. "Don't worry, we won't hate you for something like that - especially not something we all have in common."

Cameryn's mouth opened wide. "So you can both make things explode too?" he asked, but they both shook their heads.

"No, hon, but we all have powers. There are more of us at the castle. You'll love it there. People just like you with abilities, and we're all like family," Ellie replied. "And by family, I mean an actual family, not like what you're used to - as in people who love and treat you good, no matter what."

Cameryn nodded. "I guess whatever is waiting there for me is much better than what I have now."

"It is. Trust me," Ellie said.

Shadow smiled. "Cameryn, I want to let you know that you don't have to come with us. I'm not forcing you to do anything you don't want to. You do have a choice. I hope you'll come. I want you to come."

"Me too!" Ellie added.

"Of course, I'll come with you guys," Cameryn replied. "There's nothing left here for me anymore. I don't think there ever was. Besides, in the past ten minutes, you guys have treated me better than I have been treated in my entire life, all fourteen years. I'd be crazy to stay here, when you guys offer me something that I've always wanted… a home."

"Well, that settles it," Ellie said. "Shadow, make a portal for us! I don't know about you, but I'm sick of this town."

Shadow shook his head. "We have to find Tereya, remember?"

Ellie gasped. "I almost forgot! I hope he's all right. I haven't seen him since we came in here."

A loud rumbling sound shook the ground under them. Suddenly, the entire wall of the cathedral crumbled away. "Hey, guys!" Tereya said, waving happily.

Ellie blinked. "Well, I guess he's here now."

"Wow, Ellie," Shadow said. "Maybe you should try wishing for a million dollars next, or world peace."

"Oh, hush. It was just a coincidence. Either way, thank you, Reya, for providing such an awesomely awesome distraction."

"Yeah, we couldn't have done it without you," Shadow said, ruffling the boy's hair. "You did an amazing job."

"Aw, it was nothing," Tereya said, blushing slightly. He looked over and saw Cameryn. "Is that him?"

Cameryn looked Tereya over carefully before nodding. "My name is Cameryn. Nice to meet you, Tereya."

"Nice to meet you too," Tereya replied, smiling. "You can call me Reya, by the way. All my friends do."

"Friends?" Cameryn repeated. "It sounds so strange. I've never had any before."

"Well, you do now," Shadow replied. "Let's go home." He pointed his hand to the ground, and a portal appeared.

Ellie and Tereya made their way over to the portal and jumped in.

Shadow walked over to Cameryn and held out his arm, picking him off the table, allowing the boy to lean on him so that he could stand up.

"Hey, Shadow?" Cameryn asked.

Shadow looked down at him. "Yeah?"

"Why are you helping me?"

"I don't know. Because it's the right thing to do?" Shadow replied, shrugging. "Somebody had to, and I'm glad I could be the person. Nobody deserves to go through that. Nobody."

"I just don't understand why you're any different. Growing up, nobody's ever loved me or cared about me before. I've never known affection or trust - or friendship. What makes you different from all the rest?" Cameryn asked, blinking back tears. "I never thought I deserved those things."

"What makes me different is that I know how you feel. I know what it's like to not feel good enough or strong enough, or to blame yourself for other people's ignorance and bigotry. But eventually you come to understand that it's not you. It's them. They're the problem, and you're perfect. As one of my favorite human singers, Lady Gogra says, you were born as you are; there's nothing wrong with you."

Cameryn shook his head and smiled. "Actually, it's Lady Gaga."

"You've heard of her? That's funny. I didn't take your parents as the type who would let you listen to anything but gospel."

"Well, when you've heard them complain enough about somebody, you tend to remember the name," Cameryn replied, scratching the back of his head. "Besides, I may have gone behind their back and listened to a few of her songs. They're pretty good."

"See, we're going to get along great," Shadow said, smiling. "Now let's go. You have more friends to meet."

"All right. But do me a favor?"

"What is it?"

"Promise me that you won't let anything bad happen to me and that you'll always be there for me?" Cameryn asked.

"I promise," Shadow said. He led Cameryn to the portal. As they both jumped in, he prayed, harder than he had for anything in his entire life, that he could keep his promise.

Michael Chulsky

CHAPTER 5: THE BLACK MARKET

Thousands of miles away from the dark castle, a mansion stood looming high upon a hill. Inside the mansion, in the largest room, a woman was sleeping in a bed that was large enough to fit ten people. Dozens of shoeboxes littered the floor around it.

The woman stirred and then woke up. Her wild red hair was askew, even more so than usual. She yawned and rubbed the sleepiness out of her eyes. "Mezmir!" she yelled.

The tiny demon in question ran into the room, panting heavily. He carried a tray of food in hand as he stumbled up to the side of the bed. "Lady Maedara," he wheezed, giving her a curt nod, "I hope you slept well."

Maedara smiled down at him and took the tray from his hand. "Breakfast in bed. My, my, my. How delightfully unexpected!" she swooned, an air of dramatic shock filling her voice.

"But last night you told me to bring you breakfast in bed or you would rip my legs off and beat me to death with them!"

"Oh, hush, you fool. I would never say something like that. Idle threats aren't becoming for a lady of my stature."

Mezmir sighed and bowed his head in shame.

"Oh, Mezmir, don't be sad in my presence. You know how sensitive I am to the pain of others," she said, biting into a piece of toast.

"Forgive me," Mezmir replied, "but didn't you just kill a guy in a shoe store because he didn't have your size?"

Maedara slapped him across the head and laughed. "Oh, Mezmir, you're such a comedian," she said, taking a sip of the orange juice. "I didn't kill him. Any ordinary ruffian could kill somebody. I like to look at it as… soul liberation."

Mezmir rubbed his head and frowned. He watched her eat the eggs and then, in mid-bite, groan. "Are you not enjoying the food I prepared for you?"

"It's as horrible as usual, but the food isn't what's upsetting me. I just really wanted those shoes the other night."

"Shoes? Master, what about the Dragon's Eye?"

"Oh! The Dragon's Eye," Maedara replied, glaring. "Yes, thank you for bringing it up. One of my strongest demons died in the attempt of stealing it and, as a result, I don't have it. But thank you again, Mezmir, for reminding me of a failure that was soooo traumatizing for me."

Mezmir stepped back, nervously muttering his apologies. They unfortunately were unheard by her, and he saw she was getting more hysterical with every passing second.

"You don't know what it's like, Mezmir!" Maedara cried, tears falling down her face. "I'm supposed to be this sexy, powerful woman with a stunning body, but no one knows how I feel. No one knows how hard it is to be evil. Crime doesn't pay unless you work hard at it, and I do. But no one seems to notice!'"

"B-b-but I notice how hard you work. It's all right. You're doing a great job as queen of evil!"

"Good. I'm glad you feel that way," Maedara said, instantly cheering up. She breathed a sigh of relief and patted him on the head gently. "Now I don't have to kill you."

Mezmir blinked. "Well, thank you for that. But what are we going to do about our little problem, those teenage brats who have been getting in our way? They've held up our plans. What are we going to do?"

Maedara stood up and walked over to look out the window. "You know, Mezmir, lately you've proven to be quite the mood dampener. I was just getting over losing the Dragon's Eye, and now you're again bringing up something that you know will cause me emotional stress. Do you hate me?"

"Hate you? What do you mean, Master?" Mezmir replied, slightly taken aback.

"Well, you seem to get some cheap, sick thrill out of bringing up things that make me upset, like some little sadist. So I ask you again, do you hate me?"

Mezmir shook his head and then realized that her back was to him. "No, of course, I don't hate you," he said, "I'm just worried about these kids and the threat they pose!"

Maedara laughed. "Oh, Mezmir, I love how you assume that those brats are problems worth stressing over! Don't you understand that I could kill them anytime I want to, if I actually cared?"

Mezmir nodded carefully, his face not betraying any emotion. "If I may ask, why don't you just kill them now, and save us trouble later?"

"I owe you no explanation on why I do the things I do. You are a servant, not an equal. Remember your place."

"I apologize once again, Master. I did not mean to question your methods. I only wanted to. . .assist your decisions in removing them as a potential threat. I know you are the most powerful, the toughest, and the most. . .beautiful!"

Maedara opened her mouth wide, joy etched in every inch of her face. It was almost like Christmas had come early. "Y-you really think I'm beautiful, Mezmir?!" she gushed, batting her eyelashes.

"Yes, of course. You are the fairest in all the land, " he replied, frowning at having to use such a clichéd line.

At any rate, she appeared to have taken his word for it, as she began to dance around the room. A few moments later, she stopped dancing. "Mezmir, pack my traveling case. I wish to set off in a few minutes," she said, walking over to her closet. "I have errands to run."

"Master, may I ask where you're heading to?"

Maedara frowned impatiently while riffling through her clothes. "I'm heading to the Black Market. I'm in a shopping mood. Maybe I can even buy some nice, new things to make me feel better," she said, flicking her hair.

"Besides, what are you, my mother? I'm being rhetorical, by the way. I know you aren't my mother, because I killed her. You're still alive. At least for now, anyway."

Mezmir shrugged and went to go fetch her traveling bag. As he was walking out the door, she called his name, so he stopped. "Yes, Master?"

"While you're getting my traveling bag, go to the treasury and put about…" she paused and thought for a moment. "Put about 150,000 charlocks in my bag."

Mezmir frowned.

"Oh, Mezmir, what have I told you about pouting?" Maedara asked, looking at him in the mirror. "Hello, worry lines!"

"Forgive me for pouting in your presence. I just wonder if it is wise to bring so much money with you, especially with the kind of people that hang out there."

"Mezmir, it is not healthy for you to wonder if something I do is wise or not, nor is it part of your job description. You are a minion. If you'd like, I can get you the dictionary so you can look up the definition of it there. Or better yet, I can take that dictionary and bash in your head."

"No, that won't be necessary. I'll go get the money and your bag at once," he stammered, rushing out of the room.

Maedara continued to rifle through the hundreds of designer dresses that filled her closet. She smiled when she found the perfect dress to wear for the occasion. The dress was long and flowing, cut right below the knees, flaring out on the sides to create the illusion of multiple layers. It was deep lilac, with a spider embroidered from real spun silver on the center of the dress. The spider was adorned with precious jewels: emeralds, rubies, and diamonds.

Maedara slipped off the dress she was wearing and pulled the new one on, adjusting the straps. She bent down and put on a pair of shoes that matched the color of the dress. She reached into her jewelry drawer and picked out a pair of amethyst earrings.

Mezmir walked back into the room as she was putting the earrings in. "Your traveling case, Master," he said, holding the bag above his head.

"Did you put in the exact amount of charlocks that I asked for?"

Mezmir nodded as he looked directly in her eyes. "Of course."

"Wonderful. I'm dressed to kill and have tons of cash!" She ripped the bag out of Mezmir's hand and walked to the door. "Now, Mezmir, don't break anything, and I want the place spotless when I return. I'd hate to eviscerate you after a long journey."

 CR&OCR&OCR&OCR&O

A short while later, Maedara exited her car and pressed the little button on the key chain to auto-lock it. She walked into the kiosk building.

"Hello, there. How may I help you today?" the ticket man asked, a bright smile on his face.

Maedara frowned. His chipper attitude was bugging her. She had no time for happy people or things. "Clearly, somebody is much too happy to be working in retail," she replied, rolling her eyes. "Anyway, I'd like a ticket to Hyael, preferably a boat that's leaving soon."

"I must have misunderstood you," the man said, ignoring her blatant rudeness. "Are you completely sure that you want a ticket to Hyael?"

"I'm sorry, but did I stutter?" Maedara asked softly. Anybody who knew her well knew that if her voice went soft, she was getting angry. "I'm quite sure that I didn't stutter. So unless you have hearing problems or are a bumbling idiot, there shouldn't have been a misunderstanding of any kind. So, yes, I'm sure. I want a ticket to Hyael."

The ticket man blinked, no longer able to disregard her rudeness. Sighing, he punched a button and ripped off a ticket that came out of a slot. "That will be 15 charlocks, ma'am."

"15 charlocks?!" she asked incredulously. "That is a complete and utter rip-off. How dare you charge such a crazy price and expect me to pay that? It's so crazy and outlandish that I will pay it only because I don't wish to anger a crazy person. They tend to have violent outbursts!"

"I'm sorry, ma'am, but I don't set the prices."

Maedara pursed her lips. She took a stack of charlocks out of her bag, counted out 15, and threw them down on the counter. "You're lucky I'm

101

such a refined woman, because if I wasn't, I would rip off your legs and beat you to death with them."

The ticket man's eyes widened, obviously affronted. "So I'm guessing you wouldn't want to purchase our new sailor's saving card? The more you sail, the less you pay."

"Yeah, how about no? If I wanted to save money on sailing, I'd kill you, lowly ticket peasant. That, or buy my own boat," she said, flicking her hair casually. She waved goodbye to him and skipped to the dock.

Once she reached the dock, she gazed out and saw a huge ship in the distance. The ship sailed in, gradually coming to a complete stop.

A man waved to her from the deck. "Hey, there! I am the ship captain," he said. "Where are you heading?"

Maedara flashed him a dazzling smile. "Hyael. Have you heard of it?"

The captain looked startled. "Nobody ever goes there. It's a dangerous place filled with ruthless criminals and evil creatures of all sorts. It's not a place for a petite lady such as yourself."

Maedara glowered, sucking her teeth. "If I wanted your opinion, I would have asked," she said. "Can you get me there or not?"

The captain nodded. "Not a problem. It's my motto," he said, pointing to a large plaque on the side of the ship. "You name a place and I'll sail you to it."

"Good, because I don't have all day," she replied.

CЗ ঙ CЗ ঙ CЗ ঙ CЗ ঙ

She was, at last, on the outskirts of Hyael. "I have arrived!" she announced.

"Oh, my God! It's her!"

"What's she doing back here?"

"This can't be good."

"If she's back, I'm getting a one-way ticket out of here!"

"I don't wanna die today!"

"I can't believe it," Maedara thought. She could hear the people whispering, and a smile spread across her face. *"They're actually talking about me, little ol' me."*

"Maedara, what are you doing back so soon?" a man asked. He took a few steps back, making sure to keep his distance.

"Back so soon? That's crazy talk. I haven't been back in many years. I didn't want to keep my adoring public waiting!"

"It seems like only yesterday," the man muttered. He could almost still see the destruction and chaos from her last visit. Taking her confusion as an opening, he pushed his kids inside the house. He slammed the door shut and locked it.

Maedara shrugged and continued walking. To her disdain, people were standing in her way. "Can I help you idiots with something?" she asked, stopping. Her eyes narrowed. "Why are you all being so rude and standing in my way?"

"We're not," a man said. "My wife and I are just passing by. We don't want any trouble, all right?"

"Maybe we wouldn't be standing here looking if your dress wasn't so hideous," the man's wife said, frowning in disgust.

Maedara gasped, eyes widening in shock.

The man pulled his wife behind him. "Forgive her," he choked. "She's not from here. She didn't mean it!"

"So my dress isn't ugly then?" Maedara asked, batting her eyelashes.

"It's beyond ugly," the woman answered. "In fact, it's so ugly that the person who sold it to you should be arrested and sent to jail for life."

Maedara's eyes closed. She trembled as if she were about to cry, her body rocking back and forth. "You're a liar," she whispered. Suddenly, her mouth opened wide, and a torrent of a green acid-like substance shot out of it, drenching the couple. Their screams were loud and piteous as their skin melted off, leaving nothing but piles of scorched bone.

"You killed them!" a woman screamed.

"Stop looking at me! I just want to blend in like everybody else!" Maedara cried, putting her hand to her forehead. The people scattered in different directions. Taking this as a sign that they listened to her wishes, she shrugged and continued to walk on.

As she strolled through the town, she noticed the people acting differently. Instead of going about their business, the town's residents were now running away in scattered directions. *"Why do people always run away from me? It's like I'm diseased or something. It's not fair. I just want to be loved like everybody else. Is that so wrong?"*

All of a sudden, she reached out and grabbed a man who was running away by his throat. The man struggled, both his hands trying to pull her one hand off, but his strength was no match for hers. She smiled as she lifted him in the air.

"P-please. . .don't kill me!" he whimpered, fear etched in his voice.

Maedara scowled. *"That's what I'm talking about! Why does everyone automatically assume that I'm going to kill them? I'm totally not that violent!"*

She looked at the man and stared into his eyes. "Why is everyone running away from me and screaming?" she asked, her voice reverting to its soft, Valley-girl mode.

The man attempted to reply so that he wouldn't be killed, but her grip tightened and he began to struggle, gasping for air.

Maedara waited impatiently for his reply, watching him struggle. "Okay, now, that is just rude!" she said. "Not being able to breathe is no excuse for bad manners. Answer me!" She waited, and he became limp in her grasp. "Fine. If you want to be a jerk and pass out while I'm trying to conversate with you, then I don't want to conversate anymore!"

She threw him away with all of her strength. The man's body flew from her hand and collided with the side of a house, bricks shattering down around him. She watched the bricks pile over the man's body. "How utterly rude of that man to not get up and apologize for his disdainful behavior," she thought, shaking her head. "I guess people just don't raise their children right anymore."

CR&CR&CR&CR&

"Where the hell is this portal?" Maedara wondered a short while later. She knew that the portal entrance to the Black Market used to be in the center of the town, but it apparently just vanished. "This isn't fair!" she said, stomping her foot on the ground. "Why can't I find the portal? Why are they trying to keep me, of all people, out?!" she yelled. In the middle of her temper tantrum, she noticed that there was a new building to the side of the town. *"Hmm, I've never seen that building before. I'd better check it out."*

The building was small, plain, and ordinary. It was obviously intended to be inconspicuous, but it failed, because it grabbed her attention. This brief moment of clarity calmed her down, and she stared at the building, noticing that it was well guarded. *"Hmm, why aren't those guards trying to stop me from ruining the city? Maybe, just maybe, they're trying to guard something,"* she thought. Pausing only to smooth out her dress, she brushed off the dust and walked over to the guards. "Hello, there!" she called, waving her arms.

The guards cast confused looks in her direction but kept silent. Maedara took a few more steps forward until she was mere inches away from them. Gazing at them, she picked out the one who had a different uniform, the leader. "Hey, there, cutie," she said. When she received no answer, she frowned. "You know, it's rude to not answer a lady when she's speaking. So terribly rude!"

The guard flushed but almost instantly regained his composure. "Sorry about my manners, Ms. . .?"

"Maedara. My name is Maedara!" she replied, throwing her hair back. "I'm like royalty; all should know my name."

The guard looked at her for a second. He frowned. Now he knew who he was dealing with. He had been warned.

"Ah. Well, my apologies, Ms. Maedara, but this area is restricted, unfortunately. You'll have to leave now," he said cogently. His voice held the firmness of someone who was well used to giving commands.

Maedara giggled like a little girl. "You're...ordering me?" she asked. "That is just so adorable!"

The guard shook his head. "It's no laughing matter. My orders are clear. This is a restricted area; no civilians allowed. You must leave," he repeated.

"Yes, I heard you the first time, and I'm sorry to say that it just wasn't as funny the second time you said it," Maedara replied, "Now, tell me. . .you guys, you're guards. Would I be correct in assuming so?"

The guard blinked at her and gave a curt nod. "Yes, you would be correct. We are the lead officers force of Hyael."

"Good, good," she replied, with a mocking smile. "Now, you guys are guards; hence, you are guarding something, which means it has to be important enough for it to need guards to guard it," she stated, her voice getting lower. "So…you're guards guarding something. Right?"

"Why, yes, that is accurate. But I'm afraid that information is classified. So unless you have the password or proper authorization, you must leave."

Maedara looked him up and down and tilted her head to the side. "Or what, may I ask?" she questioned, her voice careful. "You're not threatening little ol' me, are you? Because that just wouldn't be gentleman-like. And I'd hate for you to spoil the friendly dialogue we have going here."

The man shook his head. "It's not a threat, ma'am. Leave now or you will be forcibly escorted off the premises. This is your last warning."

Maedara smiled yet again. Abruptly, she thrust her hand forward. Her palm connected with the man's chest and propelled him backwards, sending him smashing into a wall. The guards drew their weapons from their holsters, and she watched them, interested, the same way a lion watches a gazelle. "It seems that your captain is, as they say, down for the count," she said, flicking a piece of hair out of her face.

"You're under arrest! Any movement, and we'll shoot," a guard yelled.

Maedara smiled because she could hear the fear in his voice. She darted forward and elbowed him in the chest. The man doubled over in pain, and she slapped him across his face, knocking him onto his side. This was all the guards needed to open fire. As the bullets flew towards her, she grinned and jerked her hair down in front of her like a veil. To the surprise of the guards, the bullets rebounded off her hair and rebounded at them. She laughed as the guards fell to the ground, one by one, bullets in their chests.

"Oh, dear. I guess I used way too much hair spray this morning," she said, looking down at the bodies in front of her. "Or maybe it's Maybelline."

She was about to move forward, but she turned around when she heard a groan. The leader of the guards remained alive, the cut on his head still bleeding. "I missed one? How embarrassing. This just isn't my day."

The guard struggled to crawl away from her, but he lacked the energy. "Go...away," he panted.

Maedara walked over to him, casually slow. She kneeled down by his body, her knee resting on his arm. "Now, if you're lucky, I'll kill you fast. Really lucky, I won't kill you at all. But that's only if you're a nice man and tell me what you guys were - as in the past tense - guarding."

The man let out a gasp of pain as she ground her knee deeper into his arm. This continued until he screamed.

"I'll talk!" he yelled, and the pressure on his arm ceased. "We. . .we were guarding the entrance to the Black Market. We were told to not let anyone in unless they have a password."

Maedara smiled. "I see. Well, you failed," she replied coldly. "You have got to be the worst guard ever. You're a shame to your hometown, your parents, and everybody you love. If I don't kill you, which I am probably going to, FYI, suicide is probably a good option."

The man winced. The pain from the head wound and his arm were taking their toll. "What do you want from me?" he asked, his voice strained. "I already told you everything."

"Nothing, really. I'm just having fun at this point."

The man attempted to speak, but all that came out was a scream, and then he lost consciousness.

"Hmm. Well, isn't this upsetting. It's always less fun if they aren't screaming in pain or begging for mercy," Maedara said, getting up and stepping over his body. Taking a second to survey the area, she pushed open the large black door in front of her. "I wonder what was so important that the king would need to guard the market," she said.

As she walked further into the building, she saw two sets of stairs, which came together at a balcony above her head. "I believe that's my destination."

She walked up the stairs, following them as they curved. When she reached the top, she could see a shimmering black light on the balcony in front of her. The portal. "Time to see why they put up such a fuss keeping me out." She ran right into the energy, and it dispersed, surrounding her.

C3❧C3❧C3❧C3❧

Maedara appeared in a large ballroom-type area. Lights illuminated the floor, and candles decorated the walls. She wiped the dust off her dress and then began to walk across the ballroom. She could hear a commotion on the other side of the door, so she pushed it open. As she entered the room, she noticed quite a few people, all of whom were very well-dressed. They were standing and talking and held wine glasses in their hands. They all seemed to be waiting outside a door.

"Oh, they're having a party. How lovely. But why wasn't I invited?" she wondered. When she had almost reached the door on the opposite end, a woman called to her.

The woman was shorter than her, but not by much. She had bubble-gum-pink hair, which was styled upwards like some sort of bizarre pineapple. She definitely seemed to favor the color pink. Her nails, skirt, belly shirt, and five-inch high-heeled shoes reflected that well. Her voice was high, nasally, and giggly all at the same time.

"Maedara, girl, is that you? I haven't seen you in, what, two centuries, right?" she asked, rushing over. This was quite a feat, however, as she had very high heels on and wasn't graceful enough to pull them off.

Maedara turned around to look at the woman and was shocked. "Lydia!" she squealed. "I can't even, right now!"

Lydia smiled and nodded as she looked Maedara up and down. "Wow, girl, wherever did you find that dress?" she asked, waving her hand. "It's fabulous, so chic. I swear, I'm gagging so hard that I could just die!"

Maedara shrugged and gave an aw shucks look. "Well, you know how I am. Would you expect any less? I got it off of this nice woman in Naoua. She was a doll."

"Naoua? That's, like, so very far away. You must have paid an arm and a leg!"

"I didn't, but the woman did!" Maedara said, smiling darkly. "You'd be surprised how little people will charge you when they're begging for their life. In the end, she practically gave it to me."

"Oh, girl, you're too much," Lydia replied, and they both laughed loudly. Their laughter attracted the attention of the people surrounding them, and some gave disapproving grunts or coughs.

Maedara frowned and glared at the people. "These people are so rude," she said, rolling her eyes. "You talk about slaughtering a few innocent people for fashion, and they act like you're a criminal or something!"

"I know exactly what you mean, hon. These people just don't understand the price one must pay for fashion," Lydia replied. She narrowed her eyes and glanced around the room. "Whatever. You can't expect good insight from peasants. Anyway, I'm surprised you even came to this little shindig, especially considering the king gave specific orders to keep you out!"

Maedara opened her mouth in disbelief. "What do you mean, the king didn't want me to come?" she asked.

"Darling, I have no idea. I only heard the word on the street. The word is that you weren't invited, ya know?"

Maedara growled. "I cannot believe such a thing. Of course, I would be invited. Obviously, there's been some kind of mistake. Yeah, that's it, a mistake!" she said, throwing her hands up in the air, flustered. "Whoever is in charge of invitations deserves to be fired for making such a mistake. I've never felt this insulted in my life! And I had a homeless person touch me once!"

Lydia rubbed her shoulder. "I'm sure that's just what it is, Maedara. All that matters is that you're here in time for the auction!"

The door in front of them opened, and a man walked forward. "The auction will now commence!" he said, and beckoned everyone forward. "Please come forward, single file. Take the first seat available. No fighting. Yes, thank you."

Maedara and Lydia walked into the new room. Everything in the room was gold-accented. The rug looked to be spun out of real gold, and the chairs and table were fashioned from solid gold. Even the lighting in the room was dim and gold-colored. The room was very large, but it had a strange, static feel to it. There were eight or nine rows of chairs, with twelve chairs in each row.

They rushed to grab seats nearest to the podium, sitting down in the front row. People seemed to avoid the row they were sitting in completely and filled in the rows behind them.

"So, Lydia, what do you suppose will be sold today?" Maedara asked, readjusting her traveling bag, which was sitting on her arm. "And don't play coy. I know you know all of the hot gossip. Dish, girl, dish!"

Lydia looked around to see if anyone was eavesdropping before she responded. "I'm not entirely sure, but I hear it's something dangerous, something that they don't want to fall into common hands."

Maedara smiled. "Well, that's a good thing, because I'm very dangerous and not at all common," she replied, flipping her hair dramatically to the side.

The auctioneer walked into the room. He was a demon, over eight feet tall, and his green skin looked as if it were stretched almost too thin to fit him. He had thick claws on both his hands and feet that curved. If his appearance wasn't off-putting enough, his voice seemed to 'boom' in the sense that he sounded like he was talking into a microphone.

"Once again, I welcome you all to the Black Market!" he said, pausing to clear his throat. "The one place where your dreams can come true, at a price; that is, if your dreams include causing pain and suffering to hundreds of thousands of people."

Maedara tilted her head to the side and smiled. *"That's me!"*

The auctioneer cleared his throat once more, which made the murmuring crowd fall quiet. He motioned to a guard in thick plate armor, who proceeded to walk behind a curtain. When the guard came back, he was carrying a tiny bottle filled with a pale, red liquid. The bottle seemed to emit a strange orange glow.

"Now, the first item up for bid. . .is a potion!" he said, and then paused for a second to create dramatic effect. "Now, I'm sure you're all wondering what makes this particular potion so special. This potion gives you the ability to shoot…" he paused for another second, "flames out of your hands!" he finished, and the crowd gasped in awe.

People were now whispering; most in shock, but a few in excitement. Once again, however, they were hushed by the auctioneer's booming voice.

"Shall we start the bidding at 2,000 charlocks?" he asked, scanning the crowd. A few people raised their hands, and the bidding started.

"It's a shame it's so expensive," Lydia whispered, leaning over to Maedara. "If it wasn't, I would buy it for myself."

"You want it?" Maedara asked. "I'll buy it for you. You could always pay me back, or not. Whatever."

"You mean it?"

"Of course. What are friends for?" Maedara replied. She raised her hand to bid. "15,000 charlocks," she declared, and the crowd exploded with noise.

"15,000? Is she crazy?"

"Too rich for my blood!"

"Oh, great, now she can shoot fire. As if her hands weren't deadly enough!"

The auctioneer gave a longer pause and looked desperately around the room. "Are we all absolutely sure we want our lovely current bidder going around shooting fire? Really, now?"

He paused for one more second before letting out a huge sigh. "Very well. The fire potion, for 15,000 charlocks, goes to Maedara!" he said and then struck his gavel on the podium.

Maedara dug through her bag for a second or two as a guard walked over with the winnings. She pulled out a large wad of bills and handed it to the guard. He handed her the tiny bottle and took his place back on the stage. Passing the bottle to Lydia, she waited for the next item to be announced.

C3ᏰᏰᏕᏰᏕᏰᏕᏰ

A few hours later, many different items had been auctioned off. Maedara bought a few minor items, but she was waiting patiently for the last item, rumored to be the most dangerous ever auctioned, to be announced.

"All right," the auctioneer said before clearing his throat. "Many magnificent rarities and items have been won today. I hope all of you make good use of them. However, none of them will compare to the next item up for grabs."

He beckoned to a guard standing in a corner. The guard went behind the curtain and returned with a chest, placing it on a small table next to the podium. The chest was quite large, carved out of solid sapphire. The chest had a human skull where the lock was, the eye-holes adorned with opals. Tapping it, the auctioneer nodded to the crowd. "Yes, the rumors are true. For those who don't recognize it, allow me to be the first to say, the Chest of Ondeyr is not just a product of legend, but real!"

The crowd broke out in whispers. A small, silent figure in the third row, wearing a huge black cloak and mask, shifted in its seat when the auctioneer announced this particular item.

"Everyone, quiet, and let us start the bidding," the auctioneer said. Even though his voice wasn't booming as usual, not a single sound could be heard. "Thank you." He paused yet again to clear his throat. "Now, how about we start the bidding at 60,000 charlocks?" The crowd muttered loudly. "I realize the price is a bit steep, but this particular item is rare."

A large skeleton demon raised his hand. "80,000."

The auctioneer nodded and pointed his gavel at the demon. "I have 80,000 to the Valacti demon." He paused and cleared his throat. "Does anyone want to bid higher?"

The room went silent. No one moved an inch or made a sound. The logical reason for this was likely because the Valacti demon was so physically imposing.

The auctioneer raised his eyebrow and surveyed the crowd. "People, people. The contents of this chest can cause worldwide destruction and misery!" he said, motioning to the chest. "So do I hear 90,000?"

The figure in the third row raised a hand, still covered by the cloth of its cloak.

"I have 90,000 from the grim demon!" the auctioneer said. "I believe that's as high as we're going to get, so—"

"How about 120,000 charlocks?" Maedara announced, raising her hand. "Cash, not charge."

The auctioneer cleared his throat again to hush the crowd. Everyone was in an uproar because of the sudden jump in bid. "120,000 charlocks going once. . ."

Maedara glanced around the room and smiled. "No one in this crowd could ever hope to outbid me."

She whispered to Lydia, "It's as good as mine."

The auctioneer looked around. "120,000 going twice?" His eyes narrowed as he scanned for potential bidders. "Come on, people. You have in front of you a chance to rule the world. Someone bid!"   He went to bang the gavel a third time, but it 'slipped' out of his hand and landed on the floor. He called for a guard to pick it up and then asked for a glass of water.

Maedara coughed. "On. . .with. . .the. . .bidding…" she said, stretching the words out, her voice rising higher with each syllable. "Or do I need to come up there and shove my foot way up your–"

"The winning bid goes to Maedara," the auctioneer proclaimed and then struck the gavel before she could finish her threat. "For the price of 120,000 charlocks!"

"I won? Did I really?" Maedara exclaimed, placing her hands over her mouth. "Dear me, this is quite a shock. I'm absolutely and utterly speechless!"

The auctioneer looked as though he had swallowed something sour and then made a motion to the guard to his right. The guards of Hyael were trained by different hand signals. This particular motion meant for them to call backup.

"Excuse me?" Maedara said, her eyes narrowing as she saw more guards pile into the room. "I won the bidding. Where's my friggin' prize?!"

The auctioneer moved a few steps back and hid behind the line of guards. "I have specific orders from the king himself. We are not to sell you this particular item."

Maedara slowly pulled herself out of the chair and smiled pleasantly. "Oh, really. How interesting. Well, I guess if you won't be a gentleman and hand it to me, I'll have to go up there and take it myself."

"Maedara, wait!" Lydia said, grabbing her by the arm. "You can't fight all of the king's best guards!"

Maedara tilted her head to the side. "Why ever not, Lydia?"

Lydia frowned, pointing at Maedara's shoes. "You cannot get blood off red Italian heels," she said, with a flick of her hair. "Are those guards really worth ruining $4,000 shoes?"

Maedara gasped. "Oh, my God, I was almost so careless," she said, shaking her head. She reached down and took off the shoes and then handed them to Lydia. "Be sure to take care of them while I… take care of business."

"But, hon, there's over fifty of them," Lydia said.

"What's your point? So what if there are fifty guards? Why ever would that make a difference?"

"Maedara, I know you're tough, girl, but there are so many of them and just one of you. The odds aren't good at all!"

Maedara smiled. "Not for them," she said. She skipped happily down the row, making her way to the stage. When she reached the stage, she looked the auctioneer directly in the eye. "Well, you have two choices. Either you give me my prize, or give me your life. . .and my prize. Whichever choice you pick, I get what I want. So choose wisely, very wisely."

The auctioneer cleared his throat and shook his head. "I'm sorry, I can't. I'm not –" he began, but was interrupted as a set of doors behind them burst open.

"Enough!" somebody yelled. The voice caused everyone to turn in its direction. A man was standing in the doorway. He was a tall man with an imposing presence about him. He radiated with an aura of power that seemed to scream exactly what he was: the king.

He grimaced, his eyes narrowing as he looked at Maedara, who returned his hostility with a tiny wave. "Maedara," he said, his voice full of anger. "You're not welcome here, and I suggest you leave on your own, or you will be forced out."

Maedara turned from the auctioneer and faced the king. She curtsied and smiled sweetly. "Why, Your Highness, I meant no disrespect. . .what with the whole 'coming into your city and killing your subjects' thing," she said, and her voice went back to the cutesy Valley-girl tone. "But they were mean to me, honest. And anyway, I'm more than twenty percent sure that they were going to die anyway of natural causes."

The king's face flushed bright red. "You – you were banished!" His voice boomed as he pointed his finger at her. "You know you're no longer welcome in this city."

Maedara rolled her eyes. "Why, King, I'm not sure what you mean. Why ever would I be banished from my hometown?"

The king frowned. "Maedara, don't you remember what happened the last time you attended the auction?" he asked. "Don't you remember how you purchased the ability to grow your nails longer, and how you then used it to slice the throats of twenty people in the room?"

"I don't know what you're talking about, Kingy," she replied, batting her eyelashes, attempting to look innocent. "I would never do such a horrible thing."

The king just stared at her. "Maedara, are you telling me you don't remember buying that power and killing people with it?"

Maedara shook her head. "I could have gotten that power anywhere."

"We have a record of the transaction."

"It's probably a forgery."

The king sighed. "There are eyewitness accounts!"

Maedara bit her lip and stomped her foot on the ground. "That's just circumstantial evidence. Clearly, the jealous people are out to frame me!" she said, brushing her bangs to the side. "Who are you going to believe? Them or me?"

"Fact of the matter is that you killed over sixty people today alone, and just one murder is punishable by death," he said. "That law is in place to protect our organization. If we didn't have it, it would be chaos."

"Oh, Kingy, tell me, who here doesn't like a little bit of chaos?" she asked, growling seductively. "It's the spice of life."

"Maedara!"

"Okay, so maybe I did kill all those people, but I had to test out my new power. I mean, what if it didn't work and I was ripped off? I had to test and make sure!"

"Testing is one thing, damn it. You didn't test; you made a project of it!" he snarled. "Maedara. You have left me with no choice. You are hereby exiled from not just the Black Market, or Hyael, but you're exiled from all of Zytrihr!"

Maedara was livid. She rocked back and forth on the stage, pulling her hair. "It always happens. It never stops," she whispered as tears streamed down her face. "People always reject me, always try to push me away." With every word, her voice grew louder, until she was screaming. "They're jealous! You're all jealous! You cannot handle how great I am!"

She fell to her knees and rested her head on the floor. She dug her nails into the stage and scratched them along it, making a loud screeching sound. "I'm... me. I'm... wonderful."

"All right. That's enough of her antics. Guards, if you please, take her away," the king said, with a lazy flick of his hand.

As the guards approached Maedara, she sprang into action. She lifted herself off the ground and was on her feet in an instant. "Don't," she said softly. "I haven't received my prize yet."

"Come with me," a guard said, grabbing her wrist and jerking her to her feet.

"You're so rude, you know that?" Maedara asked, her eyes going wild. "Didn't your mother ever teach you anything? You never touch a lady unless you buy her dinner first." She jerked his hand to the side, and twisted. A loud cracking sound could be heard. As the man screamed out in pain, his shattered bone jutted through the skin of his arm.

The other guards were stunned for a split-second, which was all the time Maedara needed. She used the man's arm as leverage to do a flip into the air. She landed behind him and thrust her hand into the back of his neck. He screamed in pain as blood sprayed from his mouth and the wound. The guards prepared to kill, pulling out their guns.

Maedara flung her hand forward, and the man's body flew forward and slammed into two other guards. As the remaining few opened fire, she did several cartwheels. The bullets missed her with every flip. When the sound of the guns clicked empty, she landed catlike on her feet. She extended her nails and raked them across another guard's throat.

The remaining few took a few steps back, staring in horror at the bodies on the ground. She smiled sweetly at them, specks of blood decorating her face. "Do you two want to play as well?" she asked, her voice returning to the soft Valley-girl tone.

The guards looked at each other, at her, at the king, then back at each other, and then ran away.

"It really is so hard to find good help these days, wouldn't you agree, Your Majesty?"

The king trembled. "Maedara, what are you... you can't..." he muttered, backing away from her. "I am the king here. Y-you're supposed to obey me."

"You haven't learned anything yet, have you?" She wiped the blood off her face and looked at it curiously. "Nobody tells me what I can or can't do. My parents tried to order me around when I was younger, and I killed them: my father first; then my little brother; finally, my mother. I liked my mother. That's why she went last. And I only liked her because she gave birth to me. Tell me, King. What have you done for me lately? Nothing. That's what."

The king looked at her for a second and then turned and tried to run away.

Maedara was suddenly in front of him, lightning quick. She grabbed him by the front of his shirt. "You know, I don't enjoy this... being the bad guy. I don't enjoy having to get pretty clothes dirty while fighting. Ladies don't fight, they talk. So do you want to talk?"

"Let me go, this instant!"

"So you don't want to talk then?" she asked, frowning. "Pity. I could have done with a nice chat, but I guess you are right. It is kind of rude to conversate, especially with all of these people here."

The king gave a sigh of relief when she let go of his shirt, thinking he was pardoned. "I'm glad you've come to your senses."

Maedara grabbed him by the throat. "You're lucky, you know? I normally don't do this on the first date. Consider yourself lucky." She pulled him closer and placed her hands on both sides of his face, as if she were going to kiss him. "Now, pucker up, Your Majesty." Before he could respond, her mouth opened wide, and a large wave of green acid shot out and drenched him completely.

The king's final scream could be heard throughout the entire kingdom.

CHAPTER 6: THE DESCENDING DARKNESS

"Mother!" Shadow yelled, jolting awake. He was in a cold sweat, his heart pounding. That same nightmare had haunted him at least twice a month for as long as he could remember. Rubbing his eyes, he picked up the alarm clock that was sitting on the dresser by his bed. 12:57 p.m. *"I overslept,"* he thought.

Getting out of bed, he ruffled his hair and yawned. He did not want to let the fact that he had overslept ruin productivity for the day. He proceeded to pick out an outfit from his closet, the typical for him: tight black tank top and black pants.

Yawning, he glanced at the clock again. 1:15 p.m. He shook his head. *"I have to get the team together so we can do some patrolling. The sun being out just means that I can't patrol; doesn't mean that they can't,"* he thought. He left his room and walked into the living room, frowning when he saw that nobody was there.

"Guess I'll have to find them all now," he sighed. He headed into the gigantic hallway and knocked on each door, one after the other. He waited at the end of the hall. When there was no change, he went back down the hallway, knocking quite a bit louder this time. After waiting for what seemed like forever, he heard the sound of doors opening and watched as his confused team walked out of their rooms and into the hall.

"Shadow, man, what's with the knocking? It's, like, 1:40 p.m. on a Sunday. I usually like to sleep until seven," Ryan yawned, rubbing his eyes. "Where's the fire?"

Shadow shook his head in disapproval and motioned the teens forward, signaling them to follow him into the living room. His team, with the exception of Cameryn and Kay, had all followed him, wondering why they were called there.

"Hey, Shadow, what's going on?" Ellie asked, her blue eyes filled with concern. "Did something happen?"

Shadow smiled. This was one of her best features. Nothing could stop her from worrying about her friends or people she cared about. "It's nothing major, Ellie. Don't worry."

"Shadow, you'd tell me if something was going on, right? I mean, if we're sitting on a volcano, I would kind of like to know about it before it erupts."

"Trust me, everything's fine. I just need to talk to everyone."

Ellie looked at him for a few seconds and then nodded. She turned and walked over to the couch, plopping down on it. "Let's hear it."

"Well, as everyone's aware, we have this great evil to fight," Shadow said.

"Yes, this great big evil thing," Ryan said, smiling.

"Thing? You make it sound like it's a teddy bear or something!" Tristan blurted. "Like an evil teddy bear of doom!"

Shadow growled, shaking his head. "Really, Tristan?"

Faith, seeing how annoyed he was getting, decided to come to his rescue. "Tris, will you please do us all a huge favor and keep your mouth shut if you have nothing useful to add to the proceedings?"

Tristan blushed and nodded. "Sorry. I didn't mean to be annoying."

"Sure, you didn't," Shadow replied. "Now, as I was saying before I was rudely interrupted," he glared at Ryan and Tristan, "we have this evil psycho out there. We have to put an end to her once and for all or the whole world as we know it will be doomed. Meaning, this is no time to sleep in or to play video games."

Ryan groaned. "No sleeping in or video games?" he asked in horror. "Why don't you just kill me now?"

"Don't tempt me," Shadow replied.

"Shadow, where's Kay?" Faith asked. "Shouldn't she be here for this? I mean, she is part of the team, after all. This concerns all of us."

Shadow blinked. "I could have sworn she was here," he replied, looking around. "Hey, Isaac, do you happen to know where she is?"

Isaac shook his head. "No, I haven't seen her since last night."

"Cameryn is missing too!" Tereya exclaimed. "We both fell asleep out here last night, watching TV. I left him right here. I thought he would be okay. What if something happened? I'll never forgive myself. It will be all my fault!"

"I wonder where Kay and Cameryn could have wandered off to," Ethan said. "Or if their disappearances are related in any way."

"Maybe a gigantic beast came in and kidnapped them or something," Crystal replied, shrugging.

"Yeah, because a gigantic beast totally could have broken in and taken them without any of us hearing the commotion. Real likely," Ryan said, rolling his eyes.

Shadow cleared his throat so that once again all eyes were on him.

"Is everyone definitely, without a doubt, sure that they don't know where Kay and Cameryn are?"

He frowned when nobody replied. *This isn't good. Cameryn is too fragile to be alone for too long, and I am supposed to be keeping a close eye on Kay.* He couldn't hide the fact that he was worried. If only they knew what was in his mind, what he was thinking. Like always, his pessimism was getting the best of him.

"Shadow, why are you worrying?" Isaac asked. "I'm sure that if Cameryn and Kay are both missing, then that must mean that they are together, which means that he's in good hands. So you have nothing to worry about!"

Shadow shook his head. "I just want to find the both of them to make sure that they are safe, is all." He frowned. *I don't trust him in anybody's hands, not after what he endured. I hope he's all right,* he thought.

"You guys wait here. I'll be back. I'm going to go track them down."

"What makes you think you'll find them?" Tristan asked.

"I don't think. I know," Shadow replied. "I have enhanced senses. I can follow their scents, their energy signal." He turned to leave, but paused.

"If I'm not back in thirty, you all are ordered to vacate the building. Someone or something could be in here."

He left the living room and followed the long hallway which led to the left wing of his home. He didn't go down this wing often because his room was in the right wing and he had nothing compelling him to go to the left. The only reason that he had to go there now was because it was where Cameryn's and Kay's rooms were located.

Shadow didn't isolate them intentionally; it just happened that Kay picked a room where she could be away from the others, wanting her privacy. Cameryn, however, was forced to have a room on this side, simply because all the other rooms had been filled up.

He went up to Cameryn's room first and knocked three times, pausing for an answer, and then knocked again. After a short time with no reply, he opened the door and looked inside. To his dismay, the room was empty.

He then walked over to Kay's room, which was across the hall and two doors down. He knocked, paused, and then knocked again. He got no answer there either, and he realized that he might have a problem on his hands. *They're the only ones missing, and they're the only ones who have rooms in this wing. I doubt it's a coincidence.*

Going down the hall, he glanced into the doors of open rooms, checking for any sign of Kay or Cameryn. With every empty room, he grew more worried. When he came to the end of the hallway, he had reached the staircase that led to the higher floors.

When the teens had come to live with him, he told them all, including Cameryn, that the staircase in the left wing was off-limits. Thinking that the chances that two teenagers would disobey a direct order were likely, he climbed the stairs, swearing under his breath at how naive he had been. He should have known that if he told a teenager to not do something, they would be more compelled to do it. He knew that it probably would have been better if he hadn't mentioned the staircase at all; maybe it would have been ignored altogether.

He was more worried about Cameryn than Kay because he knew that she could take care of herself. It was Cameryn that concerned him. He had just rescued the kid from a horrible situation, one too terrible for words. If anything happened to Cameryn, he'd never forgive himself. *"I refuse to let anything happen to him. He's been through too much. I promised him that he wouldn't be hurt ever again, and I always keep my promises."*

When he reached the top, a loud scream pierced the silence. It chilled him to the very core. It was a sound that was all too familiar to him, having heard it before, the day he rescued Cameryn. Fear gripped at him as he ran. "Cameryn!" he shouted, running down the hallway, looking into each room. The rooms were all beginning to look the same to him; a blur of colors, but no Cameryn.

When he came to the end of the hall, he heard a loud crash coming from the door to the far left of him. In one fluid movement, utilizing every bit of his superhuman speed, he pulled the door open so forcefully that it tore right off its hinges, and he threw it aside. Glancing into the room, he saw Cameryn on the floor, with Kay standing over him.

"This isn't what it looks like," Kay began. "I found him like this, I swear."

Shadow growled. He flicked his hand, and the shadows in the room came to life. They flooded towards Kay, surrounding her like a cocoon. She was lifted off the ground and held in the air by a gigantic blackened hand, clenched in its fist. "What did you do to him? Tell me, now!"

Kay struggled in the grasp of the shadow hand. Seeing that her efforts were in vain, she stopped. "I didn't do anything to him, I swear! I found him like this," she said. "Now, let me go!"

Shadow's eyes darkened. "You're a liar." He waved his hand forward, and the black hand pushed her against the wall. "Tell me the truth, Kay."

"I am telling you the truth. Why don't you believe me?!"

Shadow shook his head and kneeled down over Cameryn. He tapped the kid's arm gently and placed his hands on his face. "He's unconscious. People don't just fall unconscious. You had to have done something. So cut the bull crap and tell me what happened."

"I didn't do anything. I found him like that, I swear! I just wanted to do some exploring, that's all. I didn't hurt him. I heard him scream, and I came running in here. That's all."

Shadow raised an eyebrow. "How did you manage to get in here before I did? I heard the scream and ran in here. I didn't see you."

"I took that door," Kay replied, pointing to another door. "There are two entrances in here. You took one, and I took the other."

Glancing over his shoulder, Shadow walked to the door in question and pulled it open. It was indeed another entrance to the room. A motion on the ground caused him to look down. Cameryn was stirring. The kid groaned in pain, his eyes opening.

Shadow kneeled back down beside him. "Are you all right?"

Cameryn blinked. "Yeah... I'm fine. What happened?"

Shadow looked from Cameryn to Kay, and then back to Cameryn. "You were unconscious. What happened to you?"

Cameryn's face scrunched up in thought. "I'm not sure. I mean, one second before I felt this intense pain, I saw Kay. Then the next moment I woke up and saw you staring at me. So I'm really not too sure."

Shadow frowned. "Kay," he said, "this is your last chance to tell me what you did to him."

Kay shook her head. "I didn't do anything, but I bet that vase did," she said, pointing to a bunch of glass on the floor. "Clearly, oh, esteemed leader, the vase fell and smashed Cameryn on the head, knocking him out. So you can let me down now."

Shadow looked down at the glass. "Cameryn, is that what happened?"

Cameryn glanced at Kay and then looked at the floor. "I don't know, Shadow. It sounds right, I guess. It's not like Kay has a reason to hurt me," he said as he struggled to get off the ground.

"Careful," Shadow said, rushing to help him up. "Take it slow. You don't know how badly you're hurt. We'll have to get Faith to heal you."

Kay glared. "Um, hello," she said loudly, "can you please let me down now that I'm innocent?"

Shadow nodded. He put his hand forward and then pulled it back. The dark hand faded back into the shadows.

Kay dusted herself off and went towards the door.

Hesitating, Shadow walked forward and grabbed her by the shoulder. "Kay?" he asked. "Wait."

Kay sighed. "It's whatever. Just don't jump to conclusions again. I would never do anything to hurt anybody here."

"I know. I'm sorry," he said. "I just made a promise, and I intend to keep it. I'll be more careful about my accusations in the future, so don't worry."

Kay opened her mouth and then closed it. She pulled out of his grasp and walked out the door.

"Are you okay?" Shadow asked, turning back to face Cameryn.

Cameryn nodded. "Yeah, I'm fine. Really, it's all right," he said. He absentmindedly brushed his hand against the gash on his head and winced.

Shadow nodded. He put his hand around the boy's shoulder. "Come on. We'll get Faith to heal you."

"All right, you win. Let's go," Cameryn said, sighing.

Shadow chuckled. It was blatantly obvious that the kid thought that by needing to be healed, he would look weak. "Cameryn, needing to be healed is not a sign of weakness," he said, shaking his head. "It's actually a sign of intelligence."

"Really?"

Shadow smiled. "Yeah, really."

Cameryn looked up at Shadow. It was a strange new thing, somebody actually caring about him. It had been a long time since he had given up hope of somebody ever caring for him, somebody to make everything better, to show him how it felt like to be treated like a person, to be loved. Yet that day that Shadow and Ellie had rescued him was the day that all his dreams came true. He had a new family and friends. It was all thanks to Shadow.

"Thank you. For everything. Really, it means a lot. I don't know what I would have done if you hadn't come along and saved me."

Shadow nodded. "Don't mention it. You deserve it. I mean, you deserve someone actually treating you right for a change," he replied, as they both headed for the stairs.

ଔଞୠଔଞୠଔଞୠଔଞୠ

They reached the living room. Glancing around, Shadow was proud to see that everyone was still where he left them. "I'm back, everyone."

"Is everything all right?" Ethan asked, eyeing them.

Shadow nodded and then motioned Faith over.

Faith walked over. Reaching them, she gasped.

"Ohmygodwhathappened?!"

"Air, Faith," Ellie said. "Deep breaths. Remember to breathe."

Shadow smiled. "It's all right, Faith. Calm down," he said. "He had an accident. Nothing major. Nobody's to blame; everything is fine."

Faith released the deep breath that she was holding. "All right. I was just worried," she replied, much calmer. "Cameryn, let me heal you."

Glancing sideways at Shadow, Cameryn saw him wink and then sigh. "Go ahead. I mean, if you want to."

Faith raised an eyebrow. "It will feel better, I promise." She placed her hands above the wound and closed her eyes in concentration. Purple waves of light flowed out of her hands and doused the injury. Within seconds, the cut looked days old, months of recuperation done in seconds. After less than a minute, Cameryn's head had returned to normal. There was no sign any injury had taken place.

"Thanks, Faith!" Cameryn said, rubbing the area where the cut had been. He then walked over and started talking with Isaac and Tereya.

Shadow nodded in agreement. "Yeah, thanks, Faith."

Faith smiled. "It's no problem at all. Healing is kind of my thing."

"Shadow?" Isaac asked suddenly, standing up. "Where's Kay? How come she didn't come back with you? Cameryn said that you all were in the room together with him. How come she's not here?"

Shadow shrugged. "I'm not sure. She rushed off after we had a - " he paused, trying to think of the word to use, "a tiny disagreement."

Isaac frowned. "Are you sure that's all that it was? You didn't upset her or anything, did you?"

Shadow shook his head. "We had a bit of an argument, if you want to call it that," he said. Following the look of horror on Isaac's face, he frowned. "Don't worry. We made up. She told me that everything was fine.

126

I'm guessing she just wanted to be alone or something. She's probably in her room."

"Maybe you're right. I'll go check on her later, in case she wants to be alone," Isaac said, although he sounded distant.

"It's all right. I know you're worried about her. I'm sure she values how much you care about her. I sure as heck do. But trust me; she does fine. Don't worry yourself to death."

Isaac smiled. "All right. Thanks. I didn't mean to get all crazy with the overprotectiveness."

Shadow nodded. "It's fine. Once again, it's really good that you are overprotective of Kay. I'm glad, and I'm sure that she is too."

"Thanks again, Shadow." Isaac muttered, walking back across the room and taking his seat.

"Now, if we can get on with the issues at hand - " Shadow began. To his dismay, he was interrupted by someone loudly clearing her throat. Glancing around the room for the cause of the interruption, his eyes fell upon Crystal. "Yes, Crystal?" he asked through clenched teeth.

"Sorry for interrupting, Shadow, but I think that we all deserve, well, a break," Crystal said. "We're all tired of being cooped up in this boring, dark, and dreary place."

Shadow's eye twitched. "What do you mean, a break, Crystal?"

Crystal shrugged. "Maybe we all deserve just, like, a chance to blow off some steam, you know," she said. "Like a trip. . .maybe to the mall?"

Shadow laughed, glancing at Crystal like she was crazy. "You. . .you're not serious?" he asked, hoping she wasn't, but it was evident that she was, and he frowned. "You are serious."

Seeing the look on his face, Crystal shook her head. "What is it?" she demanded, hands on her hips.

"I just don't understand it. Weren't you the one who, a day ago, told Ryan and Tristan off for not being serious? For being easily distracted when it came to our mission?" Shadow asked, sighing and putting his face in his hands. "Now you're doing the same?"

Crystal shrugged. "Yes, I said those things. I believe without a doubt that our mission is important, but still. . .I've been here for three months and have the exact same wardrobe as I did when I first got here."

Shadow lifted his head up and raised an eyebrow. "So?"

Ethan shook his head. "Oh, dear."

Faith looked confused. "What's wrong, Ethan ?"

"He's got her started now…."

Crystal flushed bright red. She was shaking like she was about to go into convulsions. "Shadow, do you have any idea how horrible it is to wear the same outfit more than once?" she asked, glaring at him. Looking at him, she saw that he was wearing the same things he always wore: a black shirt with a black pair of jeans.

"Okay, so maybe you do know what it's like to wear the same outfit more than once. But I absolutely refuse!"

Shadow sighed. "Somebody please tell me she's joking."

Ethan scratched his head. "I'm sorry. I wish I could."

"Please, Shadow. We'll train extra hard if you let us go," Tristan said, his hands clasped together, begging. "We never get to have any fun. It's so boring around here."

"I'm sorry if life-threatening situations aren't exciting enough for you guys," Shadow replied.

"Sorry, man, but I gotta agree with crazy Crystal," Ryan said. "Even though she usually has bad ideas, this ain't one of them."

Shadow scowled. "You guys, do you know how dangerous it would be to go out in public when there's evil on the loose?"

"Shadow," Crystal said, glaring, "this trip to the mall is much needed for all of us, especially me, and I demand that you allow us to go!"

"This must be a record," Shadow thought. *"I've sighed more in the time that I've known these kids than in my entire life."*

After a few moments of consideration and enduring begging faces, he shrugged. "Fine. You guys can have your little field trip. Just make sure you're back before. . ." he paused to look at the clock. 2:40. "Be back before 5:30. Can you do that?" he asked.

"Thanks, Shadow!" Crystal exclaimed, Ryan and Tristan cheering in the background.

Shadow slipped out of the room as they were all chattering about the trip and getting ready to go. He walked to his room and entered, closing the door behind him. He flopped onto the bed. Minutes later he heard a light knock on the door. "Who is it?" he asked.

"It's me," a familiar voice called out. "Ellie."

Rising to a sitting position on his bed, he glanced at the door. *"Why does she keep coming to my room? What could she possibly want now?"* he wondered, partially frustrated. It wasn't that he had any problems with Ellie, per se. It was mostly that he didn't have as much privacy as he was used to. "Come in," he   answered.

Ellie walked into the room. "Sorry for interrupting your, er, private time," she said. "I just wanted to apologize."

Shadow looked at her, confused. He wasn't aware of anything that she had done to him to make him mad or warrant an apology. "What do you mean? You didn't do anything wrong."

Ellie frowned. *"Why does he always have to be difficult? It would have been less problematic to just accept the apology."*

"I meant that I'm sorry for the way they all acted in there, jumping at the chance to go out and leaving you behind," she explained.

"It's really fine, Ellie. Trust me. I want you to go and have fun, okay?" he said, walking over to the door.

Ellie looked at him, affronted, feeling like he was forcing her out. "You want me to go, Shadow?" she asked, a tiny bit hurt.

Shadow sighed. He hated that she got so easily offended or hurt by little actions that he did, and hated more than anything that she had the knack to make him feel bad for doing said little meaningless actions.

"No, Ellie, it's not that at all. I just don't want you being confined to this room like I am. This room, this house, is like a prison. Do you think I enjoy it?"

"No," Ellie said, trying not to add more oil to the fire, but her efforts were in vain. The fire had been raging for years.

"Do you think that I enjoy not being able to be like everybody else? Not being able to go out and feel the warm sun on my skin or the nice day's breeze on my face? No. You don't. You couldn't."

"Shadow, I –"

"No, Ellie, it's fine. Go with them to the mall before they leave you behind. We have a lot of work to do when you guys come back."

Ellie glanced at him, trying to decide the right thing to say to him to make everything better. She ultimately decided that there was nothing she could say to come close to making things all right. She gave him one last fleeting look and then walked away.

Shadow sighed. He hoped that he didn't upset her too much, but the fact was that he already had too many troubles on his plate to deal with the inner workings of a teenage girl's mind. He had to stop some great evil from rising, and he had to make sure that his entire team survived the big confrontation, not to mention he had to find out what the strange woman was up to before she actually went on with her plans. It was a lot to handle. The situation with Ellie could wait.

CЗ&ОCЗ&ОCЗ&ОCЗ&О

Meanwhile, everyone, with the exception of Shadow and Cameryn, was inside a huge limousine.

"Crystal, do I even want to ask how you got this limo in such short notice?" Faith asked.

Tristan shook his head. "Sis, she got us a li-mou-sine!" he exclaimed. "Don't question it!"

Ryan nodded in agreement. "Yeah, seriously. When life hands you lemons, don't question it. Just make lemonade."

"It's all right, Faith. I didn't do anything illegal," Crystal replied, smiling. "I simply told the limo company that if they didn't send us a limo, they would never rent in this town again."

"All right. Mind telling me how we're all going to buy stuff without any money?" Faith asked.

Crystal opened her wallet and pulled out a few large bills. "Here, there's a hundred for everybody who isn't me. I'm not so limited."

Shrugging, Faith leaned back and sipped her bottle of orange juice. She looked over and noticed Ellie, who was glancing out the window. "What's wrong, Ellie?"

Ellie didn't answer at first. She was admiring the beautiful fields of wildflowers that grew along the roads. "It's nothing, nothing important."

Faith, being a girl and a partial empath, knew that Ellie was lying, but she also knew better than to press somebody when she wasn't ready to talk. "Well, if you need to talk, I'm here for you."

Ellie nodded, not taking her eyes off the scenery. "Thanks. I'll remember that."

C3E0C3E0C3E0C3E0

After nearly twenty minutes of Tristan complaining about how long it was taking to get there and Ryan whining about having to use the bathroom, they finally reached the mall.

"All right, guys. It's 3:30," Ethan said, examining his watch. "We promised Shadow that we'd be home by 5:30, so make sure you all are back at this entrance by 4:30 and not a minute later. All right?"

Everyone agreed.

"I'm going to go check out a bookstore," Faith said. "It's terribly boring to live in a house where there are no good fantasy novels to read."

"You'd think that you would have your fill of fantasy," Ellie remarked. "I mean, our lives are practically a fantasy novel."

Faith laughed. "Not quite. We're not interesting enough."

"Let's go, Ethan. I need somebody to help me carry my bags!" Crystal said, pulling him with her. "Ooh, and Kay, you can come with us!" she added, grabbing Kay with her free arm.

"Why do you want me to come along, Crystal?" Kay asked. "I'm sure I would just get in the way or something."

Crystal laughed. "Not at all. I need another girl with me to help pick out cute outfits," she replied. Before Kay could object further, she was pulled along with Ethan and Crystal into the mall.

Ellie looked around. Tristan and Ryan had rushed off somewhere. *"Probably to cause trouble,"* she thought. She watched Tereya and Isaac hurry along, muttering something about going to check out video games and movies. She walked into the mall herself and noticed that Kay had ditched Crystal and Ethan and was walking alone.

Filled with curiosity, Ellie moved behind a pillar and continued to watch Kay. *"What could Kay be doing?"* she wondered. Truth be told, her stalking wasn't unwarranted. Kay was acting very peculiar, constantly looking around to make sure she wasn't being followed. After a minute or so of walking, Kay came to a stop. Throwing another quick glance over her shoulder, she walked into a store.

Ellie walked on and came to the side of the store that Kay had entered, Animus Magicka.

She was confused. *"Why would Kay be going into this store, of all places? A shop of magic? It doesn't make any sense,"* she thought. The shop was not a magic shop like the ones that sold card tricks and cheap illusions; it was a shop of true magic. The shop had books for sale on spells, and it had various herbs and crystals used in rituals and incantations.

For a normal person with no special powers, the shop was something like a tourist attraction, since all the stuff in there would only be for decoration. But for someone like Kay, who was gifted, the shop could prove to be very dangerous. Magic only worked for those who were blessed with special abilities.

Making sure that Kay wasn't watching, Ellie rushed into the store. The owner gave her a weird look as she hid behind a wall of charms and amulets. He starting heading towards her as if he was going to yell at her, and she frowned. *"This guy telling me off would definitely get me noticed,"* she thought. She turned to a rack of dream catchers, pretending to be browsing. Obviously fooled, the shop owner walked away and began dusting off glass orbs.

Ellie continued to watch Kay while still managing to examine the items for sale with feigned interest. She moved on to the shelves of various potions to keep a good eye on Kay. To keep up with her act, she was examining a bottle of Chaney root, which supposedly was guaranteed to bring health, happiness, and prolong your life.

She put the bottle down and walked over to an aisle where strange bags of herbs were sold. The sign promised that the bags would do a various amount of effects, such as get a friend to fall in love with you, ward off demons, chase away bats, and prevent the common cold. Taking great care to stay behind a wall of spell books, she watched Kay look in a glass case. *"What are you up to, Kay?"* she wondered, edging closer to get a better view.

Kay glanced around the shop before making her move. Pointing her finger at a large, skull-shaped crystal ball on a high shelf, a jet of light shot from her finger to the ball. She moved her finger downwards, and the crystal ball fell off the shelf and landed on the floor with a crash, sending glass and smoke   everywhere.

Ellie channeled her energy into her fingertips and began drawing the water in the air into her. Breathing out, she released the water and it formed a protective barrier around her so that her vision was not impaired by the smoke that was now rising into the air. Her eyes darted back to Kay, who, taking advantage of the confusion caused by the crystal ball, smashed the glass case that she was standing by. Kay reached into the shattered case, grabbed something, and darted out of the store.

Outside the store, Ellie looked around. *"Where did she go?"* It seemed as if Kay had disappeared into thin air. *"The whole situation is fishy,"* she thought. Checking her communicator, she noticed the time. "4:10. Darn it. I'd better go meet the others."

Leaving the mall, she saw some teammates waiting by the limo, including Kay, who looked like she was bored. "Hey, Kay, did you enjoy your mall visit?"

Kay shrugged. "I guess so."

Ellie took a few steps closer. "Cool. So what did you do? I didn't see you around. Whatever did you do to occupy your time?"

Kay frowned this time, her eyes narrowing. "Nothing much; just looked around for a bit. Just a little window-shopping, you know."

Ellie nodded. "All right, then. I was just curious, is all. I mean, I saw you go off with Ethan and Crystal, but now you're here and they're not. Why is that? Hmm?"

"Crystal was all for shopping in these rich, boring stores. I'm not into that scene," Kay said, glancing at an airplane that was passing overhead.

"Is that so?"

"Since when did you become so interested in my life, anyway, Ellie?" Kay asked.

It was Ellie's turn to shrug. "What, am I not allowed to be interested in the lives of my friends? I mean, Kay, we are friends, aren't we? Don't friends tell each other everything that happens in their lives? No secrets or lies between them?"

"What are you—"

"Oh, my," Faith said suddenly, pointing in the distance. "Can you believe Crystal?"

Turning to look where Faith was pointing, Ellie saw what had made her gasp. Crystal was carrying a small shopping bag. This wouldn't have been exciting except for the fact that Ethan brought up the rear, carrying a little over twenty large bags.

"Crystal, what in the world?" She was awestruck. She had known that Crystal wanted to buy more clothes, but she had no idea that this was her idea of more clothes.

Crystal beamed at them with pride. "Isn't it all amazing? I got such a perfect deal on all of them, and I couldn't leave such beautiful outfits in the store for someone less attractive than me to purchase," she said, climbing into the limo.

"Oh, no," Ellie said, shaking her head. "All of this will NOT fit. How do you suppose you're going to get this stuff home?" she demanded, angry at Crystal's lack of foresight.

"It's all right. I'm going to fly with it in my hands," Ethan said.

Ellie sighed. "Crystal, how could you even ask him to do that?" she asked, throwing a glance at Ethan, who was carrying much more than a normal guy would be able to.

"It's fine, Ellie. He doesn't care. He always carries my stuff home for me. He's my guardian angel , remember?"

Ellie looked from Ethan to Crystal and then back at Ethan. "Ethan, are you sure you can handle all of that?"

Ethan, who had dealt with Crystal for many, many, years by this point in time, simply gave his usual calm smile. "Trust me, Ellie, it's completely fine. I'm used to Crystal's shopping habits. I will be more than able to deal with it," he replied. Making sure that no people were around to witness it, he launched up into the air and was gone.

"Where are the others?" Kay asked, yawning. "I wanna go home already."

Ellie rolled her eyes. Kay was beginning to annoy her. Even if she hadn't seen Kay's secret theft act, her attitude was bordering on obnoxious and disrespectful. If somebody didn't straighten Kay out, she decided that she would be the one to do so.

"We cannot leave yet, Kay. Tristan and Ryan aren't back yet; Isaac and Tereya either," she said through gritted teeth, trying not to make her resentment obvious. "You would think that you would be a little more concerned about Isaac."

Kay shrugged, got into the limo, and lay down. "I'm sure he's fine. I told Tereya if anything happened to Isaac, I'd hurt him."

Ellie opened her mouth to respond with a number of clever insults when two familiar faces came strolling up the walkway.

"Hey, Ellie!" Tereya said, smiling. He glanced at Kay, and his smile wavered for a split-second. "I had tons of fun today. Isaac and I browsed video games and bought a movie for us to watch together, and we even had churros!"

Ellie smiled. "Glad you had fun," she said. "What about you, Isaac?"

Isaac nodded in agreement. "It was really great!" he exclaimed. "Reya is super cool. I had more fun with him than I've had in a long time. I can't wait for us to watch that pirate movie together."

Kay looked out of the limo with a lazy smile. *So Isaac's made a friend? How sweet,* she thought.

"Glad you had fun, Isaac."

Less than a minute later, Ryan and Tristan came bursting out of the mall with a man in blue following them. When they reached the limo, Ellie raised an eyebrow, but her questions were immediately answered.

"You two punks are banned from the mall from this day forward!" the man yelled, who evidently was a security guard of some kind. "Don't ever come back!"

Ellie glanced from Tristan to Ryan, not knowing who to yell at first. "What in the world could you two possibly have done?"

"It's whatever," Ryan said, eyeing the security guard with dislike as he walked back into the mall. "He's just a buzz kill."

Ellie glared and smacked him on the back of the head. "Idiots!"

"Ow! Ellie, what was that for?!" Ryan exclaimed, rubbing the back of his head.

Sighing, Ellie clenched her fists in anger. "Apparently, you two can't even go on a simple trip to the mall without causing mayhem. Do you have any idea what low profile means?! What the hell did you guys do to warrant being banned from the mall? Inquiring minds have got to know."

Ryan looked at Tristan, and then Tristan looked back at Ryan and shrugged.

"Well, what had happened was. . ." Ryan began, and they ping-ponged details until finally Tristan finished with, "And it wasn't even that lady's real hair!"

Ellie gave a cry of frustration. She didn't know whether to laugh at their stupidity or be angry with it. In the end, she couldn't decide, so she just turned away from them. "You two, limo, now!" she growled.

Shaking her head, she checked her communicator. It was almost 4:45. With luck, they would be home before Shadow's curfew.

As they were getting in the car, Ryan stopped them. "Wait. Why did I get hit and Tristan didn't?" he demanded.

Tristan smirked. "Maybe it's because she likes me better than you. In fact, I'm pretty sure everybody likes me better than you," he said. Suddenly, he was hit in the back of his head by Faith.

"Happy?" Faith asked, and Ryan gave a smile of appreciation, although the act of equal play caused Tristan to frown the entire way home.

136

CЗ♥Сʒ♥СʒѸСʒ♥

Once they arrived at home, they all piled out of the limo and went inside with their bags and left for their rooms to put their stuff away, all except Ellie. She walked down the hallway to Shadow's room and knocked. She felt a bit of déjà vu, having done the exact same thing just hours before.

"Come in, Ellie," he guessed, not even looking up. He heard her walk in. "How was the trip?"

Ellie shook her head. "Not good," she said, glancing everywhere but at him.

Shadow rose from the chair and studied her face. "What happened? Is someone hurt?"

Ellie sighed. "No, no, no. It's not like that at all. Just something fishy happened."

"What do you mean by 'something fishy'? What the hell happened?"

Ellie filled him in. She told him about how she stalked Kay to the store and the strange way that she was acting. She also told him about the unknown item that Kay stole from the store in question.

Shadow considered everything that Ellie told him and shook his head. "You're putting me in an awkward position. I'm not sure how to handle this."

Ellie blinked. "What do you mean, you don't know what to do? It should be obvious!"

"I've already accused the girl of doing mischievous things once already today and was proven wrong. How would it make me look accusing her again?"

"You can't be serious. I gave you information. I told you what I saw. I can't believe you don't trust me, of all people, on this! Why would I lie?"

"The only thing we have proof of is that she's a shoplifter, not evil incarnate. Without proof, there's nothing I can do except watch her closely. Okay?"

Ellie stared at him for a second, her anger fading. "But what if she hurts somebody while you're out playing detective?" she asked. "You have no idea of the risk that you're taking, the danger you're putting us all in!"

"Are you seriously suggesting that I would allow the very people that I've sworn to protect be harmed right under my nose?"

"No, I didn't mean that," she blushed. "I just meant that maybe you're not taking everything into consideration, is all."

"I promise you, I'm taking everything into consideration that's humanly - or superhumanly, in my case - possible. Trust me," Shadow said, with an air of finality in his voice.

"Shadow," she said, her eyes going wide.

"I don't want to hear anything else about Kay tonight, all right?" he asked, part request, part demand.

"But Shadow - "

"Enough!" he shouted. "I told you, just drop all of this Kay nonsense. All right?"

"L-l-look," she said, pointing out the window.

Shadow only obliged because he heard how scared she sounded. Turning around, he stared out the window. He saw the sun setting in the distance the same way that it always did, although something strange was happening.

He saw a dark circle in the center of the sun that was expanding. It spread out until it covered the entire surface of the sun, engulfing it. With the sun went the light that kept the Earth illuminated. All that could be seen in the sky was an endless pool of black.

"Ellie... I'm sorry," he said, his body shaking. "I thought you were going to press the Kay issue."

Ellie shook her head. "It's fine," she said, her voice distant and lost. She couldn't blame him for assuming the worst, that she was going to continue to argue with him. Neither he nor anyone else could have guessed what actually had happened. Darkness had descended upon them.

CHAPTER 7: REVELATIONS

"Shadow, can you fill me in on why the sun, after so many years, suddenly decided to take a vacation?" Ryan asked.

It had only been twenty minutes since the strange event occurred. They had all gathered in the living room after it happened.

"As Ryan not so eloquently put it, I, too, am curious as to why the sun disappeared," Ethan said, gazing into the sky. "It's quite peculiar. I don't recall this ever happening, not in the thousand years I've been around."

"It's barely after 6:00," Faith said, checking her cell phone. The sun usually doesn't set for another half hour or so."

Shadow walked over to the window and laughed bitterly. True, this event had given him something he had wanted for quite some time now, the ability to go out in the daytime, but at a price. *I'm not sure what exactly this is, but irony comes to mind,"* he thought. Any other day, he would have loved to be able to go out before the sunset. Today, the mere thought of doing so made his stomach tight and uncomfortable.

"Guys, I'm not sure how this happened, but I am sure of who did it."

"Who did it?" Ellie asked.

"Yeah, who?" Kay asked.

Before Shadow could reply, Ellie cut him off. "Are you absolutely sure you don't know, Kay?"

Kay frowned. "What do you mean?" she asked. "How would I know who did this?"

Ellie narrowed her eyes. "I don't know. You tell me."

"What's going on?" Isaac asked. "Is something wrong?"

Shadow whistled. "Enough," he said. "It's rather obvious our mysterious evil woman caused this little problem. Ancient magic is at hand here, the kinds of which I cannot be certain of."

"I wonder where we can find out more about magic," Ellie said, feigning deep thought. "Hmm, maybe Kay would know."

"Ellie," Shadow said, "I thought I said–" he began, but he was interrupted by a loud thrashing sound coming from the entrance hall.

"What the hell was that?" Ryan asked, glancing around. "It sounds like somebody just let a bomb off."

"Everyone be on guard," Shadow said, drawing his sword.

The team all rose out of their chairs and spread out, preparing for a fight. Suddenly, the door to the living room was kicked open.

A teenage girl walked into the living room. She appeared to be about seventeen or eighteen. She was quite short, much shorter than the average girl for her age would be.

She had long, jet-black hair with vibrant purple highlights that fell in neat waves to her shoulders. Her dark hair contrasted beautifully with her skin, which was the color of ivory. She wore a short plaid skirt and a plain white blouse. She looked like an Asian schoolgirl, minus the ethnicity.

"Excuse me, but who the hell are you?" Shadow asked, annoyed. "And what are you doing here?"

"So this is the base, huh? Not too impressive, though, is it?" the girl asked, ignoring him. "You'll definitely need to boost up your defenses a bit. I was able to get in with little trouble. The only thing in my way was a door that I had to destroy, but I'm sure you'll find some way to get it fixed." She smiled at them all. "So how's everyone doing today? You know, besides the whole sun going bye-bye thing. Real bummer, right?"

"I said, who are you?" Shadow asked again, getting angrier.

"I'm sorry, but I cannot talk to you if you're going to take that tone with me," the girl replied, shaking her head. "You know, you catch more flies with muffins than you do with broccoli. And right now, you stink of broccoli."

"Can you please tell me who you are?" Faith asked.

"You're polite. I like you," the girl said, smiling. "My name is Niki, but you can call me Niki. That's Niki with one 'k,' not two. Okay?"

Shadow's face fell. If the girl's unexpected entry wasn't annoying enough, her way of talking would be the icing on the cake. *She sure is a strange cookie,* he thought.

"You do realize you're breaking and entering, right?" Tristan asked.

Niki gasped. "That's against the law, and I am no lawbreaker. I am Niki, remember?" she said, twirling a piece of hair.

"She's certainly interesting, that's for sure," Ethan said.

"Ditto," Kay said.

"That's one word for what she is," Shadow said, rolling his eyes.

"So these are the teens you picked?" Niki asked suddenly. "Nice work, I mean, especially since it was last-minute and all."

"How do you know about that?" Shadow asked, but she didn't seem to hear him. She was too busy examining the computer.

"Hey, don't touch that!" Tristan yelled, rushing over. "That's our computer. It's top secret and nobody but members of this team can use it."

"Tristan is correct," Ethan said. "You really should ask permission before touching the possessions of others."

Niki pouted. "Fine. Can I use the computer?" she asked, giving puppy dog eyes. "Pretty please?"

"If you can guess the password, you can use the computer," Shadow replied. "And good luck. Only the people in this room know it, and trust me, nobody is volunteering that information out."

"Hey you, candlehead," Niki called, turning to face Tristan, "what's the password?"

Tristan laughed. "As if I'd ever tell you."

Niki let out a slow breath and stared him in the eye for a few seconds before smiling. "Interesting password," she said, punching in letters. With a beeping sound, the computer unlocked. "I'm sure that nobody would ever guess that it was Armarois."

"How in the hell did you know that?" Ellie asked, interested.

"It's quite simple, you see," Niki said. "I have the power to read minds, in addition to other things. Of course, it's not perfect. I mean, anybody with an above-average intelligence can keep me out, and I can't read everything, just small bits and pieces."

"Way to go, Tristan," Kay muttered, walking out of the room.

"Well, a deal's a deal," Shadow grumbled. "And thank you, Tristan, for having the mental capacity of a walnut."

"Get off that computer!" Tristan shouted, walking over to Niki. He grabbed her arm, whipping her around to face him.

"Brother!" Faith exclaimed.

Niki just blinked. "Can I help you?"

"Tristan, be careful," Ethan said. "You don't know anything about this girl. She could be dangerous."

Tristan scoffed. "Don't tell me what to do," he said, tightening his grip. "As for this one, I think I'll show her the door."

"Brother, wait!" Faith said, eyeing Niki hesitantly. "You don't know what she's capable of!"

Tristan laughed. "Don't worry, Sis, I'll be fine. It's not like this little girl can beat me in a fight."

Niki smirked. She jerked her arm out of his grasp and then lowered herself to the ground. Before he could react, she swept his feet out from under him with her right leg, spinning her body.

Tristan fell to the ground, crashing through a wooden table. He struggled for a moment to catch his breath. "L-lucky... shot."

Niki rose to her feet. She glanced down at him with a piteous look. "Let me guess. He's a virgin, right? They're always so angry."

Shadow raised an eyebrow and smirked. "Could be," he said stiffly, looking down at Tristan. "Either way, he needs to learn how to control himself."

Tristan got up and looked around the room, stone-faced, almost daring anybody to laugh at him. "She caught me by surprise!" he yelled.

Niki ran her fingers through her hair. "Boy, you don't quit, do you?"

"Don't talk down to me!"

Shadow watched as Tristan prepared to charge again. *"Maybe I should intervene here before something bad happens,"* he thought. "Um, Tristan?"

"What?" Tristan snapped, glaring.

"Nothing at all," Shadow replied, his voice icy.

"This will be good for Tristan, good in the sense that he can really use an attitude adjustment, and maybe this Niki could be the one to give it to him," he thought.

Ellie moved next to Shadow. "You're not going to stop this?" she whispered, gesturing at Tristan and Niki. "He'll get massacred."

"Not really. If he wants to be an idiot, then he deserves it."

"So there are no objections?" Tristan asked, waiting for a response. "Good. Now, watch as I show this chick who's boss," he said, placing his hands out, palms facing her.

Niki kept the same calm smile on her face. "You know, chronic anger is often a sign of insecurity. I suggest chocolate or therapy."

"Are we going to talk or fight?" Tristan roared.

"I love fights!"" Ryan said, voice filled with glee. "Don't start without me. I'm going to get a soda real quick," he said, rushing away.

"Tristan, don't do this!" Faith cried, but it was in vain. Nothing could stop him at this point, and she knew it. Tristan's own stupid pride wouldn't let him stop, especially after he was embarrassed.

Tristan rushed at Niki, fist flying.

Niki's face, which once held a strange peace, shifted immediately into an expression that was both calculating and indifferent. When his fist came at her, she grabbed it and kicked him squarely in the chest, knocking him off balance.

Tristan groaned in pain as her foot connected. He quickly grabbed her foot and made to throw her by it.

Niki thrust her foot forward into his chest. Using his body as a platform, she threw two fast kicks at his chest and shoulder. She flipped back in midair, landing a few feet away. "Be smart," she said. "I don't want to hurt you, but I will. And I suspect a few people will be grateful."

Faith made a motion as if she were to move forward, but she was stopped by Ethan, who grabbed her arm. "Why are you holding me back?" she asked. "He's my brother. I have to help him."

"I know that you believe that, but nothing bad will come of this. If anything, it will make him a better person. You'll see."

Faith looked mutinous, but she stepped back in place. "Fine. But if it goes any farther, I will intervene."

Tristan breathed in and out heavily as he stared at Niki in utter resentment. He had never been bested in an all-out fight before, especially not by a girl. He didn't know how to handle it, nor could he even fathom how to accept it. He rubbed his arm across his face, wiping the sweat away. "You won't beat me… I won't let you."

"That will be enough," Shadow said crossly, grabbing the back of Tristan's shirt. He glared at them both. "From the two of you."

Niki nodded. "Why didn't you just ask me to stop from the beginning?" she asked. "I would have, no matter how fun it was."

"She sure is weird," Shadow thought.

Tristan glared at Shadow. "How are you going to let her just come in here and attack me?"

Shadow shook his head and sighed. "Tristan, if I recall correctly, and forgive me if I'm wrong, but you attacked her first. She simply defended herself to the best of her ability." He paused before adding, "which was quite impressive."

"So just like that, you forgive her?" Tristan asked. "For breaking in and for invading our personal property?"

"No, but I'm not just going to throw her out. She could be useful. I definitely want to hear what she has to say. I highly doubt she's here for no reason."

Scowling, Tristan was led off into a corner by Faith, while Niki smiled triumphantly.

"So your name is Niki, right?" Shadow asked.

"Yes, I am Niki."

"All right then. What are you doing here?"

"Surely you didn't come here just to beat up on Tristan?" Ellie said.

Niki stretched out her arms and yawned. "No, I'm definitely not one for drama. I don't like it at all," she said, throwing Tristan a quick smile. "But

I will settle it if it comes my way, and you can take that check to the bank and cash it."

Shadow, not wanting the diffused situation to get out of hand again, moved to the side, blocking Tristan's view of Niki. "Well, that still doesn't answer why you're here. What was the point of even coming?" he asked.

He was very curious to find out Niki's motives; after all, it wasn't daily that somebody came along and impressed him, or broke into his home.

Niki shrugged. She looked around, pulled a chair out, and sat down in it. "Why am I here... Let's see," she said, pausing as she heard footsteps getting closer. They belonged to Ryan, who was just now returning from the kitchen.

"Aw, man, did I miss the fight? Who won?"

"She did," Tereya muttered, pointing at Niki.

"It probably was epic," Ryan said, frowning. He sat down next to Niki, a grape soda in his hand. "Oh, well. I'll have to wait for the next time somebody is beating up Tristan, which will probably be in the next hour or so."

"I'm thirsty," Niki said suddenly, eyeing the soda.

"That's nice," Ryan replied. "Get your own."

"But I want it. Give it to me. If you don't, I won't share my secret."

"Oh, come on, now. Don't pout," Ryan said.

"Ryan, give it to her," Shadow said.

"Why should I?" Ryan asked.

"Because she knows something important. We can't find out what that is unless you give her that soda."

Before he could respond, Niki snatched the soda out of his hand. She popped the tab open and took a large swig. She turned to him. "Thank you. I was terribly thirsty."

Ryan glared. "Don't mention it. So glad that I could help."

"Anyway," Niki said, winking at Ryan as she took another deep sip of the soda, "I heard from this lady that you were recruiting teenagers with special powers."

"Lady?" Shadow asked, his voice trailing off. "What lady?"

"Yes, lady. And I think that I certainly qualify for the job. I mean, aren't I both unique and powerful?" she asked, her head tilting to the side.

"Well, you are powerful."

Niki nodded rapidly. "You see?"

"And you're not going to tell me who this lady is, are you?"

"I'm afraid if you don't know, you're not allowed to ask."

Shadow looked at her and sighed. "You're right. You do qualify. But we cannot have any more fighting between you and Tristan. You guys are going to be on the same team, so you'll have to get along."

Niki nodded.

Shadow nodded. "Tristan, come here."

"What do you want?" Tristan asked angrily.

. "You know, I think that somebody's cranky and needs a time out," Niki said. She paused and glanced sideways at Shadow. "I meant Tristan," she whispered.

Shadow ignored her and faced Tristan. "Tristan, you two are teammates. There will be no animosity. Do you understand me?"

Tristan growled in frustration. If he didn't like being around the girl for a few minutes, how could he bear to live with her for what could be a very long time? "I don't know," he said blankly, fighting back his anger.

"Trist, please?" Faith asked softly. She walked up to Tristan and grabbed him by the shoulders, turning him to face her. "Please do this. . .for me?"

Tristan looked at Shadow. Shadow had done a lot for him in the past few months, giving him a place to stay, food, and a new family. He then looked at Faith. She loved him unconditionally and was always there for him when he needed it, never asking anything of him. Yet here she was, finally asking for something, something so small and something even stupid that could easily be done. He sighed.

"Fine. You win. I can bury the hatchet if she can."

Faith smiled. "Thank you, Tris."

"That's very mature of you, Tristan," Shadow said. "Thank you," he added, after a few moments' thought.

Niki sipped the grape soda loudly, obviously indifferent to the touching scene going on in front of her. She didn't care if Tristan liked her or not. It was all about respect and understanding. She was practical like that. "Glad that everything's totally arctic."

"Arctic?" Tereya questioned.

"Arctic as in cool."

"Do you have anything else to add, Niki?" Shadow asked, giving her a long, calculating look.

Niki took another sip of her soda. "Well, what if I told you that I know why we're dealing with the night that will never end?" she asked.

"What would you know about that?" Shadow asked.

"If she knows more about what happened, then obviously she must be involved in it somehow," he thought. *"Or at least know of who did it on a semi-personal level."*

Niki didn't say anything at first. She took another sip of her drink and then frowned, discovering that the can was empty.

"If you know something, please tell us, Niki," Ellie said.

"Any information at all could be crucial to returning things back the way they belong," Shadow said.

"Well, I definitely do have that information for you guys," Niki said, tapping her soda can impatiently. "First off, there is woman that you all have been after, right?"

Shadow nodded. "Yes. We don't know her name or where she is or even what she's up to."

"Right. Well, your search is over, partly. Her name is Maedara, and that name is definitely one that you'll all want to remember," Niki said. "She lives on Om'erah, the continent to the far west. Most people don't go there anymore, fearing the slight chance that they might run into her. She truly is one of the most evil beings that exist in this world… and don't forget crazy. Definitely don't forget that."

"What does this Maedara have to do with the eternal darkness thing?" Shadow asked. "How is she tied into it?"

"I was fortunate enough to be 'invited' to an event that took place a few days ago. It was the yearly opening of the Black Market," Niki said. A quick glance around the room told her that nobody except Shadow even knew what that was. Sighing, Niki hastened to explain to them exactly what it was.

"The Black Market is a place hidden deep within the continent of Zytrihr, the place where all the big baddies like to roam and where their government is. Once a year, for only a month, the Black Market opens up. All sorts of evil creatures from different dimensions gather there to exchange valuable artifacts and abilities. It's quite the tourist attraction."

"And how did you come to be 'invited' to this gathering of evil beings, Niki?" Shadow asked, with raised eyebrows.

Niki sucked her teeth. "You're not seriously insinuating that I am evil, are you?" she asked. "I am not evil. I am Niki. We've been over this."

Shadow frowned. "I didn't mean that you were evil. I just find it hard to believe that you would have been invited to an event which took place in the most evil city in the entire world."

Niki beamed. "It's okay. In the spirit of friendship, I am willing to look past the fact that you just called me evil, and I forgive you."

Rolling his eyes, Shadow moved his hand in a 'go ahead and continue with your story' motion.

"So, as I was saying, the Black Market just opened, and I thought that it would be a good opportunity to see what the bad guys are up to. Yes, I did. So I decided that I would be on the guest list if it would kill me... and it almost did. Basically, I jumped this grim demon, which you all know, I'm sure, are tiny creatures who wear big cloaks and never show even an inch of their body. This was so that I could sneak around and go in unnoticed and without suspicion. I had a few close calls, but in the end I succeeded in getting in.

"I was there, sitting in the third row, watching the auctions take place. Naturally, I was waiting for something interesting or even uber-dangerous to be sold." She stopped abruptly and eyed her empty grape soda can in a strange, sad, longing sort of way.

Shadow bumped the nearby Ryan in the ribs. "You. Get her another soda."

"No. Make somebody else go get it," Ryan replied.

"If you don't get it, I swear… I'll make you share a room with Crystal."

Ryan's eyes widened. Without another word, he ran to the kitchen. After a few minutes, he came back with another can of grape soda. He handed it to Niki in an exaggeratedly unenthusiastic manner.

"Thank you!" Niki said, popping the tab and taking a huge sip.

"Now, please continue," Shadow said politely. Even though he was getting slightly annoyed, this wasn't something that he wanted to articulate. It would take manners to get this particular girl to talk. She gave off the strong vibe that she couldn't be intimidated and would certainly not take orders.

"So where was I?"

"You left off where you told us that you were at the auction at the Black Market and that you were sitting in the third row," Shadow replied, and then added, "Now, please continue."

Niki nodded. "So anyway, I was watching people buying different kinds of potions and whatnot until finally one of the most legendary items that I've ever heard of was sold. It was the infamous Chest of Ondeyr," she said, her voice going quieter than normal.

Everybody in the room looked puzzled, with the exception of Shadow, who had a look of horror on his face. "No. It can't be. It just can't," he breathed, shaking his head. "The Chest of Ondeyr. . .How did they even find it? It was supposed to be lost in the sands of time."

"All right. For those of us who aren't history buffs, what's so bad about this stupid box of Ondeyr?" Ryan asked.

"The Chest of Ondeyr is a highly dangerous artifact, Ryan," Shadow replied flatly. "It's said to have powers beyond the realm of mortal comprehension."

"It was always said that it was able to bring about an endless night," Niki said. "But evidently, judging by the way the demons and bad guys were acting, it was a huge shocker that the chest was even available to bid on. It also didn't help that Maedara made a bid and won it. Apparently, though, Maedara wasn't even supposed to be there!"

"Why?" Shadow asked. "Why would her own kind ban her from the auction?" he wondered.

"Maybe even bad guys have a crazy quota?" Ryan suggested.

"I'm not sure, but whatever the reason was, it was obvious that they didn't intend for her to get the chest in the first place," Niki replied. "The king of the Kvana himself was there, and he had his guards attack her, trying to remove her from the place. She took them all out, effortlessly. If that wasn't bad enough, she also killed the king. She is now the ruler of the entire continent, in charge of all the demons."

Shadow grimaced. It was bad enough that Maedara was obviously very mentally unstable with deadly abilities, but now she was in a position of power. With her power and the entire force of the Kvana behind her, she could easily sweep the world into a dark, ruined shell.

"So… you're saying that this woman is pretty unstoppable?" Tristan asked.

Niki smiled. "Aww, you're learning."

"So what are we going to do, Shadow?" Ellie asked.

Shadow frowned. "I. . .I don't know. I really don't know," he replied, his gaze falling to the ground. He could not meet her eyes and tell her that he had nothing - no plan, no course of action, no faint clue on how to make things better.

"Well, it's obvious, isn't it?" Niki asked. "Because I thought it was quite obvious."

Shadow looked up. "What do you mean, it's obvious?"

"You can't be serious, leader dude! It's obvious. We find Maedara, kick her ass, and then set the world right!"

Faith smiled. "At first I didn't like you because of how you were with my brother, but you're definitely okay."

"And I like the way you put things," Ellie added, grinning.

"That's what she said," Niki replied, sticking her tongue out.

Shadow rolled his eyes. "How are we supposed to find her, let alone beat her?" he asked. "You understand, I'm sure, that since she's in possession of what was inside the Chest of Ondeyr, right?"

Niki nodded. "Yes, the Scepter of Ondeyr."

"Then you must know that the scepter is rumored to make the wielder as strong as the sorceress who originally crafted it. If that's the case, then Maedara is a few hairs short of immortal, meaning it would take a hell of a lot of effort to stop her. In short, almost impossible."

Niki smiled. "You know, something impossible is just that, because you took the unnecessary extra effort to put the 'im' before the word 'possible'."

"Meaning?" Tristan asked.

"Meaning, when one says that something is impossible, it's only because they themselves deem it to be," Niki said dryly.

Tristan gave an involuntary laugh. "Nice to know that your endless optimism will allow us to fight Maedara."

Ethan shook his head. "You would do well to have faith, Tristan. It's an important attribute."

"You'd think he, of all people, would have faith," Ellie remarked.

"Niki's right," Shadow said. "We have to do whatever we can to stop Maedara, even if the odds are stacked against us, even if it looks impossible."

"Shadow's right, you guys. If we work together, we'll be fine," Faith said. Suddenly, she was knocked down by an invisible force.

"Faith!" Tristan yelled. He ran over and kneeled on the ground by his sister. "What's happening to her? Somebody, please, help her!"

Suddenly, to everyone's surprise, Faith's body slowly lifted off the ground and hovered in midair, floating up and down.

"Faith! Faith!"

"Faith, please answer us!"

CЗ৪ОCЗ৪ОCЗ৪ОCЗ৪О

Faith heard the worried calls of her friends, but she was too far away to answer. No longer in her body, she found herself on the floor of the same ancient, moss-covered temple she had been in a few months ago.

Walking on, Faith still heard the echoes of her friends calling her name. She knew that they were worried about her, but something told her that she couldn't answer them. Not yet, anyway. A strange force had to have brought her here, someone or something. Her intuition told her that she needed to be here.

"What's going on?" she wondered, walking forward through the strange temple. As soon as she thought it, her question was answered. She had reached a room that mirrored the stars in the night sky. It was as if she were standing in the sky itself, a surface of black with tiny, glimmering specks of bright white, a constellation made of roses at her feet.

"Hello, Faith," a voice called.

Turning around, Faith found the source of this voice. It was a woman, or at least it appeared to be a woman. She had ghostly-pale white skin and long, glowing, golden hair that radiated with a bright light. Her eyes were blue-green. They appeared to be live pools of water, the color rippling with every blink. She was wearing long, flowing robes of the deepest pink. She was arguably the most beautiful woman that Faith had ever seen.

"Greetings, daughter of time," the woman said.

"Who. . .are you?" Faith asked. She had never seen this woman in her entire life, yet there was a strange feeling inside of her heart. The feeling spoke of familiarities; a goodnight kiss, being tucked in at night, and drinking hot chocolate on a cold winter's night.

"My name is Harathune. I am one of the Haati," the woman replied.

"Why did you come to me?" Faith asked. "What do you want from me?"

"Do not fear me. I am here to help you. There will be great suffering in your future, and important things for you to know," Harathune said. "I was the only Haati ever blessed with the gift of future sight. It is a rare gift, even today. I'm here because, through our shared power, there's a link that tethers me to this realm. I come bearing a gift."

"What gift could you possibly have for me?" Faith asked.

"My gift to you, child, is knowledge. You must prepare for what's to come. Your destiny is written in the stars. There are great troubles in your future. . .and you must do whatever you can to protect your world from what's to come."

Faith shook her head. "How can you be so sure that I can do it? I'm not very strong physically, nor do I have a power that is suited for combat."

"Faith, your power is in your knowledge of things that have not yet come to be. Your power exists in that you and you alone can alter the destiny of those around you. You and you alone can change what is written in the book of time. Trust in yourself."

"I will," Faith replied. "Thank you."

"Do not thank me yet, Faith," she said. "There are a few more things I must tell you. One will help you restore your world to normal; the other is something that I will simply tell you; the last is something that I can't tell you yet."

"So then you'll tell me later?" Faith asked.

Harathune nodded. "Yes, one day. You are not yet equipped to see the vision that I have seen. But when I do finally show you, then and only then will you be able to understand your destiny clearly."

"All right. What can you tell me then?"

"The woman, Maedara, she is pure evil. You must remember and warn your teammates that there is no reasoning with her. Her mind is not stable. Maedara knows nothing of compassion, love, or mercy.

"There is a way to stop the Scepter of Ondeyr, but it will be no easy task. You must destroy the heart of the one who caused the endless night. It will be difficult because my sister, Ondeyr, forged the rod to make the wielder impervious to most forms of damage. It will take great cunning and teamwork to defeat Maedara.

"Lastly, I must warn you to beware of blue fishes. They will lead you to grave disaster."

"What do you mean by that?" Faith asked, but the woman didn't answer. Suddenly, the floor was ripped out from under her, and it felt like she was being thrown through a long tunnel. Then, almost immediately, it was though she collided with something solid. She opened her eyes, gasping for air.

"Faith!" Tristan cried. "Are you all right?"

"Y-yeah, Brother," Faith said. "I'm fine."

"Thank God," Tristan said, pulling her up to a sitting position and then hugging her. "I was so worried. I thought you had. . ."

Even though he didn't finish his sentence, she understood all too well what he was going to say. "It's all right, Brother. I'm fine. I just had a vision."

153

"What was the vision about?" Shadow asked.

"She told me –" Faith began, but she was interrupted by Isaac, who burst into the living room suddenly.

"Kay's not in her room!" Isaac shouted. "I haven't seen her since she told me that she wanted to be alone."

Shadow's eyes widened at this news. "Did you just check her room or - "

"No," Isaac replied, "I checked everywhere."

Shadow frowned. Kay was nowhere to be found. He wondered to himself if Ellie was right to worry earlier. He wondered if Kay's mysterious disappearance had anything to do at all with the sun going away. The only thing on his mind wasn't where Maedara was or what she was doing, but where Kay was and what she was doing - and what he was going to do when he found her.

CHAPTER 8: THE FIRST TEMPTATION

"Has anybody found her?" Shadow called. After Isaac's announcement that Kay was missing, he had everyone go out in groups and search around one last time to find her. He couldn't fathom where she had disappeared to or even why she had left the protection of their home, especially when the sun had been blacked out.

"Nada," Niki replied, shrugging. "I checked around the building, but I found a whole lotta zip."

"She's not in the training room," Ellie replied. "It's like she just disappeared."

This does not look good. I doubt she went out for a midnight stroll. She has to be up to something, Shadow thought.

"What about you, Ethan ?"

"I'm afraid I haven't had much luck in my search either," Ethan said. "She has truly performed quite the vanishing act."

"What do you think happened to her, Shadow?" Ellie asked.

"I don't know for sure. All I can say is, I should have listened to you earlier. I'm sorry, Ellie. It was stupid of me to ignore something that you felt so strongly about."

"Don't beat yourself up," Ellie said. "For all we know, you could just be jumping to conclusions. We don't know for sure that she's up to something malicious. She could have just gone out for some alone time. I mean, she's not exactly Ms. Reliable or anything."

Shadow looked thoughtful for a moment and then shook his head. "I just have a bad feeling about this. She was acting weird when I met her a few months ago and again when we went to Draconia Isle. Even if you ignore those things, stealing something from a magic store is very suspicious. And now the sun... I can't shake the feeling that these things are somehow connected."

"You can't be serious!" Isaac exclaimed, rushing into the living room. He ran up to Shadow, anger spread across his face. "You can't seriously think that Kay had anything to do with what happened. You just can't!"

"Isaac, don't get upset," Tereya said. "He didn't say that Kay was definitely to blame. He's just concerned. Don't take it personally."

"Stay out of this, Reya," Isaac said, pointing his finger at Shadow. "He basically just accused my best friend of being evil! How do you expect me not to take that personally?"

Shadow met Isaac's eyes. He had nothing but sympathy for the young boy. He understood that the boy would be upset at the prospect that Kay, somebody who had always been there for him, was capable of such evil.

"I'm sorry, but it doesn't exactly look good for her. She's missing, less than an hour after the sun disappeared. What are we supposed to think?"

"What's going on?" Crystal asked, coming through the living room door.

"Well," Shadow began, "I suspect that Kay is working for the other team. There have been a few events that have taken place over these past few months that make me question her integrity. She has lied quite a few times to me and has even resorted to stealing."

He paused as he saw the distraught looks on their faces. Isaac, however, seemed to be the only one who was not sad but instead was angry at him for revealing what his suspicions were.

"Don't give me that look, Isaac. The team had a right to know. It wasn't only you who Kay betrayed. It was them too."

"She didn't betray me!" Isaac roared. He threw his fist forward, and it smashed into the right side of Shadow's face.

Ellie, Faith, and Crystal gasped collectively at the sight of Isaac, usually sweet and calm, actually resorting to violence, especially against the one who had treated them all so well. Even Tristan and Ryan, two who rarely took anything seriously at all, were both shocked.

Shadow brushed his hand gingerly against his face. It hurt, but not too much. "I see that the training isn't paying off. You still need to work on that left hook. Put your weight into it."

"Oh, yeah?" Isaac growled. "Well, how about another demonstration?"

"Isaac!" Tereya yelled. "Stop!"

Cameryn, who was the last one to enter the room, had caught the display. He walked in front of Shadow and stared daggers at Isaac.

Isaac returned Cameryn's glare with his own. "Move. Now."

"No. I won't," Cameryn replied. "Shadow promised to never let anybody hurt me, so what kind of friend would I be if I let somebody hurt him in front of me? A bad one, that's what."

"This is between me and Shadow; you're not involved at all. So get out of my way, or else."

"No, Isaac," Cameryn said, "I can't believe you're trying to hurt Shadow over Kay. If you had any idea of how she really is, you wouldn't be acting like this."

"What do you mean, Cameryn?" Shadow asked.

"Yeah, Cameryn," Isaac flared, "what do you mean?"

Cameryn frowned. "Promise you won't hate me, Shadow."

"I would never hate you, okay?" Shadow replied. "Just tell me what you have to say. It could be important."

"I lied about what happened between me and Kay in the room where you found me," Cameryn said, blushing slightly.

"You did what?" Shadow asked, eyes widening.

"I lied about what happened, but please don't be mad. I'm sorry, Shadow. I just didn't want to cause any problems for the team. Kay told me that if I said anything, she would call me a liar and you all would believe her and I would be kicked out. I didn't want to lose all my new friends and be forced to go back to that town. I just couldn't go through that."

Shadow opened his mouth and then closed it. He looked Cameryn over and then sighed. "It's fine. Tell me exactly what happened, then."

"I left my room to get a snack. I saw Kay going to the stairwell in the left wing. I know I shouldn't have, because you told us to never go there, but I followed her. When I found her, she was talking to somebody on this weird sort of device. It looked sort of like the cell phones you gave us, but it was different. She was talking to somebody, although I didn't hear their whole conversation.

"She realized I was there, and she turned on me and attacked me. I don't remember what she did to me, but the next thing I do remember is waking up with you standing over me."

Shadow blinked. He looked as though he was going to be sick. "How could I have been so stupid? How could I have trusted her? I put you all in danger. Damn it!"

"Don't blame yourself. You couldn't have known!" Ellie exclaimed. "Beating yourself up isn't going to accomplish anything."

"Ellie's right, Shadow," Faith said tenderly. "What Kay has done is not your fault. Don't allow yourself to carry the weight of her sins on your shoulders."

"He's a liar!" Isaac yelled. "You're a liar, Cameryn. Kay wouldn't have done anything like that. She just wouldn't!" he said, frowning. "Shadow bringing you here was one giant mistake. You're just a troublemaker. You should have never been rescued."

"Isaac!" Tereya cried. "That's cruel. You shouldn't have said that."

Cameryn flushed bright red. He smiled spitefully. "Don't get mad at me because your friend is a lying skank."

Isaac bowed his head as if he were about to cry, and then suddenly threw another punch, this time hitting Cameryn squarely across the mouth.

"That's enough," Shadow said, flicking his hand forward. Immediately Isaac was knocked backwards and thrown through the air, landing roughly on the floor a few feet away. "Are you all right, Cameryn?"

"Yes, I'm fine," Cameryn replied, rubbing the corner of his mouth. "It's a good thing Isaac can't throw a decent punch."

Shadow smiled. "Good," he said. Then he turned to Isaac, nostril's flared. "Hitting me is one thing, but don't you ever touch Cameryn again. Do you understand me?"

"He. . .shouldn't. . .have. . .said. . .those. . .things. . .about. . .her," Isaac growled through clenched teeth.

"You're acting like a child," Shadow replied. "Grow up."

"Shadow –" Ellie began, but she closed her mouth when he held up his hand.

"No, Ellie, he needs to hear this," Shadow said, glaring at Isaac, who was fighting to get up. "Stay down," he said. Shadows from the corners of the room crept over to Isaac and bound his wrists and ankles to the floor, forcing him back onto the ground.

"Let me up!" Isaac shouted. He lay sprawled out on his back, staring at Shadow with hatred in his eyes. "I'm done with this stupid team. I want out."

Ellie walked over to Isaac and put her hand on his shoulders. "Isaac, please. We cannot do this without you. We need you."

"Ellie's right. We need you, cutie. You're a part of this team," Crystal said, glancing down at him. "Like it or not, we're a family. However dysfunctional, we're in this together."

Isaac's face softened. "I. . .I can't. I can't do this without Kay. I just can't," he said, sounding as if he were on the verge of tears. He turned his face away from them all, determined not to let them see him cry.

"It's all right to be upset, Isaac. We understand," Faith said. "I know she hurt your feelings."

"You could never understand!" Isaac cried. "Kay meant the world to me! She means everything. My parents died when I was still very young. Demons killed my parents. I escaped and Kay found me, and she's taken care of me ever since. She's fed me, gotten me clothes, protected me from anybody who threatened me, and made sure that I had a roof over my head every night before I went to sleep. You don't know the real Kay. If you did, then you wouldn't accuse her of any of this stuff."

"Isaac," Ellie muttered, "it's all right, buddy."

"And how do you think she did all that amazing stuff, Isaac?" Shadow asked coldly. "Did Kay have a job? Did she have anybody giving her money?"

Isaac shrugged. "I don't know, all right?"

"You don't know," Shadow repeated. "She probably stole it and stole everything that she ever gave you."

"I - it's. . .not true. It. . .she wouldn't. . ."

"How pathetic," Shadow said.

"Shadow!" Ellie exclaimed. "Why are you being like this?"

"Yeah, Shadow, calm down," Ryan said, shaking his head. "I mean, it's one thing to be tough, but you're bordering on cruel."

Shadow frowned. "I can't just keep treating you all like babies and telling you that everything is going to be all right. I'm here to make sure you all survive. We can't expect to survive if Isaac would rather sit and cry than fight."

"But I can't fight without her. I need her," Isaac said. He was no longer trying to be strong. He was now crying. Tears streamed down his young face in tiny waves.

Shadow scoffed. "You need Kay to fight? I wasn't aware that your powers only work when she's around, I guess I missed the memo."

Isaac just stared, at a loss for words.

"One second," Ellie said abruptly, pulling Shadow to the side. "Can't you just go easy on him? It's obvious that he's going through a lot right now, what with his best friend in the entire world being evil. It's a lot to handle."

"Ellie, I'm sorry, but pity isn't going to cut it here. If we pity him, then he'll be weak, and we cannot handle the slightest bit of weakness right now. Every single one of us needs to be at the top of our game if we even hope to survive."

"I understand that. Trust me. I do. But you've got to understand that pushing Isaac to his breaking point is not the way to do that. He's lost without Kay."

"That's precisely the problem!" Shadow said, shaking his head. "He shouldn't be relying on anybody but himself. He shouldn't have so much faith in another person, so much so that he cannot think to function on his own without that person around."

"You're right. He has issues he needs to work on. But is being cruel really the way to go about things?"

"Ellie, I am trying to help him. Just trust me. I promise you that I am not doing anything to harm him, nothing that I believe is against his best interests."

"I do trust you, Shadow. You know I do."

"Good," Shadow replied, walking back over to Isaac. "Listen, kid, I'm not going to sugarcoat things for you. We need you at your best. And if you aren't, then you need to stay here and not come on any more missions with us. You'll get hurt, and we don't want that."

He waved his hand over Isaac, releasing him from the dark restraints.

Isaac got off of the floor and looked thoughtful. "I know that it all seems like Kay is bad. I know that you guys wouldn't go against her if you didn't believe she was truly bad. But how can we be sure? We don't have her word. Can't we give her the benefit of the doubt?"

Niki twiddled her index fingers together. "Isaac, the likelihood that Kay is completely innocent, when all the odds are stacked up against her, is the same as hotdogs being able to fly. And I've tested them. Trust me. They can't."

Shadow whistled. "Isaac, I need you to decide now. Either stay here from this point forward and miss out on the missions or opt to come with us. Just know that if you come with us, you may have to come up against Kay. It's a reality that you need to face. Can you handle it?"

Isaac didn't answer immediately. He looked away as if he were trying to gather his thoughts. "I need time to decide for myself. I don't know for sure yet. All I can do is promise that I will try to do what's right."

Shadow looked at him carefully. "I have complete faith in you, Isaac. I know you wouldn't let us down."

"Thanks. I just, I still have trouble believing that Kay would do this. She's never done anything like this before."

Shadow shook his head. "You don't know if she's done stuff like this before, Isaac. Let's be honest. You don't know everything about her, only what she's told you. I'm aware you spent tons of time with her, but she's good. She's very good. It wouldn't be hard to hide things from someone of your age, especially if she was trying her very best. She fooled us, so don't be upset that she fooled you as well."

"Yeah, Isaac. It's not your fault at all, we promise," Ellie said.

"So what do we do now, Shadow?" Crystal asked. "It's not like we can just go after Maedara. We can't even go after Kay. We have no idea where either of them are."

"I never thought I would say this, but Crystal is right," Ryan said. "I mean, the world is huge. How are we going to find either one of them?"

"I already told you guys," Niki said, crossing her arms. "I told you where Maedara's home is. We can go there and be all, like, We caught you. Now, give us the sun back or we'll have to take you out, gangsta style."

"That's a nice plan, Niki," Faith said, "but we don't know if she's even there right now. I mean, if you were a psycho and just stole the sun, would you go home or go out and celebrate?"

"Faith's right," Ellie said. "I doubt she's there now, and it would be a huge waste of time to go all the way there for nothing. I think we should focus on finding Kay. Thing is, how do we find her?"

Shadow smiled. "Oh, but I have a very good idea where Kay is right now."

Isaac's eyes widened. "But you told us that you didn't know where she was!"

"Well, it's true that I don't know where she went, but I can find out," Shadow replied, pulling out his own black cell phone. "You see, there are tiny tracking chips in each and every one of your phones. It's how I can locate one of you if you're far away and in trouble."

"Shadow, you're brilliant!" Ellie exclaimed.

"Thanks for the compliment, but I don't deserve it. I can't believe that I failed one of you this much," he said. And then, before she could respond, he added, "I know I can't save everybody, but that doesn't stop me from trying."

"I don't blame you for this, Shadow. Nobody does," Ellie said. "I truly wish you believed that."

"I know you don't think it's my fault, but can you be so sure about the others?"

"I don't think it's your fault," Tristan said. "I know that you try your best, and that's all that matters."

162

Faith nodded in agreement. "I know in my heart that you would never do anything to purposely endanger any of us. You would go to hell and back for any of us, and we'd do the same."

"They're both right, Shadow," Tereya said meekly. "You are one of the most amazing people I know. You saved me from that woman who was trying to harm me, even though you didn't know me. You didn't owe me anything; yet you still felt obligated to save me. I wouldn't be here today if it weren't for you."

"Nor would a lot of people, Tereya," Ethan said. "Shadow has saved not only just our lives but the lives of countless others. He's been protecting people for many years now, and he's done quite a good job."

"I can't add anything to what they've said already," Ryan said. "But I've known you longer than most of them, and I know that you have always watched out for me."

"Thank you, guys. It means a lot."

"What do we do now?" Faith asked.

"I think it's time we all take a field trip," Shadow said.

"A field trip?" Tereya asked.

"We're going to find Kay."

Isaac looked up at the mention of Kay's name. "What are you going to do when we find her?"

Shadow shrugged. "I'm not exactly sure. But don't worry. I'm not going to attack her on sight. I want to talk to her, find out things, fill in the blanks: what she told Maedara about us, if she told anything; what she stole from that store; why she lied about what happened between her and Cameryn; and why she left the castle."

"All right. As long as you promise not to hurt her," Isaac said.

"Don't worry. Kay was somebody that I had grown to care about too. I swore to protect her. My first instinct definitely isn't to hurt her. All I want are answers."

"Speak for yourself," Ellie muttered under her breath.

"What was that, Ellie?" Shadow asked. His enhanced hearing allowed him to hear what she said, though he was pretending not to.

"Nothing, nothing at all. I was just talking to myself."

Shadow gazed at her for a few moments before looking away. "All right, let's get ready to leave. Ellie, Ethan, and Faith, I want you three to help get everyone ready to leave in a few moments. I have to take care of something."

"I'll go get the jet ready," Ethan said.

"It's as good as done," Faith said.

Waiting until Ethan and Faith were out of earshot, Ellie pulled Shadow to the side. "What do you have to take care of?"

"Nothing. It's really not that important."

Ellie frowned. "Well, I'm just wondering if it has anything to do with Kay."

Shadow sighed. "No. I want to check on Cameryn. He walked off after the whole altercation with Isaac. I want to make sure he's all right."

"All right then."

Shadow patted her on the shoulder. "It's fine. Trust me. Would you please have everybody ready by the time I come back?"

Ellie smiled. "I'm on it," she said. "I'm sure Faith and Ethan are wondering where I am right now."

"Thanks again," Shadow said. He gave her a quick smile, watched her walk away, and then left the living room himself. He walked down the left wing hall and came to the door of Cameryn's room. "Cameryn?" he called, but he received no answer. He took that opportunity to knock on the door, three quick raps. He had a weird surge of déjà vu. His mind jumped to how Ellie always went to his room looking for him.

"Who is it?"

"It's Shadow," he replied.

"Come in."

Shadow turned the handle and pushed in. Walking into the room, he realized that he hadn't ever really looked inside Cameryn's room, not since the kid had moved into it and made it his own. The room was quite different than what he had remembered. The walls were now painted sky blue, the trimming a sharp turquoise. On the walls were pictures from different bands and singers. "Wow," he said, looking around. "I see you've decorated the place."

"You don't like the room?" Cameryn asked. He was lying down on the bed, throwing a ball up, catching it, and repeating. "I mean, I hope you like it… like, you don't think it's too dorky or something."

Shadow shook his head. "No, the room is fine. Really."

"Thanks."

A few moments of awkward silence passed. Shadow just watched as Cameryn played catch, absentmindedly following the path of the ball with his eyes as it went up and down.

"What's up?" Cameryn asked, as if the awkwardness had finally gotten to him.

"I wanted to see if you were all right, you know, after what happened."

Cameryn rolled his eyes. "Oh, you mean with Isaac? Never better."

"Are you sure?"

"Yeah. I'm fine. Never better."

Shadow nodded slowly. "All right. Well, if you need to talk or anything, let me know. All right?"

Cameryn nodded, not taking his eyes off of the ball. "Yeah, I know. Thanks."

"The guys and I are going on a mission. Do you want to come or stay here?" Shadow asked, and then shook his head. He waved his hand, and black energy covered the ball, freezing it in midair.

Cameryn turned and looked at him. "Why did you do that? I was having fun."

"I wanted you to pay attention to me," Shadow replied. "You seem distracted. Are you sure nothing is wrong?"

"Why do you keep asking if something is wrong?" Cameryn asked. "Can't I just be annoyed for no reason?"

"I don't know. You tell me," Shadow replied. "Are you just annoyed for the sake of being annoyed, or is there a deeper reason?"

Cameryn sighed loudly. "I'm sure it has nothing to do with the fact that I was just punched in the face. That probably has nothing to do with my anger, nothing at all."

"I'm sorry for that. You know I am," Shadow said. "I promised you that I wouldn't ever let you get hurt again, and I'm doing my best to keep that promise. It's not like I can control the actions of others. I never expected that he would hit you like that."

"I don't blame you for Isaac hitting me. I'm just mad that you got involved so I couldn't return the favor."

Shadow raised an eyebrow. "You're telling me that you're mad because I disciplined him for hitting you, because why? You wanted to do it yourself?"

Cameryn nodded. "Yeah."

"You're acting tough, but the thing is, I know that's all it is. An act. You don't need to put on an act for me. You and I both know that you don't like violence because of what you went through. I know that you wouldn't have hit Isaac back, and that's why you're really mad."

Cameryn slowly let out his breath. "You're right," he admitted, shaking his head. "I want to hate you for it, but you're right. I couldn't hurt him even if I wanted to, because I'm not that kind of person."

"I'm aware," Shadow said, smiling. "So why are you angry at me?"

"I'm... not," Cameryn said, clenching his fists. "It's just that I'm worried that the others will think I'm weak because you needed to protect me."

"Don't worry about what the others think," Shadow said, rubbing his shoulder. "All that matters is what you think and what I think. And you know what? I think you're a cool kid who's been through more in fourteen years than most people go through in their entire lives. So, yeah, I think that makes you pretty tough."

Cameryn smiled. "All right, you made your point. I was being dumb."

"Good," Shadow said, laughing. "Now that you understand that, are you sure you don't want to come with us?"

"I would, but I'm... not up to going out yet. I'm not ready to face the world and deal with... people yet. It's too soon. What happened left me scarred, and not just physically. I don't know if I'll ever be okay again."

"I know that you're still uneasy about everything. It's fine; there's no pressure. I just hope that–" Shadow said, but was interrupted by a loud

166

beeping noise coming from his pocket. He reached into it and pulled out his communicator, a tiny red light on the top flashing.

"What's going on?" Cameryn asked.

"I forgot. You're still not used to them. It's the cell. Somebody is contacting me," Shadow replied. He opened it and pressed the large talk button in the middle under the screen. "Who is it?"

"Shadow, it's Ellie. Where are you?" Ellie asked, her voice resonating from the speaker.

"I'm in Cameryn's room. Is something wrong?"

"No. I just wanted to let you know that everyone is waiting and ready to leave."

"All right. I'll be there soon. Later," Shadow said, and clicked the device closed. "Are you sure you'll be all right, Cameryn?"

"Yeah, don't worry about me. I'll be fine," Cameryn replied. "Just promise me you'll all be careful, okay? It would kill me if anything happened to you."

"I promise," Shadow said. He walked over to the door. He turned to look one last time at Cameryn almost as if he wanted to say something but couldn't. He gave a curt nod and closed the door behind him.

CRBOCRBOCRBOCRBO

"What took you so long?" Ryan demanded as Shadow walked into the jet and closed the door behind him.

"Don't concern yourself with how I spend my time," Shadow replied.

"Shadow?" Ellie asked. "Is everything okay?"

Shadow nodded. "Yeah. Why would something be wrong?"

"I don't know. You're just acting on edge."

"I'm fine. I swear. I just really want to find Kay," Shadow said. He beckoned Ellie closer, lowering his voice to a whisper. "I'm just a tiny bit tense, all right? I'll continue to be until I find her and find out how much she told Maedara."

Ellie nodded. "I understand, and don't worry, we'll find her."

"I'm sure of it," Shadow said. He got up and walked down the aisle towards the pilot's room. Once inside, he pulled out his own cell and clicked the huge black button to turn it on. Once on, he pressed a few buttons, and then a tiny map appeared on the screen. "Locate Kay," he muttered into the speaker.

Almost immediately, a tiny yellow dot appeared on the map, a bright red one a short distance away. *"If I remember correctly, the yellow dot is where I'm located and the red dot is where Kay is located,"* he thought. Double-checking the communicator's mini-map to see if he had the coordinates right, he punched in Kay's location and hit the button to begin the launch sequence.

03க03க03க03க

A short while later, they all disembarked the jet.

"Where are we?" Ellie asked.

"The continent of Lunarai," Shadow said, attempting to keep his voice calm. The place held bad memories for him. He was unable to completely keep his anger passive.

"What's wrong?" Tereya asked.

"It's nothing," Shadow said flatly. "Really," he added, when he received looks of disbelief. Ellie especially gave him a look that clearly said that she knew he was hiding something. "Let's just say that I have a history with this place, and that's all I'm going to say on the subject, so let's move on. I believe that she is in that building over there."

"Right. So what do we do?" Faith asked.

"Simple," Shadow said. "Ellie, Faith, and Niki, I want you three to head around back and make sure to not let anybody get away if they come running out. Got it?"

"Aye, aye, Captain," Niki said with a wink. Faith and Ellie nodded in agreement. The three of them rushed to their ordered positions.

"Crystal and Ethan, I want you two to stay at my back. If there are any loud noises, like screaming, rush in," Shadow said, looking over the remaining members carefully.

He pointed to Tristan and Isaac. "You guys will wait out front in case a problem occurs; in case somebody runs out of the front doors; in case Ethan, Crystal, and I are swarmed. Ryan, you're coming in with me."

"Wait a minute!" Isaac exclaimed angrily. "This is crap!"

"Isaac, calm down," Ethan said.

"Kay is my friend. I should be there when he confronts her," Isaac said indignantly.

"This isn't a debate," Shadow said coldly. "Either go where I told you or you can wait back on the jet."

Isaac glared at him, and for a split-second it looked as if he were about to argue. Instead, he rolled his eyes and looked at the ground. "Fine. I'll stay here with Tristan."

"Thank you," Shadow replied, and then he, Crystal, Ethan, and Ryan walked up to the front door. He went to turn the handle and found that the door was locked.

"Now what do we do?" Crystal asked.

"You really think a locked door can stop him?" Ryan asked. "Watch. You may learn something."

Shadow placed his hand a few inches away from the door. Slowly but surely, tiny wisps of black smoke were coming out of his open hand, trailing inside the lock. After a few seconds, the smoke stopped, and he placed his hand once again on the door. Turning the knob, the door opened for them.

"You certainly never fail to impress," Ethan said. "Well done."

Shadow nodded and then pushed open the door. He tensed up, swiftly scanning the room for any danger. When he was satisfied, he beckoned to them. "Move forward and stay on guard," he whispered. "Do not make a sound."

"Wait a moment!" Ethan whispered. He brought his hand to his chest, and a sphere of light appeared within it. The sphere sank into the ground, expanding until it surrounded them with a bright light.
Ryan blinked. "Well, isn't that nifty."

"Ethan, you're so handy!" Crystal exclaimed.

"Crystal, are you trying to wake the dead?" Shadow growled as quietly as possible. "Keep your voice down. We don't want to lose the element of surprise."

They walked down a long hallway that ended at a single door; the only door in the entire house, yet it somehow seemed out of place.

"Call me crazy, but I'm thinking that Kay is behind this door," Ryan said.

"All right. I'm going in," Shadow said. He then pointed to Ryan. "You're coming with me. Crystal and Ethan, you two wait out here and keep a lookout."

"Leave it to us, Shadow," Crystal said.

Ethan nodded in agreement. "We'll let you know if anything suspicious occurs."

"Thanks," Shadow said. He took a deep breath and then turned the handle, pushing in.

The light from Ethan 's hand filled the dark room eerily. The further the door opened, the more light entered the room, pushing the darkness away.

Shadow walked inside the room. He quickly searched it, checking to see if the coast was clear. After a few seconds, he seemed satisfied and gave Ryan the signal to follow him inside. Suddenly, his body tensed as he caught a tiny movement in the corner of his eye. He whipped around to face whatever it was, but there was nothing. Nothing appeared to be in the room except for a large pile of cardboard boxes.

"Why would this house have only one room, completely empty, except for boxes?"

"It could be a garbage dump or a recycling building," Ryan muttered. "That, or a trap."

Shadow frowned. "Something about this seems all wrong."

"Wasn't Kay supposed to be here?"

Shadow paused, hearing another noise. "Oh, she's here," he said, and in one swift motion he knocked the mountain of boxes over, revealing Kay.

"Oh. Hey, guys!" Kay said, giving them a weak smile. "How's everything going?"

"Everything's fine, but I can bet your night is about to get a whole lot worse," Shadow replied, gazing down at her in extreme dislike. "Where have you been, Kay?"

Kay flushed bright crimson. She took a while to speak. Her lips occasionally opened and closed as if she was trying to think of what to say. "You know, just around."

Shadow scoffed. "And you have nothing to do with the darkness that swallowed the sun. Is that right?"

Kay blinked. "Nope, I'm as confused as you are. In fact, I decided to go out on my own and do some detective work."

"Right," Ryan said. "Shadow, I don't know about you, but something sure smells like lies."

"I'm not lying. I swear," Kay said, although less convincing this time. "I don't know what happened or why it did."

"So you just happened to disappear after the worst thing that's happened to the world since Friends being cancelled?" Ryan asked. "I don't buy it."

"And Cameryn just happened to catch you talking to a mysterious person?" Shadow asked. "You going to tell me that he was lying? Because I believe his word over yours."

Kay flinched. "I didn't do anything. I promise!" she said, tears forming in her eyes.

"Can the waterworks, Kay," Ryan said, shaking his head. "It's a poor gimmick, and you know it."

"Okay, fine," Kay replied, wiping her tears away. "You got me. I surrender."

"Very funny," Shadow said. "Now, tell us what you know about all of this."

"I don't know anything. And even if I did, what makes you think for a second that I would tell you anything?"

"There are ways of getting you to talk," Shadow said, his voice going cold.

"W-what do you mean?" Kay asked, a touch of fear penetrating her voice.

Shadow smiled darkly. "I mean that I have ways to force somebody to talk, somebody who won't cooperate."

Kay's eyes narrowed. "You wouldn't do anything. You're bluffing."

Shadow didn't respond. He turned his back on both of them, gazing out of the only window of the room. Looking outside, he saw some of his team members, all eagerly awaiting his word to spring into action. It was for them, and for the rest of the people in the world, that he had to get the information that she had. It was for all these reasons that he had to do whatever it took to get said information.

Kay ran for the door.

"Hey!" Ryan shouted. He flicked his hand forward. Air swooped around Kay, twisting itself at her feet like a mini-tornado, causing her to lose balance and fall down.

"Going somewhere?" Shadow asked. Before Kay could answer, his eyes flashed black, and small, shadowy tendrils reached through the ground and wrapped around her waist. "How about you stay a while."

Ryan gave an appreciative whistle.

Kay didn't struggle. She remembered from the last time that it was futile. "You can't do this!" she growled. "You can't hold me here!"

"Oh, but we can," Ryan replied. "You put all of us in danger. We know, even if you won't admit it. So we don't owe you anything, not anymore."

Kay looked offended for a second before laughing. "You're speaking as if I owed you guys something in the first place. I didn't owe any of you jack."

"Owed us something?" Shadow asked incredulously. "I took you in. I gave you a home. I made sure that you were kept safe from anybody who wished to do you harm. I risked my life to protect you again and again, and you betray not only me, but everybody who was like a family to you!"

Kay closed her eyes and shook her head. "I didn't ask you to do any of that. It was your choice. Nobody forced you. You're the idiot who trusts total strangers."

Shadow took a deep breath, his eyes shifting to swirling black pools. "I'm only going to ask you this one last time. Tell me what you know, or else."

Kay shook her head. "I already told you what I know, which is nothing. You're wasting your time."

Shadow sighed. "Fine, have it your way. I'm not leaving until I find out what I need to know. And if you won't tell me willingly, I'll have to resort to much less conventional means to obtain it."

Kay squirmed in the tendrils that bound her to the ground. "Let me go, now!"

Shadow ignored her cries and walked closer to her. Darkness began pouring from his eyes and mouth, his face hidden behind a wall of the thick, coarse smog that was flowing out of him. When he was in touching distance of her, he bent over, allowing the shadows to fall onto her body. She screamed, but it was muffled by the blanket of darkness that was now covering her. After a few seconds, he pulled away and, with him, the darkness receded.

"Just stop it," Kay whispered, her voice hoarse and her face pale. "Please."

Shadow's eyes and face returned to normal. "Just tell me what I need to know and I'll stop," he said. "Don't mistake me for a cruel person, Kay. I'm not. The only thing that matters to me right now is the safety of those kids. You've compromised that safety, and I need to know how much so."

Kay gave a bitter laugh, the color returning to her face. "Are you sure that you care so much about their safety?"

Shadow frowned. "I try my best to protect those who put their faith in me. Can you say the same? No, you can't. You make me sick."

"How dare you look down on me like you're something special, something spectacular!" Kay exclaimed angrily.

"I may not be anything special, Kay, but I'm certainly worth a damn, more than you are. You're nothing but a traitor. "

Kay's face turned bright red. "Oh, yeah? Well, at least I'm not the one who left his most fragile teammate alone and vulnerable."

Shadow's eyes widened. "W-w-what?!"

"Don't act so surprised. I mean, after all, you would think that the great Shadow would know not to leave one of his own by himself at a time like this."

"Cameryn," Shadow thought, frowning. He knew that she was right. He had no business leaving Cameryn alone, especially now, with what was going on. "Kay, what did you do to Cameryn?"

Kay smirked. "Maedara knew that you would come here searching for me. In fact, she counted on it."

"S-s-she knew I would come for you?!"

"Yes. There isn't much that she doesn't know. In fact, you might say that she knows what you'll do before you even think of doing it."

Shadow was dumbfounded. "Have I really been playing into Maedara's hands all along? Did I really allow myself to play the fool so that her own plans can be furthered?"

"Now, I believe you asked me a question about Cameryn, right?" Kay asked.

"Yes," Shadow said, struggling to contain his anger. "Is he okay?"

Kay looked thoughtful. "If I'm right, which I know I am," she said, pausing to smile, "as we speak, some of Maedara's most powerful demons are on their way now to your castle."

Shadow felt as if he were falling through the ground. His heart practically stopped as he thought of the dangers that Cameryn could be facing at that very moment. "How much time do I have?" he asked.

Kay checked her cell phone. "They should be there in ten minutes."

"You know, there's a special place for people like you, somewhere nice and toasty," Ryan said.

Kay laughed. "Maybe, but I won't have to go there for a very, very long time. After all, I'm still young and I've got my health."

"Well, maybe you'll be going sooner than you think," Shadow replied.

Kay rolled her eyes. She turned to face the door as she heard footsteps approaching. She smiled as Ellie walked into the room.

"Shadow, what's —" Ellie began, but her eyes fell on Kay. She clenched her fists and took two steps forward. "You!"

"Me?" Kay asked mockingly.

"Ellie," Shadow said, putting his hand on her arm. "Our suspicions were true. Kay is working for the other team. We have to leave and head back immediately."

Ellie studied his face for a few seconds. "What's happened?"

Shadow looked at the floor. "Ellie, Cameryn is in danger. Maedara has her men on their way to the castle at this very moment."

"How did she know? There's just no way," Ellie said. "You've done your best to hide it."

Shadow shook his head. He glanced quickly at Kay and then back at Ellie. "It's not important. What's important is —"

"Kay," Ellie said emptily, noticing Shadow's eye movement.

"Ellie, no. Wait," Shadow said.

"You stupid bitch!" Ellie screamed, darting across the room. She closed the gap between her and Kay in seconds and slapped her across the face.

Kay raised her hand and placed it on her face. "Nice to see you again too, Ellie. So glad that you missed me."

Ellie backhanded Kay, slapping her on the other cheek. "How dare you? We trusted you. We treated you like a friend."

Kay sneered. "You shouldn't waste your time roughing me up. Don't you have a team member to save?"

"I'm gonna —" Ellie growled, taking another step forward.

Shadow dashed next to Ellie and put a hand on her shoulder. "Ellie, no. Now isn't the time for this," he said softly. "You getting revenge on Kay isn't doing anything except wasting time that we could be using to save Cameryn."

"But Shadow. . ."

"Don't let anger cloud your judgment. Violence against Kay will gain us nothing," Shadow said, whipping her around to face him. "Kay, you'd better hope we don't ever see you again." He pulled Ellie out of the room.

Ryan went for the door and paused, looking back at Kay. "This isn't over, Kay; far from it. I promise. Know that when I finally do catch up to you, I intend to pay you back fully for all the suffering you've caused us all."

"Oh, I'm shaking," Kay replied, rolling her eyes.

"You should be," Ryan said. "I'm not like Shadow. Next time we meet, I won't hesitate, and you can count on that."

He ran out of the room, sprinting after Shadow and Ellie. As he reached the jet, everybody was already on it, waiting for him. As soon as he got inside, he closed the door behind him, and immediately he felt the takeoff. "Sorry I'm a bit behind. I had to say my goodbyes."

"Any trouble?" Shadow asked, looking slightly concerned.

"Nothing at all. Not yet, anyway."

"Do you think Cameryn is all right?" Ellie asked.

"I hope so, Ellie," Shadow said, glancing at his communicator. "I don't know for sure. He didn't answer his cell when I called for him."

"Don't sweat it. I'm sure the kid's fine," Ryan said bracingly. "He's strong. He's been through way too much to give up now, you'll see."

"Yeah, you're probably right," Ellie said.

"I know I am," Ryan replied, sticking his tongue out.

The jet lurched forward much faster than it had ever gone before. The people inside felt incredible turbulence as it hurdled quickly to its destination.

"Uh, Shadow?" Faith asked. "Who's piloting the jet?"

Shadow blinked. "I could have sworn Ethan was."

Ethan leaned over Crystal from his window seat. "I am not. Niki is."

"Ethan," Shadow said slowly, "are you sure that it was a good idea to allow Niki to pilot?"

Ethan nodded. "She assured me that she was more than capable of flying. I generally give everyone a chance to prove themselves."

"I see," Faith said, rolling her eyes. "Well, I suppose you will have no problem with the knowledge that she's never flown a jet in her life?"

Ethan looked taken aback for a second. "Are you absolutely sure, Faith?" he asked, and she nodded. "Well, you did try to talk her out of it, right?"

"That's right," Faith said, tilting her head to the side. "Obviously, it didn't work, though."

Shadow blinked. "What did she say?"

"Well, she told me that she had things totally under control and to not worry because she could handle it. She then went into some weird story about muffins and how hobos are people too," she said, biting her lip. "And then she told me not to judge her. I kind of just walked away after that. Sorry."

"Right," Shadow said, trailing off slightly. But at that moment, the fact that Niki was acting as pilot was the least of his worries. Even if she crashed it into the side of his castle, it wouldn't hold a candle to the amount of tension surging through his blood at the moment. His mind was on nothing else but Cameryn. "Hang in there, kid. We're almost there."

Michael Chulsky

CHAPTER 9: DREAMING WHILE AWAKE

"Are we almost there?" Shadow asked. He had tried the door, but it wouldn't open, so he was forced to talk through the cockpit door screen. "Also, why is the door locked?"

"We are close, yes," Niki replied. "And the door is locked because I can't have distractions. Being a pilot is a very difficult job, especially if you have no training."

Shadow rolled his eyes. "All right, but please hurry. Cameryn's in danger. We can't waste any time."

"Don't worry, Captain. It's all whip."

"Whip?" Shadow asked.

Niki scoffed. "Yeah. Whip, as in cool."

"Whatever you say, Niki. Whatever you say," he muttered, walking back to his seat. He was well beyond worry, bordering on insanity. He couldn't think of anything but what was going on at home and what was happening to Cameryn.

"Are you okay?" Faith asked, sitting down next to him.

Shadow jumped slightly in his seat. "What? Oh, it's you, Faith," he muttered. "Yeah, I'm okay. Why do you ask?"

"It's okay, Shadow. You don't have to pretend. We all know you're worried about Cameryn, and for good reason. But you need to have…" She paused and smiled. "You need to have faith, especially in him."

Ethan walked over and stood by them. "I know it's hard. Believe me, I do. But even when surrounded by darkness, the light will never abandon you."

Shadow rolled his eyes. "Easy for you to say, Ethan. You're literally an Ethan. You have never been human. You don't know what it's like to have faith and be let down; to hope and dream for something for so long and never have it come true. How could you possibly understand?"

"I understand perfectly, Shadow," Ethan replied. "You may not think that I'm a human, but I am closer to it than my brethren... much like yourself. I was born into this body. I've lived nineteen years on Earth as a human, and I've reached incredible understanding. I know how it feels to wish, dream, hope, and want. I've seen people lose faith and then, by great miracle, have it restored, stronger than ever. Trust me, I know."

Shadow opened his mouth, closed it, and then nodded. "Ethan, you're right. I didn't mean to get angry with you. It's not your fault that any of this is happening. I'm sorry for taking it out on you."

"I know, and I forgive you," Ethan said, placing his hand on Shadow's shoulder. "Even the best of us can lose our temper when faced with a loved one being in danger. Just try to stay rational. It will help out more in the long run."

"Like I said, none of us hold it against you," Faith said. "We know how much you care about him. But you have to believe me when I say that all of us are worried too. We don't want anything to happen to him."

"They're right, you know," Ellie said. She had returned during Ethan 's speech but decided to remain silent until then. "Everything you're feeling is natural. You just don't know that because you've never felt it before. You've never had anybody to care about, have you?"

Shadow looked fixedly at the ground. "No, I haven't. I've spent my entire life isolating myself from other people, and then this crazy shaman told me that I had to find you guys and protect you and let you all live with me. She stressed how important it was that we all form a strong bond so that nothing could tear us apart."

"And we have," Faith said, casting a fleeting glance at Ethan. "You've done a wonderful thing, Shadow, bringing us all together. You'll never know exactly how grateful we all are, how much joy you've brought all of us - not just because of how happy we are to be safe, but because of the friendships we've made."

"How could you say that?" Shadow replied, hostility returning to his eyes. "If it wasn't for me, you guys would be safe. I've done the most horrible thing ever by bringing you all together. If it wasn't for me, then Kay wouldn't have been able to betray you. Do you have any idea how much restraint it took to not rip her limb from limb back there? How much I had to fight not to—"

"You saw Kay?" Isaac shouted, jumping out of his seat. He bumped into Ethan and stood right in front of Shadow. "Why didn't you tell me?"

"There was nothing to tell. I saw her, we talked, and that was it."

"That couldn't have just been it. There's more to the story," Isaac demanded. "Tell me. I deserve to know."

"Isaac, please calm down," Ellie said. "Getting angry won't help the situation. It will only make it worse. So take it down a notch."

"Nobody asked for your opinion, Ellie," Isaac spat. "So sit down and shut up."

"Isaac!" Faith gasped, placing her hands over her mouth as Ellie's eyes widened.

"Isaac, apologize now," Shadow said, his voice low.

"Not until you tell me what happened with Kay."

"No, Shadow," Ellie said stiffly. "If he doesn't want to apologize, then I don't want to hear it."

"Isaac, I saw her, and she informed me of what she did," Shadow said. "She admitted to everything: stealing and betraying us. I'm sorry. That's all I can say. Ask Ryan, if you don't believe me."

Isaac turned and looked at Ryan. "Well?"

"Well, what?" Ryan asked, raising an eyebrow. "Shadow told you everything. You would think that his word alone would be good enough."

"Well, it wasn't."

Shadow sighed. "If my word means nothing to you, then why are you wasting time asking me about what happened?"

"Because you know more. You're lying, and I know it."

"Isaac, you're being selfish," Ryan said. "There are more important things to worry about than your bruised pride."

"Ryan's right, Isaac," Tereya said softly. "I know it's not my business, but you're being insensitive. Cameryn is in danger. Don't you care?"

"I do care about him, but you're right. It isn't your business."

Tereya flushed. "Like I said, I know it's not my business, but it needs to be said. You're being incredibly immature right now. We're supposed to be friends, and friends tell one another when they're wrong. You're wrong right now."

Shadow smiled in appreciation. It was nice that even though Tereya was the most shy and mild-mannered kid of the entire group, he spoke out. "Thanks, Tereya, for speaking out. I appreciate it. Can you please go to the front and ask Niki how soon until we'll be there?" he asked.

He watched Tereya nod and walk away and then turned back to address Isaac. "I can't add any more onto what they said, because they're spot-on. I'm too worried about Cameryn to have another Kay debate with you. Save it for later."

Isaac growled in frustration. "No, I'm not just going to drop it. I refuse to. I know Cameryn is in danger and he could be hurt. I'm sorry about that. But Kay means more to me than he does, so I'm not putting my feelings in the back seat for him, not for anybody."

"Well, then I guess I have no choice," Ethan said softly.

"What are you going to do?" Isaac asked, taking a step away from him.

"Yeah, Ethan, what are you going to do?" Shadow echoed. "As much of a jerk as he's being, you can't hurt him."

Ethan shook his head. "Don't worry. I have no intention of doing anything that will hurt him."

"Stay away from me!" Isaac yelled, moving further back.

Ethan flew forward, gliding along the floor. One second he was standing a few feet away; the next, he was directly in front of Isaac. "Sleep," he whispered. And then Isaac fell forward into his open arms.

Shadow's eyes opened wider in half-amazement, half-wonder. "Ethan, what did you just do?"

Ethan smiled and placed Isaac down into a seat. "It's another small ability of mine. You've already seen my power to calm others down? Well, I can take it a step beyond that. In certain cases I can actually will a person to let go of all tension and drift off to sleep. It's a shame I had to resort to such methods to calm Isaac down, but I felt it would ease the burden off of you a bit."

"Yeah, he used to do that to me until I threatened him," Crystal said matter-of-factly.

Shadow smiled. "Well, it definitely helped. I appreciate it."

"You're most welcome," Ethan replied. "However, be aware that you're going to have to deal with Isaac and his Kay issues at some point. What I did for you was only to give you some breathing room to think more clearly about what you're going to do when it comes time to cross that bridge. I only pushed that time slightly farther away, but it will come soon."

"You know, I liked it better when he was the strong, silent type," Ryan remarked, a smile spreading across his face. "After all, strong and silent Ethan is much less scary than knock-you-out-with- a-touch Ethan."

"It's not scary so much as it's practical," Faith said. "After all, imagine how useful that ability would be if I could control my brother with it."

"Speaking of Tristan, why has he been so quiet?" Shadow asked. "I've just been wondering why I haven't had a headache today."

"He's out like a light; you know, catching some shut-eye," Ryan said.

"I had nothing to do with it," Ethan said before Shadow could even look at him. "Faith has begged me multiple times, trust me, but I haven't. I only use my abilities for good reason."

"Dude, it's Tristan," Crystal said, shaking her head. "His mouth is the only reason you need."

"That's beside the point," Ethan said, shaking his head.

"Shadow, Niki said we'll be there in ten minutes," Tereya announced.

"Thank you. Now, hurry and sit back down," Shadow replied. "It's Niki we're talking about. Chances are, landing is going to be bumpy."

CB&CB&CB&CB&

The jet landed roughly into the flight bay and everyone rushed out.

"I told you I could land it," Niki said, bringing up the rear. "I call shotgun next time. Being a pilot is a stressful endeavor."

"Niki, you almost crashed into the side of the castle," Ryan said incredulously.

"Almost doesn't count - except in horseshoes," Niki said.

"Yeah, and in near-death experiences," Ryan replied.

Niki smiled and waved her finger at him. "Key word being 'near' death."

"If it's all the same to you, Niki, Ethan will pilot it next time. Besides, now isn't the time to discuss your piloting skills or lack thereof," Shadow said, frowning.

"It's quiet," Ellie said softly. Her hands were out in front of her, ready to fire at any given moment. "Almost eerily so."

"Yes. Quite ominous, considering the fact that this place is apparently supposed to be swarming with demons," Ethan said softly.

"Are you sure that Kay wasn't just making up lies so that she could get away?" Faith asked.

"Yeah, I'm sure," Shadow replied. "Stay on guard, guys. I don't trust this at all."

They walked through the hallway leading to the living room, taking great care to not make a sound. Before they reached the doorway, they heard a loud crash and then the sound of fabric tearing.

"What was that?" Tereya cried. He turned and looked around for the source.

"It's our friends," Shadow replied, unsheathing his sword. "I believe they're waiting to give us a Welcome Home party."

"A party?" Crystal exclaimed. "I love parties."

Ethan sighed. "Crystal, it's not that kind of party." He took a deep breath and then let it out slowly. Power flared within him and he let it out, pushing it forward into the living room. "There are definitely demons in there. Unfortunately, I cannot sense Cameryn."

Shadow frowned. "If it's ugly and moves, kill it. And I swear, if Cameryn's hurt, their deaths will be something for all demons to write home about."

"Well, there's no point in just standing around here," Ryan said. "Let's go kick some demonic ass."

Shadow motioned to the others to follow him and Ryan forward. As they reached the living room, they saw the demons. They were Dominyv, similar to the kind that Shadow had encountered when he first met Kay and Isaac. They were tearing up the place; ripping apart couch cushions and smashing furniture.

Tristan let out a cry of anger as a large object flew across the living room and shattered on the wall. "Please don't tell me that was the TV," he growled, his eyes filling with fire.

"It was the TV," Ryan said, shaking his head.

"I told you not to tell me."

"Sorry, couldn't resist," Ryan replied stiffly.

"Why are we just standing around and not kicking their demonic faces in?" Niki asked.

"Niki's right," Ellie said, turning to face Shadow. "So can we commence with the butt-kicking?"

"Don't let me stand in your way," Shadow said. "Just remember to be careful. Watch out for each other and–"

"Forgive me, Shadow, for interrupting what I'm sure was a very compelling speech, but we've been spotted," Ethan said, gesturing to the demons.

The demons had stopped their destruction of the house to look at them. Since they were alive, they were a much more compelling target than the house.

"Go, now!" Shadow shouted, and the rest of them dashed in different directions, each picking out a target. He broke through the battlefield that was once his living room. Explosions and chaos littered the room. He didn't join the fight, because they had it covered. They weren't the ones currently in trouble. Cameryn was.

Dodging a flying ball of fire, Shadow left the living room and made his way to Cameryn's room. As he approached his destination, he could hear voices.

"Don't be stupid, Cameryn," a female voice said. "You know that I'm right." A pause and then a gasp of pain. "Do you really want to make me upset?"

"I-I. . ." Cameryn muttered, his voice strained.

"Do you really want me to continue?" the woman asked. "I have all day and multiple methods of torture, all of which are fun for me... less for you. Perhaps, if you're lucky, you'll live through a few of them."

Shadow had heard enough. He kicked the door open.

Cameryn was kneeling on the floor. Sweat covered his neck and forehead, and there two long scratches across his left cheek. He smiled upon seeing Shadow, relief spreading across his face.

Shadow returned the smile and then turned to face the woman. She was wearing a bright neon-pink dress and had long bubble-gum-pink nails. "Who are you?"

"You don't know who I am?" she replied, opening her mouth in shock. "Well, aren't you just a sad little rude person. Anybody who's anybody knows my name. But I'll humor you. Allow me to introduce myself: Maedara, at your service, though you may refer to me as Her Royal Lady Maedara."

Shadow's mouth went dry, and his eyes opened wide.

"You're... Maedara."

"Ah, so you have heard of me?" she asked, smiling. "It's good to see that years of hard work and dedication pay off."

"You could say that," Shadow said, recovering from the shock. "I'm surprised I didn't put two and two together when I first saw you, but it caught me off guard. Kay told me that your minions would be here, but she didn't tell me that you'd be joining them."

Maedara ran her hands through her hair. "Ah, yes, Kay," she said thoughtfully. "Useful little girl, she is, even though she looks like she dresses in the dark. She told me a lot about all of you, the pests who keep trying - and failing, I might add - to ruin my plans. Do you know how rude you are,

Shadow? How much work I put into those plans only to have them ruined by you?"

"You're breaking my heart," Shadow replied.

"You're funny," Maedara giggled. "Know what else will be funny?" She took a step towards Cameryn, stepping on his hand. "This one bleeding to death."

"Shadow!" Cameryn cried.

"That's enough, Maedara," Shadow said, a bitter coldness taking over.

"I'll tell you when it's enough," she replied softly, the echo of a dark smile lingering on her face. "I'm not quite done."

Shadow took a step forward and held out his hand. An invisible force pushed Maedara a few inches back, off of Cameryn's hand. "I think you are."

"You're going to regret interrupting me like this," Maedara said, flicking her hair. "Do you have any idea how much I want to just knock you silly for wearing all black? It's so hideously out of style. What do you call it? Funeral chic?"

"Shadow, she told me all these horrible things," Cameryn said. "She kept telling me that you wouldn't come, that you didn't care enough to save me. But I knew she was wrong. I didn't stop believing."

"I'll always be there for you, Cameryn. You know that," Shadow replied. "Nothing or nobody can ever change that, I promise."

"Oh, please," Maedara said, giggling loudly. "You really should tape yourself. You'd be perfect to run a self-help seminar. That way, people from all over the world could listen and take solace in the fact that they aren't as pathetic as you."

Shadow frowned. He carefully maneuvered around the room, taking great care not to go within touching distance of her. He pulled Cameryn up off of the ground, moved the boy behind him, and drew his sword. "If I were you, Maedara, I'd leave now."

"Honey, if you were me, you'd be sexy and fashionable," Maedara replied. "It's going to be such a shame when you're gone. All those kids alone in this big, bad world without somebody to defend them. Oh, how tragic."

She took a step forward. "You know, it would be less annoying for me if you would just stab yourself. In fact, I encourage it."

Shadow tensed his sword hand, prepared to fight. Before either of them could begin, a loud beeping sound pierced the intense silence.

"Oh, crap," Maedara said, reaching into her pocket and pulling out a cell phone. "I cannot believe the timing. This little engagement has held me up way past what I thought it would, and I'm late for another appointment."

"Appointment?" Shadow asked. "What other trouble is she going to cause?"

Maedara flashed him an annoyed look and put her cell phone away. "Not that it's any of your business, but I am actually late for this gigantic sale at my favorite store. Everything is thirty-five percent off."

Shadow rolled his eyes. "Right. Wouldn't want to miss that."

"I'd love to stay and continue our little chat, but duty calls," she said, throwing her hands up.

"Yeah, totally," Shadow said. "Just make sure you don't come back, or I'll kill you. I swear."

"You, kill me?" Maedara asked mockingly. "I highly doubt it," she said, flicking her hair. "But then again, keep dreaming. I'm not one to squash the dreams of others. Everyone needs something to live - or in your case, die - for."

Shadow growled. "I promise you, if you come near any of these kids again, I will find a way to kill you. If I have to search the entire planet, I will find a way."

"Oh, Shadow, don't fret. Do you want to get worry lines? You'll be seeing me sooner than you think. And trust me, our date will be a killer," Maedara said. She threw her head back and laughed as she faded away.

"Is she gone?" Cameryn asked. "Like, really gone?"

"Yeah," Shadow muttered, looking around the room. He sheathed his sword and turned to face Cameryn.

"I'm lucky you came when you did. She's really horrible. You have no idea, Shadow."

"I do. Believe me, I do," Shadow replied, and his face softened. Looking down, he smiled, relieved that Cameryn was all right. "But don't worry about her. She's gone, and you're fine. That's the only thing that matters, right?"

"I guess you're right," Cameryn said, smiling brightly. "Where are the others?"

"They're fighting the demons."

"Well, let's go help them!"

Shadow nodded. They both left the room and headed back down the hallway that led into the living room. Once they reached the living room, they saw that it was more in shambles than before. "Everyone okay?" he asked.

"Yeah, except for the fact that we had some ugly demons attacking us," Ryan replied, rolling his eyes. "But besides that? We're all just peachy!"

Ellie shook her head at Ryan in disapproval. "Ignore him. We're all fine, just a little bit exhausted. I actually got through without a scratch, but Tristan, Crystal, and Tereya got banged up a bit."

"Are you sure they're all right?" Shadow asked worriedly.

Ethan and Faith walked into the room. They both looked extremely exhausted, sweat dripping down their faces, dust covering their clothes.

"Ethan? Faith?" Shadow asked.

Ethan nodded, knowing exactly why Shadow was addressing him. "Yes, they're all right."

Shadow looked at Faith for confirmation. Faith smiled half-heartedly. "Yes. I can attest to the fact that they're all right. I just spent the past couple of minutes healing them and draining myself to physical exhaustion."

Shadow gave a sigh of relief. "Thank goodness they're all right. I would have never forgiven myself if anything had happened to any one of them."

"What happened?" Ellie asked. "You disappeared when the fighting started and—"

"Not that we're annoyed or anything," Ryan interrupted. "It was a welcome change from you not letting us fight at all. I mean, it's obvious you went to go check on Cameryn, but what happened when you found him?"

"Oh. About that. I —" Shadow began, but he was cut off by somebody clearing their throat from behind him.

"No, it's all right. I'll tell them what happened," Cameryn said. "If it's okay?"

Shadow nodded in approval. "Go ahead."

"Before you guys returned, the demons came. I was fighting one, but then more came, so I had to hide in my room. Then, all of a sudden, she appeared."

"She?" Ryan asked, confused.

"Maedara," Shadow said, and that one word caused everyone in the room to freeze.

"She's not here anymore," Cameryn said quickly, and a wave of relief broke out through the entire room. "Shadow made sure she was gone before we came to check on everyone else. He was amazing. She backed off quickly."

Shadow coughed. "It wasn't like that."

"So why did she appear in your room, Cameryn?" Ethan asked.

"She was trying to get me to join her side. She said that my powers of destruction would make a wonderful addition to her team and that I belonged to her."

"You. . .belonged to her?" Shadow asked. "What did she mean by that?"

"Shadow, it obviously means nothing," Ryan said. "I mean, are we seriously going to take advice from the woman who blocked out the sun?"

"No. It's more than that," Cameryn said quietly. He turned his back to them.

Ellie walked over and patted him on the shoulder. "Cameryn, whatever's wrong, you can tell us. You know that. We're your friends now, your family. We won't turn our backs on you, no matter what happens."

Cameryn turned around and searched Ellie's face. "Maedara told me why everything happened to me in my home village. I was born as a weapon for her to use," he said. Tears glistened in his eyes. "I was raised, put through hell, and abused. . .all for her, all for Maedara. I hate her so much. Shadow, we have to stop her."

Ellie pulled Cameryn close to her and hugged him tightly. "It's all right. It's all okay," she whispered.

Shadow blushed slightly, not knowing what to do or how to help the situation get better. He pulled both of them into a hug and rubbed Cameryn's back consolingly, and that small gesture was the best that he could do to show how much he cared.

Taking this as a sign that they should leave, the others slowly slipped out of the room, muttering something about going to bed. It was, after all, late at night.

After a few minutes of crying, Cameryn lifted his face from Ellie's shoulder, looked up at Shadow, and then sighed. "They all probably think I'm weak, and you two probably think I'm stupid."

Shadow shook his head. "On the contrary, Cameryn. I actually believe that since you cried in front of us all, it proves how strong you truly are."

"You mean that?" Cameryn asked

Ellie smiled warmly. "Of course, he means it, silly. I said it before and I'll say it again. We're all your friends. We won't ever judge or turn on you for anything, especially something that stupid."

Cameryn smiled in spite of himself. "You're right. I'm just being stupid, aren't I?"

"Yup," Shadow replied, "pretty stupid."

"Shadow!" Ellie laughed, slapping him hard on his arm.

Cameryn broke the merriment with a loud yawn.

"I guess somebody's tired," Shadow said, punching him lightly on the shoulder.

Cameryn nodded, answering with another yawn. "It's not my fault. It's kinda late." he replied defensively.

"It's okay. It doesn't make you a baby if you're tired. It makes you human," Shadow said, and there was a hint of a joke in his voice.

"I think Cameryn has the right idea. I could use some sleep also," Ellie said, ignoring Shadow's slight attempt at dark humor. "What do you think, Shadow?"

Shadow shrugged. "I could actually sleep. Strangely enough, I am quite tired, which is rare for me. I don't actually require sleep, but I feel almost compelled."

"Well, why ignore your compulsions?" Ellie asked. "I say we all go to bed so we can prepare for what's to come. We'll be no use to anybody with any energy."

"Perhaps you're right, Ellie," Shadow said, and he yawned.

"No, I know I'm right," Ellie replied, sticking out her tongue.

Hiding a smile, Shadow rolled his eyes. He walked Cameryn to his room and said good night. He walked back into the living room and saw Ellie still standing there. "Ellie?" he asked. "What are you still doing here? I thought you were heading to bed."

Ellie shrugged. "I was, but I was waiting for you."

"Waiting for me?"

"Yeah," she said. "I wanted to say good night."

He raised an eyebrow. "Just to say good night?"

"Yeah. Good night!" she said, waving to him.

"Oh. Good night, then," he said, walking past her and heading to his room.

"She was acting different than usual, quite unlike herself. It felt sort of like she wanted to tell me something. Why didn't she?" he wondered. He entered his room and closed the door behind him, taking great care to lock it. He unlatched the necklace that he always wore and put it inside the wooden jewelry box that sat on his dresser.

Yawning, Shadow took off his shirt and vest, laying them both on the nightstand, and then fell down with a plop onto his bed. The events of the day buzzed, swarming around inside his head like a colony of angry bees. He wanted so much to know the answer to all of his questions: how to bring back the sun, how to stop Maedara, how to find Maedara, how to make sure his entire team survived the great battle, how to figure out what was wrong with Ellie, and how to find his father.

None of these answers appeared to him. The only relief he obtained was the pure bliss of the blackness that consumed all of the thoughts and worries, the one thing that made all of the questions in his head fall silent: the sweet release of sleep.

⊂ℨ⊱⊂ℨ⊱⊂ℨ⊱⊂ℨ⊱

Shadow was in some mysterious place. This place was different from any other that he had ever seen. It seemed to go on for miles, nothing but white in every direction. The floor had a white smoke rising off of it. Curiosity got the best of him and he bent over to touch the ground, but his fingers didn't meet anything solid. *"Where am I?"* he wondered.

"To find out what your heart doth hide, you must, in yourself, look deep inside," a voice called out in a singsong voice.

The first rise of anger reared itself in Shadow. He was starting to get annoyed by the combination of the voice and the mysteriousness of his situation. "Enough with the games. Come out and face me!"

A swirling white ball appeared in the middle of the room. "Child, you need to learn some patience." The voice seemed to be coming from the white ball.

As Shadow walked towards it, the orb expanded and a woman appeared. She had long waves of hair so dark brown that it would have been mistaken as black from a distance. Her eyes were a bright gold, two shades lighter than the golden robe she wore. Her skin was a light caramel color.

"Greetings, child. Allow me to provide an introduction for myself," the woman said. "I am Alvita."

"Alvita?" Shadow asked, confused.

"Yes, that's who I am."

"Well, who is that?"

Alvita searched his face for a few seconds, then nodded curtly. "I am Alvita, Goddess of Dreams. I have traveled a great distance to meet with you here in your mind."

"In. . .my. . .mind?" Shadow repeated.

"So I'm not crazy. I really am still safe in the castle, in my bed. I'm just dreaming," he thought, and let out a sigh of relief. As long as everything was still normal, then this was the least of his worries.

"Don't worry, child. You still are fast asleep in your bed," Alvita said. "Nothing to worry about at all."

"So why did you come here?"

"I am here to teach you a lesson, something important that you all can take with you into the battle that is coming up."

Shadow didn't even try to hide the surprise on his face. "What did you come to teach me?"

"I would have thought that, for the good of your team, you would accept any and all help to deal with what's to come. I mean, after all, you do wish to protect them, don't you?"

Shadow rolled his eyes. "No, of course not. I want them all to die."

"Be serious, child. Now is not the time for joking. If you don't stay on your guard, you will lead all of them to death. Is that what you want?"

"No!"

"Then what do you have to do?"

Shadow frowned. "I must win."

"Exactly."

"So this whole thing was—"

"This whole thing, child, was for you to see that losing is not an option. Winning is the only option that is available to you, for the sake of every single life that has been entrusted to you. Those kids count on you for so much, and you must see to it that they keep their lives. The fate of the entire world rests in your hands, Shadow. I hope you understand what a great honor and burden it is and why you cannot go into battle thinking that failing is a possibility."

"I understand," Shadow replied. "I refuse to fail them all. My team and all of the innocent people in the world are counting on me. I can't let them down."

"I must go now," Alvita said suddenly, then slowly floated away from him. "There is much that I have to do tonight, more people that I must visit. I do hope that you've learned something from this encounter."

"Wait. . ."

"What is it?"

"Do we win?"

Alvita looked thoughtful. "I am not a psychic. However, I can say that the stars will be on your side in the confrontation. Destiny is yours to hold." She gave him a comforting smile. "Now I must be off."

Shadow nodded, watching as she faded away. He definitely had learned something important, and it had made all the difference in the world to him. There wasn't a doubt in his mind now. They were going to win.

Michael Chulsky

CHAPTER 10: ALL HAIL THE QUEEN

The next morning, Shadow woke up. After the events that had taken place within his dreams, it was surprising that he was able to get any rest at all. He looked over to the digital clock on his nightstand. 10:35 a.m.

"Was it just a dream, or was it real?" he wondered, rubbing his eyes. He glanced out the window; he found that the sky was still the same blackened color, devoid of all light. Normally, when he looked out of his window, he could see the sun in the distance, its harmful rays held at bay by the special windows.

"I will make sure to bring the warmth back, even if it means I can't go outside like a normal person, and even if it sacrifices my own happiness."

He left the room and walked down the hallway, entering the living room. Looking around, he saw Cameryn and Tereya sitting on the floor, chatting away. "Hey, guys," he said.

"Hey, Shadow," Tereya said.

"What's up?" Cameryn asked.

"Not much. Do you guys know if the others are awake?"

"Most of them are on the roof, training. Tereya and I saw them heading up as we were leaving," Cameryn replied.

"Why do you need them?" Tereya asked. "Is it something important?"

Shadow forced himself to keep a calm demeanor. He didn't want to make too much of the situation by showing tension, although he didn't want to make light of it either. "I need everybody ready. We are facing something tonight, something powerful and dangerous. Probably the most dangerous thing any of us will ever be up against in our entire lives."

"You don't mean—" Tereya began.

"Maedara," Cameryn finished, eyes going wide.

"Calm down, you two," Shadow said quickly, attempting to mollify the situation. He didn't want them to be stressed out because it would throw them off their game. For his plan to work, everyone needed to be at their best if they could hope to stay alive.

"If what I'm thinking is correct," Tereya said, pausing and licking his lips, "then we're going after Maedara tonight. Is that true, Shadow?"

Shadow nodded. "Yeah, Tereya, you're right. We have no choice. Kay told Maedara everything, so she can attack us at any given moment. I'd rather surprise her with an attack than have her surprise us. Last night was the final wake-up call, when she was in Cameryn's room, hurting him. I need everybody ready."

"I'm glad to be a wake-up call," Cameryn replied. "But don't worry. You can count on me. I want to pay her back for all she's done to me."

"Me, too!" Tereya added.

Shadow nodded. "Head to the flight bay. When I locate the others, we'll all meet you there."

He watched as the two of them left, and felt a surge of pride that his two most unstable team members had grown so strong. Smiling, he walked into the side corridor which led to the hidden elevator. He laughed in spite of himself that he hadn't known about its existence before Faith. Taking it was a more convenient way of reaching the roof than walking up several flights of stairs, and teleporting used too much energy. Pushing the button to close the door, he let out a loud yawn as the elevator doors closed.

The elevator dinged and the doors opened. Stepping out, he was greeted by his teammates. They appeared to have stopped in mid-training to see who was coming out. The tension in the air was almost tangible. "Hey, guys?" he asked. "What's with the staring?"

"It's nothing," Ellie said. "Everyone's just on edge because we've been training hard all morning."

"Are you sure that's all it is?" Shadow asked.

"Seriously, man. It's nothing at all, really," Ryan said. "We just wanted to be careful, you know? What with the sky being all black and whatnot, you never know who could come creeping up behind you when you least expect it. Right? I mean, it is what you taught us. Right? To be careful and to always watch each other's backs. Right?"

Shadow blinked, obviously puzzled. "Umm, Ryan?"

"Yeah?"

"I don't think I've heard you say 'right' as much as you just did in the entire two years that I've known you. What's going on?"

Ryan shook his head. "I'm not sure what you mean. I'm fine."

Shadow rolled his eyes. He didn't have time for Ryan's crazy antics. "Would anybody care to tell me what all of this is about?"

Ethan sighed and walked forward. "Shadow, I'll tell you what's wrong."

"Please do," Shadow replied, his voice holding the slightest bit of impatience. "If there is anything wrong, I need to know."

"It's nothing wrong, per se, but there is something you should know. Last night, all of us were visited by a being."

Shadow's eyes widened. *"No, it couldn't be. . .could it?"* he wondered. *"Is it possible that they were visited by the same person that came to me in my dream?"*

"Shadow?" Ethan asked. "Are you all right?"

"I'm sorry. I was just thinking about something."

Ethan nodded. "Just checking. You went unresponsive for a second. Are your thoughts something you'd care to share with all of us?"

"Well," Shadow began, taking a deep breath, "this person that visited you all. it wouldn't happen to be a 'she,' would it?"

"She called herself Alvita," Ethan replied.

Shadow gasped. He couldn't believe his ears. The same thing that happened to him really had happened to them also. "I guess I can't be too surprised. She did say she had others to visit, didn't she? But still, I didn't think that she meant other people in the castle. I thought she meant others in the world."

"She definitely met with all of us," Faith said. "I liked her. She was nice."

"I think it was friggin' weird," Crystal said. "She was all strange, and she kept calling me 'child,' like I was a little kid. I am NOT a little kid. Can you believe that?!"

"What did she say to you, Ethan ?" Shadow asked.

"She told me that I would have to make a decision soon, a very distressing one. She would not specify."

"Did she say anything significant to the rest of you?"

"She told me something," Ellie replied softly.

"What did she tell you?" Shadow asked.

"She told me: 'Nothing but the straight truth will pierce the darkness. This occurs to the cold front, three hundred sixty-five. The darkness will shatter and will need to burn brightly in cold fire.' "Weird, huh?"

Shadow blinked in confusion. "Do you have any idea what she meant by it, Ellie?"

Ellie shrugged. "Not in the slightest. She seemed to like hearing herself talk, though."

Shadow rolled his eyes. "Yeah, you could say that."

"If you two are done flirting, I believe Shadow came up here to make an announcement of some sort?" Ryan asked. "After all, it did look like you were in a hurry when you came up."

"Yeah, you're right," Shadow replied. "I did come up here to tell you all something."

"What's wrong?" Faith asked. "Has something else happened?"

Shadow shook his head. "No, nothing like that." He paused, taking a deep breath. "I wanted to tell you all that today is the day."

"What do you mean?" Crystal asked. "Is it, like, your birthday or something?"

"Of course. How could we have been so dense?" Ryan asked, putting his hand over his mouth mockingly. "That must be exactly why he ran all the way up here, to inform us that we forgot his birthday."

"When you put it that way, it sounds kind of far-fetched," Crystal admitted.

"Just be quiet!" Faith exclaimed.

"Whoa," Tristan muttered.

"I think it's fairly obvious what he means," Niki said serenely. "He means that we're finally going to be confronting Maedara today. Is that right?"

Shadow opened his mouth and then closed it. "Yeah, that's right, Niki."

"Are you serious, Shadow?" Ryan asked.

"I wouldn't joke about something like this. You should know that."

"What are we going to do?" Faith asked. "Do you have a plan of some sort?"

"Yeah, Shadow," Crystal chimed in. "It's not as if we all rehearsed a battle plan or whatever. How are we going to win this thing?"

Shadow sighed. "I know you guys are scared. Trust me, I am too. But we cannot linger on the problems. We have to think up solutions, turn the improbable into the possible."

"So we're actually going to do it then?" Faith asked. "We're really going to take on Maedara tonight?"

"Yeah, we are," Shadow replied. "It's hard to believe, I know. But we have no options left. She needs to be stopped. We're running out of time."

"Wait!" Isaac called and stepped forward

"What's wrong?" Shadow asked, forcing himself not to add a "now" at the end of his statement. He hadn't noticed the kid before and had assumed he was still sleeping.

"Well, we're taking on Maedara, right?" Isaac asked, his voice suddenly low and quiet.

"Yeah, that's been established already," Ryan said, glaring in extreme dislike. "So what's your point?"

Isaac's face flushed. "My point is," he replied, his eyes fixed determinedly on Shadow, "that if we're going up against Maedara, that means that Kay will be there."

Ryan frowned. "Again, I ask, what's your point?"

"My point is, I won't do anything against her," Isaac replied. "She's my friend, and I won't hurt her. I refuse."

"Are you friggin' serious, Isaac?" Crystal asked in disbelief. "Kay's lied, cheated, and played us all. What in the deepest pit of hell makes you think that you're special? What makes you think that you were the one person who she was up front with?"

"Crystal —" Ethan began.

"No, let her talk," Faith interrupted, to general astonishment.

"You're all wrong about Kay!" Isaac yelled. "You guys don't know her. I do. I swear she's not like you think. She's just not."

"Isaac," Shadow said, struggling for a neutral tone. "You weren't there when we found her. You didn't hear the things she was saying, the things she confessed doing.

"You're aware of how she planned to take out our base while we were gone, right? How she almost got Cameryn killed for the second time? Even with all this evidence, you don't care, do you?"

Isaac blushed for a split-second and then gave Shadow a dirty look. "No, I don't. I just want my friend back. I want Kay."

Shadow smiled bitterly. "Fine."

"Shadow. . .don't," Ellie pleaded. She knew he would never harm Isaac. She was sure of that. However, she also knew that he would kick the boy out of the castle in a heartbeat if he suspected that he was a danger to them all.

"No, I'm sorry," Shadow said, shaking his head. "This seems to be what Isaac wants, so why should we try to reason with him?"

Ellie looked at him in disbelief. "Why should we try to reason with him?" she repeated, her voice getting higher. "Shadow, you can't be serious."

"I believe he is most definitely serious," Faith said in a distant voice quite unlike her own.

"Ethan, aren't you going to act as the voice of reason like you always do?" Ellie asked.

Ethan smiled sadly. "You know, normally, I would. My conscience tells me that I should argue to keep Isaac with us, but my head and heart are bringing up a different argument. They're both telling me that I should ignore my conscience and speak about what's best for the team. I cannot support the idea of keeping somebody with us who very much wishes not to be. Likewise, I refuse to help keep somebody around, endangering those I've sworn to protect."

"Ethan's right," Shadow said. "I don't want Isaac here if he's going to put the rest of you in danger."

Ellie sighed in defeat. "Fine. Let him stay here then."

Isaac scoffed. "So, what, you're kicking me out?"

"Why, because you don't deserve it?" Ryan asked.

"Oh, no, he deserves it," Niki said. "Go ahead, Shadow. Make with the kicking."

"No, Isaac, I'm not kicking you out," Shadow said. "But you're definitely not coming with us when we confront Maedara. We need all the help we can get, and you're definitely not help."

"You're making me out to be some horrible person, when I'm not," Isaac said.

"It's not that you're a horrible person, but that you're incredibly stupid," Niki replied. "But it's okay. We totally understand."

"Can we get back on more important matters?" Ryan asked before Isaac could respond. "Like when we're leaving?"

"Yes," Shadow said. "Well, I've sent Reya and Cameryn to the flight bay. They're waiting for us."

"So we're leaving now?" Crystal asked. "Are you sure we're all ready?"

"Yes, I'm sure," Shadow replied. "You've all been training for months now, getting ready for this exact moment. I have nothing but faith in all of your abilities, and I know you all are strong enough to help me stop this psycho."

"Shadow, how are we going to find Maedara's base?" Tristan asked.

Shadow smirked. "The same way we did last time, by following our little friend Kay's communicator location signal. I've actually been watching it for a while, and her location has jumped. She's now in the same general area as where Niki informed us that Maedara's home is rumored to be."

"So you're using Kay again?" Isaac growled. "You give up on her, then you use her?"

Shadow sighed. "Isaac, I really don't have the patience or the energy to deal with you. If you want to act like Kay's an innocent victim in all of this and I'm some kind of evil being, go ahead. I don't have to defend myself to you. You've made your choice very clear, so please just get the hell away from me. Go take a nap or something, like the child you're being."

"Whatever," Isaac said, rolling his eyes. "I don't care. You just better not hurt Kay."

"I'm sure Shadow will be looking over his shoulder for the rest of his eternal life," Ryan said sarcastically. "But for right now, we have a serious problem to take care of."

"Let's go, guys. This whole thing ends today."

CR&OCR&OCR&OCR&O

Minutes later the group met up with Cameryn and Tereya. They both looked very impatient.

"What took you guys?" Tereya asked. "We've been waiting for almost an hour!"

Shadow sighed. "Trust me, you don't want to know."

Tereya frowned for a fraction of a second. Then, seeming to accept it as an answer, he nodded. "All right. When do we head off?"

Shadow took in a deep breath and let it out slowly. "We leave now."

They all boarded the jet. Making sure everybody was seated, Shadow entered the cockpit, pressed the necessary buttons, and the vehicle took flight.

He threw himself down into the pilot's chair and gazed out the window absentmindedly. *"So it's all come down to this: the final confrontation. I hope we're all ready, because tonight it's do or die,"* he thought.

Ellie walked in. "Hey, Shadow."

Startled slightly, he was jolted back into reality. Pressing a button on the side of his seat, he turned the chair to face her. "Hey."

"What were you thinking about?" Ellie asked. She knew that Shadow had a tendency to get testy when asked about the inner workings of his mind, but it was just something that she felt she had to ask him.

"I was just thinking about the big battle today and what's going to happen."

"Don't worry. We're going to do this together, and we're going to win."

Shadow chuckled. "I know we're going to win, because I refuse to believe anything otherwise. I'm just worried about us all making it out alive. I can promise we'll win, but I cannot ensure a hundred percent that we'll all be fine. I couldn't do that even if I was a fortune-teller."

"Nobody is expecting you to know what's going to happen, Shadow. Trust me when I tell you…" Ellie paused, looking out the window. "The only thing we expect of you is to lead us. Lead us, and trust that we are strong enough to survive. It's all we expect."

Shadow looked at the ground and sighed. "I just couldn't stand it if one of you guys got hurt."

Ellie surveyed him and shook her head. "Just trust us. We will be fine. You've taught us well, and we've trained. Plus, even if one of us does get hurt, we have Faith. Remember?"

He smiled. "I guess that's the silver lining I was looking for."

"So cheer up," she said, and then she immediately hugged him.

"Uh, thanks, Ellie."

Ellie pulled away, blushing slightly. "Don't mention it."

They both remained rooted to the spot in awkward silence. After a long while, Ellie turned to leave. "I'll see you when we land. I want to get a little bit of rest. All right?"

Shadow understood; anything to break the air of discomfort. "Yeah, it's fine. I'll see you later."

Ellie lingered at the door, almost as if she wanted to say something but just couldn't find the words. To his displeasure, after a few moments, she walked out, leaving him alone.

There are moments, just moments where I think I understand her perfectly and know where she's coming from, he thought. *Yet there are other moments where she leaves me with more questions than certainties. I don't know what it is that I'm feeling. The worst part of all is that these strange feelings I have scare me. They scare me more than anything, even more than the upcoming battle.*

"Destination reached. Landing will proceed in twenty seconds," a calm female voice said, that voice belonging to the jet's computer. With a lot of programming and help from Crystal, the resident computer expert, it had worked. The jet could talk and voice important announcements.

"Looks like we're here. I hope they're all ready for this. I know I am," Shadow thought, bracing himself as the jet landed. Exiting the cockpit, he walked down the aisle and watched as the others slowly started to rise out of their seats.

"You guys ready?"

"Not for nothing, Shadow," Ryan said softly, "but I think we're all as ready as we're ever gonna be."

"I believe Ryan is right," Faith said. "I think we're all over-anxious about what's to take place today, and I'm confident that we're all up for any and all challenges that may present themselves."

Shadow nodded. "I know you guys won't let me down."

"Shadow," Ethan called, stepping out into the aisle. "Since Ryan and I can take to the skies, I think it would be best if we scout ahead. Would that be all right?"

"Yeah. Just be careful, you two. We can't afford for any of us to be discovered until we're ready to make our move."

"We'll be as careful as a mouse in a room full of fat women wearing high heels," Ryan said, smiling slightly at his own joke. "And trust me, that's careful."

Ethan shook his head. They both departed from the jet. Ethan 's wings sprouted and began beating furiously, lifting him up. The wind itself coiled around Ryan's feet like a tornado and lifted him up into the sky.

Watching from the door as Ethan and Ryan left, Crystal came back stone-faced. It was obvious that she was worried. The possibility of him being captured weighed heavily on her. "I'm so worried. I know that I'm mean to him sometimes, but Ethan really does mean the world to me. He's been around me for so long, ever since I could remember, and I don't know what I'll do if I lose him."

"Don't worry, Crystal." Shadow said consolingly. "They'll be fine."

"Are you sure?"

"Nothing in life is a surety, no matter how perfect the idea or how flawless the planning. I have faith in them both. They're both intelligent guys and are powerful enough to defeat anything that would threaten them."

"Shadow?" Crystal asked. "Are you absolutely sure they'll be okay?"

Shadow nodded and patted her shoulder.

"Thanks. I appreciate it. It's just, like I said, he's been there since I was born, just watching over me. I don't know what I'll do if anything happens to him. I mean, yes, I'll go shopping, but that's just a temporary fix."

"Crystal, I promise he'll be fine."

Seemingly accepting the answer, Crystal went back to her seat.

Shadow whistled loudly, calling everyone to attention. "All right now. I'm going to have us disembark now. We'll wait outside for Ryan and Ethan to come back with their news. I'd rather us not remain in such a huge target."

"You think Maedara knows we're here already?" Faith asked.

"I don't believe she does," Shadow replied, "but I'm not one for taking chances. The thing I'm definitely sure of is that she's aware of a jet landing on her territory. More than likely it will interest her, and she will investigate by sending a few of her soldiers to check it out."

"So you want us to be gone before Ms. Crazy-pants comes a'knocking," Niki said blankly.

"Yeah, exactly."

Niki shrugged. "Works for me. I could do with some fresh air."

"I know what you mean," Tristan said. "I hate jets. They're so uncomfortable."

"Easy, tiger," Niki said, rolling her eyes. "I think we should wait for Ryan and Ethan to come back. That would be the smart thing to do. And, while it's hard for you to do smart things, I suggest you comply."

Tristan glared at Niki in disbelief. "What did I do to you, anyway? You always treat me like I'm stupid," he asked. "I thought we dropped the whole incident. Why do you hate me?"

Niki stared at Tristan unflinching. "To be horribly honest, I don't hate you," she replied. "Hate is far too strong of an emotion for me to feel it for you, because I don't know you like that. You are a part of a team that I am on as well, so I respect you on that level.

"On a personal level, I don't particularly care for you. I think you're far too hotheaded to be taken seriously. Until you can be taken seriously, I couldn't possibly hate you."

Tristan blinked, dumbfounded.

"That was a tiny bit harsh, wasn't it?" Faith asked carefully, not wanting to cause another argument.

Niki smiled. "Not at all. Now that we have that settled, I say we get off of this jet and wait for our friends to return!"

Tristan sighed, watching Niki disembark.

"Is the altercation between Niki and yourself getting to you?" Faith asked.

"Yeah," Tristan said. "I mean, I know I made a bad first impression with her. I get that. But I've been trying hard to make up for that ever since, honest."

Faith sighed. It was always hard for her to see her brother upset, especially in the situations when there was nothing she could possibly do to fix it. "Don't worry. I'm sure Niki will come around soon. You've just got to give it time."

"I guess you're right, Sis."

Faith smiled. "Are you sick or something?"

"No, I'm not sick," Tristan replied, frowning. "I'm allowed to admit when I'm wrong and others are right, aren't I?"

Faith paused, raising an eyebrow slightly. "You're allowed to say whatever you want, and you do. It's just that this particular thing is a bit out of character for you."

"That's fair. But from this moment on, I'll try to control my temper better."

"And?" Crystal asked from her seat.

"And. . .I promise to think before I speak," Tristan added, his eyes narrowing.

"And?" Shadow asked.

"I promise to try to not be a jerk."

"Good!" Faith said loudly, before anybody could add anything else. After all, Tristan was her brother. She didn't want anybody else chiming in with things that they thought he should change, for fear of discouraging him. Any bit of change was good, and more change would come in the future.

"Let's go," Shadow said to the few that were still on the jet. "We've been in here too long."

"Finally," Tristan said. "Another minute of waiting, and I would have lost it."

"Do you think they're coming back with good news or bad news?" Faith asked.

"I don't know. You're the psychic. You tell me," Shadow replied with a grin.

Faith rolled her eyes. "You know it doesn't work like that. The visions don't always come immediately. They're random most of the time."

"I know. I was just kidding; a bit of humor to ease the tension. But if you want my honest opinion, I'm expecting bad news."

"Dark and cynical. There's the Shadow that we've all come to know and love," Ellie said, smiling.

"I'm allowed to joke sometimes."

"You're right, I guess. But try not to make a habit of it," Faith replied. "But on a serious note, let's go. I see Ethan and Ryan in the distance flying back to us."

"Well, let's go meet them." Shadow said.

"Right behind you," Tristan said.

On his way out, Shadow noticed Tereya fast asleep. He walked over and shook the kid gently and whispered in his ear. "Reya, wake up. Come on, it's time to go. We're here."

Tereya rose out of his seat. "We're here?" he asked, yawning and rubbing his eyes wearily. "Cool. Can't wait."

"You sure you're up for this, Reya?" Cameryn asked, grinning. "You seem more ready for bed than for a big battle. We wouldn't want you falling asleep during combat."

Tereya let out a loud yell. "You know that I'm up for it, Cameryn. No way did I train hard for so many weeks just to sit up here."

Cameryn laughed. "I knew that would be your answer."

Once they had all left the vessel, they watched as Ethan and Ryan slowly came through the air, heading towards them.

"Good news?" Shadow called, watching as they landed on the ground a few feet away from him.

"Hardly," Ryan answered, stone-faced.

"Explain?" Shadow asked.

"Allow me," Ethan said. He took a deep breath. "We didn't have to fly far to see the extent of the damage that Maedara has caused to this continent. Om'erah was once a beautiful land, but now it has become nothing more than a desolate wasteland. The fields are scorched and ashen, the plants shriveled and dying."

"Is that the bad news?" Tristan asked.

"Not quite," Ethan replied. "We've found the location of Maedara's palace."

"That's good news, though," Shadow stated. "How is that bad news?" He was struggling to hide exactly how excited and nervous he was.

"Well, you see…" Ethan began, desperately searching for the right words to use that could accurately describe what Ryan and he had seen. "We were able to spy on a meeting that occurred outside of her home."

"It's hard," Ryan said softly. "I doubt that we could even verbalize what we saw. Nothing we could say would even begin to do it justice."

"Show us then," Faith said.

"Show you?" Ryan repeated. "How are we supposed to show you? It's not like we're DVD players or something."

Faith rolled her eyes. "You can use my powers."

"Of course," Ethan replied.

Shadow nodded in understanding.

"Maybe you three can read minds, but the rest of us are lost," Crystal said.

"No need to be lost, Crystal," Ethan said. "Faith is quite a remarkable girl. In addition to her normal powers of healing and seeing the future, she can also transfer memories."

"Well, then what are we waiting for?" Crystal asked. "Help them show us, Faith!"

Ryan rolled his eyes. "So glad you were here to provide us with the intellectual design capable of finding a solution, Crystal."

"Enough, guys," Niki said, slightly annoyed, before Shadow could. "Can you guys stop going at each other's throats and just let Faith show us what we need to see?"

"Sorry," Ryan murmured.

"Faith, will you show us now?" Shadow asked.

"Of course," Faith replied. She walked over to Ethan and Ryan, pulling them in closer to the group. "To do this, it requires us all to be touching. We must maintain a strong conductor of energy. So, to begin, I need all of you grabbing the hand or shoulder of the person next to you until we form a circle."

They began to follow the directions given to them. Shadow grabbed Ellie's hand, who grabbed Tereya's, and so on until they all had grabbed somebody's hand.

"Ready?" Faith asked.

Everyone nodded in unison.

"Let's get this going, already," Ryan said. "Tristan's hand is all gross and slimy."

"Shut up, Ryan!" Tristan exclaimed. "It's not my fault that my hand is sweating."

"Hush, both of you." Niki said. "You're lucky you have hands. A starfish isn't as lucky. No hands at all; they only have those pointy thingies. And people capture them and kill them to be sold as gift shop items. Count your blessings. You could have been born a starfish."

Shadow rolled his eyes. "Faith, just go ahead."

Faith began to concentrate, focusing her energy into her mind as she always had done to tap into her power. Her eyes began to glow as violet static energy crackled around her body.

"Ryan, Ethan," she called, "think of the memory you wish to share, then bring it to the top of your minds. Do it, NOW!"

Ryan and Ethan hastened to obey. They dragged the memory, the sight that had unsettled them both from the very moment they saw it, to the surface of their minds. No sooner had they remembered than the images began to flood the vision of all of them, appearing right in front of them as if they had been there themselves.

A large palace could be seen in the distance. All around the palace were legions of demons and creatures, their numbers going well into the hundreds. Standing in front of the crowd of creatures was a tall figure.

"Today marks the final day, which cements the rule of our queen," it said, and the crowd broke out in cheers. "Lady Maedara will sweep across and lay waste to this pitiful world. She will give rule back to those who deserve it. Our kind will no longer be forced to hide; we will rise and enslave the entire human race. With Maedara and the darkness on our side, we will be triumphant. Nothing can stop us!"

More cheering, followed by a short silence.

"I see you're giving one of your little pep talks again." Maedara said, walking up. She flicked her bangs to the side. "How cute."

"Lady Maedara!" the creature said, bowing. "We did not expect to see you so soon, not until the dawning."

"I honestly don't care what you expected, idiot," she replied. "All that matters to me is that you do your job and guard the palace until the clock ticks away and my sky makeover thing is permanent. That's all I care about."

The creature nodded furiously. "Why, yes, of course, Lady Maedara. We will keep guard and kill all of those who wish to get in your way."

"I said guard, not kill. Or are your ears not working properly?"

"But—"

"Are you questioning me?" she asked. "Because I sincerely hope I do not have to kill you. Finding a replacement army leader this late in the game will be a headache."

"No, Lady Maedara, I would never question you. We will capture any and all who try to enter. We will hold them until we get final orders from you."

"Good. Now we have proper communication. And proper communication is the key to life, literally," Maedara said, and then she turned to address the crowd of demons. "I want each and every one of you miserable creatures to know that if anybody so much as approaches within a few inches of my home, I will make sure that the demon responsible suffers unimaginably. So if you don't want to die a horrible death, I suggest you not disappoint me."

The crowd began to chant her name over and over again. She did a little curtsy and walked back into the building behind them.

The memory faded and everyone separated.

"Whoa," Tristan muttered. "That's… just whoa."

Niki blinked. "I can see why you both couldn't explain what you saw."

"I think there are more demons there than I've seen in my entire time of being with you guys," Cameryn remarked. "How many do you think there were?"

"There must have been over five hundred in total," Faith said slowly. "How are we going to get past them?"

"Yeah, Shadow. What are we going to do?" Tereya asked.

Shadow didn't respond. He had absolutely no idea.

Michael Chulsky

CHAPTER 11: THE LAST TEMPTATION

"Shadow, you can't be serious," Crystal said. "You have to have a plan. You totally have to. You're our leader, remember?"

"Crystal, please," Ethan said. "It's a lot to take in, more than any normal person could ever hope to. Don't hold it against Shadow that he doesn't have a plan, especially not right after seeing all of that."

"I think I can sum it up in one word," Ryan said. "Wow."

"Ryan, how could you joke at a time like this?" Faith asked.

"Well, we knew this wasn't going to be easy," Ellie said. "I mean, I highly doubt that anybody really thought that we'd be in, out, and back before dinner." Murmurs of agreement echoed all around her. "We all knew what we were signing up for, what we all spent months and months training for."

"I'm not backing down," Tereya said. "I agreed to help protect our world, no matter what the cost. I knew long ago what I was getting into, as did everyone else here. Ellie's right. This was never meant to be a walk in the park."

"Yeah, me either," Cameryn added. "Shadow saved me. He protected me when he didn't even know who I was or if I was worth saving. He invested so much into me, and I refuse to let him down. He saved me, so I'll return the favor and fight with him and the rest of you. It's the least I can do to pay him back for all he's done."

"I honestly don't believe any of us are going to back down," Faith said. "We're all together in this."

"I may not agree with everyone in this group all the time, but like it or not, we're a family," Tristan said.

"And families stick together," Tereya said.

"Well said," Shadow replied. "And you're completely right. We're going to do this together. And make no mistake, we're going to win."

"I'm all for the new resolve, Cap-i-tan, but how exactly are we going to get past the plethora of demons?" Ryan asked. "It's not as if we can rent a magical bulldozer to just kill them all, though if we could, I'm all for it."

Shadow sighed. "That does put a damper on our plans," he admitted. "But as they say, where there's a will, there's a way. So either we'll think up a plan or we could just go in, fists flying, and hope for the best."

Ryan started to say something but paused, noticing a strange look crossing Shadow's face, somewhere between anger and hatred. "Shadow, you look like somebody just stole your cookies. What's wrong?"

"Kay," Tereya said softly.

"Hey, guys," Kay said, waving. "How's tricks?"

Crystal let out a huge breath. "Excuse me. But, Kay, what the hell are you doing here?"

"I must admit that I, too, am curious as to how you happened to show up when you did," Ethan said thoughtfully. "It's almost as if it were planned out, though the chances of that are quite slim. After all, there's no way you could know the exact point of our landing."

"It wasn't by accident," Kay said. "You can be sure of that."

"How wasn't it by accident?" Faith asked. "You're not giving us much; more like you're just talking in circles."

"Just spit it out, Kay," Ellie demanded. "What do you want from us? Because we sure as heck don't want anything from you."

"Really, Ellie?" Kay asked. "Even if it meant that I could solve the mess you all have gotten yourselves into?"

"Just shut up and tell us what we need to know," Cameryn said.

Kay smiled. "Oh, it seems that the little weakling finally discovered a backbone. Isn't that cute?"

"Leave him alone, and explain yourself," Shadow replied curtly. "I have no patience to deal with your games."

Kay rolled her eyes. "Fine. What if I could help you get past all those demons over there?" she said. "Because I'm assuming you don't have a plan. You never were that good of a leader."

"How could you do that?" Shadow asked incredulously. "And more importantly, why would we accept your help? So you could, what, betray us a second, or is it a third, time?"

"I guess you'll just all have to go on faith, now, won't you?" Kay snapped.

"Strangely, I'm not feeling much like having what my name suggests," Faith said. "You haven't exactly been the most reliable person in the world."

"Faith's right. You're going to have to give us a little more than that," Ryan replied. "I'm sorry, but unless you can walk on water, cure the blind, or rise from the dead after three days, you'll get no faith from me."

Kay shook her head. "Being funny isn't going to save you. Although maybe, just maybe, you can make the demons laugh to death before they rip you apart with their bare hands."

"Want to know exactly what I think about you?" Ryan asked. "I promise, there's nothing funny about it."

"Enough, you two!" Shadow yelled. "Stop with the immature pettiness. We don't have time to deal with it."

"I agree with Shadow," Niki said, playing with a dead flower that she had picked from the ground. "This fighting isn't productive. There's no point in it."

"So, what, Shadow, you're going to trust her?" Crystal asked disbelievingly. "Just like that?"

"Crystal, calm down," Shadow said. "I'm sure you think I'm taking Kay at face value. . .and I'm not. I will hear her out because I don't have a better option. But make no mistake. She's beyond me ever trusting her again."

"All right, then," Faith said calmly. "Let's hear her out - if not for us or for her, then for Shadow. We owe him at least that much, guys."

"Agreed," Cameryn said. "We should trust him, even if it's hard."

"Thanks," Kay said.

"Don't thank me; I didn't do it for you," Faith replied, glaring. "I did it for Shadow. He's our leader, and if he says we should hear you out, then I guess he believes you have something useful to say. For your sake, you'd better hope you do."

"Once again, I agree with Faith," Cameryn said. "You're not a good person, and everyone here knows it. We don't care about you; we just care about stopping Maedara."

"Wow, such hatred for me. I think if I didn't find it so incredibly funny, I would actually be kind of hurt. It's surprising how it doesn't take you all that long to turn on somebody."

"Kay," Ellie said slowly, "say what you have to say, or I will shred you to pieces."

Kay narrowed her eyes. "I know of a way around those demons over there." she said, pointing in their direction. "It's very simple. All you guys have to do is do exactly what I say, and it will be a piece of cake."

"Why would you want to help us, anyway?" Shadow asked, taking a step towards her. "After all, didn't you say that Maedara's side was the winning one?"

"I know, but–"

Shadow took another step forward. "And you expect us to believe you're helping us go up against her?"

Kay sighed. "No. If you'll just let me–"

"Do you think I was born yesterday?"

"No!" Kay yelled, anger rising for the first time since she appeared. "It's not like that at all."

"Then why, Kay?" Ellie asked. "What's it like? Try honesty, for once in your life."

"We know it's a foreign concept to you, but who knows, it may work," Ryan said.

"I'm trying to help because she wants you all dead!" Kay blurted out. "Including Isaac."

"Oh. So that's it, isn't it?" Shadow replied coldly. He finally understood. "You're only helping us because of your own selfish reasons. You don't give a damn about any of us, do you? You only care about Isaac."

"So what if that is the reason?" Kay said, staring at the ground. "It doesn't change the fact that you'll be getting help that is well-needed. The reason doesn't matter."

"Who are you to make that choice?" Ethan asked. "The devil will assume many different guises to offer many different promises. Just because the offer is good doesn't mean you're not setting us up for trouble."

"While your argument or lack thereof is compelling, I'm sorry to say that I'll have to decline," Shadow said.

"Oh, really?" Kay asked. A dark smile slowly spread across her face. "Even with the Scepter of Ondeyr's hidden clause?"

"What are you talking about?" Shadow asked. "What hidden clause?"

"The great leader doesn't know something that could literally make or break the world. Truly amusing."

Shadow scowled. "Cut the small talk and just get on with what you're taking about."

"Well, since you asked so nicely," Kay replied, rolling her eyes. "Basically, if it's not stopped within a certain amount of time after it begins, it will last forever."

"And how much time do we have left?" Faith asked.

"You have exactly three hours and forty-five minutes, give or take a few minutes. So can you really take the chance that you'll find a way to get to Maedara and stop her before it's too late... all without my help?"

"You're so twisted," Crystal said angrily. "While you're playing your little mind games, we're running out of time."

"Crystal," Ethan said, a hint of warning in his voice. "It would be unwise of you to lose control right now."

"I'm fine, Ethan, really. I'm just tired of this skank wasting our time."

"I'm sorry, what was that?" Kay asked.

"It was nothing," Shadow said. "Just tell us what we need to know."

"There's a simple way past all of those demons. I've explored most of the castle, and the guards know me as part of Maedara's crew. I will go and tell them that there are a large band of intruders on the eastern side of the land. When I give the signal, and you'll know it when you see it, that's your cue. Any questions?"

Everyone stood there and blinked at Kay for a few moments before Tristan broke the silence. "I have a question."

Kay rolled her eyes but gave a nod of consent. "Fine. What is it?"

"Well, so what if we get rid of all the demons? What about Maedara herself?"

"Maedara's not on the battlefield, so you don't have to worry. In two minutes, it will be her relaxation hour, which is time that she takes each day for her own personal relaxation, meaning she'll be unguarded and not expecting an attack, or any interruptions, for that matter. Hopefully, if you guys are smart, this will be the time you strike and take her out."

"That still doesn't change the fact that she's a crazy psycho who you've told us is quite powerful."

"Yeah, Maedara's broken the cardinal rule." Ryan said.

"What's the cardinal rule?" Tereya asked, confused.

"Powerful or psycho; pick one, not both."

"And why is that the cardinal rule?" Faith asked.

"It's just not safe for anybody to be both at the same time."

"Well, Tristan, oddly enough, has a point," Kay said. "Maedara prides herself on how strong and enduring she is. I've heard the other demons talking, and rumor has it that she's immortal."

"What does immortal mean?" Cameryn asked.

"It means that something cannot be slain, by any means," Ethan replied. "Though true immortality is rare. Angels, like me, are actually one of the few things that are immortal."

"Nothing is truly immortal," Shadow said. "Everything can be killed. It's just a matter of how."

"Are there really that many different ways to kill something?" Crystal asked.

"You'd be surprised," Niki answered. "For were - creatures, it's a silver bullet, or anything silver, really. If there's nothing silver on hand, then a wooden stake with the tip dipped in the blood of the real animal that the particular were - creature's DNA contains may be used.

"Speaking of wooden stakes, those, although quite old-fashioned, work well on vampires. And not just any wooden stakes, either. I mean, it's not like you can just pick a branch off the ground and stab a vampire with it. For a wooden stake to be effective, it has to be dipped in holy water or blessed by a clergyman.

"Besides that, silver weapons work too, such as knives and guns, as well as anything blessed by any faith, or good ol' fashioned sunlight for a nice vamp BBQ."

"Gee, Niki, why don't you just announce to the whole world the many ways to kill our leader," Ryan said. "Maybe next you can print out pamphlets and hand them out to those demons over there."

"No offense there, Captain," Niki said, giving Shadow a thumbs-up. "I just was trying to emphasize your point that nothing is immortal."

Shadow smiled darkly. "No offense taken. However, if anybody here comes at me with a pencil blessed by a Catholic priest, I'll blame you."

"If you all are done joking around, I think we should get started now, seeing as how it's now almost three hours until the sun goes bye-bye permanently," Kay said. "Or just stay here and joke around. I don't care either way. All I know is, if you can't stop Maedara, I'm taking Isaac and we'll be gone."

"Fine," Shadow replied. "But if you do anything like betray us again or get any one of us killed, I will personally come after you with every ounce of my power. Do you understand me?"

"You don't have to worry about me, Shadow. I wouldn't do anything to put Isaac in danger." Kay glanced around the group. "Wait a minute. Where is Isaac, anyway?"

"Isaac is at home," Ellie said. "We didn't bring him."

"Yeah, he couldn't make the trip." Ryan chimed in.

Kay blinked. "You all. . .you didn't–" she stammered. "You guys didn't hurt him, did you?"

"We're not you, Kay," Shadow replied coolly. "None of us here would ever hurt somebody that we've sworn to protect."

"Wait, Kay," Crystal said suddenly. "Where is Maedara's relaxation room located?"

"It's on the second floor, third room on the right. You can't miss it. It's the only door in the entire mansion that's painted black."

"As much as I'm sure the answer is a stupid one, I'll bite," Ryan said. "Why is it the only door in the entire mansion painted black?"

"Because black doesn't go with the rest of the décor, and it's a sign that whoever enters that room who isn't Maedara will die," Kay replied. "I'm going to head over there now. Watch for the signal, and good luck." She started off, and within moments, she was gone.

"You sure we can trust her?" Ellie asked.

"Not in the slightest," Shadow replied. "But it doesn't matter. Trust or not, this is our only option. And either way, we'll be on guard."

"I say we follow the plan," Niki announced.

"You're not seriously suggesting that we put all of our trust in Kay and just walk blindly into a potential trap, are you Niki?" Crystal asked dubiously.

"No, not at all. But we can and should most definitely have a wild card that we can use to turn the tide at any given moment, if the need occurs."

"And I'm guessing you have those just lying around?" Tristan asked sarcastically. "Let us see this magic wild card of yours. I hope you managed to bring it with you."

Niki smiled. "I believe I do happen to have one on me, and I did remember to bring it!"

"Well, don't leave us in suspense or anything. What is it?" Ryan asked.

Niki dug her hands into her pockets and then pulled out a small glowing glass orb. "Ta-da," she said.

Tristan frowned. "Niki. . .I don't think –"

"I said, ta-da."

"But that's not–"

"TA-DA!"

"Okay, okay," Tristan said, throwing his hands up in defeat. "You win."

"For what it's worth, Niki, I trust your little orb thingy, whatever it is," Crystal said. "I just hope it doesn't get us killed."

"Don't worry about that," Niki replied. "There's a ninety-nine percent chance that it will do something amazingly cool and helpful with only a less than one percent chance of it causing total chaos and destruction. But there's honestly nothing to worry about."

"Check it out!" Cameryn yelled, pointing towards the mansion.

There was a huge commotion going on and tons of murmuring going on throughout the crowd. The group of demons parted and began to move away.

"I guess Kay really did keep up her end of the bargain," Tereya said. "I guess this means that we can trust her."

"No," Ellie said swiftly. "That doesn't mean anything. If anything, it only means that getting us to think that we can trust her was part of her plan."

"It doesn't matter right now," Shadow said. "We have less than three hours now before the world as we knew it is gone forever. We cannot let that happen. We have a fight to win, and nothing, not even Maedara, will stand in our way. Let's go!"

CR80CR80CR80CR80

They walked up a pair of grand white stairs, which led up to the front door of the mansion.

Shadow held up a hand, signaling the rest of them to wait behind him. "I wouldn't be surprised if Maedara booby-trapped this door somehow." He hesitated, his hand positioned slightly above the doorknob.

"It just seems so anticlimactic," Ryan said.

"Hush, Ryan," Shadow replied.

"Since we're running out of time, allow me to do the honors," Niki said. She walked right up to the door and kicked it full force. It burst inward and fell off the hinges with a loud crash.

"Well, there goes the element of surprise," Ryan remarked.

Ellie blinked. "Nice kick."

"Niki, are you crazy?" Shadow thundered.

"I've been called that," Niki replied, shrugging. "But I stand by my original decision. Let us now proceed."

Sighing, Shadow took a step forward. After a few seconds of nothing happening, he decided that there wasn't any danger. He beckoned the others to follow him forward.

The mansion interior was beyond beautiful. The walls and floor were white, the tiles on them decorated, speckled artfully with gold. The ceiling appeared to be professionally painted. It looked like the sky before the darkness had come, with clouds that looked realistic, almost as if you could reach out and touch them. In the center, there was a great staircase, which led to the second floor and parted, leading to two different wings.

They crept carefully up the stairs. When they had reached the top, Shadow turned back around to face them. "Listen, guys," he whispered. "If what Kay said is correct, then Maedara will be up here, inside the black door. We just have to find it."

"Yeah, we know. We got the memo," Tristan said.

"Tristan, keep your voice down!" Shadow replied, still whispering. "Are you trying to get us all discovered?"

"Yeah, Tristan," Ryan said, his voice low. "Why don't you just announce to the demons that we're trying to sneak up on their leader? I'm sure that will go over quite well."

Tristan bowed his head. "I'm sorry," he muttered.

"It's fine; just keep your voice down," Shadow said softly. "Anyway, guys, Kay didn't mention on which side of the place that the room was, so we're going to have to split up and do a full search of—"

"Or we could just try that door over there," Niki said, pointing at a door on the left side of the hall.

Shadow nodded and walked up to the door, the rest of them closely behind him. He braced himself, turned the handle, and pushed.

It was an oversized bathroom. The mirrors were huge and covered large sections of the wall. The bathtub was the size of an aboveground swimming pool, and curtains were draped around it, matching the rest of the room, which was a bright bubblegum-pink.

Inside the bathtub, water was running. Music was coming from a radio on the edge of the sink.

"Be careful," Shadow whispered, so softly that the others behind him could barely hear. He took another step forward and pulled his sword out. He continued until he was just a few inches away from the tub.

Faith shuddered, a shiver going down her spine. Suddenly, the room was becoming too hot. She couldn't breathe.

"Faith!" Tristan exclaimed, struggling to keep his voice low. He moved over and grabbed her left arm, holding her to her feet. "What's going on?"

"I–" Faith muttered, her voice strained. She didn't know what was happening. She felt like her skin was going to crawl off. "I... c-can't... breathe."

Ethan moved forward and grabbed Faith's other arm, holding her still. "Calm, think calm thoughts. Breathe," he whispered, willing his voice to soothe her, but it did not.

Shadow took a deep breath, not noticing what was going on behind him. He raised his blade, preparing to strike. *"In a few seconds, this will all be over,"* he thought triumphantly. "As soon as I strike, the world will be saved, and none of them will have to lose their lives fighting."

"Faith, can you hear us?" Ethan asked.

"She's not responding!" Tristan cried, forgetting to keep his voice low. "Something's seriously wrong with her. This isn't how she usually gets when she's having a vision. Something's not right."

Faith leaned forward. She swallowed and blinked a few times to clear her vision. When her eyes finally opened, she found herself staring at the floor. She noted that the tiles were pink, much like the rest of the bathroom, except the tiles were decorated with a pattern of tiny blue fishes. "Oh, my God..." she whispered, her eyes opening wide. "No..."

"Faith, what's wrong?" Ellie asked. "Did you have another vision?"

Faith shook her head. "We have to leave. We have to get out of here now."

"We can't. We have to stop Maedara." Ryan said. "Don't you remember?"

"Sis, what's wrong?" Tristan asked. "What just happened?"

"This is all wrong. We have to leave. I… I was warned. I was told to watch out for this. It's a sign. We have to go."

Shadow grabbed the curtain and slowly pushed it to the side. The tub was empty, aside from the water. "She's not here," he said blankly. "Kay told us she would be here, but she isn't. Something is wrong."

Faith ran up and grabbed his arm. "We're leaving now," she said. "Something definitely is wrong here. This was a trap, and I was warned of it."

"What do you mean?"

"I mean, my vision from before, back in the castle," Faith said. "I was told by that Haati to beware of blue fishes. And guess what? They're all over the tiles."

"We should leave at once then," Ethan said.

"We can't have just come this far only to be stopped here. Maedara has to be somewhere in this place, and time's running out," Shadow thought, and frowned. "Faith, are you completely sure?"

"Shadow, what's that noise?" Tereya asked, moving away from the door.

"What noise?" Shadow asked and then hit the power button on the stereo. "I couldn't hear it because of the stupid radio. I can hear it now." He paused, listening. "It's like a strange ticking sound."

"Guys, now is not the time to play look-around!" Faith yelled. She sighed when she realized that she was being ignored.

Cameryn moved around as if following something. He stopped right in front of the bathroom cabinet. "It's coming from inside there."

Ethan walked over to the cabinet and opened it. He pulled out a black box. It was roughly the same size as a shoebox. He placed it on the counter and began examining it.

"What is it?" Tristan asked.

"I'm not quite sure. I've never seen anything like this," Ethan replied. He flipped it over and looked at the other side. "I've found the source of the ticking. It's coming from some sort of clock."

"You guys seriously don't know what that is?" Niki asked, backing up. "It's a bomb. Like, you know, 'boom.' And we have to leave now."

Ellie's eyes went wide. "Oh, my God."

"It's at fifteen seconds." Ethan said.

"Everyone, out now!" Shadow yelled.

They all ran for the door, running back the way they came. As they reached the bottom step of the staircase, everything happened all at once: a loud booming sound above them, and Niki pulling the small glass orb out of her pocket, shouting some strange words. The entire palace exploded, and then their vision faded to black.

CRWCRWCRWCRW

The remains of the palace were nothing more than debris, scattered over the scorched earth. Pillars, bricks, and large planks of wood littered the ground.

A pile of bricks stirred, and Shadow rose from it, digging his way out. His arm was bleeding from a large gash, and several cuts were across his face. He ran his hand over himself, checking for any serious injury. When at last he seemed satisfied, he trotted out of the wreckage and began looking around.

"Ellie! Cameryn!" he called, his voice hoarse and weakened. He listened but heard no answer. He called out the names of his other friends as he continued to search.

Seconds later, Shadow saw a large piece of wood move, and he ran over to it. He grabbed the slab with his good arm and threw it away, effortlessly. He bent down and looked at the person under it.   "Tristan, are you all right?"

Tristan groaned in pain and struggled to get up.

"Take it easy," Shadow said. "You're lucky to be alive. Don't put too much strain on yourself right away."

"Where's. . .my. . .sister?" Tristan coughed, forcing himself to a sitting position. "Where's Faith? Is she safe?"

"I'm not sure," Shadow admitted. "You're the first and only one I've found. I don't know if anybody else is even alive."

227

Tristan shook his head furiously, the pain of which made him wince. "She's not… She can't be dead. She isn't," he said. "We'll find her. We have to."

Shadow nodded, holding a hand out to him. "Don't worry, we'll –"

A person making pained sounds could be heard nearby. From the tone, it sounded like it was a girl.

Tristan pulled himself up, holding onto Shadow's arm. "Do you think. . .Could it be Faith?"

"It could be," Shadow replied. "Or it could be Crystal or Ellie. Any one of them could be the source. Let's go check it out."

They walked over in the direction of where the noise was. It was coming from under a large pile of rubble. They both began working at it, throwing bricks and other pieces of debris aside until they reached the person who had cried out.

Shadow glowered. "Kay," he said, his voice dark and low. "I wish I could say I'm surprised, but I'm honestly not. What the hell did you do?"

Kay blinked at him for a few moments until she seemed to find her voice. "I. . .I don't know what went on. One second I was inside, and then next, I woke up out here. What happened?"

"You seriously expect me to believe that you weren't behind all of this?"

"I'm telling you, I'm not. I swear I don't know what happened."

"I hate you, Kay," Tristan said coldly. "I hate you for betraying us, I hate you for betraying us the second time, and most of all, I hate you because you're not Faith."

Kay rolled her eyes. "I honestly don't care how I make you feel," she replied, moving into a sitting position. "I'm just glad that stupid explosion, or whatever it was, didn't kill me."

"Fine, Kay. Let's pretend you're innocent in all of this," Shadow said. "Let's pretend that you didn't lie and tell us that Maedara would be inside of a room that had a bomb in it. And let's also pretend that you're not just concerned about your own selfish ass and actually care that the other people that were on the same team as you could possibly be dead."

"Hmm. Let me think about that for a second," Kay said, feigning deep thought. "Isaac wasn't in there, so he's alive. I was in there, and I'm alive. So, no, I don't care about anything else."

"My sister was in there," Tristan snarled. He aimed his fist at Kay's hand and opened it, a red glow appearing in the center. "You should have died in that blast, but you didn't. But I'll fix that."

"Tristan!" Shadow exclaimed, grabbing his arm. "Don't. She deserves to be punished, but not like this."

Kay looked amused. "Saving me, even after all this? I'm touched."

"Shadow, let me go. She deserves to die," Tristan growled. "My sister is, was, a damn good person. She never hurt anybody, not in her entire life. She did her best to help as many people as possible. Back in our village, she had many sleepless nights, staying up late to heal those who had even the tiniest injury. She sacrificed so much of her time to give help to anybody who needed it. Why should she be gone, while this... pathetic thing still lives?"

He let out a quivering breath, tears forming in his eyes. "How in the hell is that fair?"

"Tristan, she's not... We don't know if she's dead for sure."

"Yeah, your sister is probably fine," Kay said, rising up from the ground. "And you were about to attack me, which was for no reason, because this wasn't my fault. I didn't know that the damn bathroom had a bomb in it."

"You're a liar," Tristan said, spitting on the ground at her feet. "And I swear to God, if my sister is dead... I'll kill you. Even if I have to go through Shadow to do it."

Kay laughed skeptically. "Yeah, whatever," she said, turning to leave.

"Kay!" Shadow shouted. "Wait."

"No, I don't think I will."

Shadow rushed over and grabbed her by the arm. "You're staying here until we find the others. And if, and only if, they're all okay, then you can leave. But until we find them, you're not going anywhere."

"First of all, don't touch me," Kay replied, ripping herself out of his grasp. "Second of all, I don't have to do anything. My advice to you, Shadow, is to cut your losses and run. Your team is dead and gone. You've lost this fight."

"I wouldn't be so sure of that."

Shadow turned in the direction of the voice and smiled. "Ryan!"

"Yeah, it's me," Ryan said, walking over to them. "Please, please, stop the applause. It's too much. I don't deserve it."

"Ryan, you jerk!" Shadow exclaimed. "You're alive."

"Well, yeah, obviously," Ryan replied, poking Shadow in the chest. "See? I'm solid, not a ghost."

Shadow shook his head. "Well, yeah, obviously. But we thought we lost you, with the others."

"The others?" Ryan asked. "I actually found Cameryn, Tereya, and Faith. They're a bit banged up, but otherwise good."

"My sister's alive?" Tristan asked, his eyes going wide.

"Yeah, that's what I just said," Ryan replied, nodding slowly. "She was healing Cameryn and Tereya when I was leaving. I actually left to search for any others."

Shadow breathed a sigh of relief. *"Cameryn's fine. He's still alive. I didn't break my promise to him."* he thought.

"Great, everyone's happy," Kay said. "Tristan's sister is alive, and Shadow's little orphan is fine and dandy. Now can I go?"

Ryan frowned, catching sight of Kay for the first time. "Oh, Kay," he said, looking thoroughly disappointed. "You're still alive? That's wonderful."

"Yeah, yeah, Ryan. You don't like me; I don't like you; you want me dead. Sing a new song. Whatever. It doesn't matter. I'm leaving anyway."

"No, you're not," Shadow said. "I told you already. You're staying with us until we find the others. That means each and every one of them. Crystal and Ethan are still missing. Ellie, too."

Kay smiled unpleasantly. "I see now. You're just worried for your little girlfriend, aren't you?"

"I'm not like you, Kay," Shadow replied. "I'm worried for all of them. I want them all to be okay."

"And we are," Ethan said. His clothes were tattered, there were holes in his jeans and shirt, but he otherwise looked unscathed. "We're fine."

He was supporting Crystal, who wasn't conscious. Standing on the other side of him was Ellie.

"Ethan! Ellie!" Shadow exclaimed, rushing over to them. "You guys are alive!" He paused, and frowned. "What's wrong with Crystal?"

"We found her like this," Ellie said. "She hasn't woken up. We think that she could have some internal bleeding... or something. We've been trying to find Faith to see if she can heal her."

"I know where she is," Ryan replied. "I'll take you to her."

CB&CBCB&CBCB&CBCB&CB

"How much longer until we get there?" Shadow asked. "We don't have too much time left until our window is closed, only about an hour and a half. We have to get everyone together, find Maedara, and kill her before then."

"Shadow, you have eyes. Use them!" Ryan exclaimed, pointing in the distance.

Shadow frowned. He looked in the direction Ryan was pointing and saw Faith. She was kneeling down by Cameryn, who was awake, and Tereya, who was unconscious, her hands glowing and waving over them.

"Faith!" Tristan called.

Faith's head jerked up and, upon seeing him, her eyes lit up. She jumped to her feet and turned around. "Brother!" she replied, rushing forward and pulling him into a hug. "I thought you were dead!"

"I thought you were dead too, but I was wrong, and I'm glad. I don't know what I would have done if I had lost you."

Ryan smiled. "Just because he's brain-dead doesn't mean that he's actually dead."

"Shut up, Ryan," Tristan replied.

"Shadow," Cameryn said, rising from the ground. "I woke up with Tereya, surrounded by huge piles of junk. He was bleeding really bad, and I was alone. I was scared. I thought that you had all died and that I was going to have to watch him die too."

"I'm sorry you had to wake up to that," Shadow replied. "But everything is fine now. Faith healed him, and she'll heal us."

"I thought I had lost you," Cameryn said softly.

"You didn't. I'm still here. And as soon as Faith heals everyone, it will have been like this never happened."

"Speaking of healing, Faith, Crystal is badly injured." Ethan said.

Faith pulled away from Tristan. "Let me take a look at her."

Ethan laid Crystal gently on the ground. "I've tried my best to protect her for all seventeen years of her life. If she can't... If anything happens–"

"Ethan, it's fine," Tristan replied. "My sister can fix this. I know she can."

Faith nodded. "The wounds may be serious, but they're not beyond my power. I can sense it. Give me a minute."

She placed her glowing hands over Crystal and began to channel energy into her. After a few moments, the glow faded. "I believe she's fine."

Ethan looked down at Crystal. "Crystal, are you all right?" he asked, nudging her on the shoulder.

After a few moments, Crystal's eyes slowly opened. "What happened?"

"You were in an explosion," Ethan said calmly. "Do you feel all right?"

"I... I think so. Wait. Did you say explosion?" She jolted into a sitting position. "It was the bomb, wasn't it? Is everyone else okay?"

"Crystal, relax," Shadow said. "Everyone's fine, except Niki, who I haven't seen yet."

"But she's probably fine," Ellie said quickly. "After all, we all were fine."

"It was sort of odd, don't you think?" Ryan asked. "I mean, what are the chances that all of us were in the same building as a bomb, it exploded with us in it, and we all survived? I mean, yeah, we got kinda scratched up, but otherwise we're good. So what gives?"

"I think it's a miracle." Ethan replied.

"Ryan has a point, though," Shadow said. "It's almost too perfect. All of us survived with a few scratches and bruises? It's weird."

"I think Crystal would beg to differ," Faith said. "It wasn't just a few scratches and bruises that I healed just now."

"Fine. She's the exception, then," Shadow replied. "But that doesn't change the fact that we all survived a huge explosion."

"It's not good to look a gift horse in the mouth," Ethan said.

"What does that mean?" Crystal asked.

"What I mean is that when you're given a blessing, don't assess it. Don't try to understand it. Just be glad that you were blessed in the first place."

"He's right," Faith said. "We're being stupid. We shouldn't be trying to explain why all of us are all right. We should be happy."

"Speaking of all right, it looks like Tereya is waking up," Ryan said.

They all gazed down at Tereya, who was stirring feebly. He groaned and then opened his eyes, staring up at all of them.

"Before you ask, the bomb went off and it exploded," Crystal said.

"I think that's a bit self-explanatory, unless bombs that are detonated do something other than go 'boom,'" Ryan said.

"Actually, they can fizzle out," Ellie replied. "It's rare, but it does happen."

"Thanks, Ellie," Crystal said. "And you're a jerk, Ryan."

"And we're all okay?" Tereya asked, before Ryan could retort.

"Yeah, we're all good," Shadow replied. "Everything's okay."

"Now, Shadow, lying does not become you," Maedara announced. She clapped her hands slowly and sarcastically. "I must say, I'm surprised. Each and every one of you survived. There wasn't a single death. It's so upsetting. I wanted a nice funeral celebration, but I guess that can't happen now - or, rather, yet."

Shadow moved in front of everyone to face her. He grabbed his sword and pointed it towards her. "The only one who's having a funeral today is you, Maedara."

Maedara laughed, a sudden burst of sound. And then, as quickly as it came, it faded, like thunder. "If you think that making me laugh will distract me from killing you all, you're sadly mistaken. All of you have been this constant annoyance to me. You're all like a tear in a pair of really good stockings or underwire in a bra that has been constantly poking at me. I'm tired of being frustrated and annoyed by those who are beneath me, who aren't even fit to lick the dirt off of my pumps. But you know what? Enough is enough.

"I'm going to have to beat each and every one of you to death. And then, if by some unlucky chance any of you are still alive, I'm going to beat you to death again. It's going to really suck, me beating you all to death. Not just for you, but for me. I'm going to have to work up a sweat, and it's going to make me all smelly and nasty, and it's totally annoying. In fact, it might just be better for all parties involved if you guys just kill yourselves, right now. Yes, do that. I would love to watch."

"Shut it, Maedara," Shadow said angrily.

Maedara brushed him off with a wave of her hand. "You know, that kind of rudeness is simply poor etiquette. Didn't your mother ever teach you proper manners? Oh wait, that's right. I just remembered. She died before you could even say her name, didn't she? How terribly tragic." She took a few steps forward, and then stopped. "Oh, and I see that our guest of honor is here."

"What do you mean?" Shadow asked.

"Don't play dumb. You're standing right by her. Why don't you take a bow, Kay."

"Kay's here?" Ellie asked, looking around. "I'm going to rip her apart."

"Sorry, Ellie," Shadow replied. "Tristan and I found Kay earlier. We left her behind because we really didn't want to bring her around you, especially not if you were injured. We didn't want you to get upset."

"Why don't you all give her a round of applause. She deserves it. After all, without her, this lovely rendezvous could have never happened!" Maedara exclaimed. "She's so convincing, isn't she?"

"It's not true," Kay announced, walking towards them. "I didn't plan any of this. It was all her."

"Kay, I'm brilliant, but I'm not that brilliant," Maedara said. "I mean, come on. It takes a special talent to pull off backstabbery like this. Sadly, I wasn't blessed, but you were. I'm sure your little friends believe your innocent act as much as they believe in buying decent, non-price-reduced clothes."

"You're right. We don't believe her, at all," Shadow replied.

"Yeah, she's been nothing but a liar since day one," Crystal said. "And, by the way, I'd like to go on record saying that I never buy discounted clothes."

"Crystal, that's not the point," Faith said, shaking her head. "The point is, Kay's a traitor. We'd all sooner believe in ghosts than believe in her."

Tristan frowned. "Ghosts actually do exist."

"Tristan, there is absolutely no evidence that ghosts are real." Crystal replied.

"Children, there's no need to argue," Maedara said. "You'll find out the answer after I kill you, which will happen momentarily."

"You're not killing anybody, you skankbiscuit!" a voice yelled, and a flash of light hit Maedara and knocked her off her feet, sending her flying a few yards.

"Shadow, it's Niki!" Ellie exclaimed.

"Hey, everyone. Sorry I'm late to the party, but I did bring a gift," Niki said. She motioned to Isaac, who had separated from her and had run over to Kay.

"Isaac, what are you doing here?" Kay asked.

"Kay, I had to come. They were talking about hurting you, and I had to come to protect you."

Kay shook her head. "I can protect myself. You're the one who needs to be protected, and it's my job to protect you. When the coast is clear, we need to get out of here."

"But Kay–"

"No, don't argue with me. I need to get you out of here before you get hurt."

Shadow smiled when he saw Niki. Then he frowned, noticing Isaac. "What's he doing here?"

"Relax. I didn't take the jet back to go pick him up or anything. He was a stowaway, hiding in the engine room," Niki said.

"Just what we need," Shadow replied. "It was incredibly dumb and risky, but thank you for intervening when you did."

Niki smiled. "Anytime."

"Don't look now, but she's getting back up." Ryan said.

Maedara rose to her feet. She looked herself over and then scowled at Niki. "Okay. Well, that was unpleasant. Perhaps you're the first one I should teach a lesson to."

"Cry me a river," Niki replied. "And if you think you're skilled enough, then come over here and show me what you got."

"Oh, no. I want to be the first to kick her ass," Ellie said.

"You're both wrong," Shadow said, stepping forward. "If anybody is going to fight Maedara, it's going to be me."

Ellie frowned. "Shadow, we've talked about this. You're trying to shield us from everything again. We can handle this."

"No, it's not that. I'm the leader; it's only right that I fight first. If I don't succeed, then one of you can try. But unless that happens, let me handle this." He walked forward.

Maedara smirked. "Oh, Shadow, the brave and powerful leader. Always trying to keep everyone out of trouble, no matter what. How admirable." She advanced as well, going to meet him.

"Yeah, that's right. I'm their leader and I won't allow you to lay a hand on any of them. I will destroy you before that happens. You'll be nothing but dust in the wind when I'm through with you, Maedara."

"You talk a good sell, but I don't know if I'm buying it."

Shadow sneered. "Too bad, because you have no choice." He braced himself as he reached her and prepared to strike. Taking a step backwards, he jolted forward and brought down his sword.

Maedara grabbed the sword with one hand and grabbed his throat with the other. She tossed him carelessly to the side. He flew headfirst into a metal fence and fell down, lying motionless. "Wow, and he calls himself a leader."

"Shadow, no!" Cameryn cried. He went to move forward.

"No, she's mine," Ellie said coldly. She ran forward at Maedara, aiming a kick at her chest.

Maedara moved to the side, dodging the kick. She then slapped Ellie across the face, the pure power of it almost knocking her over. "Manners. You should remember them. You don't just charge at people like that. It's absolutely barbaric."

Ellie rubbed her face and laughed. "If you think that your little slap was enough to hurt me, you need to check yourself. I've been waiting for this for a long time. I've saved up so much anger, from dealing with Cameryn's parents and Kay, that I need a good punching bag, and you've pissed me off enough that you'll do perfectly."

Maedara flicked her bangs to the side. "I'm glad you have a good reason for fighting, aside from the fact that I just knocked your boyfriend out."

"First off, he's not my boyfriend. Secondly, I'm going to make you wish that your mother never laid the egg that you hatched out of."

"I'm going to teach you to respect your elders," Maedara replied. She whipped her head forward, and her hair seemed to come to life. It lashed towards Ellie and struck her across her shoulders and chest.

Ellie fell backwards into a backflip and landed on her feet a short distance away. She shot a beam of ice out of her palms at Maedara, and it hit. The beam spread out and formed a thin cocoon around her. "That was for hurting Shadow."

She then ran forward and roundhouse-kicked the ice block, shattering it and sending Maedara flying backwards onto the ground. "And that was for slapping me."

Maedara huffed, getting back to her feet. "Okay, I'm done playing games." She closed the distance between her and Ellie, lightning fast, and scratched her across the face.

Ellie growled in pain, reeled back, and then kicked Maedara in the stomach. When Maedara bent forward in pain, Ellie grabbed her hair and punched her twice in the face and kneed her in the stomach again. "Had enough yet, bitch?"

Maedara grabbed Ellie's arm, twisted it, and jerked her off of her feet. "No, but you're definitely about to, you little brat. I think I'm bleeding. Am I bleeding? Oh, you're so lucky I'm not bleeding. I swear, if there is any permanent damage from your barbarous assault… I don't know what I'll do."

"Put me down!" Ellie yelled, kicking at her legs.

"Oh, I'll put you down. And just like the little animals in those shelters, you'll never get up again." She wrapped her fingers around Ellie's throat, closing tightly.

"Ellie!" Tereya cried. He threw his hands up into the air, and the ground began to rumble loudly. The area underneath Maedara's feet cracked, and two gigantic stone pillars sprouted from both sides of her.

Maedara tilted her head to the side and smiled at him, as if he were a puppy who had done a really interesting trick. "Apparently, I was misinformed. I was told that you were nothing but a little crybaby."

"Let her go. Now." Tereya's voice was shaking slightly. "If you don't, I'll crush you."

"I wouldn't want that," Maedara replied, casually tossing Ellie away. "There. Are you happy now?"

"Ellie, are you okay?" Tereya asked.

Ethan walked over to her and placed his fingers on her neck, checking for a pulse. "She's still breathing. She's just unconscious."

Maedara sighed. "Don't any of you ever die? This is just too much. I sent demons after you. I detonated a bomb and blew up my entire house with all of you in it, and that didn't even work. And now, when I try choking one of you to death, you survive. Just please tell me what it takes to kill one of you guys. I'm curious. Poison, maybe? Come on, give me something."

"You can thank me for your little explosion not working," Niki replied. "I had brought some insurance with us into your palace because I didn't trust you, and I certainly didn't trust Kay. So I brought something that I bought at the black market. When you say the magical words, it instantly creates a thick shield that absorbs heat damage.

"I bought it right after you purchased the power of fireballs because I thought it would come in handy. It was pure luck that you would just so happen to use a heat-based bomb."

"Well, that's unfortunate," Maedara said. "but it doesn't matter now. Here's what's going to happen. I'm going to kill you for spoiling my plan right after I kill this little one for making me throw away my toy before I was done playing with it."

"No, you're not hurting Niki, because you're not getting past me," Tereya replied. "I'm not going to let you hurt my friends anymore." He brought his hands down, and the two stone pillars rushed towards each other to sandwich her between them.

Maedara put her hands straight out to the side, palms facing outwards. The stones smacked against her hands, but she held them at bay.

"Tereya, push harder!" Tristan shouted.

"I'm. . .trying," Tereya replied, gritting his teeth. "She's really strong. I don't know if I can hold her much longer."

Maedara flipped forward, out from between the rocks, and they smashed together. "It was a nice try, really. But you're going to have to do much better than that. So much better."

Tereya backed up and motioned towards a pile of rocks, and they lifted into the air and flew at her, one at a time.

Maedara whipped her hair forward with every rock that came towards her, and they broke as they made contact with her hair. "I believe you owe me an apology," she said, advancing on him. "And I promise, if you apologize now, I will try my best to restrain myself and make your death quick and painless."

Tereya glanced back at Shadow and Ellie, neither of whom had moved since Maedara attacked them. He took a deep breath and let it out slowly. "You're trying to intimidate me, but it won't work. I've been afraid of a lot of people my whole life, but I'm not going to be afraid of you."

He watched as she made her way towards him. He blinked, and she was standing directly in front of him. His mouth was opened wide in shock.

"Are you intimidated now?" Maedara asked. She sent her hand crashing into his chest, and he fell onto the ground at her feet. "Because you should be."

Tereya coughed and gasped for air.

"Giving me the silent treatment isn't going to make me go away. It's just going to make me even more annoyed. Now, you don't want to do that, do you?"

Tereya shook his head and then spit on her shoes.

"You little brat, these shoes cost me a fortune! Well, they were free, but I had to kill the previous owner to get them!"

"Don't you get it?" Tereya choked. "It doesn't matter... how attractive the wrapper is... if the food inside. . .is rotten."

Maedara glared. "I think it's nap time for little Reya," she replied, kicking him in the stomach. He was knocked backwards and remained motionless.

"Tereya, no!" Cameryn cried.

"Don't worry, Cameryn," Maedara said. "You can join him, if you want. Well, actually, Niki's next. But if you want, you can be after her. See? You can't say I'm unreasonable."

"There won't be a next one, Maedara," Shadow said. His eyes had faded to black and his face was stony. "You caught me off guard, but you won't again."

Maedara glowered. "And tell me exactly how you're awake?"

"It's my secret. Maybe if we were better friends, I'd tell you."

"Do you honestly think I'm dumb?" Maedara asked. "I know damn well that Faith can heal. Kay told me."

"Of course, she did." Shadow replied.

"Kay, is that true?" Isaac whispered.

"Isaac, keep quiet," Kay whispered back. "If she notices you, you're as good as dead. If we're careful, we can walk away, and I can get you to safety."

"We can't just leave them. She's going to kill them."

"And what can we do to help, Isaac?" Kay asked. "Nothing. She's too powerful for either of us. As soon as we have an opening, we're out of here."

Isaac shook his head. "Kay, I can't. It's not right."

"And again, what are we supposed to do?"

"I can't do anything, but maybe you can. You know Maedara better than any of us. Maybe you could talk to her, get her to stop."

"Just because I know her doesn't mean she's any less crazy. Isaac, she's not going to listen to me. Nothing I say will make her suddenly decide to be all cupcakes and sunshine. Nothing."

Isaac sighed. "Then the world is doomed, and we're dead anyway, even if we get away."

"I tire of your games, Shadow," Maedara said coolly, "so maybe it's time for one of my own. Here's the game. Tell me if you like it.

"Kay also informed me that, in addition to healing, Faith is a psychic. So how about we see if she can see what I'm about to do to her."

"You're not going to do anything to her."

Maedara laughed. "Right, because you totally stopped me from mopping the floor with them already. Your delusions are entertaining. But lock in your answers. Time is ticking."

She hummed the Jeopardy theme as she pointed her finger at Faith, who was then lifted up into the air.

"Faith!" Tristan exclaimed.

"Any ideas? Time is almost up. If you get this one right, we'll go into the lightning round. . .which involves actual lightning striking one of you."

"Put her down!" Shadow yelled. He charged at her, and she swiped at him, knocking him back twenty feet. He landed on his knees and cursed.

"Okay, time's up. If you guessed that she would be dropped from about fifty feet in the air to her death, then you were correct!"

"Maedara, wait!" Kay yelled. "Please don't hurt them anymore!"

"You've got to be joking," Maedara replied, shaking her head. "The traitor has a conscience. Be still, my heart."

Kay shook her head and moved forward. "I'm tired of all the violence and pain. Just please stop. You've gotten your wish. Nobody here can stop you. Just let us leave."

Maedara tilted her head to the side. "Perhaps you're right. Maybe we should stop all of this nonsense." She lowered her hand, and Faith fell, landing in Ethan's outstretched arms.

"Really?" Kay asked. "You're going to end all of this?"

"Of course. I'm not completely cruel. You're obviously very upset, and I don't like it when others are upset around me. It's totally not good. It creates worry lines."

"Kay, don't listen to her!" Shadow yelled.

"That really hurts my feelings," Maedara said, pouting. "He paints me out to be some kind of backstabbing person, but I'm not. I've never stabbed anybody in the back - unlike you, Kay."

"I know what I did, and I feel bad for it," Kay replied. "The only thing I can do now, to make everything better, is to try to fix this."

"Well, you're doing just that, aren't you?" Maedara asked. She strolled forward and placed her hand on Kay's face. "Do you really not want to see any more violence?"

"I just want . . .all of this to be over," Kay replied. "I just want all of this to stop."

"Then you shall get your wish. You will not see any more violence."

Kay turned around. "See, Shadow, I told you that you all could trust me again. I just had to reason—"

Three long, sharp objects jutted through Kay's body, piercing her throat, chest, and stomach. A gurgling sound escaped from her mouth as blood traveled to the surface, finding its way through the hole in her throat. Abruptly, the objects retracted from her body, and she fell to the ground, like a puppet whose strings had been cut. Behind where she was standing, Maedara was licking the fresh blood off of her now-short fingernails.

CHAPTER 12: DEATH WITHIN, LIFE WITHOUT

Shadow was rooted in place. Cold swept over him like a winter's breeze, yet his chest burned like a flame was raging inside of him. The last few moments replayed over and over again in his mind. It was as though his brain just couldn't fully process the fact that Kay had just been murdered right in front of him. He was powerless to save her. She was truly gone.

"Kay!" Isaac yelled.

"Oh, how rude of me," Maedara called. "You probably want to pay your respects, don't you?" She kicked Kay's body, sending it flying forward, and it landed at Isaac's feet. "There you go. I'm so sorry that she's leaking."

Isaac growled, picking Shadow's sword off of the ground. "Maedara, I'll kill you!"

"Isaac, no!" Faith cried.

"Shadow, snap out of it!" Ellie exclaimed. "Isaac is going to do something crazy."

"Wait," Shadow said suddenly, grabbing Isaac's shoulder. "Don't. She just wants to get a reaction out of you."

Isaac shook his head, tears glistening in his eyes. "I don't care. I'm not going to let her treat Kay like that. You failed to protect her, and now she's gone. All I can do now is defend her memory."

Shadow froze, letting go of Isaac's shoulder.

"Don't be foolish," Ethan said. "You're going to get yourself hurt, or worse, killed."

"Please, Isaac, don't do this. We can't lose you too!" Tereya cried.

Isaac ignored them. He ran forward until he was a few feet away from Maedara. "I swear, I'll kill you."

"Oh, how touching. It's the BFF," Maedara said, tilting her head to the side. "It's so cute how much you care about her. You must have really loved the little bitch, didn't you?"

"Shut it."

"Oh, now, now. Don't be rude. It hurts my feelings. I'm just trying to support you in your time of need, what with your friend's unfortunate passing. It's such a shame, really. The good always die young. Though she wasn't good, was she?"

"I said shut up!" Isaac yelled. He raised the sword and charged at her. When he was within touching distance, he slashed upwards, aiming for her stomach.

"Do you truly care about Kay this much, enough to commit suicide? It must really hurt to know that she never really cared about you. I know, because she told me. We talked about it all the time, her lack of any emotion for you. We sat down, drank tea, and talked about how much she hated you. Good times."

"You're a liar!"

"Isaac. . ." Ellie muttered, turning towards Shadow. "You've got to go help him. You can't leave him at Maedara's mercy."

"I know, but what am I supposed to do? She's crazy, powerful, and able to pretty much take out any of us with a single punch. Just rushing in blindly isn't going to cut it."

"I honestly don't know, but you have to try. We don't have much time left. If we don't stop her now, her reign of terror will never end."

"I'm afraid Ellie's right," Ethan said. "We have less than forty-five minutes until the curse is permanent. If that happens, everything is lost."

"Faith, are you doing all right?" Shadow asked, ignoring them. He had an idea that hit him, and he didn't want to lose it.

Faith nodded. "Aside from being a bit low on energy, I'm doing all right."

"All right, good. Ethan, I'm going to need you to go over there and use your powers to try to heal her or help her restore some of her energy."

"I will do as you wish. I just hope that you have a plan."

"You know what," Maedara said, digging her nails into Isaac's arm deeper, causing him to cry out in pain. "I demand an apology. A true gentleman would never try to hit a lady."

"I don't see a lady here," Isaac replied.

Maedara narrowed her eyes. "Watch your mouth, brat," she retorted, slapping him across the face. Blood blossomed on the corner of Isaac's mouth. "You really need to be taught some manners. I'd say that your parents should have taught you better than this, but that would be a lie because I know you had no parents. All you had was Kay, and she was a train wreck."

Tereya took a step forward. "I can't watch this anymore. I know I'm not that strong, but I've got to do something."

Shadow shook his head. "No, Tereya, stay here. I refuse to let you go out there and get hurt like Isaac, or worse, dead like Kay."

"But he needs our help!"

"I know. I'm going to help him, but we can't just rush in there blind. Brute force is not the way."

"I've seen enough," Tristan said. "Shadow, I don't know what your plan is, but I'm not just going to wait around and see what Maedara is going to do. Somebody needs to man up and save Isaac. If you won't, then I will."

"Give me a few moments," Shadow insisted. "I have a plan, one that won't get us all killed."

"Right, because that worked so well for Kay?"

"Brother!" Faith exclaimed. "That was not his fault."

"I know," Tristan replied. "I'm not saying it is. But the fact remains, Kay's dead, and I'm not letting Isaac go the same way that she did."

"Tristan, you're being stupid," Niki said, "even more so than usual."

"Oh, she's calling you by your real name now," Ryan said. "I think that means she likes you."

Niki frowned. "Ryan, shut up. And Tristan, you're not going to help anything by charging in there like a wild animal and getting yourself killed, like Kay, or captured, like Isaac. Use your brain, for once."

"Tris, please listen to them," Faith said softly. "I don't want to lose you."

Tristan smiled and pulled Faith into a hug. "I'm sorry, but if I listened to reason, then I wouldn't be me, now, would I?"

He broke the hug, and before anyone could protest further, he began to slowly inch himself closer to Isaac and Maedara.

"Let's begin your first lesson in manners," Maedara said. "Now, what do you say to the nice lady that you've offended?"

"Go to hell," Isaac muttered, followed by a loud scream of pain as Maedara raked her nails down the side of his face.

"Now, we both know that wasn't the right thing to say. We both know that it's a word that one person says to another person when they want forgiveness. Don't you want forgiveness?"

"No. I want you to get out of my face. Your breath smells."

Maedara scowled. "Clearly, you're not learning the lesson." She stuck her pointer fingernail into his stomach and dragged it across.

"Don't you want the pain to just stop? All you have to do is tell me the magic word, and I'll make all the pain go away. Just give me the word I'm looking for."

"Is the word you're looking for, 'bite me'?" Tristan asked, from behind her. His fist came smashing into her face and sending her reeling backwards, breaking her hold on Isaac's arm. He fell to the ground and landed on a pile of broken bricks, where he lay unmoving.

"Brother, watch out!" Faith yelled.

Maedara recovered from Tristan's attack and backhanded him so hard that he went flying and skidded almost ten feet away. "There's only one word to describe that boy's actions, and that word is 'rude.'"

She looked at Isaac, who was lying on the ground, and Tristan, who was just starting to move. "Now, the question is, which one of these two should I teach a lesson to first?"

"I'm going to have to do something to slow her down," Ellie said. "She'll destroy Isaac and Tristan if I don't."

"Ellie, don't," Shadow said. "Let me."

"No, you're needed here. Stay here and formulate your plan. I'll be fine. I'm less important to our victory than you are."

Shadow sighed. "Promise me that you'll be careful."

"I'll be fine. Don't worry. I may have underestimated her before, but I won't make the same mistake twice," Ellie replied. She gave him a quick and reassuring smile before rushing forward.

"Faith," Shadow said, struggling to keep his voice calm. "Is your energy restored?"

Faith raised an eyebrow. "I think I have enough power left in me to heal one or two people, but it depends."

"Why is it so important?" Ethan asked.

"Damn it. I need her at full capacity, able to heal all of us, if need be. I. . .I think I may have a plan, one that requires you and Isaac."

Faith looked thoughtful. "If there's anything I can do to help, you know I'm up for it. Anything to help put a stop to her reign of terror. Just tell me what you need me to do."

"All right. Here's the plan," Shadow said. "We need to distract Maedara somehow, just until we can get Isaac away from her and you near him."

"Shadow, are you sure that she didn't damage something when she knocked you out earlier?" Faith asked. "You seem to be not all there."

"Yeah. I never thought that I'd see the day when you'd lose it." Ryan said.

"I haven't lost anything. In fact, I'm thinking more clearly now than before."

"Maybe we wouldn't think you're all bananas if you would actually take the time to let us in on your plans," Niki said.

"Listen, guys, I'm not crazy. I'm as sane as I've ever been. My plan might be a bit weird, but hear me out. I believe that the key in defeating Maedara isn't in brute strength, or our abilities alone. I think the only way to take her out once and for all is to combine our energy into a single force so powerful that it will obliterate her."

"And how do we do that?" Crystal asked. "We can't just combine all of our powers together. We would need a… huge power generator or something like that."

"Isaac." Ethan proclaimed.

Shadow smiled. "Exactly. We're going to get weakened up so that Faith needs to create more positive energy to heal us. If I'm correct, if she's touching Isaac, then she can channel her power through him and absorb the healing and turn it into raw power. Once it's in a raw form, it can be unleashed at Maedara. A blast like that should be enough to kill her once and for all."

"It's a good plan, but it has some serious flaws," Ryan said. "You're ignoring the fact that Faith may not be well-rested enough to heal all of us before we take a dirt nap. And you're also not accounting for the fact that, while crazy, Maedara isn't stupid. Do you really think that she'll just let Faith stroll around and heal us all?"

"Ryan, I never took you for an optimist, but pessimism? Really?" Niki asked. "It will definitely be difficult and require perfect execution, but it's by no means impossible."

"Yeah. I mean, if you have a better idea, speak up." Shadow said.

Ryan smiled. "Don't get me wrong. I'm not saying it's impossible at all, only that Tristan so kindly proved that it's not smart to just rush in. You're going to need somebody who has the skills to actually survive against Maedara long enough for you all to do what you need to do."

"Isn't that what Ellie's doing right now?" Faith asked.

"Yeah, but look at her," Ryan said. "She was already exhausted from her first encounter with Maedara, and she's pushing herself well beyond her limits. She's not going to last much longer."

Shadow frowned and turned in the direction Ryan was looking in. He saw Ellie and Maedara locked in combat, both dodging hits and throwing their own. To his dismay, he saw that Ryan was right. Ellie looked exhausted, and he could sense that her energy level was depleting by the second.

"Ryan's right. Ellie isn't going to last much longer. We need somebody else to go in and take over, and fast."

"Ooh, pick me, pick me," Ryan said.

"Are you sure?" Shadow asked.

"Of course I'm sure. Who else is going to do it? Everyone else has been knocked silly by her already except me. Tristan and I were the only ones besides Isaac who had any energy left. Tristan's already been KO'ed, and

Isaac already had a lovely conversation with Maedara, so he's clearly in no condition to do this. It pretty much has to be me."

"Excellent deduction, Ryan, but you'll find that your assessments are a tad bit miscalculated," Ethan said. "I haven't had the pleasure to fight her yet, so I also have energy to spare. I could fight her, if you don't wish to."

"Um, dude, hello!" Niki exclaimed. "You're not the only ones who can fight. I didn't get my shot either."

"This is not some game!" Shadow growled. "I don't want any of you fighting her one-on-one if it can be avoided."

"Unfortunately, it's true. I don't want to fight her, but I'm going to do it regardless. Why? Because I'm the only one who can," Ryan replied.

"Yeah, Ethan, you may have the energy, but you're way more useful than I am. You can partially heal. And Niki, you're the only one who has actually managed to actually hurt Maedara in any way. It's better if I go out there first and try my luck before you two because hopefully I can tire her out enough so that this crazy plan can work."

"We have no other choice, then," Shadow replied. "I don't know how long we'll need. How long do you think you can give us?"

Ryan shrugged. "I'm not sure. All I know is that there isn't any way I can actually last directly against her. The only way I can possibly survive is if I go pure defense."

"I agree," Shadow said. "Just distract her, and don't try to be a hero. Stay out of her reach."

"Sure, Daddy. Whatever you say."

"Ryan, I'm serious. You've seen what she can do if she gets her hands on you. I don't want to have to bury you too."

"I know. Don't worry. I'll be fine."

"Guys, whatever you're doing, hurry up and do it. Ellie's in trouble," Crystal said.

"Ryan, you're on," Shadow said. "Just remember, keep her distracted."

"I'm quite surprised that you've lasted this long against me, but your luck is running out," Maedara said. "You're going to collapse any second, little girl, and when you do, you're finished. It would be in your best interest to give up now."

Ellie breathed heavily. "Don't. . .call me. . .a little girl," she said, lifting up her arm and firing hundreds of tiny ice needles.

Maedara dodged the ice needles and moved closer. "When you die, do you think that they'll lay you on a bed of roses?"

"Nobody's dying young except you," Ryan declared. "Ellie's tapping out, and I'm coming in for her. Don't worry. I'll go easy on you."

"Oh, for goodness' sake, do you really have to do this?" Maedara asked. "Can't you morons just wait until I kill one of you before another jumps in?"

"I'm sorry. I know this must be so hard for you," Ryan said, rolling his eyes.

"Ryan… don't," Ellie huffed. "I can… handle this!"

"Listen to her, Ryan," Maedara said. "After all, there's no reason why you need to die before she does. Be sensible. Walk away."

"I wish I could, but that would require letting you kill one of my friends, which isn't cool with me."

"Fine," Maedara replied. "But I promise, this isn't over until you die. I don't care who wants to hop in next."

"If that's how you want it," Ryan said. He took a deep breath and then blew out a huge burst of wind at her. As the wind whipped around Maedara, he flew up into the air and circled around her.

"Faith," Shadow called, "how are you doing on energy?"

"I'm fine. I think I'm well enough to do what you need me to do."

Shadow smiled. "Good. Ethan, can you fly in and bring Isaac over here?"

"Yes, I'll go get him."

"Good, and try to be careful so that Maedara doesn't see you."

"I don't think that will be a problem," Cameryn said. "Ryan appears to be doing a really good job of keeping her busy."

"Not busy, but annoyed," Crystal replied. "He's really good at doing that."

"Too bad Tristan isn't up to it. I'm sure he could do a better job," Niki remarked.

Ethan landed on the ground, Isaac in his arms. "I don't know how well this plan is going to work, Shadow. Isaac is not doing well at all. He's barely breathing."

"What happened?" Shadow asked, walking over to examine him. "Why is there so much blood on his face?"

"When she dropped him, he hit his head on a chunk of brick. He must have been bleeding all this time. I sense that he doesn't have much time left."

"Can't Faith heal him?" Crystal asked. "I mean, I know she can; I've seen her do it!"

"The question isn't if it's in her ability to do so," Niki said. "The question is if she has the resilience to do it."

"She's healed worse than this," Tereya stated. "This should be a cakewalk for her."

Faith nodded. "Tereya's right, I can heal him, but…"

"But what?" Crystal asked.

Shadow sighed. He understood perfectly. "If she were to heal Isaac, then that would mean that she would use up all of the energy that she's saved, meaning that we would have to wait even longer to try our plan."

"But we don't even have that much time left, do we?" Cameryn asked.

"I'm not sure," Shadow admitted. "Ethan, how are we doing on time?"

Ethan checked his communicator. "We have about twenty minutes."

"Damn it," Shadow said. "That's not even enough time for her to gather a quarter of the energy it would take for what we need, especially not after healing an injury that bad."

"Well, then we can't do it," Cameryn said.

"It's a moot point anyway, right?" Tereya asked. "I mean, we can't even do the plan without Isaac. We need his powers."

"That's not actually true," Niki replied. "Isaac's powers of channeling exist in his entire body. He's like one big energy conductor. All that's required

251

is for Faith to touch him while healing so that the energy builds up. He doesn't need to be conscious."

"So it comes down to this," Shadow said quietly. "I have to choose between saving the world or saving someone I've sworn to protect."

"You don't have to. We'll find another way," Crystal said.

Shadow scoffed. "And what way is that? This is our only option, and it really pisses me off that I have to be so practical. It's not fair; not to me, and especially not to Isaac."

"The greater good is always more important than the lesser desire," Ethan said.

"What does that mean?" Tereya asked.

"It means that what's right is right, no matter how badly it sucks," Niki replied. "Shadow, I support you doing what needs to be done, because it has to happen. It sounds horrible, but it's the only way. We can't just make millions of people suffer and die to save one individual."

"She's right," Cameryn said. "I know that if it was me in Isaac's place, I would want you to make the right choice and save the world. If there's anything that I've learned in all the time that I've spent with you guys, it is that, no matter what, the right thing to do is never wrong."

"You guys are right," Shadow said.

"I can't believe what I'm hearing from you guys," Crystal said in disbelief. "You'd really condemn Isaac to death, just like that?"

"Crystal, you're doing it again," Niki said, "the overreacting thing."

"We're not condemning him to death," Ethan said. "You know we wouldn't do something like that."

Crystal shook her head. "There's no middle ground. Either you're talking about saving him or letting him die. You can't have it both ways."

"It's not as black and white as you're making it out to be," Faith said. "If we had a choice, of course we would do things differently. But as it stands right now, with less than fifteen minutes until the world is cursed forever, we don't. So we have to do this."

"You have to understand," Shadow implored. "I didn't want this for him. I wouldn't want this for any of you. I made a promise. I swore to keep all of you alive and to do my best to protect each and every one of you. I failed with Kay, and now it looks as though I'm failing with Isaac too. I can't be as good as you all deserve, and I'm sorry for that."

"None of this is your fault," Niki said. "But when things happen, they happen. There's no time to sit here harping on the way things could have been. Focus on what's happening now. Do something before the whole world is screwed."

"Shadow, you know there's no other way," Cameryn said.

Shadow nodded slowly, closing his eyes. "I know."

"I want everyone to remember that I'm against this," Crystal said. "But as part of this team, I won't stand in the way."

"That's all we ask," Ethan replied. "I promise, everything will turn out okay. I know it."

"Guys, hurry," Ellie said, rushing over. "We don't have much time left. Ryan is getting tired."

"Don't worry. We're ready," Shadow replied. "Faith, I need you to put your hand on Isaac and then heal us all; Ellie first, as she's the weakest. But don't use Isaac to amplify your healing. Focus your mind and use his body to absorb the energy."

Ethan placed Isaac's body at Faith's feet. "Hurry. I can feel his life force fading. He has minutes left."

Faith nodded. "All right. I'll try my best." She placed one hand on Isaac's chest and her other hand over Ellie and began to heal her. However, instead of the glow surrounding Ellie, it covered Isaac's body.

"It's working," Shadow said. "Now, go and heal everyone else."

A minute later, everyone had been healed, and Isaac was surrounded by a bright golden glow.

Ryan landed, falling down next to them. "Okay. I'm all tapped out, and she's coming this way."

"It's fine, Ryan. You did enough," Shadow replied.

"So what do we do now?" Niki asked. "How do we get this plan of yours to work? Is there a switch or something?"

"We wait until she gets close."

"You know, I meant what I said," Maedara called, glaring at Ryan. "Tired or not, you're the next to die - or, as I call it, the next to go the way of Kay."

"You're never going to kill another person ever again, Maedara," Shadow said.

"I think you're wrong. In fact, I know you're wrong. Why? Because in about five minutes, I'm going to be the queen of the world, and you all are going to be my peasants. It's definitely not a glamorous job, but somebody has to clean my kingdom."

"I swear to God, I've never met anybody this delusional," Ryan said. "I swear, you must be allergic to logic or something."

Maedara leered. "Crack all of the jokes you want; it's only fitting that you die laughing."

"Everyone, get ready," Shadow whispered. "When I give the signal, touch Isaac and push your last bit of energy into him."

"I'm sorry, but what was that?" Maedara asked, taking a few steps closer. "Are you seriously whispering when I'm talking to you? Do you know how unbelievably rude that is? I'm apparently wasting my time trying to civilize you miscreants. I don't know why I even—"

"NOW!" Shadow yelled.

They all placed a hand on Isaac and willed their remaining energy inside of him. His body levitated off of the ground and flashed different colors, like sunlight through a prism.

Maedara rolled her eyes. "So, what, you're trying to give me a seizure? Is this your big plan? You get points for originality. . .and stupidity."

"No, Maedara, this is your end," Shadow replied. "For all the lives you've taken, and for all the trouble you've caused in the world. For every family torn apart by your evil ways, and for everyone that you ever hurt in your entire life. For Kay and Isaac and every moment of their life that you robbed them of. This is for them.

"Enough chit-chat. Time to die."

A large multicolored stream of light burst out of Isaac's chest and surrounded Maedara. She was thrown up into the air, and her body ignited like a candle. She screamed when the flames expanded, and every single cell in her body ruptured, overwhelmed by the sheer power of the blast. When the blinding light faded, there was nothing left of Maedara but ashes and a pair of battered and singed red high heels. She was no more.

Michael Chulsky

CHAPTER 13: FORGET ME NOT

It had been a few months since the battle with Maedara, her death, and the curse of Ondeyr's departure. The team had been in recovery mode ever since. Most of them completely had healed, with Faith assisting with the healing process.

Isaac, who was believed to have died, miraculously survived. He was in bad shape for a few weeks, going in and out of a comatose state, but he stabilized and was quickly healed by the combined efforts of both Faith and Ethan.

Kay's body was recovered and cleaned up. She had no family or anybody to come looking for her, so she was placed in a mausoleum within the castle grounds. Isaac had visited her as soon as he could stay conscious, and he stayed there for hours at a time.

Ever since the cataclysmic battle, Shadow had the entire team working overtime. He wanted them all to train and improve their abilities, both natural and supernatural. He hoped that there wouldn't be a next time, but it wouldn't hurt for them all to be prepared. Finally, after months of vigorous training, he decided that it would be nice to treat them to a picnic as a reward for their hard work and dedication.

☙☙☙☙☙☙☙

"I, for one, am glad that you finally had a good idea for once," Ryan exclaimed happily, packing containers of food into a large brown basket.

"For once?" Shadow asked, raising an eyebrow.

"Oh you know what I meant."

Smirking, Shadow walked over and helped Ryan pack, telling him which types of blood to bring and what kinds of soda everyone liked.

Ellie walked into the kitchen. "Thanks again for the picnic, Shadow. It's super nice of you."

"Yeah. Like, totally cool," Crystal added, walking in behind Ellie. "I mean, we knew you were cool, but I didn't think this cool. You're like Alaska."

"Thanks, Crystal. I think," Shadow muttered. "But yeah, you've all more than earned it; you've been working so hard. By the way, where is Ethan?"

Ellie frowned. "He's on his way. He's carrying all of Crystal's things."

As if on cue, Ethan walked into the room carrying four large duffle bags.

Ryan blinked. "Jeez, Crystal. You do know that we're only having a small picnic and camping out for one night, right?"

"I'm not stupid, Ryan. Of course, I know," Crystal replied. "You never know what you'll need when you're out in the wild. Besides, how can we even go on a picnic outside with you, Shadow? You're super allergic to sunlight."

Shadow shrugged. "Well, I thought it would be nice if we had the picnic in the sunroom. It's outside, out back. It's the place I go when I need to think. It's like a huge greenhouse. There's plenty of room for all of us. It will be just like camping out."

"Whatever. I'm game for anything. Just don't expect me to rough it with just a tent and a can of bug spray. I prefer my cozy inflatable queen-sized bed, my electronic bug zapper, and the rest of my technology, thank you very much."

Ellie laughed. "I don't think any of us will mind. Do what you have to do. Having fun is the most important thing."

"Are we too late for the picnic?" Cameryn called, walking into the room.

"Nope, not at all," Shadow replied, smiling.

"Did anyone check to see if Isaac was coming?" Ellie asked. She grabbed the picnic basket, which was now packed full, and put its strap over her shoulder.

Cameryn shook his head. "I checked, but no luck," he replied sadly. "He didn't want to come. He never wants to do anything anymore... except visit Kay's grave."

"It's only natural that he would want closure," Shadow said. "After all, she did raise him for a good portion of his life."

"If you can even call it that," Ryan said. "She didn't really raise him, not really. She basically kept him in a huge bubble while she did horrible things. Guardian-of-the-year material, wasn't she?"

"But it wasn't just that, Ryan," Ellie said. "Isaac knew nothing else but her. To him, everything that happened was perfectly normal."

"He blames us for what happened to her," Cameryn replied. "He hasn't said anything directly, but the way he's been acting... It speaks for itself."

"Wrong, Cameryn," Shadow replied. "Isaac doesn't blame any of you; he blames me for not protecting her, for not doing my job as leader."

"But that wasn't your fault at all!" Crystal cried.

"Crystal is right," Ethan said. "You could have protected Kay from everything except the one thing that led to her downfall, that thing being her. Nobody could have."

Shadow shrugged. "I know that, and you guys know that. Somebody try to explain that to Isaac. That kid is holding some deep resentment towards me, and it's not going to go away by just talking. It's going to take a long time for him to make peace with himself."

"What in the universe is taking so long?" Niki asked, walking into the kitchen. "Come on. The rest of us are waiting." Her gaze fell to the basket on Ellie's arm. "And there so better be muffins in that basket."

"We're coming now," Shadow replied. "I'm guessing Faith, Tristan, and Tereya are waiting for us in the sunroom?"

"You'd be guessing correctly there, Captain." Niki said. "They're fed up with waiting, like hungry-cougar status."

"Well, what are we waiting for, then?" Cameryn asked. "Let's go already. I'm tired of waiting. I've been psyched for this."

Niki nodded. "Yeah, this picnic is going to be so extenscious."

"Extenscious?" Ryan asked.

"Yes, Ryan, extenscious. Like, when something is so awesome that it completely blows your mind and you just want to scream, it's extenscious. Like muffins; they're extenscious. Or Niki; Niki is definitely extenscious."

"That's not a real word. You just totally made that up," Ryan replied.

Niki returned his frown with one of her own. "Did not. Don't blame me if you're not gravitated enough to know about extenscious."

"I'm assuming, by 'gravitated,' that you mean down?" Ellie asked. She was answered by a curt nod. "Yay! I'm fluent in Niki-speak!"

"It's not a real word," Ryan repeated. "You realize she just makes them up as she goes along, right?"

"Ryan, enough," Shadow said before Niki could respond. "Today is a day of peace and relaxation. Just drop it."

"Yes, Ryan," Niki replied. "Drop it."

Ryan scowled and then sighed. "Whatever. Let's just go."

"Ryan, there is nothing wrong with taking the high road," Ethan said, patting him on the shoulder. "In fact, you'll find it leads to fewer headaches in the long run."

"Speaking from experience?" Cameryn asked, throwing a glance at Crystal.

Ethan smiled. "You could say that."

"Enough stalling. Niki is hungry!" Niki exclaimed.

"All right, guys. Let's go before Niki explodes," Shadow said. He then made his way to the sunroom, the others following him.

When they reached the sunroom, they found Faith, Tristan, Tereya, and, to their surprise, Isaac, waiting for them.

"Faith, quick question," Niki said. "What does extenscious mean?"

"It's when something is so awesome that it just completely blows your mind. Why do you ask?"

Niki threw Ryan a smug smile.

"Shut it," Ryan muttered.

"Hey, Isaac," Cameryn said, walking up to him. He looked down and saw a huge backpack. "What's with the bag?"

"It's just a few of my things."

Cameryn nodded. "Ah, cool. What are you doing here, anyway? I didn't expect you to be here, because when I invited you... you said you didn't want to come."

"Is... it a problem that I came?"

"Cameryn didn't mean it like that," Shadow said. "He just meant that it was a surprise, a good kind of surprise."

"Yeah, exactly," Cameryn said. "Why would it be a problem? We're friends. I mean, yeah, you hit me and whatnot, but that's water under the bridge."

"I know. I was just making sure," Isaac replied. "I mean, I don't want things to be any more awkward than they already are."

Faith sighed. "Isaac, I've already told you that nothing is awkward. Nobody holds anything against you."

"What do you mean?" Shadow asked. "What could we possibly hold against him?"

"It's really nothing, Shadow. Isaac is just being stubborn, as always," Tereya said. "I've been through this with him many times, and Faith and Tristan also confirmed what I've told him. He won't believe any of us."

"Tereya, I told you not to mention anything to him," Isaac said, angrily. "I don't need any pity."

"Isaac, you're being silly," Ellie said. "Why would we pity you? We're your friends. We're not here to pity you, because that's not what friends do. We're here to support you and help you work through your issues."

"She's right," Shadow said. "So you can talk to me about anything. It's what I'm here for. I'll listen. I won't judge you."

Isaac took a deep breath and sighed. "After everything that happened with Maedara, Kay's death included, I've just felt distant from everyone. . .like disconnected –"

"Well, isn't that your own fault, though?" Ryan interrupted.

Shadow held his hand up. "Ryan, please."

"No, he's right," Isaac replied. "The way I've been feeling these past weeks has been my own fault. I've. . .blamed you all for what happened to Kay. I felt a deep rage from within myself that basically consumed me. I thought it had been by some error of Shadow's that Kay had died; that maybe if he had tried harder, she would still be alive. But it's not his fault."

"I've told you that so many times," Tereya said. "Shadow would have saved her if he could. He would never allow anything bad to happen to any of us, even Kay."

"Yeah, I know. But it's not just about what's happened since then. It's also about what happened before," Isaac replied. "It started when you all found out about Kay's betrayal. I don't think it was intended, but you guys started treating me differently."

Tereya frowned. "I never –"

"I know you didn't," Isaac interrupted. "I didn't mean you so much as I meant the others."

"What do you mean?" Ellie asked. "I don't remember singling you out, at all."

"I mean, because me and Kay were so close, you all started associating me directly with her, meaning you all treated me as a traitor too."

"That's not true at all!" Shadow exclaimed, slightly outraged. "I know damn well I didn't treat you any different than I treated anyone else."

"I don't think any of us have," Ethan said quietly. "We wouldn't have judged you for the infractions of another. It doesn't matter how close you are, or were, to said person. Though it isn't any mortal man or woman's place to judge, perception is based not on whom you associate with, but the content of your own character."

Isaac shook his head. "Thanks for trying to make me feel better, guys, but it's not working. I'm not that jaded."

"Obviously, you are, because clearly, it's not sinking in," Niki said. "We never treated you like a traitor, because a traitor betrays, and you didn't do that. We treated you like the child that you were acting like."

Faith moved forward. "Niki —"

"No, Faith, I'm going to lay the cement down," Niki said. "Isaac, we didn't treat you differently because of your connection to Kay. We treated you differently because of how childish and stubborn you were acting about the situation. Every single person here saw through Kay except you. It's quite pathetic, considering that you spent more time with her than any one of us."

Isaac scoffed. "Oh, so I didn't realize that somebody who I loved and respected betrayed me because of my age?"

"No, not because of your age. Your age has nothing to do with it," Niki replied. "Tereya is roughly the same age, and Cameryn is slightly older. They're both more mature than you have ever been."

"Please don't compare Isaac and me," Cameryn said. "I was kinda forced to grow up. I wasn't so lucky to be kept in a bubble."

"Yeah," Tereya added. "Kay was all that Isaac knew. And in a way, she prevented him from seeing the truth about her. You can't see the truth if you've been surrounded by nothing but smoke."

Niki shook her head. "Sorry, but those excuses are just that: excuses. Isaac had proof; he had solid evidence. If it wasn't for Ellie telling us about Kay's little mall trip, it was when Kay suddenly vanished when the whole sun thing went down. Hell, Kay herself even admitted to doing all the bad things. Shadow and Ryan were witness to it.

"Why wasn't any of that good enough for Isaac? Because he was stubborn and simply wouldn't listen to reason. And now I'm sitting here and going off. Why? Because instead of nursing his battered ego, I'd rather be munching on a muffin."

Isaac blinked. "You all think that I'm just some big waste of time?"

"Isaac, can you please stop playing editor? You're filtering everything we say in your head," Shadow replied. "What Niki meant is that you acted a bit irrationally. We don't hate you for it, but it did make us nervous around you. We didn't think you would willingly betray us, but I must admit that I did worry that your feelings towards Kay would influence you and cause you to hesitate against her, causing one of us to get hurt. Do you understand?"

"I'm trying, but I just can't."

"See, this is exactly what Niki was talking about," Ryan replied. "You're playing the victim card and it doesn't suit you well, especially when it's you who's doing the victimizing to yourself."

"Whatever. It doesn't matter," Isaac said. "I've already made my choice, and I'm sticking to it."

"And what is that choice?" Shadow asked, his voice low.

Isaac sighed and looked away. "I've decided that I want to leave. I've been thinking about it for a while now, ever since I got better. I don't belong here. Without Kay, I have no connection to anybody here, and–"

"No connection?" Tereya asked indignantly. "We're. . .I mean, I thought that we're supposed to be friends."

"Reya, I didn't mean –"

Tereya shook his head, tears forming in his eyes. "No. Stand by what you said. You just said that you have no connection to anybody here. So you're telling me, what, that you weren't really my friend?"

"It's not like that at all. I misspoke, okay? God."

"He's hurt, Isaac, much like you are," Ethan said. "Surely you can't blame him for being upset. You yourself know how it feels when you get burned by a friend."

"Nobody asked you!" Isaac roared.

"Don't you dare yell at Ethan !" Crystal hissed.

Shadow whistled loudly. "Everyone, stop it."

He paused and turned to Isaac. "Listen, I'm not going to let this happen. Today was supposed to be all about being together as friends, as one big family. This whole thing is causing nothing but fighting."

"And again, you're blaming me for everything."

Shadow placed his hands to his face and screamed wordlessly. "Isaac, enough, already."

"Yeah, quit with the whole pity party," Ryan said. "We get that you have issues or whatever, but really, now. You're not trying to make things better. You're only vying for attention."

"We're not against you, Isaac, I promise," Ellie said. "We just want you to stop with these crazy theories that we're all trying to hurt you, because we're not. We're your friends."

"I don't care what any of you say," Isaac replied. "Like I said, I already made up my mind. Soon I won't be here to cause any more fights or problems. You'll be free of the one burden that Kay left behind when she died."

"If that's what you want," Shadow said coldly.

"Shadow, are you serious?" Faith asked. "I mean, are you really going to let him just leave?"

"I'm not going to beg him to stay here, especially if he isn't happy and feels unwanted. It's not my job to convince those who do not wish to be here to stay. It's simply to protect those who do want to be here. If Isaac doesn't want to be here, then so be it."

"Of course, you wouldn't beg me to stay. I'm not important enough," Isaac said. "If I was Ellie or Cameryn, maybe then you'd actually put some effort into keeping me here."

Shadow blinked. "Huh?"

"Isaac, that isn't true," Cameryn said, shaking his head. "I'm not treated any differently than anybody else here."

"Me, either," Ellie added.

Isaac laughed. "You both are delusional if you think he doesn't hold you higher in importance or worry more about you two than everyone else here. Ellie, I see the way he looks at you, and so does everybody else. And Cameryn? Please. It's obvious that he's more concerned about you than the rest of us. You're always the first one he asks about and the first one that he searches for when some disaster happens."

"You're just plain wrong," Shadow replied. "Ellie and I have spent a lot of time together, yes. It's only natural that we would be close. As for Cameryn, I saved him from one of the most horrible situations that I've ever seen. So, yes, I'm naturally protective over him. Other than that, there's nothing."

"You're such a liar."

"I get it," Cameryn said quietly. "You're just jealous."

"I'm jealous?"

Cameryn nodded. "Oh, yes, you are."

"And what do I have to be jealous about?"

"Maybe it's the fact that you feel that Shadows gives special attention to me and Ellie and he doesn't to you. Or maybe it's the fact that he doesn't coddle you like Kay did. That's it, right?"

Isaac took a step forward. "Don't you dare talk about Kay, not to me."

"Take a step back, Isaac," Shadow said, moving forward. "I've already warned you. But I'll repeat. If you hurt Cameryn again, we're going to have a problem."

"That won't be necessary," Ethan said, placing a hand on Shadow's chest. "Nobody will be hurting anybody."

"Ethan's right," Faith said. "We don't need any more fighting. Enough is enough. Isaac, you're practically a loose cannon. How can we trust you when you keep exploding on everybody?"

"It's fine. You won't have to deal with me anymore. I've already said I'm not staying here anymore, remember? I'm leaving."

Ellie shook her head. "Isaac, you don't mean this. You're just angry, hurt, confused, and you're just lashing out."

"I think everyone needs to take a major chill pill and relax," Crystal said. "Let's sit down and enjoy the picnic."

"I agree," Tereya said. "Let's talk about this after we've all eaten and are much less stressed out."

"There's nothing to talk about," Isaac replied. "I've made my choice. I'm leaving."

"If that's really what you want," Ryan said. "But don't be an attention whore. If you're going to leave, then do it."

Tristan nodded in agreement. "We're a team, Isaac. If you don't want to be a part of that, then you know where the door is."

"Don't worry," Isaac replied. "I will." He picked up his backpack and put it on.

"I want you to really think about this, Isaac," Shadow said. "I want there to be no misunderstandings. If you're truly going to leave, then you'll have to leave your communicator also."

"Shadow, is that really necessary?" Ellie asked, shocked. "I mean, he won't be able to contact us at all."

"I know. But that's one small price to pay in order to protect the rest of you. If Isaac leaves with the communicator, it will create a huge breach of security. Kay gave a lot of information to Maedara, and it's more than likely that some of her minions that survived the explosion know that he is or was a part of this team.

"If he's out in the open, he's able to be captured. If he's captured and they find the communicator, they'll be able to use it to listen in and learn things that they can use against us. I can't take that risk."

"Fine," Isaac said. He pulled it out of his pocket and tossed it to Shadow. "Take it. I have no need for it."

Shadow sighed, staring down at the device. "Isaac, for what it's worth, I'm truly sorry that I've failed you. I wish I could have done more."

"Wish all you want. It won't make everything just go away; all the wrong that I've had done to me, all the pain that I've experienced."

"Isaac, I guess this is goodbye," Tereya said. "I really hope that you find what you're looking for."

"Yeah, it's goodbye. And thanks, I appreciate it. You were the closest thing to a friend that I've ever had besides Kay. I can only hope that what happened to me by being with these guys doesn't happen to you. Watch yourself, because they won't."

"I know that you have your opinions on everyone here, but I trust them. They've never given me a reason not to," Tereya replied.

Isaac sighed and turned away. "Then you'll get hurt, just like I did." He shook his head and walked away.

Ellie frowned, watching Isaac leave. "Don't listen to him, Tereya. He doesn't know what he's talking about. We wouldn't ever hurt you."

"I know," Tereya replied. "He's just confused and doesn't understand, but I do. You all aren't the bad guys. You don't hurt and destroy.

Maedara was bad, and even though Isaac doesn't want to admit it, Kay was bad too."

"What about Isaac?" Cameryn asked. "Is he now our enemy?"

"It's not always that black and white," Shadow replied. "Good and evil, right and wrong; it's not always so obvious. Maedara was definitely evil, Kay was troubled, and Isaac. . .Well, he's not our enemy, but we can't count on him either. I hope that one day he'll return, maybe when he's not so confused."

"For the record, I think you did as much as you could, "Faith said. "You tried your best with Kay and Isaac, but you can't win every battle."

"My heart is telling me the same, but my mind is being stubborn," Shadow said. "It's like I can't stop replaying in my head everything that happened. I keep thinking that, in some way, Isaac is right; that I failed both him and Kay. I promised to keep you all safe, and I failed."

Cameryn frowned. "You didn't fail. You didn't. Don't let Isaac do this to you, Shadow."

"What makes you think you failed?" Niki asked. "Aside from the fact that Kay died and Isaac ran away."

"Gee, Niki, let's remind him of everything that went wrong," Ryan said, shaking his head. "While we're at it, let's throw him out into the sunlight."

"Regardless, it doesn't matter, because neither of those things were his fault," Ellie replied.

"Well, that's what I was trying to say," Niki said. "It's not his fault that Kay was a whole sack of psycho."

"Can we just drop this subject, please?" Tereya asked. "I'm hungry, and it would be nice if we could forget about all of this."

"Tereya's right," Shadow said finally. "We shouldn't ruin our picnic more so than it already has been. You've all been working so hard. This was supposed to be your reward."

Crystal nodded in agreement. "Well, it's no sweat, Shadow. Besides, there's no use in dwelling on things that we can't change. I mean, I get upset every day because, while I have tons of money, there are still plenty of things that I still don't own. If I sat around and cried over everything that I don't have, I wouldn't be able to enjoy the things I do have."

"Crystal, that was oddly perceptive," Faith said, blinking.

"Well, of course. I'm not just some shallow, prissy girl."

Ethan smiled. "And you continue to prove just that."

"Enough chatting," Ellie said. She put the basket on the ground and began digging through it. "I don't want to hear any talking, only crunching and chewing. Let's eat!"

"Now you're speaking my language," Niki replied. "Remember, the muffins are mine."

"Niki, do you think about anything but muffins?" Ryan asked.

"Yeah. Dolphins. They're pretty awesome. And carnivals, carnivals are nice."

Ellie pulled out a package of muffins and handed it to Niki. "Here are your muffins. Now you can relax." She reached back down into the basket and began pulling out containers and boxes of soda and sweets and small packages of blood. When the basket was emptied, she closed it and smiled. "Done. Everyone, take a paper plate and plastic fork and dig in!"

"I don't exactly need a fork or a paper plate," Shadow replied, smirking.

"Oh. Well, you can go —" Ellie began, but she was interrupted by a loud noise. It sounded as a bolt of lightning had struck the ground. "What was that?"

"Everyone, be careful," Shadow said. He looked around for the source of the noise. "Keep your eyes wide open."

A woman appeared, just materializing out of thin air. She had shoulder-length black hair, with beads and feathers strewn in. "Shadow, I'd put that sword away - unless you were thinking of using that on me, of course."

Shadow laughed and shook his head. "Of course not," he replied, sheathing it. "Gail, what are you doing here?"

"Pardon my language, but who the hell is Gail?" Ryan asked.

"Who the hell am I? That's an excellent question," Gail said, tapping her fingers. "Shadow, go ahead and tell them who I am."

"Well, you could say that Gail and I go way back. I met her about ten years ago. She was the healer of the town where I grew up. She was always willing to help me, and she oversaw my combat training as well as my knowledge of the spiritual. In addition, she was the one who gave me the power to sense you all and warned me of the danger that we conquered."

"So, wait," Ellie said slowly. "She's the shaman that you spoke of?"

"Yes, I am," Gail answered. "And you're Ellie, and you have the power to manipulate ice, is that correct?"

"How did you —"

Shadow smiled. "Don't let her mystify you. She's a soothsayer. She can read the thoughts, feelings, and memories of those around her, in addition to having visions of the future. Trust me, it tends to get annoying if you're around her for long periods of time."

"Hey, watch it, now," Gail replied. "Nobody forced you. In fact, if I recall correctly, you were the one who sought out my help, remember?"

"Yeah, yeah, I know."

"So, wait. Shadow actually needed your help?" Crystal asked.

"How do you think he got to be the individual he is today?" Gail questioned. "Nobody is born with knowledge. It's learned. Each mind is like a beach, with the ocean being the problems of the world that rise against you. Every single grain of information that you accumulate contributes to the sands guarding the shore."

"It's true," Shadow said. "If it wasn't for her, I wouldn't know half of the things I know now."

"It's simply brilliant," Ethan replied. "You were lucky to have a mentor as insightful as her in your life."

"Oh, stop it," Gail said. "I did nothing but light the way. He's the one who walked down the path."

"Listen," Shadow said. "I know I was very stubborn and difficult when I was younger. So if ever I made you think that I wasn't grateful for all you did for me or for all you taught me, I'm sorry."

"Well, thank you, but that's not why I came here."

"Why did you come here?" Tristan asked. "You're kind of interrupting our picnic that's already interrupted."

"Brother, please!" Faith exclaimed.

"As Tristan so eloquently put it, why did you come? I mean, I haven't seen you in a long time. What brings you here now?" Shadow asked. "Could it be that you're finally here to give me that information I asked you about?"

"I'm afraid not," Gail replied. "I'm here because I know what happened. I know about Kay's betrayal, her passing, and Isaac's departure right before I came."

"Are those... circumstances the reason for your visit?" Ethan asked.

"Not quite. Well, perhaps. They are not the initial reason for my visit, though they make me feel better about what I'm about to do, if that makes sense."

"It doesn't, but go on," Shadow replied.

"Maybe it's best if I cut right to the chase. I have two more children to leave in your care. Actually, scratch that. Not children. Two more teenagers."

Shadow blinked. "You can't be serious."

"So, what, we're getting two new roomies?" Crystal asked. "That's, like, totally awesome-sauce."

"That is the best news since, well, Maedara's death!" Ryan exclaimed.

"No. Just no," Shadow replied. "Two more is too many."

Gail frowned. "The way I figure it, the two that I have can replace the two that you've lost. You're not gaining extra; you're just getting back what you lost."

"You have to admit," Faith said, "she makes a good argument."

"Don't help her. She doesn't need it," Shadow replied. He took a deep breath. "Point is, I can't handle two more. I couldn't even handle all the ones I had."

"Now you're just being silly," Gail said. "It's not like you could have foreseen what ended up happening with Kay and Isaac. You're not psychic. Just let it go. Nothing good will come from hating yourself over things you can't control."

Shadow sighed. "All right. Fine. Can you at least tell me why it's so important that I take two more lives under my wing?"

"I can't get into specifics. All that I can say is that I've had strong feelings that led me to these two. It's imperative that you keep them with you, as they will be invaluable help. I've seen the future, and it's dark. Maedara may have been the great danger that I warned you about, but there are others - others who will try to destroy the world. These two will be helpful in saving it."

"Fine," Shadow replied. "I'll take them."

"Where are they, anyway?" Ellie asked.

"I'm glad that you're being reasonable," Gail replied. "And they can be here right now, if need be."

"So we don't have to go and get them?" Tereya asked. "Do they teleport?"

Gail smiled. "Not exactly, but you'll see." She raised her arm and brought it down suddenly. In a flash of light, two teens and two large crates appeared next to her. "I want you guys to meet Matthew and Lillian."

The girl stepped forward. "My name is Lily, not Lillian." She brushed her blonde bangs out of her face; her green eyes narrowed in contempt. "How many times do I have to repeat myself before people will remember?"

The boy standing next to her smiled. "Maybe you should wear a name tag."

"Lily, disappointment is not an excuse to be disrespectful, so please watch how you speak to your elders," Gail replied.

The boy waved. He had jet-black hair and bright blue eyes. A small scar decorated the bottom of his chin. "Hey, everyone, I'm Matthew, but I prefer Matt."

Tereya returned the wave. "Nice to meet you, Matt."

"Thanks," Matt replied. "And I just want to say that Lily didn't mean to be rude or anything. She's just been a bit tense because of all the moving."

"So you mean she's not always so testy?" Niki asked.

Matt smiled. "Yeah, that's what I mean."

"Matt, I don't need you apologizing for me. I can do that myself," Lily said.

She turned to Gail. "Sorry for being rude. I just don't like being called Lillian, at all - meaning if anybody here even thinks about calling me that, they can expect to be chewed out, followed by the ass-kicking of their life."

"Oh, yeah, we're going to get along great," Ellie said, smiling. "I'm Ellie. Glad to meet you."

"Lily, but you already knew that. It's nice to meet you too."

Gail smiled warmly. "Well, it's time for me to get going. If you need anything, Shadow, you know where to reach me."

"Yeah, I do," Shadow replied. "And don't worry. I shouldn't, because everything will be fine."

"I know. It's why I'm leaving them with you," Gail said. "I'm so proud of the man you've become." She waved and then faded away.

CЗ୧ЈCЗ୧ЈCЗ୧ЈCЗ୧Ј

Far away, in a cavern lit by wall-mounted torches, a demon sat on a throne. He was gazing down at an ancient book in his hands when a smaller demon rushed into the room.

"Lord Rokaii, I bring news!"

"What is it?" Rokaii asked. "It had better be important."

"Those brats you told me to watch have slain Maedara and restored the sun."

"That's pathetic. She should have been more than capable of killing a couple of teenagers. It seems that I've both overestimated her and underestimated the enemy."

"I'm sorry for the loss, Master."

Rokaii laughed. "What loss? So what if Maedara failed? She wasn't the best nor the last card in my hand. At any rate, I need time alone to plan. You're dismissed."

"Yes, of course, My Lord," the smaller demon replied. It walked over to the door, then hesitated. "Are you sure there is nothing you require?"

"Hmm. Now that you mention it… I need you to do two things for me. Can you handle it? I mean, normally I wouldn't ask. Maedara's blunder has really made me lose faith in people. I mean, a woman of her stature getting killed by teenagers? Really? Disgraceful. But can you handle it?"

"Yes, Master, of course. What do you ask of me?"

Rokaii smiled, flashing long and pointed teeth. "First, I need you to go to the vault and pull out the tome. Yes, the special one. I think it's time that we give those kids something to really test them."

"And the last thing?"

"Ah, yes. I also need you to prepare my ship. I need to go to Hyael. I believe they're in need of a new king."

ABOUT THE AUTHOR

Michael Chulsky grew up in New Jersey and has been writing ever since his fourth grade teacher let him create a class newspaper to channel his creativity. He is the author of The Descending Darkness and currently lives with his fiancé. When not writing he enjoys browsing Tumblr, listening to music, and devouring every piece of cheesecake that falls into his line of sight.

CPSIA information can be obtained at www.ICGtesting.com
Printed in the USA
LVOW08s2254041013

355421LV00001B/21/P